"An engrossing legal thriller."
—*Publishers Weekly*

"Taut and intense, *AfterImage* is also a novel about loss and reclamation, written with a complexity and subtlety and depth of feeling that raises it far above other novels of its kind."
—Martha Grimes

"There are many lawyers who write. Jay Brandon is a writer who practices law. The difference will be apparent to lovers of language. Jay Brandon is a fine storyteller and a gifted writer. In his new novel, *AfterImage,* the combination is unbeatable."
—Sharyn McCrumb, *New York Times* bestselling author of *The Ballad of Frankie Silver*

"Haunting, profound, and breathtaking, Jay Brandon's *AfterImage* is perhaps the finest legal thriller since *Presumed Innocent.* Sinclair's personal and professional quest is absolutely gripping and all too real. Once you've started reading this book, you won't want to stop until it's over—and maybe not then."
—William Bernhardt, bestselling author of *Dark Justice*

"I've long been persuaded that Jay Brandon is the finest writer of legal thrillers in the country, and *AfterImage* proves it conclusively. Whether you read such a book for the insider's analysis of what makes a criminal courtroom tick or for the novelist's depiction of sympathetic characters whose lives are unraveling, this riveting tale will have you searching the shelves till you find the author's earlier gems."
—Jeremiah F. Healy, author of *The Only Good Lawyer* and *Spiral*

Other Books by Jay Brandon

Angel of Death

AfterImage

JAY BRANDON

TOR®

A TOM DOHERTY ASSOCIATES BOOK
NEW YORK

This is a work of fiction. All the characters and events portrayed in this book are either products of the author's imagination or are used fictitiously.

AFTERIMAGE

Grateful acknowledgment is given for permission to use lines from the poem "A Dream of Death" by W. B. Yeats. Reprinted with permission of Simon & Schuster from *The Poems of W. B. Yeats: A New Edition,* edited by Richard J. Finneran (New York: Macmillan, 1983).

A Tor Book
Published by Tom Doherty Associates, LLC
175 Fifth Avenue
New York, NY 10010

www.tor.com

Tor® is a registered trademark of Tom Doherty Associates, LLC.

ISBN: 0-812-54044-1

First edition: February 2000
First mass market edition: December 2000

Printed in the United States of America

0 9 8 7 6 5 4 3 2 1

To my partners in (unsolved) crime
Charlie Parker and Carole Crouch Parker;
and to my professional colleagues
Sue M. Hall, Karen Ruff,
Louise Sagor, Kim Torres,
and Dina Lemus

Acknowledgments

I want to thank the following people for their help and encouragement: Jimmy Vines for his persistence and knowledge in finding a good home for Chris Sinclair and Anne Greenwald; Andy Zack for his careful attention to the manuscript; Dr. Robert Bux for his excellent tour (again) of the Bexar County Forensic Science Center; Edard W. Love, Jr., for demonstrating the wonders of modern firearm examination; and Karla Zounek and Karen Lovell of Forge Books for smoothing the way.

1

She was more beautiful than thy first love,
But now lies under boards.

—from "A Dream of Death," by W. B. Yeats

One

Some days justice nods off. Certainly there are times when the Bexar County Justice Center hibernates. Sometimes one could set off a shrapnel grenade in a hallway and not injure anyone. On such days, usually late afternoons, judges are hard to find, prosecutors have drifted back to their offices or out of the building altogether, and lawyers who do happen to meet in the echoing corridors look at each other shamefacedly, as if to say, *What are we doing here?* It is a failure of sorts just to be in the building.

The Justice Center had recently experienced a series of such days: Thanksgiving week, Christmas week, the dead end of the year. But now January had arrived, forcing the building unwillingly back to life. Jurors had been called, the courts resumed business, lawyers, defendants, and cops lined the halls. Still, justice hadn't entirely climbed back up to speed. The plea-bargaining between prosecutors and defense lawyers exhibited a desultory, let's-put-this-off-until-I-feel-more-up-to-it quality, and hardly any trials had actually got off the ground yet. So when the

District Attorney of Bexar County appeared in a court-room, people took notice.

The District Attorney, Chris Sinclair, not only entered the courtroom, he walked straight to the front and took his place at the prosecution's table. A few minutes later when the judge of the court, Betty Willis, called a case name, Chris stood and announced, "The State is ready."

At thirty-five, Christian Sinclair looked too young to be the District Attorney, but he had been for two years. He was of medium height, but looked taller standing at the front of the courtroom, where the lights caught his blond hair and strong forehead. His mouth, usually quick to twitch toward a smile, locked in a grim line as he gazed steadily across the space inside the bar, to where a defendant and his lawyer slowly made their way to the defense table.

A reporter who had spotted the District Attorney in the hall and followed him into the courtroom frowned and hurried to the front of the spectator seats to get a look at the defendant and his lawyer. The reporter knew of no big cases going to trial during this half-speed week. But if the District Attorney himself was prosecuting, it must be a big one.

However, the case didn't immediately demonstrate its largeness, and in a moment it became clear that it wouldn't even be going to trial today. "Ready on the motion to suppress," said the defendant's tall, distinguished-looking lawyer. Lowell Burke, the veteran defense lawyer, projected confidence, an appearance that sprang from his habitual air of detachment, as if he had more important business elsewhere. Some defense lawyers appear indistinguishable from their clients, huddling together as they plot a defense. Burke disdained that school of behavior. His steady gaze at the trial judge said that he had come here on a matter of law, and oh yes, that crook at his side? He was only an essential tool of the legal trade—not, certainly, a friend of Burke's.

The reporter who had come forward to watch the action

became more curious. Lowell Burke didn't take appointed cases and he didn't come cheap. This defendant obviously had money—or had had money before he'd walked into Burke's office. But he didn't look it. The reporter hadn't recognized the defendant's name when the judge called it: something Belasco. The defendant was a young man in his mid-twenties with very pale skin, ragged fingernails, and slicked-back hair. His dark suit fit him well and gave him elegant lines. Trust Lowell Burke to have his client well turned out. The young defendant wore the expensive clothing as if accustomed to it, but there was still something relentlessly late-night about his appearance. He didn't look like old money and he didn't look like earned money. The reporter waited to hear what he'd been charged with.

Judge Willis, in her mid-sixties, made a formidable impression on the bench, with her plump cheeks and bright lips. "Call your first witness," she said.

Chris Sinclair demonstrated a Bexar County oddity by saying to the bailiff, "Officer Reynolds, please." This hearing sprang out of a motion to suppress evidence, which was a defense motion, so the defense bore the burden of proof, and should have gone first in putting on evidence. But in Bexar County the prosecution had an easier time producing police witnesses, through its liaisons with the police department, and so for years had assumed the responsibility of bringing police officers to such hearings. Somehow with that burden the prosecution had also assumed the right to go forward first with evidence.

The young uniformed officer marched swiftly up the aisle of the courtroom, creaking with leather and authority, his chin lifted with all the confidence of twenty-four years of life and a year and a half of police experience. He responded with a clipped, "I do," to the judge's giving him the oath, and took his seat in the witness stand. He looked straight at the District Attorney as he'd been instructed to do.

Holding his witness's gaze, Chris said, "State your name and occupation."

"Josh Reynolds, police officer, Terrell Hills Police Department."

After another couple of preliminary questions, Chris asked, "Officer, where were you on the evening of November 8 of last year?"

"I was outside a home on Tuttle Road in Terrell Hills."

"Were you on duty?"

"I was on duty and in uniform, but in an unmarked car, parked several houses down the street from the house we were surveilling."

Hearing the word "surveillance" used as a verb tended to make Chris Sinclair flinch, even as often as he'd heard cops do it. He let it pass, unsurprised at hearing young Officer Reynolds spout jargon.

"Was anyone with you, Officer?"

"Yes sir, there were a team of us, led by a detective from San Antonio PD Narcotics Unit."

"Was this a narcotics operation?"

"Yes sir, but they needed local support since the suspects had turned up in Terrell Hills. That's why I was there."

Terrell Hills, a very small incorporated suburb completely surrounded by the city of San Antonio, had an average income level that rose much higher than San Antonio's did. The suburb also had a small police force with more experience at keeping the peace than at drug stings.

Chris asked, "Why did you have this one particular house under surveillance, Officer?"

"We had information that some suspects—"

Lowell Burke stirred himself for the first time and rose to his feet with no appearance of haste. "Objection, Your Honor. This sounds like hearsay."

"Sustained," Judge Willis ruled. In the courtroom Betty Willis displayed an absolutely blank demeanor. She strove so hard to appear impartial that she'd developed the habit of not looking at anyone. The judge stared off at the back wall of the courthouse, like Lady Justice unblind-folded but unseeing nevertheless. Young prosecutors had expressed the urge to jump up and wave their hands through her line of sight to see if she'd react.

Chris continued unperturbed. "As you sat in your car with the narcotics detective and other officers, what were you waiting for?"

"We were waiting for a signal from inside the house, sir. We had a man inside."

In Officer Reynolds's recounting of the tale, the opera-tion had become his. Chris continued, "How were you to receive a signal?"

The officer answered with exaggerated care, as if the District Attorney were venturing onto dangerous ground. "The *person inside* was wearing a hidden mike, sir."

"So you could hear conversation from inside the house?"

"Bits and pieces, sir."

"Did you ever receive a signal?"

"Of sorts. Some time after eleven P.M., I very distinctly heard one of the guests inside the home say, 'What the hell is that?' And then our receiver went dead. We couldn't hear anything else."

"What did you think?"

The defense lawyer rose again. "Objection, Your Honor. What the officer thought is irrelevant."

This time Chris responded. "It's very much relevant, Your Honor. Since Mr. Burke's motion to suppress evi-dence accuses the officers of acting illegally, their moti-vations are part of the probable cause analysis."

From the heights of her detachment Judge Willis said, "Overruled."

Quickly Chris asked again, "What did you think when you lost radio contact with your person inside, Officer Reynolds?"

"I thought the person had been discovered and was in immediate danger." The officer grew more animated, as he had that night in November. "I jumped out of the car and said, 'Let's go,' and started running toward the house."

"Did the other officers run with you?"

"They were a few steps behind, sir."

In fact, as the narcotics detective had told Chris Sinclair in the privacy of the DA's office, the detective had not only lagged behind, he had been yelling at the uniformed officer to wait. But Reynolds was not only younger than the detective, he was thinner and much faster. "He bolted like a rabbit with diarrhea," the detective had said disgustedly.

In court, Chris let none of this knowledge leak into his voice. "What did you do when you reached the house, Officer?"

"I glanced in the front window and saw several young men gathered in what appeared to be a living room. They seemed all to be looking at one man. I heard shouting. So I ran quickly to the front door, kicked it open, and yelled, 'Police! Everybody freeze!' "

"Did you have your gun drawn?"

"Definitely, sir. They wouldn't have much incentive to freeze otherwise."

"What happened next?"

"I edged forward into the room. The suspects seemed to be mostly teenaged boys. Maybe eight or ten of them. Two or three ran out a doorway on the other side of the room, but I couldn't do anything about that until my backup arrived. I quickly scanned the room for weapons but didn't see any. I also looked for someone hurt, down on the ground. I didn't see that either."

"Did anyone in particular draw your attention?"

"Yes sir," the policeman said, knowing his job as a witness. He pointed. "This man."

"You're indicating the defendant, Peter Belasco?"

"Yes sir, although I didn't know his name at the time."

"What did he do to draw your attention?"

"He was older than most of the others in the room. He was dressed about like he is now, in a suit, while the others were in jeans. So he looked like the man in charge. And he had a briefcase at his feet."

"A briefcase?"

Officer Reynolds frowned in concentration. "Yes sir, a very nice briefcase, large, with leather straps. Like a lawyer might carry in an old movie." The officer smiled to indicate a little joke.

"You say it was beside Mr. Belasco's feet?"

"Yes sir, as if he'd just dropped it. I was surveilling the whole room, but then I sensed movement and when I looked again the briefcase was farther from Mr. Belasco, as if he'd pushed it away from him. It was almost under a small end table."

"So what did you do, Officer Reynolds?"

"I told everyone to back away and I seized the brief-case."

"Why?"

The officer knew the proper answer to this question, too. A police officer is entitled to take steps to ensure his own safety. "I was afraid it might contain a weapon, sir."

"Did you open the briefcase?"

"No sir. By that time the other officers were inside, and I passed it on to the lead detective."

"Thank you, Officer." Chris stood to draw the judge's attention. "Your Honor, I believe we have a stipulation, for the purposes of this hearing, about the contents of the briefcase."

The defense lawyer nodded in unconcerned agreement. "We do, Your Honor—just for this hearing."

Chris passed the judge a short written memorandum specifying the stipulation. The briefcase had been a portable pharmacy: marijuana, cocaine, methampheta-mine—enough to keep the house party on Tuttle Road going for days. The briefcase offered enough evidence to send this defendant to prison for a long time—if Chris could get the evidence admitted. This hearing represented the real trial, because the primary issue in the case was the legal question of whether the drugs had been properly seized and could be linked to Peter Belasco.

Chris knew how difficult that would be. In spite of the confidence of the young officer's testimony, the lawyers in the room, including Judge Willis, had heard the apparent problems. It had been a bad search and a bad arrest, which meant a bad day in court for a prosecutor.

Chris could have called one of the more veteran officers on the scene as his witness at this hearing. They could have perhaps put a better legal spin on the facts. But Chris hoped young Josh Reynolds would make a better witness because of his obvious sincerity. He still didn't know that he'd done anything wrong. The drug sting had gone just as planned, as far as he knew.

Also, only Officer Reynolds had been in position to see the defendant with the briefcase close to his feet. By the time the other officers had entered, the incriminating evidence had been almost under the end table, equally close to half a dozen of the suspects.

Chris had one other, uncharitable reason for having called Officer Reynolds as a witness. He wanted to teach him a little lesson in criminal procedure. Chris let the lesson begin by sitting down and saying, "I pass the witness."

The defense lawyer smiled—in anticipation, but it appeared a courtly smile of greeting. "Officer Reynolds, my name is Lowell Burke. I represent Peter Belasco here. I'm going to ask you some questions now. If the questions aren't clear, please ask me to repeat or rephrase. All right?"

"Yes sir." The young officer's shoulders relaxed slightly, but he still watched the defense lawyer closely. Even Judge Willis had lowered her gaze to watch Burke.

Burke frowned as if picturing the scene. "Officer Reynolds, when you burst into that living room, did anything besides the people draw your attention?"

"What do you mean?"

"Well, let's put it this way: what did the room look

like? Did it look like a gang hangout? Graffiti on the
walls? Broken-down furniture?"

"Oh no, sir. It was a nice house. This was Terrell Hills,"
the officer amplified. "Nice heavy furniture. Lamps. The
walls were unmarked."

"Not one graffito?" Burke smiled.

"No sir. I believe there was wallpaper." The young officer continued his description. "At one end of the room
they had a big-screen TV."

"Ah," Burke said, not having had to pull that tooth.
"Was the TV on?"

"Yes sir. It appeared to be showing a movie."

"What was the volume like?"

"Pretty loud, sir."

"Could that have been the source of the shouting you
said you heard from outside?"

"Possibly."

"Well, when you burst into the room, was any person
in there shouting?"

"No sir, not just then."

Burke made a steeple with his index fingers, touched
the peak to his lips, then lowered his hands an inch to say,
"Let's go back to when you were in your car waiting for
the signal from your operative inside the house. What
were the words you heard?"

"Someone said, 'What the hell is that?' " The officer
quickly added, "I thought that meant someone had discovered the transmitter on our undercover agent inside
the house."

Again that blank outline had appeared in the proceedings: the informer inside the house. Both the defense
lawyer and his client glanced at Chris Sinclair, who sat
staring at his witness.

Burke turned back toward the witness as well, looking
unperturbed by the officer's conjecture about danger to
the informant. "Well, that's rather a broad speculation,
isn't it, Officer? The exclamation could have been some-

one referring to something appearing on the TV screen, couldn't it?"

The officer obviously wanted to deny that, but couldn't do so without looking silly. "Yes sir, it could have been."

"Or in fact, since the TV was producing the loudest sounds in the room, it could have been a character in the movie you heard saying, 'What the hell is that?' Couldn't it, Officer?"

Officer Reynolds chewed his lip for a second but had to concede, "I suppose now it could have been, sir. But I had no way of knowing that sitting in the car outside."

"Well, exactly. You didn't know what was going on inside the house, did you?"

"Not precisely, no sir."

"I believe you said the other thing that aroused your concern was that you stopped receiving transmissions from your broadcaster inside the house, yes? Officer, do you now know more about what caused that transmission failure?"

For the first time since cross-examination began, Chris saw an opening to try to save his case. "Objection, Your Honor, I believe that would call for hearsay."

Burke said smoothly, "I believe this witness knows this of his own knowledge, Your Honor. But if we need to waste the court's time by calling another witness—"

With most judges, threats of wasting the judge's time hit home harder than legal arguments. Judge Willis was no exception. "The objection is overruled," she said quickly.

"Officer?" Burke asked politely. "Had you lost the signal because your man inside had had his shirt ripped open and his transmitter smashed?"

Officer Reynolds coughed. "No sir. Uh—it turned out our receiver had stopped working."

"Equipment failure."

"Yes sir, I'm afraid so."

Burke switched gears, slowly gaining force and outrage as he said, "So if I'm inside my own home and police send some liar to worm his way into my home with a microphone, and then someone—anyone, including a character on television—asks what something is, and then the cops' poorly maintained equipment breaks down, in your opinion, Officer Reynolds, does that give you the right to smash your way into my house waving a gun?"

Chris stood with a weary slump before the defense lawyer had half-finished this speech. Chris let Lowell Burke rise to his peak of indignation, then said, "Your Honor, that's a speech to a jury, not a question for this witness."

Judge Willis looked at him and said, "Since there's no jury here to be swayed, Mr. Sinclair, I don't see the harm. Ask a question, Mr. Burke. Are we wrapping up?"

From that brief speech, Chris knew that he had lost the judge. The presumption at the beginning of any hearing or trial is that the prosecution will win; no judge wants to face the voters with a record of having let criminals go free. But when Judge Willis told the defense lawyer to wind it up, meaning the defense had already put on enough evidence, Chris knew he no longer had that presumption of victory operating on his behalf.

"Thank you, Your Honor," Burke said. "Officer, let's go back into that elegant living room. Was there anything in there that reinforced your sense of danger? Any guns in evidence? Anyone bleeding or down on the floor? Anyone even yelling at each other?"

"As I said, I didn't see anyone hurt or bleeding. I didn't see any guns, either. There were some beer cans on the coffee table, and drinks in glasses—"

Burke said harshly, "I asked you about danger, Officer. Did the beer cans make you feel threatened?"

Officer Reynolds sat for a moment with his jaw set, then said, "They made the situation more volatile, sir."

The defense lawyer rolled his eyes. "All right, Officer. Your backups had arrived by this time, I suppose. Did they also have guns drawn?"

"Yes sir."

"So since you and the other police officers had the only

apparent guns in the room, you were in charge of the situation, right?"

"Yes sir, at that point. Apparently, as you say."

"Did Mr. Belasco make any threats or gestures that aroused your alarm?"

The young officer felt himself being ridiculed. "No sir," he said tightly.

"Mr. Belasco didn't look like a thug, did he, Officer? You said he looked as he does today, like a businessman."

"I don't know what kind of business he's in," Reynolds said, but Burke's question had been aimed at the judge, to induce her to notice the clean-cut appearance of the defendant.

"At that point you had no evidence that any crime was going on, did you, Officer?"

"Perhaps providing alcohol to minors," Reynolds said, with an attempt to regain his earlier assurance.

Lowell Burke had been prepared for that response. "But some of the people in the room were twenty-one or older; you had no evidence of who had been drinking what, and you certainly had no evidence that Mr. Belasco had furnished the beer, did you?"

Officer Reynolds tightened his lips and didn't answer. That was answer enough. "You had no evidence of a crime at that point, did you, Officer?" Burke insisted.

"No sir, not right at that point."

"So after the misunderstanding about your radio equipment and your smashing in the door was cleared up, wouldn't it have been the proper thing at that point for you to apologize for the inconvenience and leave?"

"We had an investigation to pursue, sir."

"You had no probable cause to *begin* an investigation," Burke answered.

"We had information from the confidential informant," Officer Reynolds said. He turned to Chris, his eyes asking for help. The District Attorney sat stoically. He felt other eyes on him as well, from the defense table.

"We haven't heard any evidence of that person, Officer," Lowell Burke said softly. He waited a moment for a response, then went on, "So when you seized the briefcase you were looking for evidence, is that right, Officer?"

Reynolds hadn't forgotten the right answer to that. "No sir, I seized the briefcase for my own safety, in case there were weapons inside."

"But can you articulate for us a reason why you thought there might be weapons in the briefcase?"

Reynolds hesitated. His eyes flickered as he obviously searched his mind and memory. He began slowly, "In that situation there's always a possibility . . ."

Burke interrupted. "You're talking generally, Officer. But was there anything *specific* about this situation and this briefcase that made you think there might be weapons inside?"

Reynolds gave up. He glanced again at the District Attorney, obviously hoping Chris had more evidence. "No sir, not specifically."

"And if you had simply left the briefcase where it was and departed the premises, you wouldn't have been in any danger, would you?"

Reynolds shrugged. The defense lawyer let that answer suffice. Again, the question had been aimed at the judge. After a silence, Burke said with the sneer apparent in his voice, "I pass the witness."

"No more questions," Chris Sinclair said quietly. "The State rests on the motion to suppress."

Judge Willis looked surprised. "Rests?" she said, then regained her impartiality. "Does the defense have witnesses to present?"

"I don't believe that's necessary, Your Honor," Lowell Burke said smoothly, rising to his feet.

"No," the judge agreed. "I don't think I need to hear arguments, either. On the state of this evidence—" She turned to the District Attorney, and her voice had an undertone of imploring as she said, "Unless there's some evidence of what went on inside the house before the police officers entered—?"

Again Chris felt himself observed from the defense table. He turned and looked back. Lowell Burke had a neutral, watchful expression. His client looked more obviously eager. There had been a confidential informant inside that room in Terrell Hills, one who had obviously made a deal with the police to inform on Peter Belasco. Who had it been? The defense knew Chris couldn't win this hearing without giving up that informant. That had probably been one reason Lowell Burke had filed his motion to suppress evidence in the first place. They waited for Chris to make his choice: give up the case or give up the unknown informant who had infiltrated the defendant's organization.

Chris pushed back his chair as he began his argument. Standing, he said, "Your Honor, I'd like to raise one issue: standing."

An observer who lacked a law school education might have thought Chris was describing the position from which he wanted to make his argument. The reporter listening closely from the spectator seats knew enough to make a note of the word: *standing*.

Chris continued, "As the court is well aware, in order to challenge a search of a place, the defendant has to demonstrate that he has standing to complain of the search of that particular place. We haven't heard any evidence today that this defendant owned that home in Terrell Hills or was even an invited guest."

Chris sat down again. He had raised a point that was an intrinsic part of every search issue, but seldom came up. Usually the prosecution let it be assumed that a defendant had a stake in the place searched. Still, if the prosecution raises the issue, the defense has the burden of proving standing. Police can break into a place and rip it to pieces, but unless the person arrested there can show he had a right to be in the place, he can't legally complain.

A small argument had broken out at the defense table. Lowell Burke sat staring down at his notes, thinking furiously, while his client whispered into his ear with equal ferocity. After a moment the defense lawyer began to shake his head.

"Well, I'll testify," Belasco said, loudly enough to be heard by the judge and the District Attorney. He buttoned his jacket and started to rise. His attorney stopped him.

Chris sat quietly at the State's table. The burden had shifted off his shoulders. Not just the burden of proof, but the burden of decision. The deed to the house in Terrell Hills showed the house owned by a man who had been dead for years. Every year a corporation paid the property taxes on the house. In spite of a diligent search, Chris hadn't been able to untangle who owned the corporation.

But Peter Belasco knew. He'd come to the house in Terrell Hills by invitation. On assignment, even. Peter Belasco obviously knew the name of his employer.

Apparently he was ready to say the name on the witness stand. His lawyer, however, wouldn't let him. Burke said a harsh sentence to his client in a quick undertone, then rose to his feet. He kept a hand on his client's shoulder for a long moment, making sure the young defendant stayed down. Belasco shot an angry glare at Chris Sinclair.

"Your Honor," Burke said smoothly. "The evidence the court has already heard speaks for itself. Mr. Belasco was obviously on the premises by invitation. When the police burst in Mr. Belasco had apparently been inside the house for some time. Police hadn't seen him arrive, and they'd had the house staked out for hours. So Mr. Belasco was something much more than an intruder or fleeting solicitor. In fact, as he was the oldest person in the house, he was the one who'd *done* the inviting. Officer Reynolds even testified that Mr. Belasco looked as if he were in charge. The leader, he said. Quite obviously—"

Judge Willis shook her head. "Appearance isn't enough, as you well know, Mr. Burke. The owner of that house could have been away on a long trip and this gang broke in to use it for the weekend. Without some evidence of ownership—" She gave the defense lawyer the same thoughtful pause she'd given the District Attorney a few moments earlier. Burke said nothing, and put his hand back on his client's shoulder. "—the defendant has not demonstrated standing to complain of the search," the judge concluded. "The motion to suppress is denied. The evidence will be admissible at trial."

She rapped her gavel lightly, said, "Dismissed," and left the bench with a rustle of black robe and dress.

Lowell Burke stood stunned, still thinking fast. His client began complaining loudly. Chris walked the couple of steps to their table, looked Lowell Burke in the eye, and said, "I believe you have a conflict of interest."

That was all he said before turning and walking out the gate in the railing. The reporter stood close by. "Congratulations," he said to the District Attorney, obviously meaning the compliment as a prelude to a quick interview.

Chris looked back at the defense table. He showed no triumph. "Not really," he said, and walked quickly out of the courtroom.

The reporter stood with his hands on his hips, in the aftermath of a hearing that had left the victor obviously unhappy and the losers—the defendant and his lawyer— arguing in increasingly louder tones.

"What the hell happened here?" the reporter asked.

Chris Sinclair walked up two flights of stairs to the top, the fifth floor of the Justice Center. A receptionist behind a window buzzed him through the locked front door of the District Attorney's Offices, and he made his way along the maze of corridors and small offices back to the corner, to his own office.

Chris's private office was good-sized but not elaborate and certainly not ostentatious. A small sofa and a wing-back chair, separated by a floor lamp, occupied the corner by the windows. Chris walked the other way, to his large dark wooden desk. The desk's top held only a legal pad and a file folder. Chris removed the few contents of the folder he'd carried into court and put them back in the larger file. This larger file, which stayed always on his desk lately, held the usual contents of a prosecution case file: police reports, a lab report, some notes on yellow pages from legal pads. There was only one thing odd about the file folder. It didn't have a name on it.

Chris's first assistant, a tall, scholarly looking man named Paul Benavides, stuck his head in the door and said, "I hear you won one." But he could see from his boss's expression that the outcome in court hadn't been what the District Attorney had hoped.

Chris answered, "The whole point of the exercise was that they wanted my informant and I wanted to know who Peter Belasco works for. So neither of us got the big prize."

"No new clue to Mr. Big?" Benavides grinned.

Chris gave his first assistant a moment's study. "Gee, John, I've never known you to make jokes before." Chris didn't smile. "That's one of the things I like about you."

Not chastened, Benavides withdrew. Chris returned to his study of the file folder on his desk. The folder that still didn't have a name.

Anne Greenwald ran. Panic hadn't set in, only concern. She glanced back over her shoulder.

Eddie Garza, running beside and a little behind her, said, "You got nothing to worry about, Doc. My mama used to say if you could look back over your shoulder and not see your behind, you were still in good shape."

"Eddie," Anne said between deep inhalations, "I hate to be the one to break this to you, but I'm not your mama."

Eddie probably had a retort, but not the breath to deliver it. They ran under Interstate 10, on the edge of downtown, and started up the Commerce Street bridge, into the near west side. Crossing under the interstate seemed like crossing a border; the surroundings immediately grew shabbier and more Mexican. A closed café

announced its name in Spanish. Little shops and houses
and old cars looked dispirited. Even the telephone lines
seemed to sag more as they traveled westward.

Dr. Anne Greenwald noticed these details. But this
hour she had declared a moratorium on liberal concern in
order to concentrate on herself, for once. In her mid-
thirties, Anne had no reason to fear aging—well, only
one reason, maybe. But her skin remained smooth, her
light brown hair still bounced, and her gray-green eyes
sparkled daily, and on the same days grew sad and angry
and thoughtful. Flexibility of emotion, that was one of the
main signs of staying alive, and Anne had that flexibility
in cartloads.

At five and a half feet tall she was still slender, too—
but not as slender as she'd been two months ago. She'd
put on three or four pounds over the holidays—she didn't
weigh herself, she just felt it—and hadn't had the time to
exercise in a month. Hadn't taken the time, anyway. She
didn't panic about the extra pounds, but had decided to do
something about them. So at the end of this afternoon's
shift at Santa Rosa Hospital, where Anne did psychiatric
counseling, mostly with children, she'd grabbed nurse
Eddie Garza and told him to put on his running shoes.

Twenty-five-year-old Eddie was one of those disgust-
ing men who didn't need exercise, who wolfed down
enchiladas for lunch yet stayed skinnier than Anne, but
running alone sucked, almost as badly as running at all,
so Anne had dragged him along and Eddie didn't mind
being dragged.

After they crested the hill, from which they could see
the Bexar County Jail a few blocks away, they stopped to
pant. Eddie put his hands on his knees. Anne stopped for
only a moment, then jogged in place, keeping her leg
muscles loose.

Eddie renewed the conversation from a few blocks
back. "In fact, my mama would say you need to put on a
few pounds instead of tightening yourself up all the
time." He mimicked her jogging in place.

"I don't think your mama lives by the U.S. Health Department guidelines. And you can tell her mirrors were made for checking on the condition of one's behind."

"I'm telling you don't worry, Doc," Eddie said in a slightly more serious tone of voice. He reached over and gave her ass a friendly pat, and in fact grabbed a momentary handhold. "Spandex was made for you."

Anne shook a mock-stern finger at him. "That's the kind of thing you think you can get away with because you swish around all day and let your wrist go loose. So you can breeze into women's dressing rooms carrying towels. I'm on to your act, Eddie. You've probably got a wife and four children at home."

Eddie looked pained, and into the distance. "Don't wish ordinary on me, Doc. I escaped all that."

He lightened up as they began running again. "Besides, people always let themselves go a little bit when they're in a good relationship. It's a sign of happiness." A little silence passed at the same time an old Buick did, bathing them in fumes. Eddie finally asked, "You do still have the boyfriend, don't you?"

Anne grinned at him and picked up speed. "Last time I checked, yeah," she called back over her shoulder. "How about you?"

"Touché," Eddie muttered. He caught up to her to find Anne still smiling.

"We'd better turn around," she said. "I've got to get showered and changed.

"For him?"

"When did you get so curious? No, dear, not for him. I have more in my life than that. I've got a high school stud on the side."

Eddie laughed. "Me too," he said.

"In your dreams. And please don't describe them for me."

They gave each other inquisitive glances—who was kidding whom?—and turned and ran back into town.

* * *

Showered, refreshed, skin glowing, full of energy even as twilight fell, Anne Greenwald drove her deep green Volvo to a southside high school, parked on a side street, and walked around the school to the gym. The school had shut down for the night, but there on the back side life persisted. The gym rocked. Anne made sure which side held which team's supporters, then climbed the rickety bleachers to a seat a fourth of the way up. Fans didn't fill the bleachers—the season was still young, the team not all that promising—but still the crowd appeared good-sized and energetic. High school students sat together in clusters, cheering and yelling and calling out the names of individual players. Adults in attendance kept generally quieter, except for the inevitable few moms who leaped to their feet and screamed their sons' names when something good, or nothing in particular, happened in the game. The players didn't acknowledge these fans, but an embarrassed smile would creep onto a player's face as he dribbled.

Anne looked for a particular jersey number and found him on the sidelines, as she'd expected. She hunched down on her bleacher, folded her arms, and hoped.

She had a hard time sustaining that hope as the half ended without an appearance on the hardwood floor by number 46, but Anne stood and cheered anyway. As she sat back down she saw someone who appeared more out of place than she did climbing the risers, a graceful man in a white dress shirt who looked as if it hadn't been all that long since he'd maneuvered on a basketball court himself. "My, what an attractive man," Anne muttered half-aloud, then as Chris Sinclair spotted her and stepped across people's legs to see her she said more loudly, "What the hell are you doing here?"

"Lovely to see you, too." Chris sat beside her and gave the room a quick survey as if surprised to find that it was, indeed, a high school gymnasium. "I might ask you the same thing."

"I'm a fan, man. Don't think you know everything about me. But how did you find me?"

In a serious tone, Chris said, "I planted a bug in your car months ago, just in case of an eventuality like this."

"Eddie told you."

Chris nodded. "Eddie tries to stay on my good side. I half-suspect he's engaged in something illegal and wants to have a friend in the system."

Anne put her arm through his. "You're so suspicious."

"Yeah, it kind of comes with the job."

She kept her arm in his, and her leg warmly beside his, but when the game resumed, Anne's attention returned to the floor of the gym. In the fourth quarter, with the home team comfortably ahead by nine points, but the players sagging a little, the coach looked along his bench, appeared a little surprised to see number 46 sitting there fresh as a squirrel in spring, and gave him a nod. The boy jumped to his feet, awkwardly pulled off his warmup pants, and moments later ran out onto the court.

Anne stood, yelled, "Woooo! Go, Juan," and whistled as avidly as the craziest mother in the audience. The crowd, startled by her enthusiasm, added some cheers, so that Juan glanced up with a surprised look and almost tripped over his own shoes. Then someone passed him the ball and he dribbled down the court with the same embarrassed but happy smile his teammates displayed. Anne clapped loudly, hands over her head.

When she finally sat again, Chris said, "Gee, which one's your patient?"

Eyes on the game, Anne said, "You know I'd never reveal something like that."

In fact Anne did keep her professional life strictly confidential. In the months they'd been seeing each other Chris hadn't been privy to a glance into her counseling work. He knew how much Anne's patients meant to her, but he'd never seen it demonstrated like this before. Usually he just saw what her work did to her emotionally, not the work itself.

Anne could have said the same about him.

Chris surveyed the crowd, many of whom were teenagers who had come not so much for the game as to be somewhere together, laughing and gossiping and acting surreptitious. "You know," he mused to Anne, "I think there are drug transactions going on here."

She gently stuck her elbow into his side. "Be off duty," she said.

"I am, I am. As long as the dealing doesn't reach the sidelines."

Late in the game number 46 got the ball at the foul line and leaped high in the air, poised to shoot, which drew two defenders toward him and left a home team player free under the basket. The boy in the air spotted his teammate, shot the ball to him, and the boy under the basket made the easy layup. The crowd cheered as wildly as if it had been the decisive play, and stayed on their feet as the final whistle blew a minute later. Anne's cheer rose above the rest. Number 46 looked up at her from the court and beamed.

Anne and Chris stayed where they were as the crowd slowly dispersed, shaking the bleachers. Anne became uncharacteristically confidential. "I wish he had someone to go home to and share this with. The sad part is that he's doing pretty well. I can't do all that much for him. He's adjusted about as well as you can to having no father and a mother who no one knows where she is most of the time."

"Where does he live?"

"A group home right now. We're trying to find a relative who'll take him in, but—" Painful sadness crossed Anne's face, moistening her eye. "He doesn't seem to have anybody who cares about him."

"Yes he does." Chris put his arm around her.

A few minutes later, the gym almost empty, Anne said, "I want to go say hi to him."

So they made their way down to the cement corridor to the boys' locker room. Just outside the swinging door, Chris hesitated. "I'll wait out here."

Anne cocked an eye at him. "Don't you think the man should go into the boys' locker room to make sure it's okay for the woman to follow, instead of the other way around?"

"Ordinarily I'd say yes, but—" Chris looked around the tunnel and lifted his voice. "Sir?"

A security guard nodded authoritatively, but Chris looked past him. "I'm sorry, not you, I meant him."

A high school kid with a push broom looked up in surprise and hurried over. The boy must have been about fifteen, all arms and Adam's apple.

Chris spoke to him seriously. "Would you do me a favor, please? Go in and make sure it's okay for a lady and the District Attorney to go in. You know what a District Attorney is?"

"You put people in jail," the boy said, without apparent awe.

"Yeah, that's pretty much it. Thank you, I'd appreciate it."

The boy pushed through the swinging door, leaving Chris with his hands in his pockets and a rueful expression on his face. "Sometimes I make kids nervous. I don't want anybody to think I'm running a raid or something."

Anne's mouth pursed, as if trying to contain a secret thought. "You know that boy had never been called 'sir' in his life," she finally said.

Chris shrugged. "It takes a long time to get used to it, he might as well start now."

Anne, trying not to beam, could no longer contain it. She put her arms around his neck and said, "God, I do love you."

When the skinny boy swung the doors open and said,

"It's okay," the sight of Juan's fan in passionate embrace with a man in suit pants and a white shirt brought a louder cheer from the team than they had received themselves all evening.

TWO

Chris Sinclair trotted up the outside steps of a two-story brick building that was half the size of the courthouse but looked small compared to the surrounding hospitals of the medical center. He passed through the glass doors labeled BEXAR COUNTY FORENSIC SCIENCE CENTER into the small pleasant lobby that always smelled fresh, and across the linoleum floor to the window. The receptionist glanced up and said, "Hello, Mr. Sinclair."

"Hello, Iris." Chris congratulated himself on remembering her name. So many people knew his. "I'm here to see the gun guys today. They're expecting me."

Iris, fresh young face splitting in a wide smile, reached under her desk and said, "Why don't you surprise them playing with their toys?"

She buzzed the inner door unlatched. Chris pulled it open and said, "So you're on to them, huh?"

"Boys with toys, that's all this place is." The receptionist's voice drifted after him as Chris passed into the forensic science center. Actually the building held quite a few girls with toys too, but Chris knew what Iris meant. The fifty or so people who worked in the center always seemed cheerful in their jobs, whether they were identifying poisons or cracking open corpses. Most people, Chris included, would have considered the daily reminders of mortality depressing, but the work seemed to have the opposite effect on the white-jacketed people who performed it. One of the assistants who did the manual labor involved in the autopsies had once said, "Every time I see a body on a table I think, 'Well, here's another one I beat.' Makes you glad to wake up in the morning."

The building itself, only three or four years old, projected a competent, professional image. Chris remembered the old morgue, thirty-five hundred square feet located near downtown, as a gloomy, smelly place. The forensic science center by contrast held fifty thousand square feet of extremely modern, expensive equipment, including a DNA-identification lab.

Chris made a few turns through the white halls, nodding or saying hi when someone passed, and came to the doorway of the gun and bullet identification section, which was staffed by two police officers who fit Iris's description perfectly. Murdoch and McGuinn loved their work. Their days off often found them here, adjusting the sights on their own pistols or letting doctors use the place as a firing range.

The door stood open. The large uncluttered front room, with two desks and a long table, didn't identify the place as anything other than an office. A door in the back wall opened and Bill Murdoch emerged, dropping earphones down around his neck and breaking open the chamber of a revolver. A slight acrid smell announced that Murdoch had just been firing the gun.

He glanced up, saw Chris in the doorway, and casually said, "Hey, boss. Come look at this."

Murdoch had large sloping shoulders and a perpetually flushed Irish face—the happy model, not the gloomy one. He held up the old-fashioned long-barreled gun for Chris's inspection. "Know what this is?"

"A Buntline Special?"

Murdoch grinned, appreciating the historical reference. "It's a Colt .45 revolver."

"I've heard of it."

"Damn right. This is the gun that won the West. Used to be the most common weapon in Texas. Now you hardly ever see one anymore. Really nice to hold. I'm so damned sick of all these pseudo-Uzis and AK-47s. Anybody can kill somebody if you get to take twenty shots at him in fifteen seconds. Takes somebody with skill to carry a gun like this. You've gotta admire that."

Chris nodded, letting Murdoch have his enthusiasm. "Did he kill somebody with it?"

"Oh yes. Two shots, one right through the heart. Down in Atascosa County."

All the units of the forensic science center did occasional work for smaller counties that didn't have their own centers. "Congratulations," Chris said idly. "What about my bullet?"

Murdoch put the revolver down on the table and shifted gears easily, holding up a demonstrative finger. "Your bullet was kind of fun too, Counselor. Come look."

He led Chris not back to the firing range but instead across the office to a smaller side room that held several computers. Murdoch tapped a couple of keys on the more elaborate computer setup and its screen came to life, painting in a logo with broad computer-driven brushstrokes. DRUGFIRE, read the screen.

"Have you seen this?" Chris shook his head. Murdoch obviously enjoyed explaining. "This is the FBI's latest project. This computer's connected to the main one in Quantico, Virginia, and then to others all over the country. In about thirty states so far." He put a map of the United States on the screen with more than half the states in yellow to indicate participation in DRUGFIRE, whatever that was.

"Whenever anybody gets a bullet from a crime scene,"

Murdoch continued, "we scan it into here." He demonstrated with the scrunched-down .45 caliber bullet he had
just retrieved from the water tank in back. With a hand-
held scanner he ran an invisible beam over the bullet, top,
back, and sides, as if he were a supermarket checker
looking for a bar code. As he did, an image of the bullet
appeared on the computer screen. The back of the bullet,
the part struck by the firing pin, displayed distinctive
lines and dents.

"See there?" Murdoch said, setting the actual bullet
casually aside in order to concentrate on its screen
image. He bent over the keyboard. "Now I send it into
the system."

Chris thought he saw where this was leading. "How
long does it take?"

"Couple of minutes sometimes. Depends on how busy
the system is."

Murdoch, who would have been very comfortable as a
nineteenth-century gunsmith or sheriff, looked anachro-
nistic bathed in the blue light of the computer screen, like
a lost traveler waiting for his time machine to carry him
home. But his blunt fingers moved across the computer
keys with easy familiarity.

"No hits," he said with a frown. He'd wanted to show
off what his toy could do. "Nobody else in the system has
scanned a bullet fired by this gun into DRUGFIRE. But at
least this tells us something. Strictly a local boy carrying
the big Colt."

"Or his other victims are lying in unmarked graves,"
Chris said, to cheer Murdoch up.

The policeman brightened anyway, as he turned to
Chris's problem. "Your bullet, though, was a different
story." He tapped more keys and produced a different
image on the screen, of a shorter, shinier bullet, as com-
pacted and dinged as the .45 bullet had been.

"First of all," Murdoch said, his eyes scanning the
image with cheerful appreciation, "it's an unusual caliber.

Ten millimeter. We see a lot of nine millimeters. That's become the weapon of choice in pistols."

"Could you just have measured it wrong?" Chris asked.

"Ha ha. The unusual caliber helps us pin down the manufacturer. Relatively small company called Lowther. A semiautomatic pistol, silver-plated, pretty light to fire that long a bullet. I wouldn't like it, myself. Probably have a strong kick to it. I can tell you damn near everything about the gun that fired this bullet."

"Including who fired it?" Chris asked rhetorically. Murdoch didn't answer. Chris tapped the image of the bullet on the screen. "Whoever did was used to its kick, apparently. He put three of these into a drug dealer named Juan Garcia a week ago and then sat there smoking a cigarette and watching him bleed to death." Detectives had deduced this scenario from the way cigarette ashes had sprinkled across a line of blood from the body, the ashes changing shape as the blood flowed.

Murdoch glanced at the District Attorney, whose eyes held grimly on the computer screen. "What's so special about this one?" the cop asked.

"I wanted the dead guy, the dealer. He'd sold a batch of bad psychedelics to some high school kids. Put one of them into a psychiatric ward." Criminals could prey on each other and nobody inside the system much cared, but when children became the victims Chris Sinclair took notice.

Murdoch said soothingly, "Well, somebody got him for you."

"You know what I mean. I wanted to turn him, follow him up the line to the bigger distributor. That's probably who did this."

"That'd be my guess," Murdoch agreed. "Find me another bullet and I'll tell you if it's the same guy."

They both knew the way another bullet from the killer's gun would most likely be recovered: only when someone else had been hurt. Chris stared at the image of the squashed bullet on the screen as it revolved like a diamond on display at a gem show. Hard evidence always gives investigators such hope, but without more information the bullet would hold its secrets.

After small talk with Murdoch, Chris walked slowly out into the hall of the forensic science center, mulling over what he'd learned. He knew a little more than he had an hour ago, but still had no new clues to Mr. Big. Since his assistants had started calling Chris's elusive, possibly mythical criminal mastermind by that derogatory tag, Chris couldn't help using it himself. But the name didn't amuse him. It held too many possibilities.

He thought about looking around the building for Dr. Parmenter, his favorite among the assistant medical examiners. Instead he kept on with his job, deciding to visit the toxicology department to see what they could tell him about the bad drugs sold to teenagers by the drug dealer. He resumed his rapid pace down the white, echoing corridor. At the far end of the hallway, coming toward him, he saw a young man with a fringy beard that straggled down his sideburns and around his chin. The young man wore a white lab coat and was carrying a head. Chris knew this part-time employee of the forensic science center as the forensic sculptor, the one who reconstructed the facial features of bodies that had deteriorated far enough to be unrecognizable. In both hands at about chest level he carried an example of his art.

Chris couldn't quite remember the young man's name, but knew him enough to say hi. He raised his hand in casual greeting, glanced at the head as he drew close, then stopped in the hall. As the young man in the lab coat drew abreast of him, Chris put out his hand and stopped his progress. Chris thought he said *stop*, or something of the sort, but in fact he remained silent, staring at the detached model of a head in the young man's hands.

Chris stood dead still, staring at the sculpted face. He didn't see the hands holding the head out toward him, didn't notice the sculptor turning the head slightly to give the District Attorney a better look. Chris only saw her face.

In the hallway of the forensic science center the District Attorney of Bexar County disappeared. The sight of her face jerked Chris right out of himself, out of adulthood, made his present circumstances fade to forgotten.

Chris Sinclair became nineteen years old again, during a time when her face was the first image that filled his thoughts every morning, her name—Jean—the first word out of his mouth. Sometimes she actually lay beside him. If not, he went looking for her, before thinking of classes or study or food.

He would find her in the strangest quarters, parts of Austin he would never have known if not for Jean. That was why Jean fascinated him so completely; not just because he loved her unabashedly, with the brimming heart of a nineteen-year-old, but because he found her world so much more exciting than his. Chris had been a sophmore at the University of Texas in Austin when he'd met Jean at a party. One of those college parties that spontaneously burst out of the confines of its apartment and became an open-air scene with no boundaries. Chris wandered from the parking lot into a pebbled courtyard with a small fountain in the middle and became absorbed into the crowd, unsure whether this was the same party to which he'd been casually invited. But he waved to friends, accepted tokes from strangers, talked about school with other strangers, and looked past the heads of laughing students to see Jean moving to the raucous music.

She wasn't dancing, she just moved, shoulders and head and hips and arms flowing sinuously to the rhythm that hadn't been apparent in the music until Jean moved to it. The music lived in her, first as she got a beer in a plastic cup from the keg beside the fountain, then as she slowly made her way through the crowd, surveying the faces and waving, then stopping to lend her full appreciation to a particular passage of the song.

At that point she became aware of Chris watching her. Without looking at him she suddenly did a twirl, going up on the toes of one sandaled foot and slowly revolving, arm stretched high above her head. When she came to a stop she stood right in front of him, smiling.

"Eight years of ballet," she said, "and that's my only move."

That was a lie. Jean hadn't remotely exhausted the repertoire of her moves. Her best move was with no effort to change the life of the boy from suburban San Antonio, turning him into a slightly different person from the one he'd been when he'd come to the party, and incidentally into her companion.

Jean had reddish brown hair worn shaggy, and blue eyes and a wide mouth that smiled easily or secretively. She had a definite woman's shape but no spare flesh. The tops of her hipbones rose out of her jeans, visible below the short top she wore that left her waist bare. Chris wanted to put his arm around her waist. When she looked up at him she seemed aware of that desire, but talked to him without obvious flirtation.

"Have you seen Paul?" She had to raise her voice.

Chris looked over the crowd authoritatively, though his chance of spotting the person in question was minimal, since he had no idea who Paul might be. "Nope."

Jean called his bluff. "You don't know Paul, do you?"

"Sure. Paul Simon, right? He was here earlier."

Jean laughed. "Who *did* you come here with?"

Chris surveyed the sea of faces congesting the mild spring night. Young, young faces, kids with lots of hair, some of it on their faces, buzzing on beer and dope and making their own version of cocktail party chatter.

Chris frowned. "You know, I don't know any of these people."

Jean gave him a closer study. "You're weirder than you look," she said, which he took as a compliment.

Soon after that they left the party in the courtyard, riding in Jean's little red Subaru to another party she'd heard about. Wind streamed through the car. They seemed to be outdoors. It felt to Chris like the first time he'd ridden through the night with an unknown destination and no way to get home. Jean smoked a cigarette and told a story about somebody from the party, a friend of hers who'd decided to cheat on her boyfriend but had been interrupted by the boyfriend himself, so she'd sneaked to the phone and called Jean to come to her apartment as if it had been planned for Jean and the new boy to meet there.

"So I get dressed and run over there and act like it was all a big planned thing, and we go on this, you know, double date, and I don't know if this guy and I are already supposed to be a couple or if we're supposed to have just met—which we had—so I'm desperately trying to pick up clues. Meanwhile I get the feeling there's a lot of hand- and footwork going on under the table and I am *no* part of it."

She spread her hands, taking them off the steering wheel, laughing. Chris laughed as well. Jean still didn't flirt with him, they hadn't touched, but their legs lay close together in the small car, and in one way the situation was more intimate than bed, when Jean would pause, looking into his face as if distracted from her tale by something she saw there.

She drove them eventually to Armadillo World Headquarters, a music venue in an old Quonset hut. Chris, who hadn't lived in Austin long, had heard of the place but had never been there. Groups left over from the psychedelic era played there, as well as edgy modern innovators. Chris wasn't even surprised when Jean produced a backstage pass from her purse and put it around her neck, then talked Chris past the long-haired guard as well, so that instead of sitting out front listening and paying like the other nobodies they wandered among cables and curtains with Jean casually exchanging nods and hi's with the backstage crew. Ostensibly they were still looking for the elusive Paul, but for Chris the evening had no goal, it just served as an introduction to Jean's world.

The night passed in talk about their childhoods and high schools—hers had been in Dallas, much more sophisticated than Chris's, he gathered—and his stories had never seemed so funny or poignant. After a short long time the sun was up, and they hadn't made love, hadn't even kissed, but a part of Chris knew they would—a daring, self-confident component of his personality that had only awakened in the last few hours. Jean drove to her home, in an old mansion that had been converted to individual efficiency apartments. She parked the Subaru at the curb and they both got out, feeling suddenly sandy-eyed in the sunlight.

"You sure you can walk from here?" Jean asked, and Chris assured her he could, which was a lie; he lived miles away. But he hadn't wanted Jean to take him home, he'd wanted to see where she lived, so he could come again. She seemed to know his reasons. She smiled, and walked languidly toward him, her eyes undiminished by the long night. They glowed even brighter in the sun. She put her hand, that hand that moved so well to the music, on the back of his neck and pulled his head down slightly and kissed him with soft lips and lingering closeness. Chris didn't reach for her, didn't ruin the moment, just let his awakening emotions flow through the kiss. After a long minute Jean stepped back and raised her eyebrows, then turned and walked away without a plan or a farewell. Halfway to the back door of the old mansion she said over her shoulder, "Don't you have classes?"

That was a difficult question to answer, since he couldn't remember what day of the week it was.

* * *

Jean's world proved so much more interesting than his. Chris's friends played basketball, watched TV, often drank a lot of beer on the weekends but during the week attended classes every day, ate more or less regular meals, and occasionally went home for the weekend or holidays. Jean's friends were smoother and hipper, their music stranger, their posters more glowing, and they didn't seem to have different lives only shortly past, in which they'd been high school students and lived with parents. No, they seemed to inhabit their worlds more fully than Chris did his. They spent no time thinking or talking about what they would do when they grew up. They were already there. They lived a weird variant of grown-up lives, but seemed adult nevertheless.

And they smoked a lot of dope, at any hour of the day.

Jean never seemed stoned. Or hurried, or grumpy, or concerned that she might be late to arrive somewhere. Her life ran on no apparent schedule. One April day Chris saw her on campus carrying books and the sight surprised him, as if one of his lives intruded into the other. He hurried to catch up to her and even from the back as he drew near he felt her smiling. He knew she knew it was him. She put out her left arm and he slipped under it. She draped her arm around his shoulders and didn't greet him.

"Let's be college kids in love," she said in her languid voice, looking up at the sky, her neck stretching. When she lowered her gaze her voice had grown more southern. "My name is Clarissa, from Highland Park. I belong to the same sorority my mother and grandmother pledged. It was founded by my great-grandmother in 1866, after the unpleasantness. Have I met you at one of our mixers? Delta Upson Chucks?"

Making his voice gruffer, Chris answered, "My name is Roger Runsabunch. From Midland or Odessa. I'm a

heavily recruited wide receiver and I can run the forty in
four point something seconds."

"But don't think you're going to run out on me, big
boy." Then toning down the southern accent, as if really
seeking information, Jean asked, "Four point what?"

"I don't know. They hired some geeky math major to
keep track of the decimals for me."

Jean laughed, a sound that rose to the sky. She hugged
him more tightly and kissed his cheek, then took a quick
playful nibble of his earlobe, which shocked him with
delight, not just in the bite itself but that it came in the
daylight on the campus of the University of Texas. Jean
leaned against him. They were both smarter and better
than anyone around them. Hearing her laugh he could
also see her eyes shine, and in the laugh and the press of
her arm around him he felt her love.

And now more than a decade and a half later he saw her
disembodied head being carried down the white corridor
of the Bexar County Forensic Science Center. The young
man carrying the head coughed delicately and Chris
remembered his name. Parker Jensen had a high forehead
and glasses with thick black frames and the long, thin fingers of a sculptor. Jensen's real art lay elsewhere, but it
didn't support him, so to supplement his income he
worked for the county on a contract basis, re-creating the
faces and heads of the dead who had gone unfound so
long that they no longer had flesh.

Chris knew all this. He knew what it meant that the
sculptor was carrying Jean's head down the hall. This was
a re-creation, not her own skin, but it was in a sense real
nonetheless.

"I'm taking her to be photographed," Parker Jensen
said. "We've been having a hell of a time getting her identified; the doctors decided it's time to run a couple of pictures in the newspaper."

Chris reached for her face but didn't touch it. Jensen

had gotten the cheekbones right, and the wide mouth. The chin and jawline were too small, not as he remembered Jean's, and the hair was all wrong, too light. The sculptor had re-created something about the smooth eyelids just right. Chris had seen her sleeping and she had looked like this, as he had studied her face, waiting for her eyes to open. Jensen had given the face an innocent look that had not been part of Jean's quick, bright flashes of expression.

"You know her?" the sculptor asked, a slight hollowness in his voice. When Chris nodded, Jensen said, "Tell me about her."

That was a tall order, as Chris stood so full of memories and emotions that they clogged his throat. After a moment he said, "She had the deepest blue eyes you've ever seen. She had a tiny little scar right here"—he indicated, without touching, a spot near the corner of her mouth—"just a little white dot that didn't tan. Chicken pox scar. She had a stronger jawline than this, and her ears were bigger."

"What size was the lady you're talking about?"

"Size?" Chris felt Jean's head coming up above his shoulder. "About five eight, I guess. Very thin. She'd be about thirty-five now, so she's probably not that thin anymore. And maybe her skin—"

Jensen shook his head. He hefted the head in his hands and with a sound like relief in his voice said, "This girl's like fourteen, sir. No way she's in her thirties."

Chris felt the ground shift beneath him again. Had he made a mistake? He studied the face even more closely. No, he hadn't. He saw the dissimilarities in a face sculpted with latex, but he still saw Jean, as well. The doctors could be a few years off on the age, but even so that would mean she had been in the ground since very soon after the last time he'd seen her.

"You know I don't do the dating," Jensen said apologetically. "You'd have to talk to the doctors about—"

Chris took the head from him, carrying it very carefully. The thing felt awful, the coldness of the latex a shock to his skin even though he'd known not to expect the warmth of flesh. It was heavy, too. He knew why it weighed so much, and the thought made his heart sink.

"Let's go find the doctor," he said.

Dr. Harold Parmenter, assistant chief medical examiner, drank cold coffee and listened to Parker Jensen's explanation while watching his friend Chris Sinclair, who stood stiffly holding the head. Dr. Parmenter usually joked with the District Attorney when they saw each other here or in the Justice Center, but the doctor immediately saw today that Chris wouldn't recognize a joke if he heard one. He held the sculpted head as if it revolted him but as if a magic spell bound it to his hands.

Dr. Parmenter was tall, with long arms and a long face topped by stiff sandy hair. As a forensic pathologist—a student of the dead—he didn't usually have to speak to the bereaved, that was someone else's job, and his patients never needed tenderness, so his delicacy had grown a little rusty. But he stood and spoke very gently as he took the head from Chris Sinclair.

"She's a girl, Chris, I promise you that. Fourteen years old is about right. At that age we can get it very precisely, because they haven't stopped growing. The plates of some of the bones haven't quite grown together yet. This was not an adult woman."

He set the head down on a counter, upright on the base the sculptor had affixed at the bottom of the short neck. The three of them stood in the autopsy area where Parker Jensen and Chris had found Dr. Parmenter. The four metal tables against the walls stood empty and clean. The autopsy room looked like a very well-maintained locker room, with tile walls and drains in the floor. Under its bright lights the sculpted head looked more artificial. Chris no longer found it as spooky, or lifelike. Unreal as it now looked to him, Chris realized he was still waiting for the eyes to open.

"How long has she been dead?" he asked.

Dr. Parmenter had an answer ready. "I'd say three months. Maybe a little less. We've had her three weeks."

Chris blinked as if waking up. A fourteen-year-old girl dead only three months. It couldn't possibly be his old friend. Chris took his first full breath in many minutes. Though he seldom thought about Jean Plymouth anymore, he was glad to know she wasn't this dead, unclaimed body.

Still, that was her face molded out of plastic. A variation, certainly, but close enough that he remained sure of his original recognition. And whoever this girl might have been, she was a real child, dead and lost. The head was fake, a re-creation, but inside it lay a real skull. That was how the sculptor re-created faces, by layering his unreal flesh directly onto the skull, following its contours and taking clues from its remains. The head contained a real, extinguished life.

"Tell me about where you found her," Chris said.

Dr. Parmenter's voice held relief, as he saw his friend coming out of his daze. "Out where most bodies are found, outside Loop 1604. Not too far from where Interstate 10 crosses it. Remember back around the end of December when that child wandered away from the car while his father was changing a tire?" He nodded at the head. "One of the search teams found her instead."

"Buried or not?" Chris asked. His voice had grown more detached, like that of an investigator taking notes.

"Yes, but not very deep. There'd been a hard rain the night before that washed away some of the mounded dirt. One of the searchers saw a hand sticking up."

Chris pictured that, a white hand lifted like a signal for help. "No identification on her?"

"No. No purse, jewelry, anything like that. Although there was one thing . . . Come on, I'll show you. I'll take her, Parker, I'll bring her to the photo lab later. Thanks."

The sculptor, obviously glad to be dismissed, nevertheless stood awkwardly, hands in his pockets. "Sorry I startled you, man."

"Don't worry about it," Chris said. "It was just because you do your job so well."

With a quick smile Parker Jensen walked out. The District Attorney and the assistant medical examiner took another direction, Dr. Parmenter carrying the head. He led Chris a couple of turns through the halls to a door that when opened revealed a storage room with metal shelf units. Paper bags and boxes filled most of the shelves rather haphazardly, though Dr. Parmenter seemed to have a system. He set the head on a shelf and picked up a paper grocery sack from the shelf below. Someone had written a case number on the bag. The doctor opened it and said, "Look."

Chris didn't like being told to look when he was at the forensic science center. He even flinched a tiny bit when Dr. Parmenter opened doors and strode into new rooms. Chris wasn't particularly squeamish, but he had learned that he couldn't trust the casualness of the people who worked here and chatted over bodies or body parts, who thought nothing of saying, "Look," and holding out for observation some mass never meant to see the light of day.

But he needn't have worried about the contents of the paper bag. It held only the salvageable belongings of the dead girl: her dress, a faded violet color with tiny flower designs, her schoolgirl shoes, underwear, and the small object Dr. Parmenter groped for and held out to Chris. Chris held it on his hand: a small stuffed dog six or eight inches long, a beagle or basset with droopy eyes and long floppy ears. The brown cloth was discolored and insects had chewed part of its leg.

"This was buried with her," Dr. Parmenter said.

The stuffed dog had grown stiff, as if it had died with its owner—assuming the dog had belonged to the girl. Chris felt no warmth in the animal. But he handled it delicately as he handed it back to Dr. Parmenter, who stored it again in the sack.

"Do you have a cause of death?"

Dr. Parmenter hesitated. This might be a matter of testimony some day. Prosecutors rely on medical examiners to say confidently, "Homicide," from the witness stand. Dr. Parmenter raised his eyebrows, indicating they were speaking off the record. Chris nodded.

"She certainly didn't die of natural causes, Chris. She had a little speed in her system but not nearly enough to kill her. Without more information I can't say she was murdered. It could have been an accident. But she was certainly killed. She had a broken neck."

Chris took the news in stride, already sounding as if he were building a case as he said, "If it had been an accident, they wouldn't have taken her out to the edge of town and buried her in a shallow grave, would they?"

Dr. Parmenter nodded soberly.

Some time later Chris stood again on the outside steps of the forensic science center. The January afternoon had turned into a Chamber of Commerce day, with bright beams of sunlight piercing the clouds and the temperature straining toward sixty-five. Chris felt as if a long time had passed since he'd entered the building, because of the emotional journey he'd taken, but hours of daylight remained available. He would head back to the office.

The dead girl wasn't Jean. They had convinced him of that. Soon after that realization another possibility struck Chris forcibly, but a quick calculation destroyed it. A fourteen-year-old girl with Jean's face but blonder hair, the color of Chris's. Fourteen. Chris subtracted again. No. It had been more than sixteen years since the last time he had seen Jean Plymouth. Obviously she had gone on and quickly formed a new life for herself, but Chris hadn't been part of it. No way the girl inside the medical examiner's office could be related to him.

Maybe she wasn't related to Jean, either. There are a lot of faces in the world, with small variations among them. Faces remind us of other faces. Something might have put Jean in his thoughts, and then the sculpted face startled him with its resemblance. Chris remembered times in his life after funerals when he would see the dead person's face abroad in the world for days afterward, but when he took a closer look the resemblance confined itself to an ear or the curve of a cheek.

No, the dead girl very likely had nothing to do with him, and even less to do with his old friend Jean.

Nevertheless, he knew he had to find her.

Three

Dr. Anne Greenwald, MD, Ph.D., leaned back and to the side, torso twisting, cocked her arm back, and skipped a stone five times across the San Antonio River.

"Not bad, Doc," fifteen-year-old Henry Blevins said approvingly.

Anne enjoyed being called Doc as much as she enjoyed finding sprouts in a salad, which always made her wonder who had decided this grass was food, but young Henry was no longer her patient, so they needed something for him to call her less formal than "Dr. Greenwald," and Anne balked at promoting the boy to first-name status, so "Doc" was the compromise he had come up with and she'd accepted. She wiped dirt off her hands and watched the ripples where the stone had sunk.

"It probably bounced off sludge," she said. Where they stood in Brackenridge Park, the river between its man-made stone banks flowed maybe two feet deep.

In late January in San Antonio, the weather so yearned toward spring already that many of the trees had budded, but freezes remained possible. The air was crisp, making lungs open and hair frizz. Anne wore gray slacks and a

Lincoln-green jacket with a white knit turtleneck underneath. She had chosen the outfit carefully for her meeting with Henry, not to appear too formal or doctorish, but not dressing down to him, either. Dressing for a nondate with a fifteen-year-old boy required thoughtful care. Henry wore jeans, tennis shoes, and a long-sleeved plaid shirt. Anne knew he had probably spent time carefully selecting his clothes too, choosing his best tennis shoes and most perfectly faded jeans. And the jeans fit him, they didn't bag around his legs. Henry's light brown hair was cut short but not shaved anywhere. He looked like a healthy, clean-cut kid, which he was. He really hadn't needed much help from Anne.

Henry walked along the bank of the river, idly kicking at stones, looking down to avoid tripping over the tangle of cypress roots that snaked along the ground. Brackenridge Park, a large expanse of nature in the middle of the city, contained a golf course, the river, the San Antonio Zoo, the Brackenridge Eagle miniature train, the Japanese Tea Gardens, and generous scatterings of benches, barbecue grills, and playground equipment. Anne had picked Henry up from his huge suburban high school (carefully meeting him a few blocks away so his peers wouldn't see them) and then driven back deep within the city. Anne had chosen the venue carefully. Brackenridge Park lay on the north, more affluent side of San Antonio, but it was inner city compared to Henry's world. Actual poor people came here, with their children. Anne wanted to show Henry a different slice of the city than what he usually experienced.

She saw the boy look across the river to where a large family busied themselves hanging balloons and a *piñata* from tree limbs. One man started a fire in the grill, using a minimum of charcoal and sticks he'd gathered from the ground. Brown children bounced and laughed. From this distance one couldn't tell which was the birthday celebrant. They all looked related by blood and their delight in the day.

Not looking at her, Henry asked, "Still busy all the time, Doc? The clinic still swarming with nutcases?"

"Henry," she said sternly. "You know we have rules about that. The patients are referred to as 'the weirdos.' "

He laughed, then felt the implication. "Was I one of your weirdest ones?"

Anne put her arm on his shoulders very briefly, and walked past him to pick up another stone. "Henry, you are so relentlessly normal I felt criminal taking your parents' money."

The boy's tone of voice lightened. "You know the thing about your waiting room?" he asked, looking off into memory. "None of us talked to each other. There might be five kids in there sometimes, some of them waiting for other doctors or whatever, and we'd watch each other, you know"—he demonstrated furtiveness, eyes sliding— "but you wouldn't dare speak. 'Cause the guy across the room might be some real crazoid who'd cut your throat for saying the wrong thing. Or just as bad, the girl next to you might turn out to seem real easygoing and normal, so you'd think, 'Wow, it's really working for her and I'm still crazy.' "

"Do you feel that way? Crazy?"

Henry considered the question, as if taking his temperature at that moment. "Not too much."

"Everybody does, Henry. Look around you at school. I guarantee you every kid you see has the same thought way at the back of his mind: 'If these people knew how weird I am, they'd drive me out into the wilderness.' That's why teenagers try so hard to fit in, because each one thinks he's so strange, and tries to hide it. It takes a long time before you actually enjoy being different."

Henry looked at her sidelong. He put his hands in his pockets. "Are you sure everybody thinks that?"

"I don't know, maybe it was just me."

He laughed again. Anne tried to ease out of lecture mode and into conversation. "So your grades are pretty good and you have a fair chance of making the varsity tennis team. That sounds great. What else? Have any friends you hang out with? A girl you like?"

A quick flare of anger flushed his face. "What is this, an interrogation? Nobody's paying you to pry into my private life anymore, you know."

"Henry. I ask for two reasons. First, I figure you might want to talk about personal stuff but your parents are afraid to ask you, because they have to live with your sulking if they get you mad. I don't. Second—"

"Gah, is this your dissertation?"

"Second, I ask because I want to know. That's what friends are about. If you were my college roommate thirty-five-year-old woman friend I hadn't seen in a while, I'd ask you the exact same questions."

His face lightened as he caught the flattering aspect of what she'd said. "Really? You'd ask her if she had a girl-friend?"

Anne laughed, surprised by his quickness. "Well, people change, you know. How're you going to learn anything if you don't ask?"

They walked along the bank of the river. To their left an occasional car passed on the broad road through the park. The miniature train tracks crossed the road twenty yards ahead. The long hoot of the train's horn sounded. Anne and Henry saw it coming from the other side of the river, the engineer riding atop the engine, passengers rocking side to side in the open-air cars. The train trudged staunchly across the trestle over the river, the bridge looking barely wide enough to hold the train. Passengers waved and Anne and Henry waved back, feeling like colorful locals hired as decorations for the train set.

Still waving, staring after the train as it crossed the road into the woods, Henry said suddenly, "My parents argue a lot."

"Really?" Anne realized she'd responded with gossip-relish—those nice people?—and forced her curiosity back a notch.

"I don't fight with my friends," Henry said. "Not much, anyway."

"You don't live with your friends. It's hard for people to live together."

"How do you know, Doc? I mean, have you been married?"

"No."

"Really? And you're how old?"

Anne frowned at him. Henry lifted his eyebrows innocently. "I'm just asking, like a friend."

"Smart kid. Hey, you want to go to the zoo? Let's cut across the train bridge, it's faster."

"But you're not supposed to," Henry protested. "What if a train comes?"

"Oh, they run at least twenty minutes apart. Don't be such a weenie."

"*Now* you sound like one of my friends," Henry said, and followed her up onto the train tracks.

Stepping carefully from cross tie to cross tie, looking down through the gaps at the water twenty feet below, they made it across without being killed or having to leap into the river. As they walked on the other side, the sky grew noticeably darker, clouds bringing the day to an early close. It would be a good time to go to the zoo, when the animals wouldn't be flattened by heat, and some of the nocturnals might be waking up early.

Henry didn't have a gift for conversation. When he said anything significant he just chunked it out there, still raw from being ripped loose from inside him. "Sometimes when I come into the room from outside or something they just stop talking completely, even though I'd heard their voices from outside so I know they were arguing about me."

Anne grimaced internally. Henry would think all the family problems stemmed from him. Telling him that his mother and father were people themselves with problems of their own wouldn't help. Henry knew the kinds of things he kept secret. Thinking his parents held similar secrets would cut the ground right out from under him.

Secrets. We start accumulating them as soon as we can form words. Anne thought suddenly of Chris, as she often did, picturing him stuck inside his office on this breezy, fresh day. Chris had a face that would remain boyish until he died. He didn't look like a secret-keeper, in spite of his work. Sometimes being with him made Anne feel overly complicated. She held her own secrets, accumulated over those years of living alone, and one special one she was waiting for just the right time to spring on Chris.

That is, if a wish could be called a secret.

"I just want to tell them I'm okay, you know?" young Henry burst out.

Anne, walking behind the boy, leaned forward and rested her head on the boy's shoulder. "You are, Henry, believe me. Your parents know that, too. And I'll tell them."

"You don't have to do that," Henry said, but with relief and gratitude in his voice. So this is why he'd wanted to see his former psychiatrist again, to get her to intervene in the adult world for him. She hoped she could help, but she also saw the possibility of Henry resuming therapy again one of these months.

Nobody ever really graduates, Anne thought. They walked on down the pebbled path into the zoo, where Henry laughed at the rhinos, looked thoughtfully at the monkeys, and ate cotton candy like a happy five-year-old. Dr. Anne Greenwald did, too.

When Medical Examiner's investigator Monica Burris downshifted her Jeep Cherokee in order to drive off the main road onto a set of ruts that led into the brush, Chris Sinclair noticed the lavender polish on her rather long fingernails. Burris wore a subtle uniform, navy slacks with sturdy hiking shoes and a brown shirt with a small patch on the shoulder denoting her office. The uniform had

been designed for men. Monica Burris had a strong nose
and jawline and feminine cheekbones. She didn't do anything overtly to turn the practical uniform feminine, but
Chris wondered if the nails represented her small assertion of gender. He wondered too, if they were a nuisance
when she picked apart a crime scene.

"Maybe somebody knew the way in here," Burris said,
"or maybe they just turned off the road and kept looking
for ways off the beaten path. If you're dumping a body
you don't want to do it by the side of the highway."

"So you think she was killed somewhere else and then
brought here?"

"Oh, definitely. The doctors could tell you why from
the condition of the body, but I can tell you I found no
blood at the scene, which means—"

"Yeah, I know." When the heart stops beating, the body
stops bleeding. Chris had heard this observation in medical testimony for years.

The investigator glanced at him, wondering at his
somber tone. People in this field, whether doctors or
lawyers or investigators, usually had a very detached way
of talking about death. The District Attorney didn't have
that easy attitude, not today.

"Also it just makes sense," she said. "Why would anybody come out here except to dispose of someone?"

"To make out?" Chris offered. "She was a fourteen-
year-old girl. The end of a date, things go badly, push
push, slap, scream. It certainly wouldn't be the first time."

"Possibly," Burris said neutrally. She brought the bulky
vehicle to a stop. The spiky trees, mesquites and scrub
oaks, hemmed them in. Most of them had been turned to
stick figures by winter, though many of the oaks still bore
leaves. The landscape looked defensive, like the thorns
that had grown up around Sleeping Beauty's castle.

"Does this road lead anywhere?" Chris asked. The
trees seemed to close in on it in the near distance.

Burris laughed as she opened her door. "You call this a
road? Maybe it was once. Half a mile farther on are the

ruins of a ranch house. But other than that no, it doesn't
go anywhere. And it floods pretty badly at the slightest
hint of rain. So we didn't find any useful tire tracks."

She stretched her back as she stood beside the Jeep and
looked back the way they'd come. "A couple of guys
searching for the lost boy found this track and thought he
might have come down it, so they followed it in. If they
hadn't been on foot, looking carefully through the brush,
they probably would have missed the grave. Probably
other people did, passed right by in the three or so months
she was buried there."

As the investigator said "there," she pointed across the
hood of her car to Chris's side of the road. He had already
spotted the remains of the grave, a remarkably shallow
depression fifteen feet away from the ruts that had once
been a road. The soil in this area was black crumbly dirt
mixed with sand. The top layer would wash away quickly
in rain, but underneath it grew hard, which accounted for
the deep-rooted trees that had driven out less determined
foliage. The soil would also resist digging, especially if
the digger hadn't come well equipped. A killer in a hurry,
looking over his shoulder and improvising a shovel with
whatever lay handy, would have given up when the hole
grew just deep enough to accommodate the body. The
grave hadn't been destined to hold its secret very long.

He asked, "Could you tell from the marks in the
ground what they dug the grave with?"

Burris admired the question. That had been one of the
first things she'd looked for. "Come see." She led him the
few steps through the scratching branches to the hole in
the ground. The hole didn't deserve the dignity of the
word "grave." They squatted beside it, the investigator in
her comfortable uniform, the DA in his navy suit pants
and dress black shoes, tie loosened and jacket left in the
car. Burris noticed how he held his balance and didn't put
a hand down on the ground for support.

"See these marks? These long lines in the soil? The
body protected the bottom of the grave so they're pre-

served. A tree branch made those marks. A shovel leaves crescent-shaped bites. I found the branch over that way a few feet, just tossed into the woods after they finished."

Chris said, "So it was a rush job, he looked fast for a place and didn't take the time to get the right equipment. Probably had the body in the trunk, driving around frantically."

"She was lucky not to end up in a Dumpster," Burris said.

Chris's eyes narrowed slightly, a tiny wince. He looked into the narrow hole. Other than the marks the investigator had pointed out, the hole told him nothing. Two feet under the topsoil the dirt grew thicker, tightly packed, slightly glossy. A hard, cold place to lie, even for a minute.

Chris stood up and stared into the scrubby woods, ignoring the grave. He didn't sense her presence from that hole in the ground—neither the dead girl back in the ME's office nor his old friend Jean Plymouth. The hole had just been a temporary storage place for the dead, it hadn't absorbed any life.

But these trees took him back in time. The area looked like one of the last places he'd seen Jean, the woods near the Pedernales River not far outside Austin. Monica Burris made another observation, but Chris's attention had taken flight into the past.

He knew she dealt marijuana. Chris even helped her occasionally, carrying the package and standing by while Jean made the cash transaction. Being the bagman made Chris feel more a part of her world. A musician or stagehand would nod at him as if they shared common ground. Once a skinny guy with long stringy hair held back by a headband looked over Jean's shoulder, grinned at Chris, and said, "Are you the muscle on this deal?"

"That's right," Chris growled in his fake football player's voice, and Jean too smiled at him. For days after that she called him "my bodyguard." "The body needs guarding," her voice came softly over the phone line in one post-midnight call.

Selling grass had an outlaw novelty, like so much else in Jean's world, but it wasn't as if it were her main occupation in life, or consumed a large part of their time. Chris and Jean still went to classes, read books, drove out to the lake on Saturdays, picnicked in Zilker Park, even a couple of times swung high on the swings, unstoned on anything more sinister than youth and sunlight.

So it came as a surprise to Chris that Jean had actually been devoting thought to the business aspect of her life. "You know, I'm getting ripped off," she declared out of the blue one May day during "dead week," the few days between the end of classes and the beginning of finals. "Paul takes a big cut for what? Passing on a pound of weed from his supplier to me—and does nothing for his share except get me to do all the sales like his little messenger girl. It takes a real idiot to keep doing my part, taking all the risks, for the little bit of profit I make off the deals."

Chris vaguely knew that Paul was her supplier. Jean had pointed him out once at a party, and he'd looked more like a political science grad student than a big-time drug dealer.

"You're right," Chris answered idly. "I guess without unthinking peons like you the whole drug trade would collapse."

"Yeah," Jean said emphatically, uninsulted. She sat cross-legged on her bed on the second floor of the old mansion. She wore very short cutoff jeans and her feet were bare. Chris lay on a large cushion across the room from her, reading a history textbook.

Jean lifted a fist. "And it's time for a peasant revolution!"

The sight of Jean stirred by passion, pretend or not, brought Chris more fully into the play. "Are you going to wear your peasant blouse? And carry a rifle and wear those bandoliers that cross your chest? I've always wanted—"

"No, my boy," Jean said, eyes shining. She was off again on a project, a fantasy, and Chris delighted at being drawn along in her wake. "We need to get a gun for *you*," Jean said, staring at him affectionately. "You're the body-guard, remember?"

Which explained how he'd found himself one black midnight sitting in her Subaru on an unpaved road in the woods near the Pedernales River, which burbled some-where off to their right, a sound like the night rippling and changing—a sound, it occurred to Chris, that would cover the soft approach of thieves or murderers. The trees of these woods did not grow so thickly as to provide hid-ing places for all of Robin Hood's merry men, but the night was dark enough that a couple of men could approach very closely without Chris or Jean seeing them.

"Who are these guys?" Chris asked for the fourth time.

"Mexicans," Jean said, giving the word a thrilling for-eignness. "And I don't mean Mexican-Americans. These guys are illegals. They bring the grass across the border, they want a quick profit and a fast trip home. They'll probably seem a little nervous, since they could go to jail just for being here."

"*They'll* be nervous."

Torn between the relative safety of the car and the desire to hear and see better, Chris rolled down his win-dow. Night air flowed in, damp but not cool. He heard a snap, saw a tiny flare of light out of the corner of his eye, and turned quickly to see Jean lighting a joint.

"God, don't do that."

"Why not? It'll be good, they'll recognize the smell, they'll trust us more. A couple of narcs wouldn't be sit-ting here smoking a number."

"Maybe they would if they were overplaying the roles," Chris said, but took a hit nevertheless. The smoke soothed him momentarily, then paranoia again began to creep along his skin, raising the hairs on his arms.

Jean opened the door and stepped out of the car. He hastily followed. Jean shook back her coppery hair as if she felt an ocean breeze. She was grinning. Something about this *bandido* night deeply appealed to her. Chris stared out into it, seeing and hearing nothing human, only the murmur of the Pedernales thirty or forty yards away. In an emergency they could dash down to the river and across, and maybe their pursuers would be content to steal the car and the money in its trunk.

The way back, the way they'd driven in, might already be closed. They'd passed spots where the road narrowed so tightly that one car pulled sideways could block it. Chris could drive ahead instead, hoping the Mexicans hadn't thought of that, but anyone would. That might be where their main force would be concentrated. He scanned the trees for other possibilities.

"Maybe they're not coming," he said hopefully.

"Maybe they're not." Jean came around the car to his side and gripped his arm in both her hands. "Maybe I just made it all up to get you out here to the edge of nowhere in the middle of the night."

He chuckled, not really listening to her. Had something moved behind that tree fifty yards away? Was that a short branch or a rifle sticking out? He stared into the night.

"Look," Jean said. Chris turned quickly to see what she meant, but Jean was leaning back against the car, looking up at the sky. "This is what I mean when I call you and say to go up on the roof. These stars. Imagine them all. Imagine what's out there."

Her voice carried dreamily to his ears. He looked up too, into the psychedelic night. Jean didn't mean the stars, he knew that. She meant imagine the possibilities. Imagine what life might hold. Even what this single night might unveil.

The stars were beautiful: relentlessly pure, impossible

to sully. Under the influence of the darkness and the marijuana, he lost his sense of place for a moment. Leaning
back, he seemed to be growing upward. The stars
gleamed closer.

Jean moved over and leaned back against Chris, her
head on his shoulder. He put his arms around her. She
held his hands, then moved them along her stomach. Her
contemplation of the stars obviously grew less focused.

"What are you doing?" Chris asked with a nervous
chuckle.

Jean moved her hips, pressing back against him. "If
you don't know by this time—"

"You want to blow this off and go home?" he murmured into her ear in what he hoped was a sexy whisper.

She turned to face him and shook her head. She unbut-
toned a button of his shirt and pressed her lips against his
chest. Over her head he scanned the landscape. Nothing
moved. Of course, he couldn't see behind him. He turned
around so that Jean was the one pressed back against the
flank of the car. She seemed to like that. Chris looked
over the top of the car, but got only a quick glance before
she pulled his face down to hers.

"Let's not get carried away."

"I already am," she said.

She suddenly bounced up onto the hood of the car, sitting there with her legs hanging over the edge, and drew
him to her. She held him in place with a wicked smile.

Suddenly she reached down and pulled her own black
T-shirt off. Her breasts shone palely in the sparse light.
She stretched, arching her back, offering herself up to the
stars and to him. When Jean pulled Chris's shirt off too,
his back prickled, but not with sexual excitement. He felt
even less protected.

But the night and the moment and Jean grew insistent,
and carried him along. He nuzzled her bare skin. She
threw back her head, displaying her neck. She was fear-
less. Jean wouldn't have stopped if they'd been suddenly

surrounded by militia. She urged him up onto the hood of the car with her. She lay back on the windshield, pulling him down.

"This isn't—" Chris began once, but conversation had no place there. Jean laughed thrillingly. He kissed her shoulder. She bit his.

After a few minutes he half talked, half carried her into the backseat of the car, where he felt less exposed. Jean left the door open, their legs sticking out. The vinyl upholstery nipped and tugged at their skin. Their own scents and small sounds filled the interior of the car.

They ended up with Jean on top of him, face pressed into his neck, giggling. Chris felt a vague dissatisfaction he would never have guessed at if he'd imagined this scene.

He grew aware that he couldn't hear anything outside the car. "Shhh!" he said, sitting up. Jean of necessity sat up with him. She showed no trace of alarm, though. She didn't even look out, just stared fondly at Chris's face, two inches from hers. She drew entertainment from his changing expressions.

"Sorry. I'll be—Just let me—" As gently as he could he hurriedly slid away from her and stepped out of the car, dressing hastily. He grabbed her shirt off the hood of the car and tossed it into her, then froze.

"Jean."

She didn't answer. Chris pulled his own shirt on and stepped into his tennis shoes. "Somebody's here," he said.

Still Jean didn't reply. Chris stared through the trees toward the river, where men had appeared out of the dimness. Four men—no, five—trudging toward him like infantry soldiers. They weren't obviously armed, but all wore jackets in the warm night. They could have carried any number of handguns barely concealed.

"Jean—"

Chris folded his arms, uncrossed them, and stepped away from the car, trying to draw the men's attention away from Jean. The men were uniformly short and wiry, except for the man in front, who stood taller than Chris and sported a belly. He approached grimly. Chris coughed and sidled along the side of the car, but he had nowhere to go, no weapon to grab for.

Two of the men were smoking, a sweetly sharp smell that carried in the night. One of them said something in a low, fast tone that drew only a grunt from the leader. The other four hung back about ten feet, but the leader walked straight up to Chris, who lowered his hands to his sides and stared at the swarthy man, waiting for a quick punch or a movement for a hidden gun.

Suddenly the man grinned. "Did we keep you waiting?" he asked in barely accented English.

The man's teeth were large and feral. A chuckle slid through them. He turned and said something in rapid Spanish and the other men laughed, too. Chris felt himself blushing, and hoped the night would hide his flushed face, or that the men would mistake his color for something else. He had no ready answer. His self-consciousness focused on the fact that his tennis shoes remained untied, which must have made him look like a child.

Chris cleared his throat and tried to deepen his voice. "So, you guys have something for us?"

"*Sí*," the tall man said insinuatingly. "I have something very special—"

"I believe that's for me," said a crisp voice. Everyone turned to see Jean, fully dressed and blank-faced, coming around the car. No one had even heard the other back door open. She strode quickly, looking even in her jeans and T-shirt like a businesswoman with little time to spare for this transaction.

The Mexican man's smile, having dropped for a moment at the sound of her voice, came back broader. He reached for Jean's hand. "Oh, yes, lovely señorita," he said, then switched into Spanish. Chris knew enough to catch the first two words, "*Tengo algo . . .*" meaning, "I have something . . ." Chris could imagine the rest. He looked into the small pack of other men, wondering if he could jump among them and knock one unconscious and get his gun.

"*En tus sueños,*" Jean said firmly, shaking the man's hand.

The tall Mexican looked astonished. His face flushed much darker than Chris's, and a tendon grew more prominent in his neck. Then he burst into laughter.

The men behind him continued to look startled. One of them edged close to Chris, who tensed.

The tall man again gave a little bow, and spoke to Jean in courtly fashion. "*Sí, señorita. In mis sueños, yo estaré donde su amigo estaba.*"

Jean smiled demurely. "Can't stop a man from dreaming," she said. This time they all laughed, even, after a stunned moment, Chris. Jean walked among the other men, smiling and nodding in greeting. Good feeling became general. The man closest to Chris clapped him on the shoulder and smiled.

Jean asked, "Well, is this a social occasion, or are we going to do business?"

She looked straight at Chris and slipped him a fast wink. The tension in his shoulders eased a little and he stood taller. Relaxed, the group sauntered a hundred yards to the men's truck, down in an arroyo so it had remained invisible from the spot where Chris and Jean had parked. Obviously the men had been here for some time, reconnoitering to make sure their new business partners didn't have friends hiding in the vicinity. They must have been watching Jean and Chris for a while, wondering whether to trust them, maybe thinking of ripping them off.

Now they strolled at ease, a group of friends. The Mexicans' fears had been completely allayed. Chris and, to a much larger extent, Jean had been adopted into the fraternity. They all ceremoniously shared a sample of one of the large bales of marijuana the men removed from beneath a false floor in the bed of the truck. Chris barely inhaled. Jean dragged deeply, and nodded approval. They quickly concluded their business and left the area in opposite directions, waving to each other like old friends at the end of vacation.

As Jean drove them away Chris still felt twitchy from adrenaline and relief. Jean wore a small smile of satisfaction. She slapped a hand down on Chris's thigh and laughed triumphantly. Chris stared at her happy, lovely profile, the night behind her lightening with the approaching lights of Austin.

"What did you and he say to each other in Spanish?"

Jean smiled at the memory. That's what had put them in solid with the marijuana smugglers, her boldness and her quick tongue in their own language. "He'd said something kind of crude about me and I said, 'In your dreams.' That's when he turned kind of nice. He said yes, in his dreams he would be in my friend's place." She gave Chris a direct stare. "Your place, he meant."

"Yeah, I know."

"But he said it kind of sweetly."

Jean chuckled again. He knew she had enjoyed the adventure. A couple of thousand dollars' worth of marijuana rode in the trunk of her car, which she could resell for at least three times as much. Chris didn't even know where she'd gotten the money to buy the big investment. He also knew he wouldn't share in the profit. Finals had ended the week before. He'd be going home to San Antonio for the summer. He watched Jean's profile displayed against the night sky out her window, until she suddenly grinned broadly. Chris knew she smiled not only for the excitement of their adventure but for him, for her pleasure in his watching her. She had the joy of being the wild one.

Chris Sinclair hadn't thought of that night by the Pedernales in some time, but in earlier years he had fondled the memory often, with a powerful mix of emotions: longing and nostalgia and a continuing dread of how differently

the night could have turned out. The memory both
enticed and repulsed him. Now his memories of the night
were themselves memories.

"What are you looking at?" the investigator Monica
Burris asked.

"Nothing. Just the trees. God knows how much they've
seen over the years."

Burris nodded. "You said that exactly right. God
knows, nobody else. Some day I hope to interview Him.
I've got a lot of questions."

She turned and headed back toward the truck as Chris
shot a sharp glance of reappraisal after her. Stepping over
the shallow hole in the ground without a downward
glance, he followed the investigator out of the brush.

Four

Chris Sinclair sat in his office going over police reports. Outside, bright afternoon sunlight hit the Justice Center, but very little of it reached his office. He'd been reading reports all day, and for days before that, so that his office had the cloistered feel of midnight oil. He welcomed the sound of a crisp knock on his office door.

His chief investigator, Jack Fine, stuck his head in. "The rest of the staff asked me to come in and make sure you hadn't passed away in here."

"Please tell them how much their concern touches my heart."

"They were just hoping to take off early if you weren't here to notice," Jack said, sidling all the way inside.

Jack Fine, somewhere in the neighborhood of fifty years old, had a narrow face with a pinched nose and a mouth usually drawn closed in a small bow. The face of a man who protects himself emotionally. That kind of armor usually means the person had failed to be so careful in the past. Chris knew the source of Jack's refusal to give himself wholeheartedly to any belief. After devoting twenty-five years of his life to the San Antonio Police Department he'd blown the whistle on a minor scandal involving the mishandling of a charity fund and been rewarded with a fake promotion into a dead-end branch of the department where he could pass days at a time without anyone speaking to him. When Chris had become District Attorney, Jack had willingly given up that life in order to become chief investigator for the DA's Office.

Seeing the stack of crime reports on the desk, Jack asked, "Found any new leads on Mr. Big?"

Chris stood up without a word and walked out of his office. Jack followed. The reception area just outside, where three secretaries worked at their desks, felt much larger and brighter. Chris passed quickly through it and out into the white hallway. An aerial view of the District Attorney's Offices would have shown an expansive area, the entire top floor of the Justice Center. But inside, the offices felt confining. One could only see these narrow hallways. More than once Chris had felt like an experimental subject in a box.

"The trouble with studying those reports," he said, confident that Jack was just behind him, "is that I just have to imagine connections between them. I can interview the suspects—screw-up robbers, dumb burglars, drug dealers who sell to cops—but the kind of person I'm looking for isn't going to be known to people like that. Those police reports are a record of failures. People who messed up the crime and got themselves arrested. The successful crimes we don't even hear about."

"Well, they leave a trail of rumors," Jack answered. "Or we get a report of a theft with no suspect arrested."

Chris nodded. He turned a corner, opened a door, and walked out onto the fifth-floor balcony, an architectural nicety that in real life had been taken over by pigeons and smokers. One had to watch one's step. But Chris and Jack had caught the balcony in an uninhabited moment. Chris walked over to the stone balustrade. "I'm never going to find what I'm looking for this way." He stared across Dolorosa Street, to the plaza in front of San Fernando

Cathedral, where *raspa* vendors and napping homeless people held court. Men and women in business suits strode across the area as well, going from offices to the courthouse and back again. "I need to get out there somehow," Chris said. "Get in among them."

"What about the informant?" Jack asked. "The one who was wearing the wire at Belasco's party the night he got arrested?"

"Unfortunately, he was a new recruit. A boy they tried to get to join the gang, and he went straight to the parents and the parents to the police. He cooperated from the beginning of his involvement, but on the other hand he'd never *been* involved. He can tell us a few names of other boys he thinks committed some crimes, but that's all. No, I still need a way in myself."

"You gonna go undercover?"

Chris intoned, "*Sometimes, they say, the Phantom leaves the jungle, and walks among mortal men.* All I'd need is a trench coat and a hat."

"Maybe an eye patch and a scar," Jack agreed. "That'd fool the kind of guy you're talking about."

"You know, I didn't invent this Mr. Big idea, Jack. A police detective brought it to me. The same one who was running the drug sting on that teen gang in Terrell Hills where we caught Peter Belasco. He's gotten several leads from anonymous sources that there's someone out there, coordinating. Why do you have trouble believing that? I'm not talking about an evil empire. Just a little organized crime."

Jack shrugged. "I'm willing to believe. But conspiracy theories require a presumption of competence that I haven't seen in real life very often. Bad guys aren't that ambitious, and if they are they screw up. I just think you could find a better use for your time."

"That's exactly it, Jack. How? Who's worth going after? If you were DA how would you spend your time?"

Jack's eyes gleamed with possibility, and Chris knew he'd started that devious mind working. Chris continued,

"We put fifty people a day on probation for DWI. Convict maybe two murderers a week. People who kill their own children, beat up relatives. Where's that going to happen next, which house will be the crime scene? Nobody knows. I can't put a dent in crime like that. Maybe this other I can really do something about. Even if I'm the only one looking. Even if I look like a fool doing it and flame out in one term. Then the next DA can go on convicting drunk drivers and teenage Stop 'n Go robbers."

Chris leaned back against the balcony railing, as if he confronted the Justice Center building face to face. He looked at his investigator. "You have a lot more experience than I do, Jack. Where would you start?"

After a pause Jack spoke in a low voice, as if the information were being pried out of him. "At the bottom. Always start at the bottom, where young thugs get recruited by more experienced crooks. Not smarter, just older. And go up the chain. Most of 'em fall out along the way. Prison or dead. I don't know if there's any top to get to. But it's an ugly stew to dive into, Chris. I'll tell you that," Jack said with a surge of sincerity, as if he'd climbed out of the mess himself, and not too long ago.

"And look for a motive," he added less passionately. "You think maybe he's giving drugs to kids, ask yourself why. The profit margin there isn't enough to justify the risks. If there's a Mr. Big, Chris, he wants something. He's not just evil."

The District Attorney looked thoughtful, but not as if he subscribed to Jack's last assessment. Letting the moment pass, Chris turned back to the view of the street and said lightly, "Okay, I won't recruit you to the task force. I've got an easier assignment for you."

Jack Fine suddenly realized it might not have been aimless wandering that had brought them alone to this most isolated spot in the DA's Offices. "Is this a secret assignment, or—?"

"No, nothing like that. It's a murder a few months old—one of those successful ones you mentioned where nobody got arrested. And I want you to find somebody I think is connected to it."

"Connected? In what—?"

"Her name was Jean Plymouth when I knew her. No telling what she goes by now. She's about five eight, reddish hair—although who knows if that's true anymore—blue eyes you couldn't miss. . . ."

Jack returned the conversation to practical considerations. "Something like a date of birth or a Social Security number would be more helpful," he said.

"She'll be about thirty-five now. My age."

"Anything else?"

"Yes. She'd have a fourteen-year-old daughter. Had. And the girl's been missing since October or so but nobody filed a missing person report on her."

Jack raised an eyebrow. "This is our murder victim?"

"Yeah. I'll show you pictures. And the location where the body was found. You'll have a starting point."

Chris took one last sweeping look at the streets below, as if he searched for a particular face. His voice had changed, his expression retreated from the jokiness of his earlier conversation. Jack Fine studied him without Chris's realizing it.

They began walking off the balcony. "Sorry it's so vague," Chris said. "If I find out more I'll give it to you."

"It's okay, Chris. We'll find her." Jack laid a hand briefly on the DA's shoulder, without knowing why he thought his boss needed comforting.

Anne Greenwald looked out the front window of her pretty little two-bedroom house. The wooden frame house, fifty years old, resided in the fashionable Monte Vista neighborhood, but on one of the less grand streets. Anne sometimes said the house had obviously been built as a home for servants employed a block or two away. The front room where she stood had hardwood floors with two small, rather old, well-cared-for rugs. Art and family pictures covered the walls. Those who felt at home in the room—and there weren't many of those—thought it seemed very Anne—as if she had lived there for years and years.

Just as Anne looked out the window into the twilight, a car drove up to her curb. She recognized it as Chris's car, but no one got out of it. The car just sat there, as if it had been programmed to come pick her up. Dimly through the dusk of six-thirty she saw Chris behind the wheel, blond head bent as if he were studying a problem inside the car. Anne waited. She wore tights with a purple T-shirt, and old running shoes. She had been about to go for a run, but something had stopped her. Here sat the reason at her curb.

After a moment he stepped out of the car and came up her sidewalk at a brisk pace. Anne studied his face as it grew easier to see. Sometimes he looked very youthful. At other, more intimate times, she thought she saw the beginning of aging around his eyes. She liked that dichotomy.

"Hi," she said at the door, opening it just after he knocked. Chris looked a bit surprised.

"I'm sorry. You're going for a run. Go ahead. I'll—"

"Don't be silly," Anne said, throwing the door open wider. "I've already been."

"No, you haven't," he said, hugging her. "You'd be all sweaty and nasty and your hair would be falling down."

They kissed quickly but thoroughly. "You sound as if you'd like me like that," Anne said in a low voice.

"I like you every way I've seen you."

He smiled, kissed her nose, then walked by her into the living room. Anne stared at his back and felt an upsurge of emotion.

Chris turned and looked at her as if he knew. Ever since her burst-out declaration of love for him in the hallway outside the high school locker room—the first time she had ever said that—their relationship had deepened. Like now, when she had somehow expected him without warning, and he—

"I thought I was going home," he said, "but my car came here instead. I wasn't paying enough attention to stop it."

"What's wrong?"

"Nothing. Why does something have to be wrong?"

"You don't look like you're full of good news. You come here when you've had a bad day. I think I find that flattering."

If he were the kind of man who could put his work aside at the end of the day she wouldn't be attracted to him. Well, not *as* attracted. Both their jobs involved intimate dealings with people deep in pain and distress. Only the unfeeling could forget all those people just because five o'clock had come.

He shrugged, standing in the middle of her living room in his gray suit with his hands in his pockets. "I don't really have anything to say. Just the usual. Why don't you go ahead and run? I'll wait, or go get us something to eat, or . . ."

Anne walked by him, brushing a hand across his cheek. "I'll do the treadmill instead. You can talk to me while I do it."

She dragged the treadmill out of the second bedroom that served as a home office and storage room, and Chris sat on the couch and talked about this and that, un-work-related, a story from his teenage years that took place in a mall, and Anne walked toward him, faster and faster, but getting no closer, as if in a bad dream.

Chris hadn't shared the news of the discovered body with Anne. He wasn't keeping it secret, he just didn't talk about very many of his cases with her, as she didn't share her patients' secrets with him, except occasionally in a name-and-gender-deleted sort of hypothetical way.

He heard himself talking, telling a funny and poignant story about his own teenage embarrassment, but at some point he lost the thread of the story and trailed off. He sat on the couch lost in thought, the sound of Anne's walking like the amplified pulse of his heart, background rhythm.

When he came to himself he realized the room had been silent for long minutes. Anne hadn't broken the silence. She was looking in his direction but obviously not seeing him. Anne had thoughts of her own. He had noticed this recently. Their feelings for each other *had* grown stronger, as demonstrated by his driving here on automatic pilot when he needed comfort without explanation. But their relationship was subtly changing, too. Anne sometimes seemed to study him from a slight distance. She held her own secret thoughts. Chris felt the sense of her secrets, but hadn't consciously thought Anne might be keeping something from him. Caught up in his own concerns, he didn't notice her dilemma.

He stayed until after nightfall; Anne made a salad to which she added some leftover chicken so she could call it "chef," and they ate without talking much, both of them distracted but comforted by the other's presence. Good night took a while, holding hands crossing her living room, then a long kiss just inside the front door. Both of them seemed on the verge of starting a longer conversation, but neither did.

A few days later Jack Fine walked into Chris Sinclair's office, dropped a file on his desk, and said, "Why don't you give me a tough one sometime?"

Chris looked up at him without speaking, putting his fingertips on the file folder. Jack sat on the edge of the desk and nodded. "She's here. Been in San Antonio three years. Moved here from California."

"How did you do this?" Chris asked wonderingly, opening the file. The first page just contained a computer listing, a name, an address on the city's northwest side, and a phone number. "Jean Fitzgerald" was the name.

"You told me you were at UT with her," Jack shrugged. "I got her school records. That gave me her Social Security number, and with that you can track a person all over the country."

"Don't we have privacy laws to protect against this kind of thing?" Chris turned the pages of the file. Very little information, no pictures. A copy of a pay stub from a large insurance company, made out to Jean Fitzgerald. From the amount, Jean was not an executive.

As Chris turned the next to last page, Jack stabbed it with a finger. "And she has a fourteen-year-old daughter. Had. The girl hasn't been in school since October."

Again, the page held no picture, just a printout of a class schedule at Holmes High School, also on the northwest side of town. "Kristen Lorenz" was the name on the schedule. She had a different last name from Jean's. Chris wondered briefly about the girl's father. But only briefly. His thoughts had filled with Jean. She had been here in San Antonio for three years. She had a normal-seeming life. Except for the dead daughter.

"There *was* a missing person report filed," Jack said. "Contrary to what you told me. The ME's office didn't find it because they searched the records around the time the girl would have gone missing, and for a month or so after that. This report was only filed a month ago."

The missing person report concluded Jack's sparse file. "No one filed a report until the girl had been missing for two months or so," Chris noticed.

"Check the date."

Chris did. December 27th. It didn't mean anything to him. Jack said, "That was a week after the body was found. The medical examiner already had the body before somebody reported her missing."

As if someone hadn't taken official action until the body had been discovered. As if someone had been keeping watch on the shallow grave, and knew when it became empty.

"You want me to call on Jean Fitzgerald?" Jack asked.

"Let's wait a bit. I want to put together a little more info first."

Jack nodded agreeably, but he finally asked his own questions, first answering Chris's. "The privacy laws don't apply to a police investigation. That is what we're doing here, isn't it? Is this Jean Fitzgerald our suspect or a victim?"

Chris looked directly at him for the first time. "That's what I want to know. A girl is dead. Buried in a shallow grave and nobody made a fuss about it. What do you think?"

Again Jack didn't answer. There was no need. Chris picked up the file and they left the office, the District Attorney's posture more determined than it had been in weeks.

Neighbors and teachers gave cautiously glowing reports about the dead girl, Kristen Lorenz. Mr. Hazel, a math teacher in an advanced course, who had powerful shoulders and forearms, as if he shoved those heavy numbers around manually, first asked, "Is she coming back to school?"

"I don't think so," Chris said. He stood in Mr. Hazel's empty classroom during the teacher's early afternoon off period. Chris had the normal adult emotions on returning to high school of feeling that any moment he would be ordered back to his desk, with the slight exhilaration of knowing he didn't have to obey. The teacher sauntered around the classroom as if it were his home. He had probably long ago lost the disorientation of being an adult in a children's world.

"That's a shame," he said. "I'd hate to see her transfer again. I looked up her records. She has a very spotty school history. The family moved every few years. That's very hard on a child's education. And Kristen's a good student. I had her in second-year algebra a year earlier than most kids take it."

"Good grades?"

"Straight A's, almost. Kristen doesn't have a real gift

for math, but she's one of those kids who studies so hard that if she gets a B it just crushes her. She does very well."

Hearing the girl spoken of in the present tense gave Chris a slightly eerie feeling, as if she were listening in, but he didn't tell Mr. Hazel anything. "Did you ever meet her parents?"

"Not the father. They were divorced, weren't they? Her mother came to one parent conference. She told me she had worked for Computers Unlimited and I said maybe that was where Kristen got her talent for math. Pretending she had a talent, you know, just being nice. I remember the mother laughed and said, 'Oh no, she didn't get her brains from me. I had to go looking for that.' Something like that. I assumed everything was fine at home with Kristen. It usually shows up in a student's grades if things aren't."

Chris could picture Jean laughing with the teacher, throwing back her head. He wanted to ask how she had looked, but it would be a question not in keeping with the investigative tone of the conversation. He would find out soon enough.

"I must be wrong, though," the teacher said with a sudden penetrating stare, folding his heavy forearms over his chest. "If there's no trouble with Kristen, why would the District Attorney be here talking to me?"

"Just checking," Chris said. "We're not sure yet what's happened."

Mr. Hazel kept that steady gaze on him, and Chris felt as if he'd been caught peeking over another student's shoulder during a test.

Other teachers at the high school gave similar reports on Kristen Lorenz. A good student, no trouble. Perhaps for that reason, none of them had gotten very close to her. They couldn't say whether she'd had a boyfriend or particular friends. She hadn't participated in any extracurricular activities of the kind that keep a kid after school so the teacher learns more about the personal life. And Chris didn't want to question students about her yet. He didn't want to start rumors sweeping through the school.

"Why aren't there already?" Jack Fine pointed out as they drove from the school to the nearest site where students might hang out, Ingram Park Mall, a little way farther out Loop 410. The high school sat right next to the expressway. So would the mall. To Chris, who had never gotten very familiar with this suburban, middle-class part of town, it seemed that everything here lay within hearing of the traffic on one expressway or another.

"Why hasn't anybody noticed her missing?" Jack continued. "You know what that tells me?"

"Yes," Chris said shortly. The girl's mother should have made the loudest noise of all as soon as her daughter went missing. Not only had Jean not done that, but she must have fended off the inevitable inquiries from school officials. She must have lied.

They definitely had a leading suspect already.

"Maybe it was an accident," Chris mused.

"Someone buried her and kept it secret, Chris."

"People feel guilty and afraid even after an accident." Chris added in his thoughts, and some people who dealt in marijuana in college end up working for computer or insurance companies. They don't become murderers.

"Ready to call it a day?" Jack asked casually.

Chris gazed out the car window as they passed the mall. The huge cluster of stores looked momentarily alien to him, even though he had spent much of his own teenage years in a similar mall. Now this one seemed as odd as youth itself, so significant and so insubstantial.

"Let's try a little closer to her home first," he said.

They drove only a couple of miles, off the main road and into a neighborhood where all the street names spoke of spring and mist and landscapes more generally found in Scotland than in South Texas. "What was it," Jack asked, peering out the windshield, "Misty Glen or Heather Mist?"

The houses looked to be three bedrooms, featuring brick exteriors and good-sized plots—upscale without much individuality. They found Jean's address and parked across the street. Chris didn't feel ready to confront her. Driving down her street was a way of circling closer, but at this time of day—four-thirty in the afternoon—Jean would probably be at work.

Chris gazed at the house across the street: brick facade, picture window, narrow concrete porch, a strip of dirt for cultivating a garden, now bare as most such plots were near the end of winter. Nothing distinguished the house from its neighbors. Chris found it very hard to imagine Jean living here. Remembering her distinctive room in the old mansion near the college, with its bare floors, wooden casement windows, low furniture, posters tacked to the walls, disarrayed bedsheets, and scattered objects that only Jean's imagination saw as art, he couldn't believe she had harbored aspirations to such a comfortable, ordinary home. He wanted to see the house's interior.

"Maybe this isn't a good idea. We don't want her to hear that investigators were asking questions about her in her own neighborhood."

"Why not?" Jack asked. "There's nothing wrong with making a suspect nervous."

As it turned out, they barely had to get out of the car and set foot on the sidewalk before they had their informant. A lady past middle years, skinny arms bare in a sleeveless dress, her hands hidden in grimy gardening gloves, said, "Don't even try me. I never buy anything from strangers."

They hadn't even noticed her, half-concealed as she'd been behind a large oak tree. The tree sat in a nest made of mulch, flowers surrounding its trunk even in January. Her whole front yard was carefully manicured. That and the well-used condition of the lady's gardening gloves said that they'd found someone who spent a lot of time outside, maybe seeing what went on in the neighborhood.

Jack stood silent, naturally deferring to Chris, whose

face usually invoked more warmth in older women than did Jack's squinty countenance. "We're not selling anything," Chris said. "But I'd have to ask for confidentiality before going any further."

This request piqued the gardening lady's curiosity strongly enough that she rose from her knees and walked toward them, pushing back her sun hat to reveal deeply wrinkled cheeks and blue eyes faded but lively. "I'm famous for keeping secrets," she said. "Everybody knows how many secrets I'm holding."

As Chris still hesitated her eyes narrowed. "It's about that house across the street, isn't it?" She pointed at, indeed, the correct house, Jean's house.

Without admitting anything, Chris said, "Did you ever see the girl who—"

"Oh yes. It's her, isn't it? I knew it. That girl's been headed for trouble for as long as I've known her. No man in the house, but boys coming and going all the time. Cars in the middle of the night—"

"This happens regularly?" Jack cut in.

The lady's eyes narrowed, peering into memory. "Three times, maybe four. I don't sleep much. I don't miss much, either, not in this neighborhood."

Chris glanced at the suburban house across the street, to see if it had altered with its neighbor's characterization of the wildness within. But the house still displayed no personality.

"What kinds of activities have you seen?" Jack continued the interview in Chris's silence.

"Parties, of course. Cars parked all up and down the street—"

"Underage drinking?"

"Well, I didn't see any," the lady conceded. "But they've got a backyard too, don't they?"

"This activity in the middle of the night," Chris cut in. "What did you see exactly?"

"Just a car arriving or leaving, after the rest of the

neighborhood's asleep. You have to find out the rest for yourself."

"Yes, ma'am. Have things changed recently?"

The woman stood silent for a moment, as if dipping a foot into the stream of time and feeling with a shock how fast it flowed. "Yes, now that you mention it, the house has been quieter. And I haven't seen the girl since well before Christmas."

People may listen very closely but not hear. Chris and Jack heard the old lady say it that way: ". . . haven't seen the girl since before . . ."

They turned away with a last admonition to keep the conversation to herself, then Chris turned back. "By the way, what do you mean by the middle of the night?"

The gardening lady looked at him with the pity reserved for the dangerously uninformed. "What do they call twelve o'clock at night, young man?"

Caught off-guard, Chris searched for an answer. "The witching hour?"

"Midnight, son. It's called midnight. Now where do you think it got a name like that?"

Chris nodded thoughtfully as if absorbing important knowledge, but thinking, *A car coming or going at midnight. Three or four times in who knows how long?* Not exactly evidence of a vast criminal enterprise. He felt glad this sharp-eyed observer with her pristine values didn't live across the street from him.

Even when Anne Greenwald and Chris Sinclair spent most of Saturday together, they retired to their separate homes late in the afternoon. Neither of them could have said who had thought of this ritual separation, but Anne was the one most likely to enforce it. "Drop me off for a while, will you?" she said on this Saturday early in February, a day that had seemed so like spring it had forced them to drive to nearby Boerne for lunch and vague antique pricing and strolling by the Guadalupe River. It had been a lovely day, but Anne also enjoyed walking into her house alone. She started a bath, and as the water ran she drifted through every room of her house, straightening the thick burgundy-colored place mats on the heavy old dining table, moving glasses in the kitchen from the drying rack into the glass-fronted cabinets, both enjoying and vaguely oppressed by how familiar she found the house. When she had moved into it five years earlier the house had looked like a kid's first house after college. Now it could very easily turn into an old lady's house. Next thing you knew she'd be getting a cat.

She shed her jeans and blouse and underwear and studied herself briefly in the mirror on the bathroom door. The body remained in good shape, despite the small amount of time she devoted to maintenance. Flat stomach, taut legs. Her body had always been her friend, though Anne was edging toward old enough to suffer small betrayals. She turned sideways for a more speculative study of her abdomen, then shook her head at herself and stepped into the tub, sliding down into the almost-too-hot water.

Crises popped up almost daily in Anne's professional life, but she still could find placid time like today. She could imagine placidity growing and the crises receding as she got just a little older. The quiet of her perfect house would surround her.

But sometimes silence scared her.

The time apart on Saturday afternoons made their Saturday evenings more formal. Chris appeared at her door like a beau, dressed up as on a weekday, and Anne wore a pretty dark blue dress with silvery trim that at first glance looked demure but had a V-neck that plunged a bit, and a skirt that ended above her knees. "Wow," Chris said, and Anne tried to act as if she didn't know what he meant, but her dimples showed briefly.

They went to dinner at their favorite restaurant, La
Scala, which Anne enjoyed for its mix of fussy decoration and informal atmosphere. When she had been a girl
her parents had taken her to extremely fancy restaurants,
and she had developed a dislike of such places that took
themselves too seriously. La Scala was just right. And it
served capellini thick with cream sauce and crab.

"That was nice today, wasn't it?" Chris said. He sipped
Scotch, glanced around the full restaurant, and rested his
eyes on Anne again, smiling as if they'd exchanged some
kind of signal. "Sometimes I forget we can just take off
whenever we want. We could go to New Orleans some
weekend. Even New York."

"Or Argentina," Anne said. "Camp out on the pampas."

"I wish I'd swung on that rope," Chris said.

She knew he wished that. That afternoon they'd
walked beside the Guadalupe River in Boerne, watching
the water flowing sluggishly and the aggressive ducks
that came in clusters toward any sign of a handout. The
day had been cool in the shade, warm in the sunshine, so
one could regulate the temperature just by walking
through the patchwork under the trees.

They had come to a tree that hung out over the water.
Someone had tied a rope to one of its upper branches so
that kids could swing out over the river and drop into it.
Chris had stared at the rope for long minutes. His hands
had moved reflexively. "Go ahead," Anne had finally said,
which was when he'd laughed and turned away.

"It would have been fun, swinging out and back, even
if I'd fallen in," Chris said in the restaurant. "It's the
things you don't do in life that you regret."

Anne twirled a fork through her pasta and grinned at
the look of nostalgic loss on his youthful face. "Tell me
about your regrets. What have you not done?"

He rolled his eyes. "That opens up a whole world,
doesn't it? Other lives. Maybe I should've . . ." Jean Plymouth's young face flashed across his memory, but any

regrets he had about Jean didn't focus on anything specific. Just, as he said, another life gone unpursued.

"I thought small regrets are supposed to be the sharpest," Anne said, pausing for a sip of wine. "Not that you never saw Paris in your twenties, but that you didn't swing out over that river."

"I might've fallen in. It is still February after all. That water would be icy."

"Maybe you would've," Anne agreed. "You'd have had that swing through the air and the drop and the cold, cold water, and I would have been laughing on the bank, so you would have laughed too, and climbed out shivering, and I would've tried to help you warm up and that would've gotten me wet, too. We would have had to find a blanket in my car or buy one in a shop, and maybe you would have gotten undressed in the car and sat in the blanket beside me all the way back home, with your clothes in a little wet heap in the back."

Her speculative story had taken an unexpected direction. Anne hadn't stopped smiling, but her expression had changed. She took a bigger gulp of cabernet. Chris appeared to be picturing her imagined scene. "Let's go back."

She laughed. For a moment the glitter of the restaurant reflected in her eyes. Chris slowly joined her in smiling. Anne slipped off one shoe under the table and softly brushed his leg with her stockinged foot. "Maybe I could help you with those regrets. Do you have a list already, or could we go write one?"

He took a careful bite of scallop. "What about you? You seem to have done everything you've ever wanted. Do you have any regrets?"

After a moment in which she lost her smile, Anne said quietly, "You'd be shocked. One of these days I'm going to tell you, and you'll be speechless.

"See?" she added as he looked at her oddly, not speaking. She laughed with a touch of artificiality, finished her wine, and looked around for the waiter.

After a long, thoughtful gaze at her, Chris said slowly, "Let's start that list. I have a very specific desire I'm going to regret if I don't fulfill it. Ever since we walked out of your house with you in front of me in that dress, I've wanted to kiss the back of your knee. You know, where the tendons come into view and that little crease looks so tender. Is there some psychological root to this?"

"Not that I can think of, but I really don't go in for that slavish devotion kind of thing."

Chris frowned slightly. "I don't think you'd be so dominant just from my kissing the back of your knee."

"I was picturing me standing up, and you—"

"I wasn't."

They stared at each other as if he could convey the image through telepathy, then Anne's eyes widened, she glanced aside, tried to look demure, but her color had risen abruptly. A busboy walked by. Without seeing him, Anne said, "Waiter? Could we have a check, please?"

Later, back at Anne's house, in the bedroom Chris loved so much that it had probably kept him from asking Anne to marry him, because he so enjoyed being a guest in that simple room with its six windows and high bed with the enveloping mattress and comforter, Anne stroked his chest slowly and said, "This probably isn't the best time to tell you this."

"If it's a favor you want, this is definitely the best time to ask me," Chris said drowsily.

"Gee, I wouldn't want to put it like that."

Then she didn't say anything for long enough that Chris sat up on his elbow with some concern. "What is it? Tell me."

She didn't do the "Never mind" routine and make him press her, she knew how much he hated that. But suddenly Anne felt unready to have the conversation. She made a clicking sound with her tongue that sounded like "tick tick tick," and Chris knew what she was going to say. He felt his mouth go a little dry.

"I love you," she started. "And besides that I like the way you are and the things you care about and—oh hell."

"Anne. It's okay. Don't even—"

"I want to. I want something else, too. You know I've almost gotten married before and been in love and all that, but maybe the reason I never went through with it was because I never was sure before that I'd found somebody I wanted to have a baby with."

So it came out. When Chris didn't immediately reply, Anne filled the silence, feeling a slight sense of panic. "I don't want anything from you—well, just a little something. I'm not asking for a commitment, I definitely don't want to trap you into anything, it's not about that. It's just that I want a baby. And I think you do, too."

Chris had never felt so flattered. He knew he should have sprung up and kissed her and said of course. But a sudden image of a white hand barely lifted out of the ground held him silent. In Chris's few moments of thinking the dead girl, Kristen, might be his daughter, he hadn't lost his emotional connection to her. He still felt responsible for the girl. At this juncture in his life the thought of having a child troubled Chris as much as it thrilled him. A child out in the world, helpless and changeable. A lifelong connection to the child's mother. A responsibility that would never end, that had nothing to do with legal obligations but that he knew would hold him tightly. He'd felt the stirring of that feeling recently.

"I love you, Anne. And this is so—wonderful." He cleared his throat. "Could I have just a little—?"

"What?" Anne asked, quickly concerned. "Water? Wine?"

"Time."

Anne smiled in relief. Even rejection would be a relief. Getting past this moment in which she'd laid herself out so vulnerably would be an enormous relief. "Of course, of course. You didn't think I wanted an answer from you on the spot, did you?" She lay down beside him, on her side, and traced a finger very lightly downward on his skin, starting at his chin. Moonlight through the window highlighted the whiteness of her hip.

"Let's just lie here and think," she said playfully.

Five

There comes a time to confront the suspect. When the investigator has learned all he can from background searches and questioning of peripherals without drawing much closer to a solution to the mystery, he hopes that the suspect will reveal something more fundamental, deliberately or not. Also, inevitably, the investigator has grown curious about the suspect and wants to meet her and hear her version of events, even if it's a lie.

In Chris Sinclair's case, that curiosity was intensified. So he found himself standing on Jean's narrow front porch only a couple of days after talking to her neighbor across the street. He wore a blue suit, white shirt, and dull tie, as if for a formal portrait. His grim expression matched the suit. He looked every inch the District Attorney of Bexar County. Still, as he rang Jean's bell and waited, the occasion didn't feel like an investigation. It felt like a date.

"Yes?"

The heavy inner door of the house had opened, but the slatted outer door stayed closed. Chris felt himself observed, and for a moment just stood there. The woman didn't ask his business again.

"Jean? Jean Fitzgerald?" He remembered the name she went by now.

The outer door opened, bumping him. Chris stepped aside and Jean pushed the door wide, as if welcoming him. But she only repeated, "Yes?"

Dusk shaded the scene behind Chris's back, and the porch light wasn't on. The only light fell dimly from within the house, and in that light she looked unchanged. Her reddish brown hair, longer than he remembered, framed her face, which looked pale and unlined. Jean had wide cheeks that tapered quickly along a strong jawline to a pointed but firm chin. Her lips were full in the center, narrowing quickly to the corners of her mouth, which made her look speculative or anticipating. In the dim light Chris couldn't see the feature he remembered best, her eyes of intense blue, the color of a cloudless sky in the early morning, before the sun has faded it. Jean's eyes remained half-lidded, cautious, as she looked at the man on her doorstep.

The lack of animation in her face was what most distinguished her from the girl he remembered.

She wore the skirt from a suit, light blue shot through with threads of white, but had changed into an orange T-shirt. He knew her schedule. She hadn't been home from work long, and looked tired. Her feet were bare.

She waited.

"It's Chris, Jean. Chris Sinclair."

She stared, her eyes opened wider, then her mouth as well. Her cheeks rose in a smile that seemed to spread over her whole body. There was the face he remembered: Jean's face, alive and almost glowing.

"No," she said. "Chris Sinclair lives here—" Touching her chest. "—in my memory. You can't be real. Really alive in the world."

Chris laughed embarrassedly. Jean grabbed his shoulder and drew him in for a hug. He touched her tentatively, but she held him hard against her for a long minute. "Oh, Chris," she sighed, then pushed him back to look at him. "You look great. How did you get so distinguished?"

She drew him inside, closed the door, and flicked on a light. They stood in a short hallway. Jean led him toward a living room. "You haven't changed a bit."

The rather small living room had a deliberately sparse look. A standing lamp with a black shade aimed light toward the ceiling. A couch and two chairs with exposed wooden legs, vaguely Asian, faced a black lacquered cabinet that would undoubtedly open to reveal a television. The air carried a faint fragrance, as of lingering perfume or a spice he'd never used.

"I've seen you on the news," Jean added. She shook a finger at him as if having caught him at a shameful ambition.

"Then why didn't you call me?"

She shrugged. "I thought about it. But you're a celebrity. I would've felt like a groupie."

Chris laughed. "You'd be the first. I'm not a celebrity. Pick five people off the street, I'd be amazed if two of them could tell you who the District Attorney is."

As they chatted in the way of old friends about Chris's official title he looked for signs of uneasiness in Jean but saw nothing but her old confidence. Jean came closer and looked at him in mock reproach. "I had no idea you were inclined that way. Were you working undercover all those years ago when you knew me?"

The word "undercover" fetched up an intimate image of her college bedroom, which seemed in his memory perpetually sunlit, completely unlike this dark room in which they stood now. Jean's house made Chris feel like a teenager again, visiting one of his friends in the parents' home.

"Sit down. Can I get you anything?"

He shook his head. They took opposite ends of the couch, aimed toward each other. "I can't believe—" they both began, then laughed. Jean quickly finished, "I can't believe you're in my house."

"I can't believe you're in my city."

Jean looked upward, then around the room as if a little surprised herself. "I don't know, I always liked San Antonio. I wanted to come back to Texas. California is too . . . close to the edge." She let him take that geographically or any other way. "Texas is better for children. Dallas and Houston are too big, Austin . . ." She trailed off with a shrug and a glance at him, as if he'd know what she meant. "So here it was. I haven't been here too long. Working out at United Life, middle management kind of thing."

"That's supposed to be a great place to work. Everybody tries to get in there." Chris made small talk without effort. He had been struck by Jean's casual mention of children. He continued to watch her closely and saw no signs of hesitation or guilt, which relieved him but added to the burden of his unspoken news.

"I had some computer experience and bluffed my way in. It does seem like a good company. Great benefits."

Next they'd be sharing information about their respective company dental plans. Chris kept studying Jean, intrigued and even nervous to be in the same room with her after so many years, but finding the conversation oddly devoid of the depth he'd expected.

"So you got a degree in computer science or something?" he asked.

Jean laughed dismissively. "Didn't we all, sooner or later? I mean, except the people who went to law school."

Chris accepted that criticism of his imagination. He stood up. "I would like some water if that's okay."

"Sure." Jean led him through a small dining alcove into a good-sized kitchen that held an Early American table and chairs. The wood-fronted cabinets matched them. Chris hadn't wanted a drink, he'd wanted to look around. Jean's refrigerator was large and new, and didn't hold any drawings or school schedules affixed to its doors by magnets. He hadn't seen a photograph anywhere. On the walls were a wire basket holding fruit and potatoes and three framed prints of spices and grains that seemed to have nothing to do with Jean, as if left by the previous owner. He couldn't imagine her living in this house.

"What brings you here, Chris?" she asked, handing him a glass of water. He took a sip and set it on the counter.

"I just wanted to look you up. I heard you might be in town. It's great to see you, Jean." It was. Beneath the dull conversation he felt an old connection stir. The way they'd started the same sentence. The way she looked at him, and he looked back, as if they knew much more about each other than they were willing to say.

He wanted to ask what else besides work filled her life, whether she was happy, but that would be like torturing her, considering the news he had to deliver.

"You have children, Jean?"

He failed to say this casually. Jean looked instantly alerted. Chris cleared his throat and continued. "A daughter, Kristen?"

Jean's hands stiffened, then clasped each other close in front of her chest. "Do you know something about her? Have you—"

"She hasn't been in school for some time, but you explained her absence to school officials."

Jean inclined her head sideways and down in a kind of resigned shrug. Weariness returned to her expression. "I know where she is. She's run away from me, but she's done that before. She's with her father, I'm sure. In St. Louis. He denies she's there, but that's because he doesn't want me to come after her legally. I'm letting it lie for the time being, waiting for her to get tired of him. He's dull as dirt. She'll be back."

Chris might have refrained from telling her. He wished he could have done this visit in two stages, first the happy reunion then later, on another occasion, the bad news. He felt himself pushed along by events. Jean gazed into his

face and saw something there. Her hand went to her
mouth. Her eyes grew impossibly wide. Chris couldn't
move.

"Oh my God," she said softly. "Oh God. You're the
District Attorney. Chris?"

Her eyes welled with tears.

"I'm sorry, Jean. She won't be back."

Jean screamed something incoherent, a full-throated
unchecked scream loud enough to be heard down the
street. Her cry went on for seconds, shaking Chris and
dying in a gurgle. Jean crumpled to the floor on her
knees, holding herself. Chris knelt next to her and put his
arms around her. Jean stayed so rigid she shook, as if con-
taining an explosion within herself.

"No," she said, much more softly. Her daughter had
been missing for months, Jean had had that long to think
about the possibilities. She shook and she cried and she
mumbled "No," but she believed. After a minute she
grunted, "Uh," as if someone had punched her again.

When she finally looked up she breathed almost normally. She spoke urgently, as if she could do something.
"Where is she? Take me to her."

"She's buried, Jean. It's all right. You can have her
moved later."

"Take me there."

Chris ignored this command. The girl's body, after it
had been cut open and probed and had samples removed
and been sewn up again, had been buried in a pauper's
cemetery on the south side of town, where the bodies
unclaimed by families were stacked three deep under-
ground. Chris would never let Jean see the place.

The possibility of denial strengthened Jean again. She
gripped Chris's arm. "How do you know? Who identified
her? You've never seen her."

"It's not completely positive yet, Jean. I have a picture,
but—"

He drew the Polaroid photographs from his inside
jacket pocket. Jean stared at the white squares fascinat-

edly as they came toward her. He could see her mind working, jumping from question to question, keeping at bay the ultimate possibility he thrust on her.

One photograph showed the reconstructed head. The sculptor had taken it at such an angle that no one could tell the head wasn't attached to anything. He had laid the head back so the girl seemed to be lying on a pillow, eyes closed. A second photograph showed a side view. Jean stared at both with perplexed horror, grief momentarily dimmed.

"Where is this?" she asked. "What have they done to her?"

Chris felt himself go colder as a tiny hope died. "But that is her?"

Jean nodded. "It's her. It's Kristen. But . . . different. What happened to her?"

So many things, Chris thought. He had to make phone calls, set teams in motion. The body buried in the pauper's field, of course, lay headless. The reconstructed face, molded around Kristen's skull, still sat on a shelf in the medical examiner's office. Chris had to order the body exhumed once more and reassembled for final burial, this time with a ceremony her mother would arrange.

"Tell me about her," he said.

"Such a good girl. She looked out for me as much as I did for her. Fourteen years old, she acted like my mother. *She'd* remind *me* to make my bed. Of course, she hadn't had a father around since she was four, somehow she . . ."

Jean stopped. She had been speaking in a normal tone, almost smiling, sitting at the kitchen table with Chris. Suddenly she stopped, staring again. She made a fist and shoved it into her abdomen just below the breastbone, a sob escaping as she rocked forward.

"No! I'm not having this conversation. Talking about her as if—"

She stood quickly, knocking her chair back to the floor.

She stared accusingly at Chris. "You don't care about her. You never even saw her. You don't give a shit what kind of girl she was!"

"No. Not like you do, Jean."

Chris's quiet surrender to her on the grief scale drained the energy from Jean again. She wanted to fight. She wanted anything other than quiet, hopeless grieving. Her shoulders slumped but her fists still clenched.

"Do you have a real picture of her I can have?" Chris asked, as much to give Jean activity as because he needed a photograph. He had his positive ID.

"Yes, yes." The chore worked. Jean strode quickly out of the room. Chris followed her as far as the inner door of the kitchen and saw Jean turn down a back hallway. Chris, with equally strong urges to follow her back and to leave the house, stood in the kitchen beside a white wall phone with a long coiled cord. A white pad on the counter beneath the phone held no messages, only indentations in the paper from past ones.

Jean bustled back in carrying a shoe box. "Here." She thrust one photo into his hands. Chris looked for the first time into the real face of Kristen Lorenz. The forensic sculptor had done a good job; this girl already looked very familiar. But the living face had skin and muscle tone and the possibility of changing expressions. Kristen had turned slightly from full face, as if looking past the photographer's shoulder. Her chin was raised, displaying a short but firm jawline. She had her mother's cheeks and general heart-shaped face. Chris had been right to recognize her face in the medical examiner's office. Her coloring was unlike Jean's ruddy complexion, though. Kristen had dark eyebrows, dirty blond hair, and pale skin. But Chris saw the teenaged Jean in the photo.

"Is this recent?"

"Last year's school," Jean nodded. "She hadn't changed much."

She held the shoe box close against her, her hands covering its open top, as if regretting having brought it out, afraid Chris would seize everything for some official purpose.

He drew her back to the table and said, "Tell me about the last day you saw her."

Jean didn't need time to cast her thoughts back. She had obviously gone over that day many times. "It was a Friday. She called me at work to say she was going over to a friend's house after school. A boy named Jason."

"Were they dating?"

Jean shook her head. "They were too young to date. But they went to the mall together, hung out with friends, you know. They couldn't drive. They could only go somewhere if his parents took them or I did, so I always knew where they were."

"And you let her go to his house after school?"

Jean shot a look at him, hearing the accusation. "There were other kids going. They had some school project to work on. I had to let her do things after school, Chris. I couldn't be home for her, I had to work."

"I know, I know." He had no right to play the accuser.

"But when I went to pick her up on my way home she wasn't there. I went home and found she'd packed a suitcase and left me a note. Then I knew her father must have sent her a plane ticket."

"Had the two of you been fighting?"

"Just the usual. I think it was more about school. Kristen felt like she didn't fit in there. Some days she wanted not to go. Do you remember being fourteen?"

Honestly, Chris barely did. What Jean had said about the kids having to be driven wherever they went had struck a nerve of memory in him: nothing specific, just the helpless feeling of wanting to be independent and not having the means, of wanting to do something but not knowing what. He had made few memories at fourteen, so the age existed as a blank, dismal patch between childhood and older adolescence.

He questioned Jean a little more, but didn't want to turn the occasion into an interrogation. He'd already done enough damage. Jean looked stricken, her eyes alternately dull then casting quickly about. Her fingers trembled. She no longer looked as much like the girl he'd known years ago. This hour with Chris had aged her.

As he stood to go he said, "Do you have someone you can call, somebody who can help you with things?"

She looked at him blankly. "Should I stay for a little while?" Chris asked.

Slowly, like a badly operated puppet, Jean shook her head. Her eyes held him, giving a different answer. He sat beside her again and stayed for another hour, ordering a pizza and eating little, but more than Jean did. When she had poured herself a glass of wine and no longer looked so dead-eyed, he left. "I'll call you tomorrow," Chris said, and Jean nodded as if she expected that.

Chris stood on Jean's narrow concrete front porch for a moment looking into the darkness. Still no porch light on. No one to burn it for. He thought about Jean's explanation of Kristen's last day at home. He had no experience as a parent, certainly not a divorced one, but he thought he would have reported his daughter missing right away.

Anne Greenwald wondered whether she'd made a mistake. There's always a risk in taking a relationship to a new level. She and Chris had been doing fine until she'd sprung her desire for permanency on him. That's what a baby meant, no matter how she denied it. Chris had reacted to her expressed desire in a dismayingly typical male way. He'd said what great news this was, how receptive he was to the idea, that he loved her, but he also began building distance. His stopping by after work dwindled from almost automatic to almost never.

Anne wanted to take him by the shoulders and look clearly into his eyes, and say, *I do want a baby. I want you too, but I'm not making up the baby thing to hold you closer. You can still leave afterward if you want. I want the baby more than you.* But she hadn't yet mustered the delicacy to put this to him in a way that wouldn't make matters worse.

She sat behind her metal desk in her small office at a downtown hospital. Her patient sat across the desk in a padded visitor's chair with wooden arms. Anne didn't go in for the couch thing, which disappointed her more sophisticated charges.

Rosa shifted uncomfortably. *Knock it off*, Anne thought testily. *You're not that fat yet.*

"It was time," the girl said. "Almost past time." Rosa was fifteen. She wasn't stupid, but in her world a few special girls would finish high school, most would go into the baby-making business, and she saw little point in waiting.

Anne wore her white doctor's smock and her white doctor's expression of vast wisdom and patience and experience. "Rosa, anybody can make a baby. It's no achievement."

The cynic who lived in the back of Anne's brain, sitting with folded arms and rolling eyes, yelled, *Hypocrite!* The cynic's voice sounded very much like Anne's.

"What's important is what you decide now. It's not just your life, it's the baby's."

Rosa, with smooth brown skin, high Indian cheekbones, and long adult fingers, looked older than fifteen. Her boyfriend and fellow experimenter in parenthood was eighteen and worked for a delivery service. "Albert would never forgive me if I gave away his baby," Rosa said complacently.

"But you need to finish school," Anne insisted, "so you can take better care of the babies you'll have in the future. This baby needs more than a fifteen-year-old mother who won't be able to help him with his math homework. Rosa, there are people who can't have babies, who want a baby desperately. They could take good care of him, and you'd be free to—"

Rosa looked at the psychiatrist with pity at her lack of

understanding. "God doesn't want those people to have babies. He does want me to."

Anne sat back in her desk chair and picked up a pencil, realized she had done so, and stopped herself from tapping it. Rosa watched her with a nice open expression, waiting for the next volley to begin. Anne had never established a rapport with this child. Rosa didn't come to her voluntarily. A judge had made the counseling sessions a condition of Rosa's probation for shoplifting. She'd tried to walk out of a store carrying disposable diapers. Stocking up early.

"All right, Rosa. You know everything. You teach me. What'll you do? The first day in the hospital when they put the baby in your arms and tell you you can take him home, what will you do?"

"Take him home."

"Where?"

"To my mother's house. Just for a while, until one of the apartments in the projects opens up, or Albert gets a raise."

"Okay, and do what? Once you've got the baby home."

"Feed him," Rosa said, as if one of them were an idiot.

"Breast-feeding?"

Rosa made a face. "That's icky. I'll use bottles. That way Albert can help feed him."

Anne rubbed the bridge of her nose. "Rosa, have you signed up for a class? The parenting classes?"

Anne opened her eyes to find the girl leaning toward her. In their earlier two sessions it had grown quite obvious that the girl had noticed the absence of a wedding ring on the doctor's finger. Now with an expression that combined pity and contempt but didn't really care much either way, the fifteen-year-old said, "I've got three little brothers, Dr. Greenwald. How many children do you have?"

Anne's charges often tried to cow her or dismiss her. Anne had stopped rising to this particular bait years ago. "Hundreds, Rosa," she said. "Hundreds like you."

The girl sat back, and the contest between them slackened. Rosa's yellow blouse, on the other hand, tightened considerably. The blouse was designed to be worn loosely, but Rosa's tummy had reached the stage at which it strained against most tops. Nor did Rosa have any desire to disguise her condition with loose dresses. Even the tiny cynic in Anne's brain went silent as she looked at the mound of life across the desk from her. She wouldn't compromise the doctor-patient relationship by asking what she wanted, but Rosa read her expression easily. With enormous graciousness the girl stood up and said, "Would you like to touch it?"

Anne sat stiffly in her chair and didn't say any of the many things that came to her mind, including "Yes."

Some lives incline toward one day, one transforming moment. The moment a bullet severs the spinal cord. Election Day. The day a daughter is murdered. The possessors of these lives don't know that one certain day is coming. But forever after they will remember their lives in two segments: the happy-go-lucky before and the devastated after. Nothing that follows will be the same as any day that went before. Most people, the lucky ones, have good days and bad days but no defining days. Only crushed spirits carry the knowledge of what awful possibilities life really holds.

When Chris had been young and impressionable Jean had changed his life. Now he had helped ruin hers. He was only the messenger, but if the news was bad enough the messenger was forever associated with it. He felt responsible for Jean's emotional fragility.

He called to check on her the day after his first visit, and the day after that, and soon he was talking to Jean every day. Grief didn't make her stupid. It became apparent that Jean realized that as much as Chris might be playing the role of old friend in time of need, he also had an official function. She was the one who first brought up the question of suspects in Kristen's murder, sitting in her living room late the next afternoon.

"I called Jason," she said, clear-eyed and voice steady, "and asked him who she might have gone to meet. He didn't know. He said kids at school have wondered where she went, but no one claims to know. There aren't any rumors."

"What about Jason himself? If he's the one she spent most of her time with—"

Jean shook her head. "His mother took him to a doctor's appointment that day. She was with him all afternoon." She looked up at Chris. "She saves her calendars. It took her about a minute and a half to tell me everywhere she'd been that day." Jean's only comment on this meticulous recording of a life was a lift of the eyebrow, but Chris got the message. He shook his head ruefully as if Jean had surveyed his own life as well. In moments like that, with the sly shift of her eyes, the Jean of Chris's past gleamed through.

But he'd yet to see her old dazzling smile.

"You said Kristen packed a bag. How did you think she would have gotten to the airport?"

"She knew how to call a cab. She'd done it before, to meet me somewhere or go to the mall. And she had money saved."

"I'll have the cab company records checked. Maybe we'll get lucky." But just as likely not. If Kristen had walked to a pay phone to call a cab there'd be no retracing her.

"Chris." Jean stood and walked close to him, looking up at his face. "I want you to show me where she was buried. Can you take me—?"

"There's no point, Jean. Don't torture yourself."

"I need to see it." She spoke very distinctly. She took the lapel of Chris's suit coat as if she would pull him down. "I need to know all the days I missed. Where she's been, what it was like for her, even after she was dead. You'd understand if—Have you ever had a child?"

Looking into her eyes, he shook his head slightly.

"Then just—make it a favor for an old friend, okay?"

He felt foolishly overdressed in his suit, a fake authority figure. It wasn't his place to deny her. He shrugged and Jean knew she'd won the discussion.

Dusk had fallen by the time they reached the narrow road into the scraggly woods on the northwestern edge of the county. This time, coming from a different direction, Chris noted that they weren't far from the University of Texas at San Antonio. *College kids*, he thought. *High school girl.* Maybe he and Jack had checked the wrong campus for rumors. But it was only speculation.

Jean sat beside him, not obviously growing more tense, but she had stopped speaking miles back. She wore a simple black dress. Her hair was pulled back from her face in a tighter style than when he'd first seen her the day before. She stared out through the windshield, eyes actively seeking landmarks, appearing unfamiliar with the area. Jean took it in avidly, breathing more deeply.

"In here?" she said as he turned into the narrow road.

Chris nodded. He stopped the car a few yards short of where he knew the grave to be, and got a flashlight from his trunk. Jean waited for him to guide her, crossing her arms. It had been a sunny day, but the temperature had now fallen into the fifties, dropping quickly. Chris's skin felt as if a chill inhabited this place. He took Jean's arm and led her a few steps along the road, then deliberately released her and stopped. Jean walked on, peering into the trees on the right-hand side of the road. She stopped when she came to the vacant grave, which remained a trench a foot and a half deep, even though dirt had sifted into it. She looked back at Chris, who nodded. He walked up to her and said, "How did you know which side of the road?"

Jean shot him one sharp glance, as if she knew she must be the prime—in fact at this point the only—suspect. She said, "Because when you're burying a body

you're afraid of her. You want your car between you and
her when you get back in it. You don't want the grave
right outside your door."

Chris appreciated the insight, which rang true.

Jean went slowly down onto her knees at the edge of
the hole. She reached into it as if smoothing a coverlet.
"So hard," she said softly.

She looked around at the bare trees with their twisted
branches. "You think it happened here?"

"No," he answered. "We're almost positive not. Somebody brought her here afterward."

Jean nodded with satisfaction. So Kristen had never
seen these forbidding trees. She put her hands in the hole
again. "Was it deeper than this?"

"Yes. But not very deep." He stood with his hands in
his pockets and hadn't clicked on the flashlight. He didn't
want to give Jean too clear a view of the scene.

"Was she dressed?"

"Yes. I can give you the dress if you want."

"I remember which one." That wasn't why Jean had
asked. She looked into the hole. "Was she covered with
anything?"

"No, Jean. I'm sorry." Chris watched his old friend
staring down where her daughter had lain, Jean's hands
soothing the dirt. He remembered: "There was a stuffed
animal buried with her. It was—"

"Herbie." Jean smiled softly. "That was how I knew
she'd gone on a trip, because she took Herbie with her.
She'd slept with him all her life. A little dog about—"
She held her hands not far apart. Chris nodded.

"I can get him for you too, if—"

Jean shook her head. "I want him to stay with her."

They stayed in the woods another fifteen minutes;
Chris studied Jean's face every chance he got. She
walked away from the hole, taking the flashlight and
looking through the trees, exploring for paths or clues or
who knew what. She'd return to the hole and stare the

length of it. Her·eyes were wet, but her jaw set firmly.
Then she looked around again, as if memorizing the
place.

Chris would have sworn she'd never been there before.

In Chris's fifth-floor office in the Justice Center, Jack
Fine said, "I talked to that boy Jason. You can cross him
off the list. He did hang around with Kristen Lorenz a
good bit, but not that day. I've got his schedule down· by
the minute, and he was never out of sight of one or both
of his parents. His mother is a lawyer, securities and tax
kind of thing, and if I ask her son about two more questions she's going to hire him the best criminal defense
lawyer in the state. You should see her, standing there like
the Statue of Liberty with her hand on his shoulder,
telling me I can ask her son whatever I want, but you can
see from her face that if I get out of line she'll hit me with
her torch."

"And did Jason want to talk?"

"Oh yes. He misses that girl. It's obvious he liked her.
He wants to know where she went that last day, too. It's
funny, you can see that he's jealous that somebody else
was close enough to her to kill her."

Chris forced himself to sit at his desk and listen.
Lately he had been plagued by a constant urge to jump
up and get out of the building. "Did he give you any
other possibilities?"

Jack shook his head. "It was too short a conversation,
with Mom doing half the talking. I'll talk to him again.
Or maybe his mother'd be more comfortable with you,
lawyer to lawyer."

Chris would talk to the boy. But he felt tugged in
another, still unknown direction. He asked, "Do you feel
something missing in this case, Jack?"

The investigator didn't answer for several seconds.
Then he said flatly, "There's lots missing. What I mainly
feel the lack of is conspiracy. Or any evil intent for that

matter. This is beginning to seem to me like an accident. The girl gets mad at her mother, goes for a walk, goes to the mall or the airport, meets some other kids or maybe an older one, goes for a ride or to a party, takes some pills, and something happens. She falls or gets pushed and has really, really bad luck and breaks her neck. Whoever's with her panics and takes her out in the woods and buries her and leaves and never looks back. Goes back to a different school or off to college and we'll never find a trace of him. Unless somebody develops a real active conscience, this is starting to seem to me like one of those cases that twenty years later you're still wondering what happened."

Jack Fine's tone of voice made it clear he still carried a few such cases in his head. But Chris disagreed. Jack's hypothetical story left out elements of Kristen's story, though Chris couldn't exactly say what. He felt as if the present were a bubble that would soon burst, punctured by the penetrating past.

"Remember those boys who got arrested at that house in Terrell Hills? A few of them went to this same high school. Let's question them. The medical examiner said there were traces of drugs in Kristen's body, and those boys are into drugs."

Chris had not become so consumed by the dead girl that he'd forgotten Mr. Big. The criminal figure still lurked out there somewhere, and Chris looked for his prints everywhere. Jack walked away without comment, but Chris felt his continuing skepticism.

Anne wore a dress that no one who knew her had seen. Anne felt as if she hadn't seen it either; she couldn't recapture the person she had been when she'd bought it. It was a cocktail dress and she was meeting Chris for cocktails, so this seemed the occasion for pulling the little black number out of the back of the closet. Driving toward the restaurant, Anne could feel the top of the dress under her arms, creeping millimeter by millimeter down her breasts. "You're supposed to show a little," the saleswoman had said, telling Anne in a voice like her mother's to stop tugging at it. Then, stepping back, the sixtyish lady, who had more clothing style than Anne would ever possess, had said in an utterly sincere voice, "You look fabulous, honey. Whatever you want, wear that dress when you ask for it."

So in a wild, flirtatious moment Anne had bought the dress, but that mood had passed before the occasion for which she'd bought it. Tonight the word "cocktail" had brought the dress to mind and dropped her back into that playful spirit. Now, though, almost at her destination and feeling the dress's ever so slight shifts and shimmies, she knew that to maintain that spirit she'd better get a cocktail fast.

The valet parking guy whistled when she stepped out of her Volvo, but he probably did that for all the overdressed, overaged patrons he took pity on. Anne gathered up her tiny purse and the flimsy shawl-like thing that came with the dress and, remembering not to tug, walked slowly into Paesano's.

The venerable Italian restaurant—in the eatery business, thirty years' duration is eternity—had finally abandoned its original location and moved uptown to Lincoln Heights, a recently developed enclave of golf and shopping on the near north side. In the process Paesano's had expanded and modernized and continued to flourish. The interior was made of polished concrete, floors and ceilings, very high-tech. A hostess led Anne to the private party room, where she was enormously glad to see that Chris had gotten there first. When she saw him in his tuxedo, as on the first date they'd ever had, Anne was glad she had worn the dress.

She caught him doing one of those things men do, checking out the new arrival from the hips upward, so that he looked a little startled when his eyes arrived at her face atop the dress. He hurried toward her.

"New dress? You look great." He held her arms briefly and kissed her cheek. "Sorry about not picking you up. I was afraid I wouldn't get away from the office on time, and didn't want to make you late. You did want to come to this, didn't you?"

"The Martini Society? Of course. Doesn't everyone?"

Had that been the cynic speaking through Anne's mouth? It had sounded like her. Chris glanced at her and said, "This is your crowd, isn't it? I mean, half of them must be doctors."

Anne looked around and didn't see a familiar face among the two or three dozen people lounging elegantly in the large room with its own bar. "Not any doctors I hang out with," she said. "Where are the drinks? Is there a symbolic smashing of the first martini, or can I have one now?"

She said this half to Chris and half to a bartender as she took a stool at the bar. The bartender obliged with a smile and a last quick flip of the silver shaker in his hands, then poured the contents into two cold martini glasses that already held olives. Anne and Chris took glasses, clinked them, sipped, and felt phony.

"Do we blend in?" Anne asked.

The people in the crowd averaged under forty years of age, some of them mere kids who had discovered old vices. They grinned around cigars and toasted each other across the room. The air grew thick with smoke and self-congratulations. The society had been started a few years ago by a young plaintiff's lawyer after he'd won a big verdict in a product-liability case, which he decided made him immune to the consequences of overindulgence. The membership consisted of young professionals who wanted to play dress-up. The group was at least a little silly in both concept and execution, but the room held a significant amount of money and influence. Chris wasn't the only elected official in attendance. One wouldn't want to have one's picture taken for the newspaper here, but it didn't hurt at all to know these people. Chris circulated while Anne sat on her bar stool and appeared to enjoy sipping and nodding, wondering if her dress was responsible for the kind of people who stopped by to introduce themselves and chat her up.

"Can't be good all our lives, can we?" one tall, hearty fellow asked her, leaning over as if Anne's answer would be a private affair.

"Good at something, I hope," Anne said rather weakly, but her companion boomed laughter anyway. Then he opened his jacket to reveal a shirt pocket full of cigars, and offered her one.

Anne shook her head. He smiled slyly and fired up a fat one almost a foot long, then tried to blow a ring. He leaned close and said, "I think some women prefer not to smoke cigars because of the—the Freudian implication. Know what I mean?"

Dr. Greenwald, psychiatrist, returned his intimate smile and said, "I think so. Is that what you like about them?"

The man's face dropped from upward lines to downward ones. "Certainly not," he grumped, then walked away, looking back once as he brought the cigar to his mouth, saw Anne watching him, and dropped it to his side instead.

"I missed that exchange, but it looks like you made a friend," Chris said, returning to her side. "That guy owns six furniture stores and is the chairman of the society's cigar committee."

"They have officers and committees?" Anne said in amazement.

"Why not?"

"For a society devoted to vice, these people are a little—meticulous—aren't they?"

Chris laughed. They had another round and strolled around the room. They endured toasts and a speech by the president. They met strangers, smiled, walked through smoke. When Anne's drink grew warm, she did something that horrified the prissy purists of the Martini Society. She took an ice cube from a glass of water and dropped it into her drink. "I like it really cold," she explained to the people staring at her. She sipped and smiled and walked on.

"You offended their sense of how to do things," Chris said.

This was the new licentiousness, careful and fussy. "My God these people are particular," Anne complained. "I'd like to see how they make love."

"Now you're thinking of a different society."

They laughed, but then fell silent and a minute later separated again. Anne strolled in a casual, one-arm-outflung kind of way not natural to her, feeling Chris's eyes on her at times but resolutely not thinking about any subject related to him. She fell into a group of twenty-somethings in which the women were also smoking. After Anne declined a cigar again, one of the women, her lipstick smudged and with a continuing tilt to her head, said, "I think it's all a matter of attitude. Our parents worried too much about things like this, and where did it get them? Dropping dead while jogging instead of in bed. So what?"

Anne decided not to reply, until the girl added, "Don't you think so?" so that Anne had to say, "I think it's a matter of deposits in your liver and your lungs no matter what your 'attitude' is. Puff away, kiddos."

She walked away. Chris saw the expressions she left in her wake, and when Anne came up to him, he said, "My God, it is pure pleasure to see you work a room. Remind me to offer you a spot on my campaign team."

"Can we get out of here?" he added, just as Anne said the same thing.

They remained quiet through the process of leaving and getting her car. Anne drove aimlessly. Chris shifted in his seat and said, "Anne?"

"I know, I didn't do you any good back there. I don't

know what about those people put me off so badly, I just . . ."

"No, it doesn't matter. That's not what I'm thinking about."

Anne glanced at him, saw Chris's face troubled by something, and grew afraid.

"I've been thinking about what you said before, about . . ."

"No, don't. I'm sorry I . . ."

"No, you shouldn't be. Don't say that. I love you for it. Even more."

"Chris—" She glanced into her rearview mirror and pulled into the parking lot of a Wal-Mart, back into the far corner. She turned toward him, the little dress shifting all over the place.

He touched her arm and said, "I want what you want. Believe me. But why don't we be conventional? Why don't we get married?"

An earnest silence pervaded the car. Chris watched her, surprised to see that he had surprised her. Anne blushed. She gave a short laugh, then cut that off when she saw the seriousness of his expression. She pulled him close, hugged him, and they kissed in the close confines of the car. Chris grew relieved.

Anne drew back, smiled, and said, "No. Thank you, but no. Not now."

Anne felt a stab to her heart when his face fell. She put a hand on the back of his neck. "But I love you. Don't look like that, please. I can't explain . . ."

Actually, she could have. She felt she had trapped him into a proposal, because he was so straight he wouldn't want to father a child out of wedlock. What a word. Wedlock. Anne wanted to hit herself. She wanted to go back in time.

She almost made a joke, that mainly she didn't want to tell her grandchildren that she'd accepted a marriage proposal in a car in a Wal-Mart parking lot. Almost as bad as a pregnancy begun in a car. Actually, with her legs able to sprawl and the little black dress hiking up, that prospect didn't seem all that unattractive.

Mainly, with three martinis coursing through her veins, she didn't want to make this decision this moment.

She could see Chris resolving not to speak, and certainly not to ask why, so she tried. "You wouldn't have thought of marriage if I hadn't sprung this other on you. You weren't ready yet. *We're* not. You were right not to be ready yet. I don't want to force things."

Saying all that out loud exhausted Anne. She turned in her seat and started the car again. "My God, we're a lovely couple." Her voice achieved the lightness she sought. "Can we go have dinner somewhere?"

"Sure," Chris said, then cleared his throat. "Why not?"

A block later Anne said in a disgusted voice, "Women. What the hell do they want?"

She didn't get the laugh she'd hoped for. After a while they started talking again, about nothing significant— their food, the jerks of the Martini Society. Even later that night in her bed, it was a relief to touch each other without saying anything serious. Maybe they would never be serious again.

One of the boys who'd been arrested in the raid on the house in Terrell Hills and who also attended Kristen Lorenz's high school had been on juvenile probation for possession of marijuana. Chris talked to the boy's probation officer, who seemed overworked and clueless and couldn't remember anything about the boy, but gave Chris the name of a vice principal at the high school who supposedly kept up with the problem kids.

Chris saw the vice principal, Mrs. Strayhorn, in her office, the scene of many a lecture and suspension. Mrs. Strayhorn had grown old enough—mid-fifties—that her face fell naturally into the expression she used most, a stern frown that made Chris feel he'd gotten into trouble himself. He handed her two pictures, one of the boy,

Tommy Peters, and one of Kristen Lorenz. The vice principal nodded at the boy's photo, barely glanced at the girl's.

"What's Tommy done now?"

"Nothing that I know of. I was wondering if you knew of any connection between him and this girl. Did they hang around together? Same friends, anything?"

Mrs. Strayhorn shook her head repeatedly. "No. No chance. Kristen was a good girl. Good student, nice girl, polite, respectful. One of the ones who doesn't get enough attention because they're no trouble, you know?"

Chris knew. Kristen had left very little trail at her school. Hardly anyone even seemed to have known her. He stood up with a sigh.

Mrs. Strayhorn brought the two photos close together then pulled them apart, as if they were magnets of opposite polarity that could never be joined. "No, you're way off track here," she assured Chris again. She looked at him and said casually, "It wasn't Kristen who ran with that crowd. It was her big sister."

Six

That night, a dark one, Chris sat alone in his white modern condo, staring out the closed patio doors at the small balcony. One lamp behind him created reflections of the room in the glass doors, though occasionally a flash of headlights from Broadway shot an image from outside into his view.

The front room of the condo was a long one that ran from the front door, past the door into the kitchen, through a dining area, then opened out into the living room. The walls were white, and sparsely decorated. When Chris had first moved in he'd had no urge to make the place homey, and lately he spent more time at the office or at Anne's. The condo still felt slightly unfamiliar to him, like a transitional room.

He sat with his back to the dining area and stared at that morass of reflections and darkness in the doors. Along with the silhouettes of trees beyond the balcony, the view made a tangled backdrop for his thoughts.

Jean had another daughter. She was sixteen years old and her name was Clarissa. Clarissa Fitzgerald, her last

name the same as Jean's, different from her sister's. That
was one thing that had kept the investigators from finding
this connection. There had been nothing in the dead girl's
school records to suggest a sister.

He had tried to talk to Clarissa Fitzgerald that afternoon, but she'd been absent. In fact she'd been gone for
weeks. In her file he found a letter from Jean saying that
Clarissa had transferred to another school.

Chris remembered Jean's nosy across-the-street neighbor saying, "I haven't seen the girls since before Christmas . . ." She had said girls, plural, but Jack and Chris, not
knowing of the other sister, had heard the word singular.
Still, it was too big a secret. They would have found out
soon. Jean had in effect lied to him. She'd tried to conceal
all traces of her other daughter. Why?

Sixteen years old. Clarissa. When Chris tried to picture
her face he saw instead Jean's at nineteen, the last time
he'd seen her. After their adventure in the woods, Chris
had gone home to San Antonio for the summer while Jean
stayed in Austin. He'd changed when out of her sight,
began turning back to his old self, hanging out with high
school friends, but there was no chance of forgetting her.
Late in June he'd driven the eighty miles to Austin in his
old blue Ford Falcon to see her.

He hadn't been able to get her on the phone, but
remained confident of finding her; he knew all her routes.
Crossing the Austin city line, Chris could almost feel her
beside him. He wore white jeans and a colorful short-
sleeved shirt, and tossed his hair back from his eyes. He
grinned at the short spires of Austin and at the state capi-
tol as he neared the UT campus. Jean's city. His city.

She wasn't home, but that didn't surprise him. He tried
Armadillo World Headquarters, which looked ugly and
abandoned by daylight, Scholzgarden where afternoon
idlers drank beer, a few houses of Jean's friends. As dusk
fell he sat on the patio of a small restaurant just off
Guadalupe Street that was one of Jean's favorites, a beer

at his elbow. He smelled marijuana close at hand and raised his head to savor the smell. Turning slowly, he saw four scraggly students who were strangers to him, but they grinned as if they knew him, or what he was thinking.

Night had fallen fully by the time he returned to the old mansion where Jean had a room. He climbed once again the stairs and knocked on her door, picturing her clothes scattered on the floor of the room within, but only hollowness answered him. Chris returned to the wide porch and took up his post. Two hours later the night rewarded him. An unfamiliar car with a familiar laugh ringing from it pulled raggedly up to the curb. Chris stood slowly, listening to the confused voices from within. Finally the front passenger door opened, Jean stumbled out, laughed and slapped at the hands reaching for her. The car seemed crowded with youth and smoke and plans.

Jean wore jeans and a loose flowered top that swirled around her as she turned. Her face shone with glamour and sweat. "I'll be right back, idiots," Jean grumbled good-naturedly, then turned and saw Chris. Her change of expression told him everything he needed to know. Jean lost her happy look, became obviously confused, then walked slowly toward him, composing her expression into one of welcome. Having to put on a face for him. Chris did the same.

"Hi!"

"Chris! This is great. You look terrific. What's going on?"

He only had a shrug for an answer. His glance back over Jean's shoulder asked the same question. She grew tentative again. "Do you want—?" The car's horn honked, more than one voice called her name, and she waved impatiently.

"We're going to a party. Want to come?"

Only a moment of imagining himself shoving into that car, being stared or glared at by Jean's friends wondering who the hell he was, made Chris shake his head.

"No, thanks, I've got . . ."

"Where are you staying?"

Again he answered vaguely. He had hoped, pretty much assumed he would be staying with Jean, in her rumpled, airy room high above their heads.

They stood close for a moment, looking at each other uncertainly. Jean took his hand, but Chris sensed her urgency to move on. He said, "I'll call you," and walked down the steps, stiff with the consciousness of being watched from that damned car. Jean called his name, he turned, and they gave each other little smiles that completely lacked intimacy. He had gone home for the summer like a child and she had gone on with her life. She had grown beyond him.

He did call her again that summer, seldom catching her home, then never. In August a recording told him her phone number was no longer in service. When he returned to school in September he looked all over for her but didn't find her anywhere. She had gone, without a word to him.

Chris sat in his comfortable condo with shoulders tense, his gaze deeply abstracted into the past, remembering his last sight of Jean's face, looking lovely and lost and a little pityingly in his direction. Chris shook his head angrily and gradually focused on the view through his patio doors, particularly on a paleness within the darkness outside. Memory had invaded the present: as he stared, he saw in the glass of the doors Jean's face, as young as when he'd known her. The girl stared in at him, questioning.

A chill invaded Chris. He shot to his feet. His movement created air currents that came back to him with a sudden sense of another presence. He turned and gasped. Jean stood at his shoulder.

He looked back at the glass doors, where for a moment an afterimage of the young girl's face he had seen remained. But then the image became Jean's reflection. Shifts in the light and the background made her look young, then older. Chris's own reflection hid all of Jean except her face, which hovered bodiless in the glass. He seemed to see her through a barrier.

Reluctantly he turned away from the balcony doors, feeling his recoverable past calling to him from the reflections. "How did you get in here?"

Jean's face wore its adult expression, the deadened one that made her look like the aged relative of the young woman Chris had known. She said, "The door wasn't locked. In fact it was ajar. It was so quiet I wasn't sure you were here. I looked in and saw you not moving, like you were asleep. Sorry."

Chris couldn't remember if he'd locked his door or not. Jean must have moved quietly as a thief across his carpet. His nerves ran high with the thought of her sneaking up on him. Someone else could have come inside with her.

"Jean—"

"I got a call from the school today. Mrs. Strayhorn thought she should inquire about Clarissa again." Jean spoke briskly in a businesswoman's tone.

"Why didn't you tell me about her?"

"You didn't ask about her, and I didn't think it was important. We weren't catching up on old times, were we? Clarissa had nothing to do with Kristen being gone."

Chris circled her very slowly, studying Jean's face. Knowing his suspicion, she stood stoically, undergoing examination.

"Where is she, Jean?"

Her eyelids came down, covering up. "She's—" she began, and stopped. She looked full at Chris. Blue, blue eyes, shining with intelligence, and with a sudden sheen of tears.

"Gone to stay with her father?" He didn't bother to keep the sarcasm out of his voice.

Jean shook her head quickly, not even considering the easy lie this time.

"Then where—?"

"I don't know."

"For how long?"

"Weeks. Ever since I began to suspect Kristen didn't go to St. Louis."

"You mean she ran away? Your other daughter? Why didn't—"

Jean shook her head again, more slowly. Her hand reached up as if she would touch Chris, but she didn't. Her hand hung there, clenched. Jean was too strong to tremble, even in ultimate distress. But frustration held her tightly. She looked thinner than when Chris had first seen her again. Her eyes avoided him. It didn't seem intentional, she remained lost in thought even with Chris standing in front of her.

"Where is she, Jean?" he asked distinctly, afraid of the answer as she seemed to be.

But her answer surprised him. "I couldn't tell you. He threatened her."

"He—?" Chris had no idea what she meant.

Jean looked up at him. "Why would a woman not immediately report her child missing?"

She meant Kristen. Jean was throwing back at Chris the question he'd asked himself. What would keep a mother from mounting an all-out search for a missing daughter?

Having another child in equal danger.

"The killer has Clarissa? To make sure you keep quiet." Jean nodded.

Chris's sluggish blood began to race. He grabbed her arms. "My God, Jean, what have you gotten involved in?"

Her hands finally held him as she began to cry in earnest. "Just help me. Don't show me another grave, Chris. Help me get her back."

Her voice sounded young and frightened. Her face began to dissolve.

*   *   *

Everything else fell away as the search consumed Chris. It started that night with a call to Jack Fine, Jean standing close beside him. "What's the man's name?" Chris said to her.

"I don't know. The name he gave me was fake. I looked it up and couldn't find anyone."

"How do you know him?"

"I didn't. He was someone Clarissa was involved with somehow, or the boy she was dating knew him." Jean came out with her answers quickly. She seemed relieved since spilling her secrets to Chris. Her franticness had infected him.

"You mean this is a high school boy we're looking for? Jack, we'll have to see who else has been absent—"

"No," Jean said. "No, this is a grown man. But the boys who were involved in this stuff knew him. He sort of organized them, I think."

"Give me some of the boys' names, then. Was Clarissa dating some of them?"

"One. Ryan McClain. A boy in her class."

"Are you getting this, Jack? Tell me other names, Jean."

She twisted her hands. "Just first ones. Danny. Josh."

"Haven't you been trying to find out?" Chris barked at her. "What've you been doing all this time?"

"Yes, I have. But it's hard for me to work undercover at the high school." A burst of resentment and her old humor came through Jean's anxiety for a moment. She and Chris looked at each other with recognition before Chris returned his attention to the phone. "Let's pick up this Ryan McClain tonight, Jack. Roust him out of his bed. I don't know, something. Anything. It doesn't have to stick."

Through the phone line came the investigator's familiar voice, much calmer and more methodical than his boss's. "We don't want to start a panic, Chris. We don't know who he might call. Or his parents might call the wrong person, looking for a recommendation about a lawyer. Kidnappers panic real easily."

Chris listened a moment longer then turned to Jean, knowing he had to pass on the question but hating to ask it. Very clearly he asked Jean, "Are you sure she's alive?"

"Yes." She nodded. "I've talked to her."

Watching the momentary peacefulness on Jean's face, Chris said, "Did you hear that, Jack? Yes." Again to Jean: "Do you have a schedule? Is he supposed to call you again?"

She shook her head. "And the call was from a cell phone. My caller ID wouldn't say where it came from."

After a few more questions and answers they decided nothing could be done that night. In the morning they would try to find a way to question Clarissa's boyfriend. But the decision didn't let them relax. Chris and Jean stood close, looking again at the sliding glass doors. Their reflections were gone. A neighbor had turned on a light, partially illuminating Chris's empty second-floor balcony. The illusion he'd seen of Jean's reflection had fled, too. But there was a young girl out there somewhere in that night.

Early the next morning they met with Jack Fine in Chris's office. Chris and Jean had spent the night together, in their thoughts. Chris had slept badly, miles away from Jean's house, thinking restlessly how much of his life, and hers, had passed since he'd seen her. It had been almost a shock to see her again in the morning light, as if the horrible events that had brought them together had been forgotten for a moment and they had just run into each other, recognizing old friends in each other's faces. Jean had begun again to look familiar to Chris. He put his arm briefly around her shoulders. Jean stood tall, her mouth grimly prepared for business.

Jack Fine moved no more animatedly than usual, but he'd beaten Chris to the office and assembled some mate-

rials. He and Chris and Jean sat in the small reception
area of Chris's office, Jean on the love seat and the men in
the wing chairs. Jack spread photographs on the glass-
topped coffee table. "Do you recognize any of these,
ma'am?"

Jean was two decades younger than Jack, but because
she was a mother and a witness and possibly a victim,
she would remain "ma'am" to him. He treated her with
deference, but Chris sensed the underlying suspicion in
Jack's nature. Jack would have treated Mother Teresa the
same way.

Jean pointed at one picture. "That one's Ryan. The boy
Clarissa dated."

Chris picked up the photo. The boy had thick brown
hair that stood up from his forehead, clear eyes, and, of
course, skin unlined to the point of blankness. Jack's
incongruous photo spread consisted of school pictures, a
couple of the boys wearing ties, one with a goofy expression, and all of them looking about twelve years old.
Ryan McClain gazed back at Chris innocently.

"He wasn't one of the ones in that house on Tuttle Road
the night of the raid," Jack said, with no apparent disap-
pointment in his voice. "Or he could have been one of the
ones who got away out the back before the cops secured
the place. At any rate we don't have anything on him."

Jean pointed out another photo. "This is Ryan's best
friend. Josh Wiggins. Sometimes they call him—"

" 'Bubby,' " Jack said with her. To Chris, the investigator said, "He *was* in the house that night. They arrested
him for criminal trespass, but after we couldn't find an
owner for the house the case got dropped."

"Can we revive it?" Chris asked.

"If Josh was involved in something, Ryan was, too,"
Jean said. "I promise you that. What's this house you're
talking about? Where is it?"

Jack answered Chris's question. "Sure. You can charge
anybody with anything as long as you don't mind losing
in court later on. You know that, don't you, Counselor?"

Chris tried to calm Jean. "The house is just a place where these boys partied. Clarissa wouldn't be there. It's been empty for the last three months, I'm sure. Once the police knew about it they wouldn't use it again."

"They who?" Jean demanded. She stood up, ready to run, to jump on somebody.

"You tell me."

"I don't know!" Jean paced away from him as if stalking.

Chris gave instructions to his investigator. "I want a search warrant for that house, Jack. I want it searched this morning, for any trace of this girl. Prints, hairs." He lowered his voice. "Steam the carpets." By which he meant look for traces of blood. Jack understood. He glanced past Chris's shoulder at Clarissa's mother.

"Samples?" Jack asked.

"Yes. Send someone to Jean's house. Jean, can you give us some clothes of Clarissa's, a hairbrush she used, something she would have touched?"

"Yes, yes," Jean said impatiently. Her leg moved rhythmically. She must have had enormous energy stored, waiting for this chance to do something. Chris was glad to be able to give her tasks.

"We're going to pick up these boys, too," he said. "Find out everything we can. One of them will know who this man is."

"They might not, Chris. They might have been too far down the chain of command."

"Then we'll move up it!" Chris snapped. He too felt eager to move, and impatient with Jack's methodical slowness.

"You already have," Jack reminded him. "Remember Peter Belasco? You have a *good* case against him."

Chris snapped his fingers and pointed at Jack, a commendation. "Get on it," he said, heading for the door. "Take Jean with you."

"He's got a lawyer," Jack called after him.

"To hell with him," Chris said. He paused to look at Jean. "Are you all right? Don't worry. We'll find her."

"I should have come to you sooner," she said gratefully.

Most citizens live with the illusion that public officials can mobilize huge forces that will solve any dilemma if only they're motivated enough. Chris gave Jean a tight-lipped, Canadian Mountie sort of staunch nod, and went out.

Jack Fine, who had worked inside the law enforcement establishment all his adult life, didn't say anything, except, "Ma'am—" as he motioned Jean toward the door.

Chris had Peter Belasco brought to a captain's office at the jail. A stern sheriff's deputy whose biceps strained the dark brown sleeves of his uniform shirt asked the District Attorney, "Would you like me to cuff him to the desk, sir?"

"No thank you, Deputy. You can take them off, please."

Belasco held out his hands with a small smile at his captor, who didn't look at him as he efficiently removed the handcuffs. "I'll be right outside," the deputy said, and went out and closed the door.

Even with the handcuffs and the clanking guard gone, the small office seemed pretty metallic. The door was metal, as was the desk. The ceiling was composed of a metal grid with acoustic tiles screwed in place. The place felt very cramped to Chris, but Belasco took a deep breath and stretched his shoulders as if freed from restraint. Belasco had been in jail more than two months, with enough felonies pending that a judge had set a million-dollar bond, and Belasco's employer hadn't paid it for him.

Belasco had undergone the usual transformation, from natty dresser on the outside to the orange coverall and thongs of a Bexar County Adult Detention inmate. He wore no watch or other jewelry. Physical distinctions in here were reduced to the essentials: size, hair color, age.

But Belasco didn't appear subdued by his surroundings, the loss of his wardrobe, or the first-degree felonies looming over him because of the drugs he'd been caught with in the house in Terrell Hills where Belasco and the boys got arrested. Since Chris had won the court fight not to have the evidence suppressed, very little stood between Belasco and a long time in prison, but the inmate's manner didn't betray any concern. "You got a smoke?" he asked Chris.

The District Attorney shook his head. Belasco crossed to the desk and opened the top drawer.

"Close that."

Belasco ignored Chris, opened another drawer and rummaged inside.

"Get away from the desk."

Belasco didn't even glance up. Chris, imagining the inmate's hand emerging from the drawer holding a gun, moved quickly across the space separating them and shoved Belasco hard in the chest. The inmate fell back into the desk chair, which rolled a couple of feet to the wall.

Belasco turned his startled expression into a smirk of acquiescence and remained sitting. "When're you gonna tell me about how I can end this interview at any time and I'm entitled to have my lawyer present?"

"It's not like that." Chris leaned back against the desk and put his foot up on the front edge of Belasco's chair, between the inmate's legs. Belasco's expression turned warier. "I'm not questioning you about your own case. I'm not looking for something I can use in court. I want from you a name and an address. If you give it to me I'll give you a very reduced sentence. Under ten years. If you don't I'll go for the maximum, one case at a time, and stack the sentences. With your record I can get it."

Belasco tried to look indifferent. "What name?"

"Your boss."

"Right," Belasco said sarcastically. He pushed Chris's leg aside and stood up. "Joe Jerkoff," he said. "One Two Three Fuckyou Lane. Want me to write that down for you?"

Chris stayed close to Belasco's face. "Listen, you don't understand. Let me give *you* a couple of names. Kristen Lorenz."

Belasco was prepared, and in control of his face. He raised his eyebrows questioningly and shook his head.

"Clarissa Fitzgerald."

Belasco's face remained innocent.

"Ryan McClain."

"You could be naming TV show characters for all I know."

"Josh Wiggins," Chris said.

Belasco shrugged again.

"Now *you*'re being stupid," Chris told him. "Josh Wiggins was in the house with you the night you got arrested. Police arrested him, too."

"Those boys have names?" Belasco said dismissively.

Chris stepped away from him. "All right. Be the smart-ass. But now you know I know those names, and I'll have more by sundown today. Somebody's going to give me what I want. If it's not you you'll be losing a lot of years of your life."

Belasco continued to feign indifference, but thoughts had begun to make his eyes shifty.

Chris told him, "You think I don't know the deal? If you keep quiet you get rewarded, if you talk he'll try to hurt you, even kill you. But think about this: I want him badly. It's gone way beyond your little drugs and thievery bullshit. When I get him he's going to be in no position to do anything to anybody else. You make the right deal and he'll be in and you'll be out. A lot better than what you're looking at now, isn't it?"

Belasco didn't answer. Chris turned away.

"Uh." The small syllable stopped Chris at the door.

Belasco looked genuinely perplexed. "What's this about? What's he done now?"

Chris opened the door and Belasco said quickly, "I'll think about it."

"Yeah. I'll help you."

The sound of the office door opening had brought the tall, burly deputy back. Chris said to him, "I want this man put in isolation. No phone calls, no visitors. No contact with other inmates. If somebody does try to talk to him I want to know about it. He's going to be a material witness for me."

"Hey, no I'm not! Don't say that." Belasco sounded alarmed for the first time.

"Yes sir." The deputy smiled at Belasco and took his arm.

"Pretty soon everybody'll know you're talking to me anyway," Chris said to the inmate. "Make up your mind." Before he turned away he thought of something else. "Let me try out one more name on you. *Jean* Fitzgerald."

Belasco chewed his lip, no longer disguising his expressions. But he had a lot on his mind, and Chris couldn't tell whether the name meant anything to Belasco or not. Chris turned and strode away quickly, hearing the sound of the inmate's protests as the guard took him away.

Jack Fine said, "Man, that is one busy school. Kids selling dope to each other, parents paying for abortions, the tennis coach having an affair with the second-best player on the team. And the principal claims they hold a few classes, too."

"This is fascinating, Jack," Chris said into his cell phone as he sped along the expressway. Jack was on a cell phone somewhere, too. In the background Chris heard a bell ring. He glanced at his dashboard and saw that the afternoon had reached three-thirty. His investigator had apparently spent the whole day at Holmes High

School. "But have you found anything I can use?"

"This is how a fast investigation goes," Jack protested. "I don't have time to focus, I'm like a vacuum cleaner, I pick up everything. Everybody wants to tell me all the rumors. They think they're something out of the ordinary."

"*Are* any of them?" Chris asked. He had spent most of his day at his office and at police headquarters a few blocks away, looking up arrest records on various kids at the school. By now the day seemed to be trickling away and he'd grown too restless to stick with paperwork. He'd found out from his office that Jack remained at the school, and had headed that way. Chris sped along Interstate 10 out of downtown toward the northwest side of San Antonio. On his left he passed Crossroads Mall and prepared to loop around to switch expressways.

"There's definite thievery going on," Jack said. "That's going to take a while to track. But I did find out one interesting thing. A few months ago a boy got beaten up because he'd sold a few tabs of acid at school. And it wasn't the Fellowship of Christian Athletes who did it to him, it was rival dealers."

Chris understood the implication. "That's not high school behavior. That's grown-up dealer tactics."

"Exactly. Somebody wants exclusivity. Back in my days in Narcotics, we called that organized crime."

"So maybe there's a person organizing it," Chris said. He refused to use the silly term "Mr. Big," but knew Jack got the point.

He couldn't allow himself to get sidetracked, though. This business held layer after layer; an investigation into something this complicated typically moved as slowly as an archaeological dig, and Chris wanted speed. "Where's Jean?" he asked.

"At her house with the evidence tech. She sounds like you, in a big hurry all of a sudden. Listen, boss, I gotta go. Pops at the malt shop is supposed to have a hot tip for me."

Something about the case or about spending the day

back in high school had made Jack more jovial than usual. Chris envied him his tone. He continued west on Loop 410, passed the exit for the high school, and took the one for Jean's neighborhood.

By the time Chris pulled up in front of the pretty brick house with the yellow trim, the police evidence technician had gathered his samples and gone. Jean looked ready to get out, too. She yanked the door open before Chris could ring the bell. Her face looking restless and afraid, she spread her hands. Chris shook his head.

Jean sighed, threw back her head and shook it, and they went into her house. Jean wore black jeans and a dark brown top. Chris wondered if she'd deliberately worn dark colors of mourning or just grabbed the first clothes she'd seen. The blouse had no sleeves or collar. Jean's arms and neck looked tanned and taut. Even with its nervous anxiety, her face had grown more youthful. Eagerness animated it. How suppressed her spirit must have been for the last two months, waiting for something to happen, for the chance to do something.

"I wanted to speak to the police officer who came to collect samples."

"He's already gone," Jean said quickly. "It didn't take long."

Chris gave Jean a searching look and asked, "How are you doing?"

"Scared to death." Jean said this almost humorously, but her face remained stiff with fear. "While I just sat and did nothing I could pray that if I kept that up the girls would be okay. Just walk very slowly, go about my normal routine, hope somebody was watching me so they could see how good I was being. Now," she said loudly, almost accusingly, "I've got cops in my house and I'm spending most of my time with the District Attorney of the city. I'm scared, Chris. We've got to move fast."

"We are. Don't worry, Jean, nobody's watching you." Chris thought of her neighbor across the street. He took a step toward Jean and she turned away with a jerky abruptness. "I wish I hadn't quit smoking," she said over her shoulder.

"I'd like to see Clarissa's room," Chris said.

Jean didn't answer. She kept walking and Chris followed, through the kitchen and into the back hallway of the house. Chris had realized that Jean had deliberately kept him out of the personal part of the house on his first visit, not wanting him to see the signs of a second daughter.

The name Clarissa meant something to Chris. Jean had used it as a playful alias when he'd known her in college. Apparently Jean had been more fond of the name than he'd known.

The age sixteen, Clarissa's age, meant something to Chris, too. It subtracted from his current age back to nineteen, about the age he'd been when he'd last seen Jean.

She led him past a bathroom into the first bedroom off the hall, in which an overhead light still burned. The room was small, holding a twin bed, a tall dresser, and a small desk. Windows on two walls admitted bright sunlight through thin curtains.

The police evidence technician had uncharacteristically left the room very neat. Usually they left a crime scene looking like a crime scene, with black fingerprint powder on the windowsills, chalk marks on the floor, and furniture pulled out from walls. But either this one had treated the room much more reverently, or Jean had cleaned up. The small bed was made up with a yellow and white coverlet, the desk chair was pushed in, and there were no clothes in sight. Two shelves on the wall above the desk held textbooks, a few other books, and two trophies.

The police officer had his samples by now, they would be on their way to the lab. Samples of Clarissa's hair, her fingerprints, maybe a few threads from her clothing or mud from her shoes. The evidence tech who didn't know her in the slightest now had proof of Clarissa's existence. Chris wanted some such proof for himself.

"Can I see a picture of her?"

As Chris asked the question he looked past Jean and saw two photographs in a cardboard frame on top of the dresser. He went and picked it up as Jean said dismissively, "Oh, she was only about eleven then. When she was on a swim team back in California. They're very big on swimming there. I'll get you a more recent one."

Chris studied the two photos in the frame, a team picture of about a dozen girls in a kneeling row and a standing one. Beside it the frame also held an individual photo of a thin blond girl posed as if coming up the ladder from the pool, except that her hair and skin were dry. She grinned abashedly at the camera as if embarrassed by the fakiness of the pose. She had long thin arms, a narrow face but with a rather high forehead, and a little bump of a nose. Her eyes were deep blue like the one-piece bathing suit she wore and the pool water behind her. Clarissa looked up from the picture, from under her eyebrows, with a slightly twisted smile.

"Only eleven," Jean had said of Clarissa's age in the photo, as if eleven years were nothing, hardly worth remembering; they had passed without her noticing. And with Chris not knowing that this young life was passing. He stared at the picture for long minutes until Jean returned.

"I'm not a very big picture-taker. Here's her school one from last year, it's the best full-face shot."

"I'd like to see one you took," Chris said.

Jean gave him a sharp look and delved into the shoe box she carried, the same one she'd produced to find a picture of Kristen. This time she didn't take care to keep it covered. Her secrets were out.

If one shoe box held all the photos she'd ever taken of her two daughters, Jean had described herself accurately as not much of a photographer. She pulled out one, grimaced at it, and said, "Nah," but Chris took it from her.

Someone else had taken the photograph. Jean stood in front of a boulder or a stone wall, sunlight in her face. Her girls stood on either side of her, more solemn than their mother, unsmiling for the photograph. The older girl, who looked about thirteen in the picture, had her hip cocked and her chin lifted. The other girl, two years younger, had folded her arms and lowered her head, looking up through eyelashes darker than her sister's. The three of them looked as if they'd just had an argument, maybe over whether they wanted their picture taken.

"Can I—?" Chris began.

"No." Jean took back the photo and handed him another one, an apparently recent photo of Clarissa, dressed in a formal gown and smiling dazzlingly. The pretty girl had grown into a beautiful teenager. Her face had filled out with her mother's cheekbones and her small chin. Clarissa also had rather a prominent forehead, framed by straight blond hair worn long.

Chris looked up from the picture. "Jean."

She looked up at him as if she couldn't imagine what he might say.

"Why didn't you ever tell me?"

She did him the credit of not saying, "Tell you what?" After a moment, voice flat, she said, "Because she wasn't your responsibility. She's mine. I'm not even sure . . ."

Not finishing the sentence, she turned her head away. Her shoulders remained lifted but Jean showed uncharacteristic confusion, as if reconsidering the decisions of her life. She sat on the bed with her shoe box, still holding the one picture of herself and her girls in her hand. Chris looked around the room. It didn't hold much personality. He would have liked to see a poster of someone or a sports pennant, something to show what the girl cared about. The room held no such clues, it could have been put together anonymously by a decorator from Wal-Mart. The one wall decoration was a framed print about two feet square, showing a girl looking out a window at a view of the ocean. All that could be seen of the girl was the back of her head. The girl could have been Clarissa herself, mysteriously absent.

Jean sat silently, now watching Chris and waiting for him to speak. Sometimes he felt close to her, as if they were about to break through the lost years between them and become their old selves again, but that feeling had fled here in Clarissa's room.

Jean stood up and spoke less bitterly, but very flatly. "I'm sorry, Chris. I've made some huge mistakes, God knows. But there's not too damned much I can do about it now." Beats of silence passed while they looked at each other distrustfully, then Jean added, "Just help me, please. I don't want to get into all this other—"

"You help me, Jean. Give me this man's name. The man who has her. You know more about him."

Jean shook her head vehemently. Tears started. "I don't. I swear I don't. Don't you think I'd tell you? But I'll do everything I can to find out."

She walked quickly out of the room. A few moments later Chris heard the front door close, leaving him alone in the house, in Clarissa's room, Jean's way of demonstrating as clearly as she could that she had nothing to hide. Chris looked around and knew that if he opened the closet doors or looked under the bed's mattress he'd find nothing out of the ordinary. He put the photo in his pocket and left the house.

That evening, alone in his condo again, Chris walked all the way through the few rooms. Nothing seemed out of place, but Chris didn't feel comfortable. An invaded air still lingered, from the way Jean had walked in on him there two nights ago. He wondered if she'd developed some low-level criminal skills, lock picking and the like, either back when he'd known her or in the intervening years.

In the cell-like, undecorated spare bedroom he turned on the computer. It beeped its eagerness to serve. Chris launched his E-mail program and walked out, across the living room to his bedroom to change clothes while the machine grunted and groaned to pull in his own piece of cyberspace. As he put on sweatpants and a T-shirt he heard the computer working, then fall silent as if it had been clubbed by an intruder.

He returned to the spare bedroom, typed in his password while remaining standing, and found more than half a dozen new messages. Chris had made his E-mail address semipublic, not advertised but found easily enough by anyone who wanted to get a message to the District Attorney. He also heard occasionally from law enforcement people in other cities or states, fellow prosecutors he'd met at seminars and the like.

He didn't immediately recognize the return addresses displayed on his screen. Mostly citizens with complaints, probably. One tag caught his attention: "Krislore." It looked as if someone who had shortened or misspelled his name were compiling a dossier on him. "How 'X-Files,' " Chris muttered, and chose that message first.

The screen went to blue then filled with lines of type. The message carried no greeting, no introduction. Chris frowned as he read the first sentence, so domestic and out of context. But as he continued he sank slowly into the desk chair and absorbed the lines of text:

I had supper last night at Jason's house. We were studying and his mother invited me. I kind of wanted to stay but it made me nervous too. It would have been okay with me if Mom had said no when I called home, but she said Sure like she hadn't even started thinking about supper yet.

Jason and his sister set the table. They said I didn't have to help because I was a guest, but I watched them. They put so many things on the table! Not ketchup or pickle jars, but cloth napkins and all kinds of silverware and a vase of flowers and even candles. Instead of hot pads they used little metal things with tiny stubby legs. I was dying to know what they were called, but nobody ever said, "Hey, hand me one of those burumphas, will you?" They just set them out.

All through supper the whole family talked about their jobs and school and Jason's Mom and Dad asked about friends of the kids, using their names. I wondered if they were putting on an act for me, but it didn't seem like it.

I hope they ask me again.

The message ended as unceremoniously as it had begun, offering no explanation of who had sent it or what it had to do with Chris. But by the second paragraph he thought he knew the source. He remembered the name Jason: the boy Kristen Lorenz had said she was going to see on her last day. That explained the sender name, too; not a variation of Chris's name, but of hers. Kristen Lorenz: Krislore.

The confidential tone made Chris suspect that the passage came from the girl's diary. Its grateful wonderment over small domestic details made Chris long to take her to dinner. Quite easily he pictured Kristen watching this easygoing Cleaver-like family, wondering when the act would end or whether they could possibly be real.

Reading the short passage invoked in Chris the same response he hadn't thought of in years, of reading Anne Frank's diary: picturing a vibrant young girl eager to open up to life and then realizing that she was in the ground.

The return address offered no clue. Chris sent a short reply, with no idea where his words might be going. He printed out the passage from Kristen's diary, knowing how he would pore over it in the days to come, but he didn't see what it should tell him except how Kristen had thought. Was someone trying to point suspicion at Jason, or his family?

He hoped more messages would come. As he returned

to the main screen, his computer abruptly blotting out Kristen's words, Chris had the terrible feeling he was closing the lid over her face again.

Anne Greenwald wore an apron. It swished against her legs as she walked around her small kitchen checking her dinner on the stove and getting out plates. The apron gave a comforting feeling of enclosure and continuity, since she'd inherited it from her grandmother, but just before she walked out the swinging door she grimaced, pulled off the apron, and sailed it onto a countertop. After all, she wore jeans underneath. How much protection did they need?

Let's not go domestic goddess all at once, she thought, and called into her living room, "Ready to eat?"

After all, just her cooking a meal at home was odd enough that Chris had given her a puzzled look at the suggestion. She smiled at him now and he asked, "What can I do?"

"How about opening the wine?"

"Come on, Anne," he answered, by which she knew he meant her assigning him such a traditional male job did nothing to allay his suspicion that she was up to something odd. She smiled again, returned to the kitchen, and brought in the last of the food, a platter of beef Stroganoff and a bowl of broccoli liberally sprinkled with grated Parmesan.

Anne sat, tried to think of how her mother had begun meals, and ended up saying, "Well—" To which Chris gave the traditional reply: "Yes."

They ate. They lingered over the meal, Chris glancing around as if he'd never seen her dining room before. True, she'd had to dust the table before setting it, but he didn't have to act so weird about it. He smiled back at her and gradually they began talking about their days, people they knew, the ordinary. Chris relaxed. "This is nice," he said of her dinner.

"You must really be enjoying that particular bite, since you've been chewing on it for five minutes."

Tight-lipped, he replied, "One wants to—savor." But he discreetly moved the napkin to his mouth.

Anne poured more wine. One strand of hair fell across her cheek. Tiny lines appeared at the corners of her mouth, and as soon as she opened it again Chris knew what she would say.

"I want to thank you—" she began seriously.

"Don't worry, that offer's been withdrawn. My people will contact your people to discuss settlement terms and retreat positions."

"Oh." Anne looked down at the remains of her dinner, then up at him with falsely bright eyes. She couldn't think of what to say; a lot of remarks quickly crossed her mind but none seemed appropriate. "I wanted to explain—"

"No, you don't." Chris smiled at her.

Anne felt relieved. "No, I really don't." She took his hand off the table, squeezed it hard, and lifted it to her face.

"Okay," he said, looking at her fondly.

Chris didn't want to talk either. It would have been nice to share his turmoil of feelings, but not with Anne, not at this time. His feelings about her desire to have a baby had grown greatly complicated by his current investigation. Chris suspected he'd had a child out in the world all these years without his knowing, without the opportunity to shape her life at all or to protect her. He couldn't let such a horrible possibility happen again.

Anne came around the table and sat on his lap, resting her arms loosely on his shoulders. "But I still want what I want," she said lightly but seriously.

Chris didn't answer. Anne continued in the same tone, though slightly strained. "What's the matter, are you afraid being an unwed father would lose you votes?"

Slowly, he said, "No. I would make sure everybody knew. No one else would have a claim. Anne, if I become a father I will be a father. No matter what else, I would be here all the time. You would have to work your schedule around me. I won't be pushed out."

"I'll count on that."

"All right, then." Her chest was right in front of him, the rising triangle of golden skin above and behind the top button of her blouse. He leaned forward three inches and kissed the spot very deliberately. Anne breathed deeply, lifting her shoulders.

2

Blood calls to blood.

—Edgar Lee Masters, *Spoon River Anthology*

Seven

Chris Sinclair walked into his office early the next morning, when the chilly air-conditioned air, not yet warmed by bodies filling the offices or sun coming through his windows, still smelled of the disinfectant the overnight cleaning people used liberally. Chris wore a dark suit and conservative tie. When he talked to people today he would look his severest.

He wanted most to rush out into the streets and search frantically for the missing Clarissa, but he made himself do the harder, more useful task: sit here, organize the search, wait for calls. He felt sure that later in the day he would question the boy Jason, Kristen's classmate, especially after the diary fragment Chris had received by E-mail. That boy must know more than what he'd said—but not necessarily about Clarissa's captor. Before everything, the sixteen-year-old girl came first.

By mid-morning Chris looked more frayed, and had paced his office a dozen times and made as many lives miserable as he could. Lucky Jack Fine worked the field, talking to potential witnesses and shrugging off his boss's repeated calls.

Police technicians had compared Clarissa's hair and fingerprints with samples taken from the Tuttle Road house and found no evidence that the girl had ever been there. The carpets and walls hadn't yielded any blood traces, either, a slight relief to Chris.

Chris had time to think. He tried to remove himself and think about the crises of Jean's life as a normal case. If he were looking for someone to prosecute in a case where a woman had two daughters and one turned up dead and the other missing—correction: where the mother *said* the remaining daughter was only missing—on what suspect would the investigation naturally focus? A man, possibly mythical, who organized boys into a profit-making gang of thieves? Some classmate from high school? Any rookie cop could give Chris the answer before he finished formulating the question: the mother herself.

It had been a long time since he'd known Jean.

He pictured Clarissa as he'd seen her in the very few photographs. But Chris's memory held a hoard of terrible images after a dozen years of practicing criminal law, and it infected his imagination. He saw Clarissa's face changing, saw fear of danger. What rushed toward her, who struck the blow?

Chris decided to go out and talk to Jean, but as he stood his phone rang. Chris snapped it up. The receptionist said, "Someone calling to speak to you, sir. But the caller won't give a name. Sounds like a kid. Shall I—"

"Put it through." Maybe Chris and Jack had stirred up enough action at the high school that a student was calling him with a lead.

"Mr. Sinclair?" the voice came, and a tingle traveled up the back of Chris's neck. The voice was a girl's, and it trembled. "I think I've got him to where he's not so suspicious. But I've—I've got to help him so he'll trust me."

"Clarissa?"

"I've got to go," the girl said hurriedly. "If he finds out . . . I'll try to send you a clue when I can."

"Clarissa, just get away. Run! Get to another phone, call me again, I'll have cops there in two minutes!"

But the line had gone dead.

Chris yelled into the phone so loudly his office door opened and his secretary Irma Garcia came in staring. Chris rushed past her and through the hallways of the District Attorney's Offices, ignoring greetings and bumping one startled prosecutor. He burst through the door of the small room where two receptionists answered the phone and greeted visitors to the glass-enclosed entrance to the offices. "That call," Chris said to the young woman at the back desk. "Where did it come from?"

Looking frightened, she adjusted her headset, as if Chris's frantic question had almost blown it off her head. "I don't know, sir. The line had a block on it. Our caller ID wouldn't identify it. That was another reason I tried . . ."

But she was talking only to the curse Chris left hanging in the air. He hurried back to his office, but more slowly than he'd come, trying to think. The girl's voice repeated over and over in his head. He could picture her from the photos he'd seen. He saw her looking worriedly over her shoulder and dropping the phone, and his damned imagination kept supplying following scenes as well.

"Call Jack," he snapped at Irma Garcia, who still looked wide-eyed. "Tell him there's no more time. We need the name of the man we've been looking for right now. The kidnapper. He'll know what I mean."

Who else could he call? His fingers automatically pressed the buttons for Anne's office. "Interrupt her, please," he said after identifying himself to her secretary.

Anne came on the line a few seconds later, sounding worried. Chris had never before broken into one of her sessions with a patient. Without preamble he said, "Do you have any patients at Holmes High School?"

"Chris, you know I can't—"

"This is life or death, Anne. There's a gang of thieves

and dope dealers there who are organized by an adult man. I want his name. He's kidnapped a child, and if we don't—"

"I'll see what I can find out," Anne said without further argument. "Chris? Can I do anything else?"

"No." He dropped the phone and stood still, but with his fingers moving rapidly against his thigh. Names ran through his head, names of his assistants, investigators, cops. A network that could cover the city, but not until they knew what they were looking for. He thought of Jean but passed on.

Then he stopped on the name of the one person who definitely knew what Chris wanted to know. His mind seized the name and held it by the throat.

Peter Belasco looked different when a thin, dark deputy escorted him into the office at the jail. Smudges under Belasco's eyes indicated loss of sleep, and his chin didn't rise at the cocky angle he'd displayed at Chris's last interview.

Chris stood straight in the middle of the room, nodded thanks to the deputy, and began talking even before the door closed behind the deputy.

"Last chance. I want the name of the man, or I leave here, put you into protective isolation so everybody thinks you talked anyway, then I send you to prison for long enough that you'll be a little old used-up rag if you ever get out. I'm not screwing with you any more. Talk or I'm gone."

A lie. Chris wouldn't leave this room without a deal.

"What's happening?" Belasco asked. He still thought this must be all about him. His voice betrayed his suspicion that the District Attorney was faking all this haste and anxiety in order to trap Peter Belasco into doing something stupid.

"He's kidnapped a girl," Chris said. "That's why there's no more time."

"But that doesn't make sense. Why would—?"

Chris said, "I'm not here asking you for strategy. Just tell me who he is."

Belasco looked crafty. His jail pallor didn't support his knowing tone. "All right. But my deal first. You said probation."

"I said ten years or less. You want me to put it in writing?"

"God, no. Let's just do it. I'll get the probation myself."

"All right. The name first."

Belasco shook his head. "The deal first."

He had regained a little of his toughness. Chris didn't have time for this staring contest. "All right," he agreed. "Let's call your lawyer."

"The hell with him, he's a pipeline to—" Belasco made an angry face at himself. "Let's just do it."

Forty-five minutes later the two of them stood in front of Judge Betty Willis, who had taken an early lunch recess in her current jury trial at the District Attorney's request, and agreed to take a guilty plea in her office. She sat behind her desk, cluttered with papers and souvenirs of trips and three drawings on colored construction paper, gifts from her grandchildren. Chris Sinclair and a handcuffed Peter Belasco stood before her. The only other people crowding the room were a court reporter recording the conversations and a bailiff on the judge's side of the desk.

Judge Willis betrayed no memory of the hearing she'd conducted in Belasco's case. But she paid more than her habitual attention, looking directly at the prisoner rather than over his head. "Mr.—Belasco, is that you?"

"Yes, ma'am."

"We need to wait for your attorney, young man. If you'll—"

"I don't want him," Belasco snapped. Then he remembered that Judge Willis would be the one to decide whether he got probation or went to prison. He smiled at her, looking boyish and confused. "I'd just like to represent myself, ma'am. Can I do that?"

"Of course, if that's your choice. But let me explain to you the consequences of your decision." By rote she warned the young defendant, in legally required terms, of where his decisions to forgo a lawyer and to plead guilty might lead. After Belasco assured her that he understood, the judge turned her focus to Chris. "Is there a plea bargain in this case, Mr. District Attorney?" Then she opened the court's file, saw the array of indictments, and looked up with her curiosity increased. "I mean these cases."

"Yes, Your Honor, there is. The plea bargain is for eight years in prison on each conviction, to run concurrently. The State has no recommendation on whether Your Honor should probate the sentences."

". . . State silent on probation," Judge Willis muttered as she wrote the terms of the plea bargain in the court's file. Then she frowned at what she'd written: remarkably generous terms for a defendant the District Attorney had obviously sought to hammer with the several indictments. "Is that all?" she asked.

"There is a performance clause," Chris added. "If Mr. Belasco doesn't follow through on that, we'll be back before you with a very different recommendation."

The judge nodded with understanding, returning her attention to the defendant with no increase in interest. Since she'd become a judge, Betty Willis didn't have to care about the deal making between law enforcement and lawbreakers. After all, there wasn't much variety.

"I'll accept the plea bargain. I'll order a pre-sentence investigation before deciding whether to grant probation. Mr. Belasco, that will give you an opportunity to perform your other part of the plea bargain. Let me tell you, young man . . ."

Chris tuned out the judge's stern warning and Belasco's

obsequious promises. He even stepped away from the judge's desk and let his impatience show. Finally he opened the office door and said, "Your Honor, there's some urgency to this."

"Of course, of course," Betty Willis agreed, ushering them from her as if urging children to go outside and play.

Chris and Belasco walked side by side through a short hallway that led to the court's outer offices, where clerks did most of the work of the court. Chris suddenly opened a door and pushed Belasco into the small, empty office that belonged to the court reporter. "Now," he said simply.

Belasco started to bluster, then shut up. He looked searchingly at Chris one last time and said, "His name is Raleigh. Raleigh Pentell."

The name meant nothing to Chris. Belasco shrugged with deep sincerity. "And where does he live?" Chris asked.

Belasco shook his head. "Our deal was for a name, nothing else."

"I'll remember how precise we're being." Chris opened the door to find the bailiff standing immediately outside. "Don't let him make any phone calls," Chris snapped. "Put him in protective isolation."

"Hey!" Belasco called in outrage, but Chris didn't slow down. He hurried back toward his office, already pulling a phone from his pocket.

Within the hour a team had gathered in Chris's office, including chief investigator Jack Fine and another investigator named Olga Zamora, who looked young enough to be a high school student herself and in fact had posed as one on a previous investigation. A young prosecutor named George Stiegers also attended, because Chris wanted another lawyer's perspective and because Stiegers had been a cop before going to law school. First Assistant Paul Benavides, tall, slow-moving, and thoughtful, looked the calmest person in the room. Paul took charge of the gathering, asking, "What do we know about this Raleigh Pentell?"

"He exists," Jack Fine volunteered. "I found his picture in one of those newspaper shots of people attending a function that cost them at least a hundred bucks to get in. He owns an import-export business. Yeah, I know," he hastened to be the first to say, "that'd be good cover for a major thief. But his only record is an old assault charge that never got prosecuted. Belasco didn't just pick some name at random, that's for sure. He set you up with somebody who'll take a while to investigate."

"Does this Pentell have any children of his own?" George Stiegers asked.

"None that we know of," Olga Zamora said. Her dark blue suit made her angular face look severe. "He's been divorced for years, never remarried. You're looking for some connection between Pentell and the high school?"

"No, I— Never mind."

"What?" Chris snapped.

George Stiegers looked very young in spite of his variety of experience. Good family man with young children. "I just thought a man with children of his own would be less likely to use kids this way." He shrugged to show he knew how naive he sounded.

"Anyway," Paul Benavides said exaggeratedly, putting the meeting back on track, "*does* he have any connection to the school?"

"Not that we know of," Jack said. "I put his name to a couple of the kids we know are involved and they looked absolutely blank. Not that that was much of a contrast from their usual expressions. But if this Pentell is really the one, I don't think he has much contact with the troops."

The young prosecutor George Stiegers, the newest person on the case, asked, "What exactly are we investigating this Pentell fellow for? This thievery ring? Or do we think he's kidnapped the girl, too?"

"Yes," Chris said shortly.

"And what about the dead girl?" George persisted. "You think he's responsible for that, too?"

Everyone looked at Chris. They knew about the sisters, but of the people in the room only Jack Fine had an inkling of Chris's personal involvement. No one would guess it from his firm, controlled voice. "Right now he seems our best suspect for everything."

Jack's mouth twisted, knowing how much "everything" encompassed in Chris's mind.

Paul Benavides said, "But at this moment the living girl is what's most important. We have a very limited amount of time—"

"We know she's alive?" Olga Zamora asked.

"Yes," Paul answered. "Chris has heard from her."

The younger members of the team looked at their boss wonderingly. "Why did she call you, sir?" Olga asked.

"What difference does it make?" Jack asked. He stood abruptly, looking more restless than Chris had seen him. "We have to get in there in a hurry, that's what matters."

"And legally," the younger prosecutor added. "We need an evidentiary search warrant, and once we get one we have to camp out inside that man's house until we're done. You suspect him of so many things, that house has to be gone over with a giant vacuum cleaner. And we'll only get one chance."

In Texas, police can only obtain one search warrant to search a particular place for evidence of crime, on the theory that police shouldn't be free to invade a home more than once. Chris understood.

"Do we have enough to get a warrant now?" George asked.

Jack, who knew warrant law as well as anyone, shook his head before Chris could answer. "We have the name from one source, Peter Belasco, who's never given us reliable information before. We don't know if he has this time, either."

George Stiegers said, "Hey, why don't we just go and

bust into his house? If we don't find anything, we'll just say, 'Oops, sorry.' If he's an innocent civilian we'll never need to go there again anyway." He suddenly smiled. "Just kidding."

He had no idea that the scenario he'd just spun was the District Attorney's favorite idea of the moment. Chris wanted to move. He forced himself to do this advance planning, but he wouldn't last at it much longer.

"So let's get a second source," Paul said. "Olga, you go back to the school. Pretend to be one of them, like you're on the fringe of the gang yourself but new to it. Try the name on everybody you can think of. Take George with you, let him try more officially. I'll start writing up the search warrant. As soon as you get me more material, I'll present it to a judge. We have to have people in place at this Pentell's house, ready to move in when I've got it, and we've got to time that right, when we think the girl will be there. Jack—"

"Jack and I'll handle that," Chris said. "Let's go."

Olga suddenly asked, "Why aren't the police involved in this?" She felt the need of some backup.

"They will be," Chris said. "Paul will start informing them now. But we don't want police officers going to this Raleigh Pentell's business associates and friends asking questions. We don't want to alarm him. This has to be delicate." Chris said it, but he didn't feel much subtlety in his own urgings.

"Come on, Jack," Chris concluded the meeting, and ran out of the room ahead of everyone.

Chris had more time to think on the long walk out of the Justice Center. When he and Jack hit the parking lot in front of the building Chris made another call, to Jean Fitzgerald at her office. She answered on one ring.

"Chris," she said, as breathless as he felt. "I was about to call you."

Her voice sounded as young and eager as it had in college, when she would call him with plans for an adventure. But at the moment Chris felt no nostalgia for make-believe excitement. "We have a suspect in Clarissa's kidnapping, Jean. I'm on my way to his house now."

"Is it Raleigh Pentell?"

Chris stopped dead in the middle of the street he was crossing. Jack tugged gently at his arm, pulling him out of traffic. "If you knew it," Chris said very tightly into his cell phone, "why didn't you tell me?"

"I just heard it. One of the boys told me. Ryan, Clarissa's boyfriend. I told you he was involved in that gang. He said one night he heard—"

"Tell me later," Chris said. He and Jack walked very briskly into the county parking garage. "What else do you know about Raleigh Pentell? What can you tell me?"

"Nothing. I don't even know where he lives. But you can find it, can't you, Chris? I'll come to your office, okay? I'm useless here anyway—"

"No. Listen, Jean, I'm on my way to his house now. No, you can't," he cut her off. "We're not going in yet, we're just scoping it out. Trying to get a warrant. I'll let you know."

Chris turned off the phone as they slid into a car. He glanced at Jack, who kept his face carefully neutral, and silent.

In Jack's car they cruised to the address they'd found for Raleigh Pentell, an isolated area on a northern edge of the county, outside Loop 1604. Neighborhoods had been built out there, creating San Antonio's farthest suburbs, but much of the territory was still inhabited mainly by squirrels and possums. Driving past an enclave of clean modern subdivision, then plunging again into old oak woods gave a disconcerting effect, almost of time travel.

"There," Chris said, spotting an old road sign. The sign bore an FM number—a farm-to-market road that hadn't yet been renamed Oak Something or Stone Willow Terraces. Jack turned down an asphalt two-lane road for which the trees barely parted.

Chris read off the information Jack had given him, "The address is Twelve Four Eighty, but I don't know if the numbers mean much out here."

"Oh, I think this may be it," Jack replied, because suddenly a brick wall rose up on the right just ahead of them, interrupting the trees with sudden man-made intervention. The wall rose ten feet high, some of its bricks still shining redly to attest to the relative newness of the wall. Jack slowed the car to a cruise. The wall went on for the distance of half a city block before a gate appeared, tall, rigid with its function of denying entry, and obviously locked. But they could see the house through the widely spaced bars of the gate. Jack slowed even more, giving Chris a long look at the house, which he thought showed a variety of owners. The house stood at least two stories, made of weathered wood. Originally it had probably been a ranch house with a wide wraparound porch. A later owner or second generation had cutesied the place up with two Victorian-style turrets and other fanciful touches, which apparently the current owner sought to downplay. For example, the fish-scale shingles of the turrets should have been carefully painted in alternating colors to highlight the effect, but now someone had had them all painted gray. The house gave an overall effect of large dull solidity.

"We'll need an army to get in there," Chris said.

"And a warrant," Jack reminded him. The investigator appeared to hear something odd in his boss's voice, something that made Jack keep bringing Chris down to reality.

"Go all the way down, see how far it goes."

Jack drove slowly another thirty yards, to where the wall turned a corner and drove back into the woods. "Stop," Chris said. He opened his door, Jack said his name, and Chris said, "I just want to look."

Chris heard the car drive on out of sight as he walked

along the wall. The bricks offered no chink through which to view the house. Chris walked slowly beside it, occasionally running his hand along the wall. The mortar felt rough, the bricks almost smooth by contrast.

At some time the trees and underbrush had been cut back from the wall, but these were persistent oaks and mesquites, their long branches reaching almost to the wall above his head. Chris stumbled over an oak root that burrowed under the wall. Given a few more years the root would crack the wall and crumble it. Already the bricks above it were distorted, leaning crookedly. A crack in the wall gave Chris a very narrow view of the side of the house, which was not as formidable as its front. The side wall of the house gave more of an impression of life lived within: more windows, a side path, somehow the lawn less severe. A long aluminum ladder lay on the grass, the first out-of-place object Chris had seen about the house.

Chris explored all the way back to the corner and along the back wall. The gate behind the house was much less formidable, an almost homey affair of wooden slats. Inside the wall, fifty yards from where Chris stared through the back gate, the house had a large patio of saltillo tiles, in the middle of which a fountain tinkled, running constantly. The patio also featured two clusters of lawn furniture around tables with large umbrellas, but no swimming pool and certainly nothing like a swing set. Even at its back the house didn't look like a family place.

Chris returned to the road, but saw no sign of Jack's car. Chris stood at the corner of the wall for a long five minutes, until a hand grabbed his arm.

"Damn it, you didn't go in, did you?" Jack asked angrily.

"Of course not." Chris shook off his investigator's hand and straightened his suit coat. He continued to think about the back door of the house. He stood rigidly with the expectation of hearing a girl's scream, but if Clarissa was inside the house she would have given up screaming for help long ago. *I've got him unsuspicious*, she had said to Chris on the phone. To the point where Pentell would occasionally let her go outside? Chris wanted to get back to that chink in the wall and watch the house's windows.

He had a sudden realization. "Jack, when I called Jean she gave me this guy's name. Raleigh Pentell. She said it to me."

"Where'd she get it?"

"From one of the boys, Ryan McClain. The one her older daughter was dating."

They stood at the corner of the wall. Jack moved them a step back, to a position from which he could watch the front gate but duck quickly out of sight if anyone came out of it. "What did the boy say about Pentell?" he asked quietly.

Chris's answer came slowly. "That he organized the boys. Directed the gang's activities."

"Nothing about either girl?"

Chris knew what his investigator was thinking. They were talking about the search warrant, and Jack knew Chris wanted inside that house worse then he wanted to follow procedures. The conversation had assumed an air of interrogation. Chris chose his answers carefully. "I'm not sure what she asked him. But this is confirmation. Two sources give us this man's name."

"And say what about him?"

Chris almost snapped at his overly careful investigator. Instead he took out his cell phone and called Jean's office again. "Damn!" he said as a voice-mail recording told him she was unavailable.

Jack took the phone from him. "I'll call Paul," he said. A concession. Paul Benavides remained back at the office waiting for enough information to seek a search warrant.

As Jack spoke quietly into the phone, Chris crept around the corner and along the brick wall toward the front gate. Jack hissed at him but Chris kept going. He angled out toward the road so that he could see the gate. Maybe they were being overly cautious. The house didn't seem guarded. What if he simply walked up to the gate and rang the bell? Even the guilty often ended up talking to authorities, confident of their ability to answer suspicions.

But if Chris guessed wrong about that, he would be risking Clarissa's life.

Just as he decided to turn back, the gates slid open.

Chris stood frozen like a deer, then turned and ran, not looking back. He saw Jack at the corner of the wall, waving him on, then Jack crouched and moved out of sight. Someone must have come out of the gate. Chris put on more speed, grabbed at the wall to help him turn, and flung himself around the corner, falling and rolling on the hard-packed ground and ending up in a bush. He scrambled up. If someone had seen him—

Jack stood pressed against the wall, peering around its corner. He waved Chris back. "Car coming out," he said tightly.

Chris peered around the wall as well. The nose of a large black sedan had eased through the open gate. It sat there, as if the driver had seen something that made him hesitate to emerge. Then the car burst out into the open. Chris's heart still raced. He looked behind him, for hiding places if the car turned this way. Where had Jack parked their car?

"There it goes," Jack said quietly.

Chris looked back and saw the car's taillights as it took off back toward town. The black Mercedes's windows were tinted, concealing how many people it held.

Jack stood indecisively until Chris grabbed his arm. "They may be taking her somewhere. Go after it, Jack! How far away is your car?"

In answer Jack started running along the road in the direction down which he'd originally disappeared. Then he stopped and looked back. "Come on!"

"I'll stay here."

They stared at each other tensely. Jack wasn't fooled.

"They all just left," Chris said.

"Who knows how many people are still here?" Jack

almost shouted. "He may have killed people, Chris. He won't leave his house unguarded!"

"Hurry up, you'll lose them."

Jack turned and ran. A minute later his car came flying past. He made a gesture out the open window which Chris knew was another order not to do anything until Jack returned. Chris waited until the car drove out of sight, then he turned and crept back along the wall toward the back of the house.

Jack sped, unconcerned with the plume of dust he raised or the possibility of alarming his prey. He just wanted to catch up to the black Mercedes, and it had a long lead. But out here in the country Jack could at least guess at the car's initial direction. At the first intersection he turned left, back toward Loop 1604 and civilization. That road was long and wide and Jack sailed down it. The Mercedes driver could have done the same thing and have already lost him definitively.

Jack reached the access road of the Loop without having seen the car. He turned the only way he could turn and hurried, trying to think ahead of the car now, to its possible destinations. The high school? Downtown?

That car could have held seven people easily, including a struggling girl. Jack was about to make another call asking for backup when he got lucky. Ahead down the long access road he saw the black sedan with the tinted windows. It hadn't gotten onto the Loop, it had edged to the left and now leaned into a turnaround, heading back the other way, north toward 281, a highway that led to the airport or on into the heart of town. Jack took a long breath, feeling lucky, slowed down, and followed the Mercedes onto 1604. He hung well back, with little fear of losing the black sedan, which stood out in the sunlit day.

Just as Jack had expected, the big Mercedes took the exit for Highway 281. They glided past the elaborate church that had once housed a dinner theater, the fast food franchises that had sprung up at this major highway intersection—and the Mercedes went straight, not taking the turn onto 281. Jack eased into line behind it, wondering if the driver had spotted him. After the traffic light finally turned green the Mercedes moved slowly ahead in the right lane. Jack stayed in the middle lane, being so careful not to pass the Mercedes that an impatient driver behind him honked.

The black sedan crossed the intersection, went a little way farther, and turned into the parking lot of the large new HEB grocery store. Jack, certain now that the driver had seen him and was taking evasive measures, drove on past, moving into the right lane and keeping a sidelong eye on the Mercedes in the HEB parking lot. The impatient driver rushed past Jack on the left, honking again. If the driver had known how well armed and tense Jack was at that moment, he would have kept his horn to himself.

If the Mercedes driver was trying to lose Jack, he was being awfully slow about it. Jack continued on the access road to another entrance to the HEB parking lot and turned back. By that time the Mercedes had drifted into a slot. Maybe the driver planned just to sit there, making Jack reveal himself.

But as Jack turned into a parking space and stopped himself, the driver's side door of the Mercedes opened and a man emerged. The man didn't fit the stereotype of a bodyguard or thug. He was heavy enough, an impressive girth straining his untucked Hawaiian shirt. Below the shirt he wore long baggy shorts and huarache sandals. Past middle age and bearded, the man looked slow and sleepy. Jack had known killers with that look, but there had also been something coiled and ready about them. This man shuffled across the parking lot with no apparent awareness of his surroundings.

Jack got out of his car and walked quickly across the asphalt. By this time he had become willing to give himself away. If anyone still left inside the Mercedes saw him, he might just arrest him.

All the car's windows were tinted darkly but not, of course, the windshield. Sporting a dark windshield is illegal; the car would have been stopped by patrol cops every few miles whenever it traveled. So Jack walked past the front of the car and glanced into it, through the clear windshield. He stopped, came back, and leaned over the hood, peering inside.

The Mercedes sat empty.

Jack muttered angrily, went to the door of the car, and tried it. The door swung open; the driver hadn't even bothered to lock it. Jack quickly looked over the seat to make sure no one crouched there, then pulled a handle that opened the trunk. Slamming the door, he went to the back and lifted the trunk lid. It held very little, none of it overtly illegal and nothing like a young girl or a body. Cursing again, Jack hurried across the parking lot into the grocery store. Inside he slowed down, knowing how out of place he looked in his dark suit. But the man he sought didn't appear to have any idea that he might be pursued. The fat man pushed a cart placidly through the produce section, and stopped to pick out fresh string beans. His cart already held tomatoes and lettuce and carrots and a wealth of potatoes.

Hell. Jack had tracked down the cook.

He turned and ran out the door toward his car, hoping hard that Chris hadn't done what Jack was sure he had.

As soon as Jack's car drove out of sight, Chris crept along the brick wall to the crack in the side wall. Twisting his neck, he peered at the house. An upstairs window drew his attention. The glass shimmered in the reflection from the sun. Chris couldn't move to get a different angle of vision.

A shrill sound like an alarm made him jump. Hastily he pulled his cell phone out of his breast pocket and pressed a button to shut it up.

"What?" he snapped into the speaker, but quietly. He'd heard a sound from the house.

"Chris? It's Paul. I've got the warrant, Chris. Judge Porter signed it."

"Good, good," Chris said. He was looking through the crack in the wall again. The sun had moved slightly, he could almost see through the upstairs window. Something odd about its reflection, a twisted anomaly in the light—

"I'll get it out to you right away," Paul said in the phone. "SWAT team, or regular officers?"

"Regular," Chris said. "They won't know what we know, maybe we can do it the easy way."

"Okay, we'll be out there as soon as we can."

Chris pressed the "end" button and turned off the phone. They had the warrant. He was legally authorized to search the house now. But he had to wait. Everyone said so.

He climbed the tree that leaned against the wall so that he could see over it. From that vantage he saw what was wrong with the upstairs window he'd been watching. It was broken. Someone had cracked a small opening down near the sill.

Chris heard a sound that seemed to carry from that small opening. He saw a shimmer in the glass of the window.

But a louder sound drew his attention. The front door of the house opened and then slammed shut. Chris pressed low atop the wall. A big man with very receding black hair and blubbery, stubbled cheeks stepped out onto the front porch, smoking a cigarette. The man wore navy dress pants and a white T-shirt. He looked at home on the porch of the old house. Was this Raleigh Pentell?

Then Chris distinctly heard the sound of breaking glass. His attention returned at once to the upstairs window. A girl stood behind the window, shaking her hand. Chris couldn't see her very well inside the dark room, but the girl looked young and blond. Then she pressed her face against the glass, staring out. Her mouth opened in a silent scream. She reached a hand through the broken window.

On the front porch of the house, the dark, stubbled man looked up. Then he turned and disappeared back inside the house.

The man hadn't seen Chris, Chris felt sure of that, but he had heard something that alarmed him. The something could only have been the sounds the girl made. And who had broken the window? Was someone inside the room with the girl?

She had disappeared from the window. Without thinking, Chris jumped down, inside the brick wall. He ran toward the house, then hesitated: front door or back? Follow the big man up the front stairs, where he might have called for reinforcements, or try to beat him to the girl by going around the back. But Chris had no idea whether the house even contained back stairs.

Then he remembered the ladder he'd seen lying in the grass. He ran to the side of the house and almost tripped over the aluminum ladder lying in the slightly overgrown grass. He lifted the ladder and the green grass underneath sprang up as if in relief.

The ladder was the straight, extension type, actually two ladders attached to each other for extra height. Chris raised the tall, wobbly mechanism and rested it against the house, where the top of the ladder reached to just beside the windowsill. Hastily he scrambled up, the ladder shaking beneath his feet. Reaching the top, he peered into the room. The dimness within baffled his eyesight for a moment, but then he saw the girl. She stood indecisively in the middle of the room, looking toward the door. Then she turned and saw Chris.

Her face looked as if she had nowhere to turn. "It's all right, Clarissa," Chris said through the broken window. "Your mother sent me. I'm here to get you out."

He had said the magic words. Her face showing sudden

relief, the girl hurried toward him, turned the window latch, and raised the broken window.

"Clarissa?" he said softly, stepping over the broken glass that littered the windowsill and the floor beneath.

The girl nodded, then threw herself at him and clung to his neck. She was trembling. When Chris put his arms around her he could feel her ribs and her heartbeat as she hugged him hard. Chris felt the strangest, strongest, best, and most frightening feelings of his life. He held her tightly and almost forgot what danger they still faced.

"Clarissa."

The girl nodded against his shoulder, then pulled back to look at his face. "I'm Chris," he said hesitantly. "I'm— a friend of your mother's."

Clarissa nodded again. She looked shy as well as scared.

Still holding her, Chris took a quick look around the room. It was barely furnished, with a double bed and unmatching dresser. The bedclothes were disarrayed, but otherwise the room had no sign of habitation, not a book or a glass or empty shoes. He took Clarissa's hand and led her toward the broken window. He looked at it curiously and the girl answered his unspoken question: "I was about to try to go out."

"Why didn't you ever try before?"

Clarissa sniffled. "They told me there were dogs in the yard. Killer dogs that they don't feed enough. But I haven't seen any and I finally decided to risk it."

"Why today?" Chris asked curiously, gesturing for her to step over the windowsill to the ladder.

But they were interrupted by a sudden pounding on the door and a voice that asked loudly, "What the hell's going on in there?"

Chris helped Clarissa over the windowsill. The ladder wobbled as she caught her balance. She started down, looking beneath her for the next step. Chris swung one leg over the windowsill, careful not to sit on the broken glass, and behind him the door of the room burst open.

There stood Stubbleface, goggling at Chris. Chris ducked his head under the raised window, almost all the way outside now, but as the man recovered and rushed across the room Chris realized he couldn't pull his leg out in time to escape. Instead he stuck his head back inside the room just as the man reached him. The T-shirted thug grabbed Chris and pulled him back into the room. Outside, the girl shrieked.

"What the hell?" the man asked, staring into Chris's unfamiliar face. For answer, Chris ducked his head and butted the man's stubbled chin.

The thug fell backward, but didn't lose his grip on Chris's jacket, so Chris fell with him, and landed on top of him. The man lost his wind and his hold on Chris, but as Chris jumped up the man reached into his pocket and produced a knife.

The man scrambled to his feet, too quickly for Chris to reach the window. The knife remained closed. The thug grinned challengingly. Chris, deciding he had to move fast, turned away as if about to run, but then leaped toward his opponent and punched him again, aiming for the chin but missing and hitting the man in the throat instead. The man gurgled. Chris moved in, aiming blows at the man's stomach and face, trying to disable his opponent before he could get the knife open. But just as Chris drove a knee into his opponent's groin, doubling him over, Chris heard a snick and realized the knife was a switchblade. He leaped back as the blade came up through the airspace where he'd been standing a moment earlier.

The big man's eyes went narrow as he came forward, so confident that he didn't yell for help, and with an expression saying he didn't want anyone else interrupting this fun. Chris backed up until he was against the wall of the room. The knife wielder moved more quickly, pulling back his arm. Chris stuck out his hands as if to try to block the knife. But as the man stabbed strongly with the switchblade Chris jumped aside. The knife went into the wall and Chris drove his elbow into the side of the big man's head.

The thug grunted and slumped. Chris moved behind him, reached around the man's neck, and locked his arm around the man's throat. Chris squeezed as hard as he could, gratified to feel the man struggling for air. The thug tried to call out then, but couldn't. Chris tightened his grip, choking his opponent.

The big man struggled to pull his knife out of the wall. Chris couldn't see over his foe to his knife hand, but he heard the small thunk of the knife pulling loose. The man's hand came back, grazing Chris's leg with the blade. Chris put his knee into the man's back and pulled him backward. The thug made small choking noises. He brought his knife up toward his own throat, aiming at Chris's arm.

Chris let go, and the man almost stabbed himself in the throat. He fell down on his back, but recovered his air. Chris dropped onto his stomach on one knee. The man gushed air, and his face immediately turned deep red. Chris punched him in the cheek, and again, and stood back.

The thug didn't move. Chris reached for the knife and the big hand let it go limply.

Clarissa's face was at the window. She had come back up the ladder but not into the room. Fear showed plainly in her face. "It's all right," Chris said. "Hurry."

She went quickly down the ladder and he quickly followed. At the bottom, on the ground, Clarissa put her arms around him again. He pulled the girl close beside him, feeling her thinness and her fright. He wanted to carry her, protected inside his jacket. Clarissa kept wide eyes fastened on his face. Putting a finger to his lips for unneeded emphasis on quiet, Chris then pointed toward the wall around the house. Clarissa nodded.

Chris pulled the aluminum ladder away from the wall and lowered it until it was horizontal. He had gotten over the wall by climbing the tree on the other side, but couldn't get back the same way, and didn't want to try either of the gates. The fence stood fifty yards away. Clarissa grabbed the ladder too, and they walked quickly, feeling safer with every step they took.

A very small sound announced the failure of their escape attempt. A man clearing his throat. Chris stopped dead in his tracks. Clarissa gave a shriek and dropped her end of the ladder. It hit the ground with a clang that vibrated up Chris's arm. He dropped it too, the need for silence gone. Turning, he saw Clarissa, white as an alabaster statue, and behind her a tall man in a white suit. The man had broad shoulders, thick reddish blond hair, and glaring dark eyes. But he spoke quietly. "Who the hell are you and what are you doing on my property?"

The man was obviously Raleigh Pentell. Behind him stood three bulky men whose faces displayed anger, puzzlement, and a quietly happy expectancy. The jolliest one grinned at Chris.

Chris stood beside Clarissa and put his arm around her. She hid her face in his shoulder. Chris answered Pentell's question: "I'm the District Attorney of this county and I'm arresting you."

Pentell affected surprise, doing a good job of it, his eyebrows arching high. His manner turned toward the outrage of a homeowner intruded on. "For what? What on earth are you talking about? If this girl's accused me of anything it's a lie. What is she even doing here?"

"I know more than you think I do," Chris answered. "But I'm not talking about kidnapping. You're under arrest for the murder of Kristen Lorenz."

Clarissa looked up at Chris, her fingers clutching his shirt. Chris kept his attention focused on Pentell, who for the first time looked uncertain. His mouth opened, forming the word *who*, but he didn't say it. His eyes went sideways and his brow wrinkled in rapid thought. Finally Pentell spoke, but it had been five seconds between Chris's accusation and Pentell's response. A long, long pause.

"I don't know what you're talking about."

"Stick with your story," Chris said disgustedly, walking toward Pentell. Chris had to maintain the momentum of authority, because in fact he was at this man's mercy. Chris and Clarissa could both be dead at any second.

The bulkiest of the thugs behind Pentell, who wore a white *guyabera* shirt over gabardine slacks, stepped up beside his boss and looked at him questioningly. His hand went behind his back, reaching under the loose shirt.

Chris said, "Police are on their way here right now with a warrant."

He would have liked to keep that information secret, not giving Pentell advance warning, but at the moment staying alive was more urgent.

At his words the thinnest, youngest of Pentell's henchmen, the one who'd been grinning at Chris during the early exchange, suddenly turned and ran back toward the house. A moment later the small group on the lawn heard the house's front door slam, which increased the nervousness of the remaining two men with Pentell. The one closest to his boss stepped back as if to turn and run himself.

But by then Raleigh Pentell had made up his mind. His face went hard and blank. "No they're not," he said. "If police were on their way you wouldn't tell me. Henry. Take them inside. If he moves or opens his mouth, shoot him."

The man in the *guyabera* produced a pistol and gestured with it toward the front porch. A line of sweat trickled down his forehead. Chris faced one of the most frightening sights on the planet: a nervous man with a gun. He would have liked to keep himself between the gun and Clarissa, but the girl pressed against him, hiding her face against his shoulder as if she could turn invisible. Chris put his arm around her and gently guided her into walking past the gunman.

If he had been alone he might have tried something, but Clarissa handicapped both his movements and his resolve. The two of them stepped up onto the front porch,

closely followed by the man with the gun. Chris glanced
back, which was enough to make the sweating man even
more nervous. He raised his pistol and pointed it at
Chris's face, his hand shaking slightly. Chris lifted his
hands. He tried to push Clarissa behind him.

Raleigh Pentell stepped up onto the porch behind his
man. "What are you doing? Hurry up and get them—"

Pentell was the first to hear the sound that must have
been familiar to him, that of his front gate opening. It
unlocked with a metallic protest, then the gate began
sliding smoothly on its rail, creating a larger and larger
opening.

Everyone stared. Chris stepped closer to the man in the
guyabera and slapped aside his gun-wielding hand. The
gun didn't fall. When the man looked at him with a snarl
Chris hit him in the stomach. It felt like punching a tree.
The man swung the pistol and Chris ducked. He grabbed
the gunman's wrist, thinking that he had to get control of
the situation. The gate might be opening for Pentell's man
or men who had left in the black Mercedes.

But Raleigh Pentell put an end to the fight with a
barked syllable. "Stop."

Everyone did. Chris looked toward the gate and saw
Jack Fine, the most beautiful person Chris had ever seen,
step through the gateway. He held up a folded sheaf of
papers, gesturing with them like a talisman. In the next
moment came the whoop of a police siren. Uniformed
cops poured into the compound behind Jack, who walked
up to Pentell, hand holding the papers outstretched.
"Raleigh Pentell? I have a warrant to search your house."

"How—?" Pentell and Chris began to ask at the same
time, when Jack took a small brown plastic box out of his
suit coat pocket. "And by the way," he added, "here's
your gate opener." He handed over the electric signaler
he'd taken out of the black Mercedes.

Chris turned to see Clarissa standing in the shadow of
the house, looking as frightened as ever at the sudden
swarm of movement nearing her. Then her eyes lit on

Chris and her chest moved with relieved breath. She came toward him, arms outstretched, her eyes turning bright blue as she stepped out of the shadow and the sunlight hit her face.

Chris walked quickly to meet her.

Eight

Police took Raleigh Pentell and his men to jail, and Chris took Clarissa home. He could hardly believe in the girl's reality, in spite of having seen pictures and been in her room. He wanted to touch her face. Clarissa kept studying him as well. She let them into the house, and after Chris made sure it was empty they sat in the living room and waited for Jean, sitting sideways on the couch to face each other.

Chris asked if she was okay after her ordeal, but he wanted to go deeper into the past than the past few weeks. "Where were you born?" he asked after they'd sat for an hour.

"Fort Worth. That's what Mom tells me, but I hardly remember the place. We moved from there pretty soon after Kristen was born. That's when we went to California."

Clarissa seemed to review her answer, heard herself casually mention her younger sister, and her eyes filled with tears. "Are you sure Mr. Pentell killed Kristen?"

"Yes," Chris lied. "But I'll need you to help me prove it."

"She should never even have met him. Kristen didn't have anything to do with any of that." Clarissa hiccuped a sob. Chris stretched his left arm along the back of the couch and touched her fingers. She clutched his hand.

"Any of what?" Chris asked gently.

Clarissa's head stayed bowed. "Oh, all that—I don't know."

"Help me," Chris asked her.

She looked up at him. Her chest moved jerkily inside her thin blouse as she suppressed another sob. "The stealing and the drugs. Kristen had nothing to do with that. Nothing. She didn't even know any of the boys who were in it."

"But you did," Chris said softly, trying not to sound accusing.

They studied each other. Chris saw a girl with downy eyelashes, clear skin but a shiny forehead. With her mother's blue eyes but in a rounder shape. She had narrow lips like Chris's own. She looked at him quizzically. He wondered how much Clarissa knew about her own family history, and how much she wanted to know.

"Yes, I knew some of them," she said softly. She had a mellifluous voice, but it lost its intonations when she lowered it to a whisper. "I didn't do any of it," she added emphatically. "I swear that. But I knew some of what was going on."

"How?"

Clarissa hesitated. "Because of Ryan."

"Your boyfriend?"

She turned teenaged and coy. "We went out sometimes."

She hugged herself. "Do you want to change clothes?" Chris asked.

"I want to get a sweater." She stood up, then looked at him expectantly until Chris rose too, and followed her to her room. The room still looked much too bare and clean, even with Clarissa in it. She didn't glance at anything in the room, just went straight to her closet and pulled out a softly violet pullover sweater. She put it on, then pulled her hair out of the collar, and flipped it back in a way that reminded Chris of someone.

"What?" she asked, genuinely puzzled. Chris shook his head.

"How long have you known Mom?" the girl asked suddenly.

"Years and years. But I hadn't seen her in a long time."

"How long?" Clarissa asked, walking toward him. He hesitated, and she shifted the focus of the question. "Did you see me when I was a baby?"

"No. I wish I had."

Clarissa walked past him, out the doorway of her room. She glanced down the dark hallway and shrank a little. "Do I have to stay here?" she asked pitifully, like a shy kid in a first-day classroom.

"If your mother doesn't come home you can come stay with me."

She put her arms around him and lay her head on his chest. "Thank you" came her muffled voice.

Chris imagined that after her long captivity she had latched on to the first friend she'd seen, Chris, even though he was virtually a stranger. Clarissa felt so vulnerable against him.

Then they heard the front door opening. Jean's voice called, "Who's here?"

"Here," Chris said, and a moment later Jean appeared in the doorway. She saw Clarissa and her eyes and mouth opened wide. She threw out her arms, the girl turned from Chris toward her mother, and Jean wrapped herself tightly around the thin young girl. "Oh my baby, my baby," she moaned. Clarissa leaned backward for a moment, overwhelmed by her mother's force, but then hugged back. Chris standing two feet from them felt excluded and told himself that jealousy was unreasonable. He looked at the two pressed against each other, looking so similar but with distinct differences. Clarissa was almost the age Jean had been when Chris had known

her. The girl had her mother's tall posture and the thinness Chris remembered. But her face looked barely
formed. Chris hadn't thought that of Jean years ago.
She'd had such a variety of expressions, each one so
vivid.

As now, when she squeezed her eyes closed and
hugged her daughter tightly. "Darling, darling."

Chris brushed by them, went to the phone in the
kitchen, and called Jack Fine's office, then his cell phone.
A couple of minutes later he was hanging up the phone
when Jean hurried into the kitchen saying, "Thank you,
thank you. I can't ever—" At sight of Chris's face she
said, "What's the matter?"

"Pentell's already out of jail," Chris said grimly. "The
magistrate set a bond of a million dollars on him, but he
posted it. He barely spent an hour in jail."

For a moment Jean looked more curious than frightened. "He had a million dollars to make a bond?"

"You only have to post ten percent of it in cash," Chris
explained, then stopped abruptly because he'd caught
sight of Clarissa's face past Jean's shoulder. The girl's
frightened eyes fastened on Chris.

"Yes," he said as if she'd asked a question. "You two
can't stay here. I'll take you to a hotel tonight, and tomorrow we can make other arrangements."

"Oh, thank you—" Clarissa began, but her mother
interrupted. "No."

Chris and Clarissa both looked at Jean for clarification.
"He's not going to chase me out of my home," she said
adamantly.

Jean remained resolute on the point. Clarissa even took
her aside while Chris made more phone calls, but when
the two returned Jean had obviously prevailed. Clarissa no
longer protested. She remained quiet through the evening.

"I called the local police substation commander," Chris
said. "He'll make sure a patrol car is nearby all through
the night. And I'm having somebody else keep tabs on
Pentell, so you should be okay."

"Will you stay?" Clarissa blurted out.

Chris felt Jean's eyes on him, but he looked only at her daughter. He walked close to Clarissa in the narrow kitchen, took her hands, and said softly, "You'll be all right, I promise."

Her hands clutched his. They looked into each other's eyes. Chris said, "I'll stay just tonight if your mother thinks it's okay."

They both turned to Jean, who looked momentarily surprised, then shrugged and said, "Sure. It'll be a party."

And it was, of sorts, a combination of wake and celebration and reunion. They ordered Chinese food and ate it in the dining alcove, Jean and Clarissa next to each other, Chris opposite them. Chris and Jean had red wine, Clarissa a Sprite in a champagne glass so they could toast. "To my baby coming home," Jean said, and she and Clarissa pressed their foreheads together like cats. The evening held several moments like that when Chris felt left out, but just as often he became part of the family. Clarissa described her rescue, making Chris sound like a combination of the Lone Ranger and Spiderman.

"How did you get all the way across the yard and up the ladder without any of those people seeing you?" she asked wonderingly.

"That's my usual effect, people don't notice me. If I'm the last person at a party the hosts start cleaning up and turning off the lights and talking to each other about how the party went."

"That's right," Jean said brightly, "that's how he—" Then she decided what she was thinking wasn't for her daughter's ears. Her lips pursed in a small smile as she glanced slyly at Chris. He felt his face grow warm.

"Then he knocked out the man who tried to stop us," Clarissa continued.

"Knocked a man out? I guess I chose my bodyguard wisely, huh, Chris?" Jean said slyly, and turned aside her daughter's questions about what she meant. Chris smiled to himself.

Later on they moved to the living room and Jean played records. Clarissa seemed to know the old music as well as her mother, at times they sang the same phrase together. Chris wanted to ask them about Kristen and Raleigh Pentell, but the occasion didn't offer him the opportunity. The unspoken subject weighed the air, though. Once when a car door slammed they all looked up and sat tensely until Jean recognized the voices of her neighbors in their driveway.

Clarissa put on a record older than she was, Crosby, Stills, and Nash. One particular song, one he and Jean had liked in college, turned Chris pensive and reminiscent. After a moment he noticed Jean had fallen silent, too. They shared a glance and Chris felt sure that Jean was remembering the same time he was, of a spring picnic when they'd left Austin with no particular destination, just turning onto smaller and smaller roads until the roads tapered out altogether, and they had spread their blanket on the grass beneath an old twisted oak.

Across the living room Jean stared down at the carpet as if it were the remains of a picnic spread.

Some time after eleven Clarissa yawned and Jean became a mother. "Bedtime for you, child. God knows how long it's been since you had a good night's sleep."

Chris stood and the girl leaned against him again. "Thank you, thank you," she said sleepily. "Good night. You'll be here?"

"I'll be here," Chris promised.

Jean took her to bed, then returned with a sheet and a pillow and said, "I'm beat, too. Here's some pajamas I found, hope they'll do."

Chris looked at the man's pajamas dangling from her hand, then up at Jean, who made a "Don't ask" gesture, said good night, and left him in the living room.

Chris took a long time to fall asleep in the unfamiliar clothes on the uncomfortable couch, hearing the small noises of a house he didn't know, pursued by the urge to check the door locks again. When sleep finally did come it didn't shut him down completely, it was gray, not black, as if he continued to watch the room through squinted eyes. Footsteps crossing the carpet brought him sharply awake, with that false alertness of interrupted sleep. His body felt heavy.

She knelt beside him, wearing a short nightgown, her face made misty by the darkness and his sleep-smeared eyes. At first Chris didn't know who was waking him up, Jean or Clarissa.

"I'm sorry, were you asleep?"

"No," Chris lied.

"I haven't been able to either." Jean's voice, mellow and slightly husky, sounded clear as she leaned close to him. "I think it's because I didn't thank you. I should finally have peace now. She's home with me, and it's just because of you. Thank you, Chris. Thank God you were here for me."

She reached for his arm. Her breasts moved freely in the loose nightgown she wore, and quite suddenly he remembered her, remembered the body he'd once embraced. She touched his arm lightly, thrillingly, with her fingertips.

"I don't even know why I moved to San Antonio," she said quietly. "No good reason. I didn't know you were here. But there was something fated about me and your hometown."

There in the dimness, Chris reclining, Jean's voice soft in his ear, they could have been anywhere on earth or in time.

He almost reached for her. Jean stood up abruptly. "Good night. I—"

She stopped whatever she'd thought of saying and walked quickly away, as if she'd embarrassed herself. She left Chris to a watchful night, mired in the past and pondering the mystery of the intervening years.

Chris Sinclair quickly began preparing the trial of Raleigh Pentell. His urgency sprang first of all from the fact that Pentell remained free on bond. Until and unless Chris could convict him of something, Pentell went about his normal life, remaining a danger to Clarissa, to Jean, to the whole city. But Chris also hungered to know the connection between Pentell and Jean's family. His personal and professional curiosities coincided.

In Chris's office late in the morning, Jack Fine asked, "Why don't you try him at the same time for the kidnapping of the older sister? You've got him cold on that one, her testimony alone would be enough."

Chris had two ready answers, the legal one and the real one. "He's already hired Lowell Burke, and Burke will file a motion to have the cases tried separately. Count on that; it's what I'd do. You don't want the jury to know about all the crimes your client's accused of. Then the judge would probably order us to try the murder case first, since it's older." What Chris said was true, but he'd made this decision on a much deeper level: he himself was a witness in the kidnapping case, so he couldn't prosecute it. And he wouldn't pass off the responsibility of trying Raleigh Pentell to anyone else. Chris remembered the man's stiff face falling into uncertainty when Chris had accused him of the murder of Kristen Lorenz. That was the crime Pentell had to answer for first.

"Why did he take the girl anyway?" Jack asked. "Kidnapping's so hard to get away with, and this one, open-ended like it was—"

"He took Clarissa to keep Jean from talking about her other missing daughter."

"What did your friend know that could incriminate him? She says she didn't see him with the girl that night." Jack sat on the corner of Chris's desk swinging his leg. He spoke neutrally as if they were preparing a normal case, but he kept an eye on his boss.

"I don't know," Chris admitted. "Maybe Jean hasn't even realized what she knows about him."

"I'll talk to her again. About the search of Pentell's

house. In the room with the broken window we found a paper bag with girl's clothes in it. Clarissa identified them as hers, we gave them back to her. Otherwise zip. Nothing in the closet in that room. We found her fingerprints all over the place, of course, and Pentell's, but all that proves is what we already knew, that they were both there. No trace of anything that might have belonged to the dead girl. No blood. Of course, he's had a long time to clean up."

"What about his car?"

"Same story. Some slight blood residue down inside the door panel on the passenger side, enough for the luminol spray to detect, but too little and too dried up to have it tested."

"His car," Chris frowned. "Was he even driving it the night Kristen disappeared? Where was Pentell that night?"

"Like you said, he has a very good lawyer, so he isn't talking to us. You might ask your friend Peter Belasco, unless he's already given us everything you dealt for. But he's not the only possible source. I think the sister knows where Kristen went her last day."

"Clarissa?"

Jack hadn't raised his voice. He was a democratic cynic, his suspicion fell equally on everyone. He nodded. "When I ask her about it she says she wants to talk to you."

"I will," Chris promised, feeling unreasonably flattered. "What else?"

"Lots else," Jack replied, standing up from the desk. "The newspaper ran a story and a photo of Kristen Lorenz, so we're being flooded with tips." He rolled his eyes at the uselessness of volunteered information. "It'll take us a month just to sort through all the callers."

"No it won't, Jack."

"I know, I know." The investigator patted his boss lightly on the shoulder. "Take it easy, Chris. It's just a murder trial. You've tried dozens of them. Try to remember what it's like."

Chris nodded, unsure from Jack's tone whether his investigator was joking. Jack left the office to resume the pursuit of Raleigh Pentell, and Chris had his own appointment to keep.

Early afternoon found him in the high school gymnasium, breathing in the lost, familiar smells of humidity, sweat, and damp towels mildewing. Chris felt uncomfortable but didn't take off his suit coat. Clots of boys dressing for PE parted for him and Chris strode up to a lone boy tying his tennis shoes. Ryan McClain heard the sudden absence of voices and the click of Chris's shoes and looked up uncertainly. Chris recognized the boy from the school photo he'd seen: wavy brown hair, clear eyes, and a sprinkling of freckles across his nose. All-American and boyish-looking, even as his eyes shifted as warily as a car thief's.

"Come with me," Chris said crisply, and the boy followed him outside, where they walked the outskirts of the track under a clear blue April sky. Chris introduced himself with his title, paused to give that weight and read the boy's nervous expression, then asked abruptly, "Did you ever see a man named Raleigh Pentell with Kristen Lorenz?"

The boy's Adam's apple moved, and he looked down in thought. "No, sir."

"Look at me. Bullshit," Chris said distinctly, glaring into Ryan's wary eyes. "Here's the thing, Ryan. I know a lot about you and you don't have any idea how much I know. I can have you charged with crimes, I can send you to juvenile detention, you and I together can mess up your life beyond repair, right here, today. But I'm not after you. I'm after the man who killed your girlfriend's sister. Understand? So you can help me or you can get stepped on because you're in the way."

Oh, it gave a masterful feeling, intimidating a child. The boy's mouth fell open slightly. Chris had deliberately dropped the girlfriend remark to prove that he did know something about Ryan's life and to watch his reaction. The boy didn't deny anything and didn't ask a question. After a long moment's thought he said, "Yes sir, I did see them together once. At Clarissa's house. It was no big deal. Mr. Pentell was just leaving, and Clarissa and I were coming in from somewhere, and I just went in for a minute and saw Kristen looking unhappy."

"Did you ask her why?"

The boy looked as if the question made no sense. "Clarissa didn't, so . . ." So it certainly hadn't been Ryan McClain's place to ask the kid sister what the problem was.

"Okay," Chris said. "I have an investigator who's going to be talking to you. In the meantime you think harder about what you can remember to help me. Like what you did for Mr. Pentell in exchange for the drugs he supplied you with."

The boy's eyes and mouth opened wide in automatic denial. "I never—"

But Chris looked at him sharply and the boy subsided, remembering what the District Attorney had said about knowing things about his life.

Chris walked away abruptly then, leaving the boy as confused as he'd intended. Young Ryan would have been surprised, though, to know the mix of feelings in the District Attorney's heart at having just had his first fatherly meeting with Clarissa's boyfriend.

That night Chris realized he hadn't checked his E-mail in a few days, and remembered what he'd found waiting for him there the last time. Sure enough, when the computer in his spare bedroom reeled in its catch from cyberspace, among the list of messages was one from "Krislore." It had sat patiently waiting for him for three days, according to its date. Chris paged down to it quickly, and it seemed to take forever for the few lines to appear on his screen. "I miss Mom," the passage began, so much like a message from a cold grave that it made him shiver.

> Mom the way she used to be, when there was only the three of us and she spent all her time on us. Now she's working too hard and worrying too much. I know she worries about me and Clarissa, how to afford to raise us, but the worry takes her away from us.

> Clarissa's gone a lot too, and I worry about her. She's just like Mom, she thinks she's smarter than anybody she meets, she can handle them, but I don't think she knows what she's getting into. She is smarter, but some people are a lot meaner.

Chris printed out the message and read it several more times during the evening. It came from the same source as the last such message, the computer in the branch library in Jean's neighborhood that sat open to the public all day. Chris thought briefly of having that library staked out, but he didn't want to frighten away whoever was sending these messages. He didn't want them stopped.

By this time Chris had read letters and writing assignments from Kristen Lorenz; he recognized her style in this passage. He was sure it was an excerpt from her diary. So the girl hadn't deliberately been hiding secrets when she wrote this, she just didn't need to confide everything she knew. Still, the short segment told him a lot. What kind of girl Kristen had been, what the family relationship had been like, how it had begun to change. He pictured Jean working overlong hours, coming home to find her daughters eating frozen dinners or delivered pizza, too tired to give them much more than a wan smile. In an exclusively female household, they had probably grown even closer than most mothers and children, but the isolation also pressed Jean too hard. She had to be the sole wage-earner, confidante, protector. He could imagine Jean in that role. As her daughter had seen too, Jean always thought she was two jumps ahead of anybody else. Her self-confidence hadn't diminished, but she must have grown tired.

Chris didn't berate himself for not knowing. It wasn't his fault. But he hated having missed his chance to help support this little family.

The most mysterious part of the message from Kristen was how it had come to him. The girl spoke of fear for her mother and sister. Had she also been afraid for herself, and arranged for someone to send these messages posthumously if something happened to her? Or had someone assumed Kristen's identity?

The next day Chris met with Jason Luling, the boy who had befriended Kristen. Jason's mother, a securities lawyer in a navy blue suit and a watchful expression, insisted on being there. She shook Chris's hand firmly but quickly and said, "I know you don't have to warn him of his rights because he's not in custody, but I have anyway. If I get any idea he wants to stop or should talk to a criminal lawyer, I'm going to put an end to it."

"Fine," Chris said mildly. He didn't want to play lawyer. He had come to meet Jason and his mother at their house, a very pleasant and clean two-story modern place less than a dozen years old. The living room in which they met went up the full two stories, with windows above beaming sunlight down upon them.

Chris had left his suit coat in the car and loosened his collar. He sat on a white sofa to put himself on the boy's level. Jason sat stiffly on the edge of an overstuffed easy chair, feet together and hands in his lap. "Hello, sir," he answered stiffly to Chris's greeting.

Chris leaned back, put his arm along the back of the sofa, and said, "Tell me about Kristen."

Jason blinked several times, as if he'd had multiple-choice answers to a test memorized and the teacher had sprung an essay on him. "Well, she . . . She was a very nice girl."

Chris didn't answer, just sat there open and easy, waiting. Jason frowned in concentration, searching for a real answer. The fifteen-year-old boy looked younger than his age, handsome in a boyish way, with a little button nose and delicate chin. He stood less than five and a half feet tall. His hands, clenched together, were also small. Kristen would have wanted to cuddle him like a puppy, and Jason would be afraid of being treated like less than a man by his peers, Chris felt sure.

"She seemed very shy in class, but if you talked to her at all she opened up very fast. I just sat next to her in the cafeteria once because there was a seat there—"

And neither of them had other lunch companions, Chris inferred.

"—and I barely said hello before she started talking about herself and her mother and her sister and where they'd come from. I don't think she'd ever had a friend, or at least not for very long, she couldn't have, I think they'd moved around a lot until they got here."

Chris saw on the boy's face the remains of that first impression Kristen had made on him: Jason's hair almost blown back from the force of her talk and her springing-forth personality. Even now he looked surprised and slightly thrilled. Having a friend had obviously been a new experience for him, too.

"What did she talk about?"

"Her mother, and not seeing her as much as she used to, and her big sister Clarissa and her friends—Clarissa was so popular—and what Kristen wanted to do and be. Just things she thought, you know."

"You saw her a lot?" Chris half-asked.

"We had two classes together, and lunch, and we both stayed in the library after school. Then my mom and dad started giving her a ride home. Remember that first time she stayed for dinner, Mom?"

The mother, still standing behind her son, explained. "No one seemed to be home at Kristen's house, so she left a message and ended up eating with us." The woman's cheeks slowly lifted in a smile; she unbent and became something more than a lawyer. "She was a delightful girl, she wanted to do everything right. We didn't know we had rules about eating until we watched Kristen try to follow them. At the table if you asked her anything you got a fifteen-minute speech. She was dying to talk."

Mrs. Luling heard what she'd said, "dying to talk," and trailed off, looking down at her hands. Her son took up the slack, smiling.

"Yeah, she'd tell the strangest stories about her family, and act like they were perfectly normal. We thought she was making them up. But one time we saw her mother at school, in the parking lot, giving someone a ride—"

"Clarissa?"

"No, a boy. Clarissa's boyfriend Ryan, I guess. And Kristen stepped back around the corner so her mother wouldn't see her. All of a sudden she turned into Harriet the Spy."

"What was the matter?"

"I'm—not sure." Jason turned hesitant and his mother watchful again, fine lines appearing near her eyes as she glanced at Chris and put a hand on her son's shoulder.

"Something about her mother worried her," Jason trailed off.

Chris listened to the boy for another half hour, but heard nothing more significant than that silent pause after this remembered scene. He left the mother and son with thanks, as if he were done with them, knowing full well that one of these days he'd catch the boy alone, without his mother standing watch over his every syllable.

"She does sound like a delightful girl," Anne Greenwald said, picking up the half-empty plate in front of Chris and carrying it away to her kitchen.

"What do you mean by that?" Chris asked, his voice rising to follow her.

Anne reappeared in the doorway, looking at him a little oddly. "I mean she sounds like a delightful girl. Did I say it wrong somehow?"

Chris stood and walked to the front window, a trip not nearly long enough to relieve the tension that knotted his shoulders and neck. "I've got to take her out of that school."

"Aren't you having Clarissa watched?" Anne asked.

Yes, a police officer haunted the high school corridors outside Clarissa's classrooms. He didn't wear a uniform, and so blended in like a skunk at a Siamese cat show. A quick glance wouldn't spot him, but anything more would. That was okay, the protection didn't need to be subtle. Without telling anyone, Chris had also installed his investigator Olga Zamora as the new kid in school. "I don't think I'm the only girl carrying a pistol in her purse," Olga said after her first day on the job. "I'm just the only one who's nervous about it."

"And of course keeping an eye on this Raleigh Pentell," Anne added. Her voice traveled across her living room softly but with a tough spine, the voice she used when analyzing a patient. Chris didn't want to be worked up as a case history, but he felt like one.

"It's a little more complicated than that," he said.

When he finally turned to look at Anne she gave him an ironic look. She wore the long-sleeved white shirt that had gone with her workday suit, but khaki shorts underneath, and bare feet on her hardwood floor. April in San Antonio allowed such a costume. Chris wanted to hold her.

"Jean and I were good friends in college," he said carefully.

Anne tried and failed to keep the amusement out of her voice. "You've said that often enough with enough subtle emphasis that I think I get it, Chris. Either you're trying to tell me that as soon as you saw this Jean again your heart swelled with renewed love for her—"

"No."

"—or that you feel some longing sort of connection to her fatherless daughters."

Without answering directly, but feeling both relieved and embarrassed, Chris said, "I'm not just talking about danger from Raleigh Pentell when I say I'm worried about Clarissa. He has a connection to Jean, too. He's been to their house."

Anne walked to him, gripped his arm quickly, and passed on by. "Let's go for a walk," she said.

She stepped into shoes by her front door and Chris joined her on the porch. Seven P.M. had brought full dark, not just dusk, even after the advent of daylight savings time a week ago. The day's temperature had risen to the mid-eighties, but in spring the heat didn't linger, nightfall dissipated it quickly. Only a few wispy clouds sailed the night sky, letting the warmth rise into space. Anne hugged her arms lightly and walked quickly toward the sidewalk. Chris caught up to her, still lost in thoughts of Clarissa.

"I've got to get her out of there, but what would I do with her? I don't want to put her in juvenile detention for weeks until the trial's over, and I can't have her live with me. A sixteen-year-old girl."

They started down the sidewalks of Anne's Monte Vista neighborhood. She gave his hand a slight squeeze as, seeming to ignore his questions, she said, "Let's go to dinner or something with her. I'd like to meet the girl."

After a moment of replaying her lightly shifting voice Chris said, "Talk about your subtle emphases."

Anne laughed. "I do it better than you, at least." Her voice in the darkness lifted his worries, but only momentarily.

Two afternoons later Chris was on his way to the vicinity of the high school to meet his investigator Olga Zamora when Raleigh Pentell struck again. School had been out for forty-five minutes when the cell phone on the car seat beside Chris rang. As soon as he clicked it on, before he could even speak, Jack Fine's voice barked, "Chris? There's been a shooting. Strip center two blocks out Callaghan from 410. The ice cream place."

"Who?" Chris said in a voice that came out oddly quiet. He changed lanes, passed an old Mustang, saw the sign for the Callaghan exit.

"I don't know," Jack answered. "I'm on my way now."

Chris wanted a siren. Clutching the steering wheel and leaning forward, he veered around cars, onto the exit ramp, and down the access road, still weaving and occasionally honking. Drivers made obscene gestures at him. He passed a blur of businesses, gas station, music store, grocery store: locales that had all turned suddenly irrelevant to real life.

He could have found the location without Jack's directions, from the cluster of police cars in the parking lot of a strip center, and the crowds of people converging on the yellow tape. Chris parked as close as he could, jumped out, and ran over the asphalt to the barricade. He jostled through the crowds without seeing or hearing them. The uniformed cop on the sidewalk put a hand on Chris's chest. Chris fumbled his DA's Office ID out of his pocket and hung it on a chain around his neck. The cop let him go. Closer to the storefront, a plainclothes detective recognized Chris without the aid of the ID.

"I wouldn't, sir," he said.

Chris ignored him and stepped inside the ice cream store, one of a national chain that all looked basically alike. It was a narrow, long location with a line of chairs and small tables along the wall to the left and the serving counter and ice cream freezers on the right. The place now seemed filled, but oddly so: no one was eating ice cream. At the far end a police officer questioned the two owners, a middle-aged husband and wife with faces whiter than vanilla. An evidence technician had spread fingerprint powder along the counters and a table or two. Another on hands and knees searched for shell casings.

Directly ahead of Chris a stretcher blocked his path, with two attendants leaning against the ice cream counter. The attendants showed no impatience. They weren't paramedics, they were from the medical examiner's office, as was Officer Monica Burris, who knelt beside a covered body on the other side of the stretcher. The attendants waited for her to declare death so they could take the body away.

Chris edged past the cold counter, his back brushing it so that cold ran up his spine. He edged toward the body, going so stiff he could barely move. Thinking: *Everything I've done wasted. . . . I didn't get to have any of her life.*

Monica Burris looked up with slight annoyance at being jostled, then said, "Oh, hi, Chris. What brings you here?"

Chris knelt beside her and touched her hand as he pulled the sheet back farther from the body. He stared at the young, dead-white face on the floor.

"Know him?" Burris asked casually.

Chris stood up quickly, reanimated. "Yes," he said, then stared all around the small room. "Is he the only one? Is this it? Where——?"

"Yes, he's the only one," Burris said, looking at Chris strangely. He knelt beside her again and gave the face closer study. The boy's freckles barely showed, his body looked so drained of blood. The sheet covering him was soaked. He must have still been bleeding when police arrived, but the chest wound was one nobody could have survived.

"His name is Ryan McClain," Chris said. "He was a student at Holmes."

Monica Burris nodded. Chris stood again. "Wasn't anybody with him?" he asked loudly. "What happened?"

The detective left his questioning of the store's owners

to approach the District Attorney. The detective, only a few years older than Chris, had a weary face and an old-fashioned attitude, as if he should be wearing a fedora. "It was very efficient," he said. "The place was full of kids, the after-school rush. Two big guys in coats walked in, scanned the place, went straight through. One of them fired a shot over the counter that got everyone's attention, kind of froze everyone in place. The other one went straight to this boy, shot him twice, and kept walking. They both kept walking, right out the back of the shop. They must have scoped the place out ahead of time, because there's a back parking lot where a car must've been waiting for them. The whole thing didn't last a minute from the time they walked in the front door."

Chris felt himself start breathing again. "Was he alone?" he asked of the boy, aiming the question at the store's owners. They looked startled at being addressed. They glanced at each other, the woman shrugged, and the man said, "No, he had a girl with him. They were arguing. I noticed because he ordered for her, but when he turned around she'd left. He looked mad and gave her cone to somebody else. He was sitting by himself when the men came in."

"A blond girl?"

The man regained some of his character and his color. He was a tall man with a fleshy nose, and large shoulders that moved eloquently when he shrugged. "I think so. Really I just heard her voice. She was telling him something he had to do and he was trying to shush her. That's when she said something sharp to him and left." The man looked down at the body on the floor, diminished by death. "I guess she was right."

Chris turned and walked quickly out of the store. On the sidewalk in front he turned left, looked at the signs of the stores along that side of the strip center, saw a title company, an office supply, and a small Chinese restaurant. In the other direction he saw signs for a shoe store and a drugstore. He chose that way, walking quickly through the parting crowds. In front of the shoe store he saw the plainclothes police officer he knew, the man who'd been assigned to follow Clarissa.

The officer, a young man named Hanson with light brown hair and a wide, earnest face, had been promoted to plainclothes for this specific assignment, chosen for it because of his marksmanship scores and his relative thinness. He was a jogger. His bosses figured Hanson would move quickly in an emergency. At this moment his face looked besieged. "I'm sorry, sir," he said when he saw Chris. "When she left the ice cream place I followed her. I wasn't there to stop the shooting."

"You did exactly the right thing," Chris said. "Where is she?"

The young officer gestured with his head toward the shoe store. Chris glanced through the plate glass window, then entered the store quietly. Red carpet hushed his footsteps. Shoe racks blocked his sight and made a maze of the store's interior. Chris called, "Clarissa?"

A soft sound like a hiccup made him hurry around a rack and find her sitting on the floor, huddled against a metal chair as if it could give her warmth. Clarissa seemed to be the only person in the store. She looked up fearfully.

"What happened? They won't tell me. What is it? Is Ryan—?"

Chris just nodded. He sat beside her on the floor and put an arm around her. "Oh my God," Clarissa said loudly. She rocked forward and back, arms hugging her chest tightly, and sobbed, "I killed him."

"No you didn't," Chris said, putting his arm around her. "Raleigh Pentell did. And he was probably trying to kill you, too. You just got very lucky."

The girl shook with fear. "What happened?" she asked miserably. "I didn't want anything to eat, I told Ryan I was going to come down here and look at shoes. What—?"

Chris could imagine the scene. The gunmen must have followed Ryan and Clarissa from school, or known their habits. They'd seen them go into the ice cream store, then had driven around the center to park the car in the back. While the gunmen had circled the center on foot to enter the front of the store, Clarissa had gone out, drawn by the lure of shoes.

"What were the two of you arguing about?"

Clarissa looked startled at Chris's information, and momentarily furtive, which aged her face. "Nothing. Something stupid. I don't even know what."

"Did he tell you I'd come to see him?"

Clarissa didn't hesitate this time. "Yes. That was part of what we were fighting about. I was telling him to tell you everything he knew, but he said he wanted to talk to somebody else first."

"Maybe he did. At any rate Raleigh Pentell knew Ryan had information."

"Oh, God." Clarissa's face dissolved. She clutched Chris's collar as she had at Raleigh Pentell's house. This time he hadn't rescued her. If not for luck, Clarissa would be dead on the linoleum floor of the ice cream store as well. He held her close. Pentell knew about Clarissa, too.

"Poor Ryan," Clarissa muttered, and began crying. Her grief sounded a bit artificial, as most people's does. But when she spoke again her urgency sounded real. "I don't want to go home."

"You're not," Chris said, holding her warmly and he hoped securely. "Don't worry about that, you're coming with me."

Nine

The next morning Chris arrived at the Justice Center at nine o'clock, almost late for a court appearance. Jean must have been waiting a long time, pacing the sidewalk in front of the building. Her anger had been growing, looking for a target. She came racing toward Chris as soon as he crossed the street from the parking garage.

"Where is she?" she said loudly.

"She's safe," Chris said quietly. "You know that, she called you last night."

"That's not good enough." Jean wore a navy blue skirt suit, appropriate for her job at the insurance company, but her stance, hip cocked and arms akimbo, didn't suit the elegant clothing. Emotion made her look more like the girl he remembered from college. But at that moment Chris felt little connection to her. Jean obviously hadn't realized it yet, but Chris seethed with anger, too.

"It'll have to do for now," he said, still quiet. "I'm not letting her come home, not until this is all over."

"Like hell! She's my daughter, Chris. If I have to go to court to get a judge to order you to let me have her I will. You have no right—"

"Don't I?" he snapped. Chris's eyes flashed for the first time. Jean lost her momentum. "After she was kidnapped by a man you introduced her to? And now just missed being murdered by the same man's thugs? I'm going to trial in a couple of weeks, and you haven't given me one clue to prove who murdered your daughter. I didn't even get from you how Pentell knew Kristen. But it was through you, I know."

Jean's hesitation continued. The tip of her tongue emerged briefly, touched her lip, and withdrew. Chris spoke more softly. "Do you give a damn that Ryan McClain is dead? You of all people should know what his parents are going through. It seemed like a normal little high school fast crowd, but now two kids are dead. What was it about, Jean? Just money?"

Jean's thoughts were obviously moving much faster than her voice. "I think Pentell supplied them with marijuana," she said slowly.

"Through you. You were the middleman. Don't deny it, Jean. You were seen at the school. With one of the boys, not your daughters. Unless you tell me you were having an affair with a high school boy—"

Jean's expression showed her disdain for that explanation, but her voice turned pleading. "It was just marijuana, Chris. Just small-time stuff. They would have gotten it from somewhere—"

"So that's how you knew Pentell."

Jean still hesitated, then nodded. Chris stared at her, thinking how odd it was that she looked so familiar and in fact apparently hadn't grown far from the life in which he'd left her more than fifteen years ago, yet he felt no attachment to her. "With your own girls going to school there," he said wonderingly.

His penetrating stare changed Jean's face. Her cheeks lengthened as she looked straight back at him. "It was when we first came here three years ago," she snapped. "With two girls to support and no one on this earth to help me. It was the only job skill I had! I would do anything—

you understand, Chris, anything—to feed and clothe and raise those girls! To take care of them every damned day. You don't get a holiday, you can't say, 'Let's not eat today, girls, it's been done to death, everybody's doing it.' Or 'Let's go camp out in the park for the next month or so while I get together the rent money.' " She indicated her business attire with a gesture. "You don't just fall into a job at United Life Insurance the first time you apply. There's a waiting list for jobs, and about half a dozen interviewers to slide past. But every day there's school fees and dresses and Cheerios and the ice cream man driving by." She exhaled noisily and her slashing stare slid off Chris's face. "You wouldn't understand," she said wearily.

But Chris did understand. He'd felt the same thing as he'd held Clarissa in Raleigh Pentell's house and again in the shoe store. That feeling that there were no rules, only a fierce need to protect. It was a new feeling for Chris, and Jean had lived with it all her adult life. He had no right to condemn her. He didn't.

"I would have helped," he said.

The weariness that had invaded Jean's face lifted. With a rueful smile she touched Chris's arm. "I wish I'd—" Then her expression turned alarmed. She stared past Chris's shoulder.

Chris turned and saw Raleigh Pentell walking along the sidewalk from the other side of the Justice Center. He understood Jean's sudden apprehension. He felt it himself, staring at the man Chris thought responsible for so much crime and destruction.

"What's he doing here?" Jean asked.

But Pentell wasn't accompanied by his thugs. The distinguished lawyer Lowell Burke walked beside him, and stopped to give the District Attorney a courteous nod, which Chris returned.

"He's here for the same reason I am," Chris said. "To go to court. I've got to go, Jean."

Her grip on his arm tightened. "I have to have her back, Chris."

He looked at Jean without answering. After a moment she relented. "Is she with you? She's not just staying with some damned guard who doesn't—"

"I see her every day, Jean. I'm with her."

"All right, then." Jean let him go. She let her surviving daughter go as well. Chris knew how hard the decision was for Jean. He wanted to offer her comfort, but had no time. He hurried into the Justice Center behind Raleigh Pentell and his lawyer. Jean didn't follow.

Judge Paul Benitez, a thoughtful, watchful man in his thirties, had been a judge for three years and had never been known to raise his voice either on or off the bench. He didn't approve of emotion in the courtroom, and sensed plenty of it this morning as soon as he took his place to hear pre-trial motions in the case of Raleigh Pentell. Five minutes into the proceedings, he stared with slight puzzlement at the District Attorney. "Mr. Sinclair, why do you oppose the motion to sever the cases? You know the defendant has a right to be tried on only one charge if he chooses."

"And the people of Bexar County have a right not to be slaughtered on the streets. Your Honor, the two charges before this court, of murder and kidnapping, are not the only indictments I plan to bring against this man. As long as he walks free—"

"Then bring them," Lowell Burke interrupted. Standing tall and unruffled, the gray-haired lawyer looked the soul of reason compared to Chris. "This is ridiculous. If you had even the slightest degree of proof that my client had committed whatever crime you're talking about, you would have had him arrested again. Your Honor, could we just address the subject at hand?"

"He keeps murdering the witnesses," Chris said. He

moved out from the table to look past the defense lawyer at Raleigh Pentell. The defendant sat staring straight ahead, as if bored or even sleepy. Chris wanted to punch him. He wanted to force Pentell into displaying his true character.

Judge Benitez tried to keep the parties on track. "What is it you want, Mr. Sinclair? I plan to grant the motion to sever the cases. What is your request?"

"A speedy trial, Your Honor. If we have to try this man's crimes one at a time, let's get started."

"Are you already ready for trial?" the judge asked with genuine curiosity. Lowell Burke watched Chris with the same emotion.

No, Chris wasn't. Not remotely. But he couldn't leave Pentell free any longer. The latest murder demonstrated that risk. "Yes, Your Honor," Chris said emphatically.

"All right, then. Shall we say two weeks from today? The murder trial first, that's the older case. Agreed? Now, are there other motions to dispose of today?"

"Just routine ones, Your Honor. I don't think we need take up any more of the court's time," Lowell Burke said graciously. Judge Benitez seemed relieved to leave the bench, leaving the two lawyers and the defendant standing in place. Burke began repacking his briefcase. Chris stepped around him and said to Raleigh Pentell, "You have no conscience at all, do you?"

Burke straightened. "Come, come, Chris. You know better than to speak to a defendant who's represented by counsel. I'd appreciate it if you'd address any remarks to me. And this conscience thing isn't appropriate in any case."

While his lawyer talked, Pentell stared at Chris. The man wore a light blue suit that emphasized his ruddiness, his good-old-boy good looks. But his eyes were dark and gave off no light. Inside that flat blackness Pentell's mind moved relentlessly. Chris could see the man deciding whether to be charming or profess innocence. But Pentell apparently realized there was no point to making any subterfuge with Chris. Pentell had seen the DA outside with Jean, he must have thought Chris privy to many of his business secrets. The defendant obviously decided not to waste his charm on his prosecutor.

"I don't know what you think you know about me," he said with quiet animosity. "But you've obviously lost your mind and your objectivity. I suggest you let one of your assistants try this case. Someone who—"

"Don't tell me how to run my business," Chris snapped, moving closer to him.

"Then butt out of mine," Pentell said.

Chris stood face to face with the defendant. "I know you now," he said tightly. "I know how far you'll go. I won't give you any more slack. If you hurt anyone else I will personally get you. Any way it takes."

Pentell smiled slightly. Chris's anger both amused and gratified him. He saw Chris's personal involvement as a weakness: Chris's threat made Chris vulnerable. The defendant obviously began planning, with the District Attorney staring him in the face, how to use that vulnerability.

"Yes sir," Pentell said ironically, and turned and walked away. Chris didn't even represent a small obstacle for him.

Lowell Burke looked at the District Attorney bemusedly. "The man has a point about letting someone else try the case," he said.

Chris wanted to knock the defense lawyer down and then run and tackle the defendant. The man's arrogance was impenetrable. Chris was certain Pentell had murdered two children, but Pentell seemed to have no thoughts of funerals, bereaved parents, or remorse. He characterized his decisions as just what he'd called them: business.

Chris's only business at the moment was to stop him. And he didn't nearly have the ammunition to do so yet.

* * *

The next afternoon Chris's investigator Olga Zamora dropped her textbooks on the corner of his desk, popped her bubble gum, and said, "Clarissa okay?"

"So far."

"The kids wonder what's happened to her. Is she—?"

"How *is* school life, Olga?"

"Well, I've got biology homework I'm a little worried about."

Olga dipped her shoulder ironically. She looked even younger than she had before she'd started this assignment, her hair worn looser, her eyes more open. But it was mainly the way she moved that achieved the illusion of youth: in an unconscious glide, as if she heard music undetectable by adult ears. Chris had to smile. "Are you enjoying high school, Olga?"

"More than the first time around," the investigator admitted, looking at the photographs and certificates on Chris's office wall as if she'd never been here before. "I was a real nerd in high school, would you believe it?"

"And now you're one of the cool kids."

She turned and said, "Even the cool kids have problems. Maybe more so. Did you know that? I hate finding that out."

"So you're in with them?" Chris asked.

"Sort of. I'm hanging with a little crowd of boys and a couple of girls who talk about what they're going to do this weekend and think they're being mysterious. Your girl hangs with them too, or did until you took her out of school."

Chris felt strangely elated at hearing Clarissa described as his girl. He asked in the same lazy tone, "Do they like her?"

Olga shook her head. Chris frowned. "Oh, she's one of them," the investigator assured him. "But like isn't the word. They need her approval or fear her—something. Clarissa was the star of the crowd; I think they feel a little lost without her. The group doesn't have a focus. But

even before you took her out of school, things were
changing for her. Like, they all knew, of course, that
Raleigh Pentell's been arrested for killing her sister. One
of the other girls, this little tramp named Cheryl Peske,
said it right to Clarissa's face, like she was being sympathetic: 'Oh, Clarissa, it must be awful, how can you stand
it? Poor little Kristen, do you miss her something awful?'
The others gasped and acted shocked at how insensitive
she is, but their eyes stayed on Clarissa, looking for how
she'd react."

"And how did she?" Chris realized that with the question he joined, unseen, the crowd of voyeurs hovering
around his girl.

"I can't judge, Chris. How are you supposed to react to
something like that? I know I'd—" Olga stopped
abruptly, eyes narrowing and turning adult. "No, I don't. I
can't imagine. Maybe Clarissa looked sad, maybe she
just got mad at having to react at all. What do teenagers
know? Of course, now all they're talking about is this
Ryan McClain being killed. They wonder what Ryan
knew. Nobody seems to know—"

Chris said, "Have you learned anything other than
music and what's the coolest body part to have pierced,
Olga? Something I could use in my pathetically weak
case against Raleigh Pentell?"

"Not yet, but I think I'm getting there. Of course with
all this going on, whatever scams they had working are
on hold. But Raleigh Pentell's all they talk about. I said
yesterday that I'd read in the newspaper that he'd organized teenage gangs and that set them off, they all—"

"That hasn't been in the newspaper, we haven't
released that yet."

Olga looked at him with too much scorn. "These kids
don't know that, they don't read the newspaper. Get real,
Chris. I just said it to get them talking, and it did. They all
wanted to say what they know, which unfortunately isn't
much. I don't think any of them ever saw Pentell in per-

son. He hung way back. One of them mentioned Peter—
Peter Belasco. The boys did know him. Belasco gave a
party for them the night of October twenty-fifth."

"That's the last day Jean says she saw Kristen!" Chris
interrupted.

"I know, Chris. And something happened that night at
this party. Some kind of disturbance. It was in a restaurant, not a house. One kid mentioned it because he was
there and a man came who he thought might have been
Pentell. But it's the only time he ever saw him. Only one
of these kids ever actually had a conversation with
Raleigh Pentell. That was Ryan McClain."

"So Pentell took care of that problem this week."

"I'm sorry, Chris, but yeah. That's got to be the reason
he was killed. If anybody made his way up the chain to
the adult level of the operation, it was Ryan. He was even
into something weird and different, something the others
weren't part of, they just knew about it by rumor."

Chris sat up, concerned by "weird," hearing kinky or
dangerous.

"He was in a car wreck," Olga said disconcertingly, her
expression showing that she didn't know what this meant
either.

"Bad? Was he hurt?"

She shook her head. "No. It was a fake."

"Fake? What for?"

"I don't know."

"Who did he hit?"

Olga said, "I don't know. That may be the deal. Maybe
it was a warning to somebody—"

"Belasco?"

"I don't know, but I'm going to find out."

Chris said, "And I'm going to talk to Belasco again.
Maybe I can get him to come up with more, if he had
some hope of bringing down Pentell himself."

Chris put on his suit coat, feeling envious of Olga
Zamora in her jeans and T-shirt. "There's no time for subtlety now, Olga. I've got a court date in two weeks."

"My God, how can you possibly be ready that soon?"

"With the help of my team," Chris said ironically. He concentrated on Olga. "Find out about this party in the restaurant."

Chris Sinclair and sixteen-year-old Clarissa made a homey scene that evening in his condo, he on the sofa with a book, she at the round glass dining table working on homework, in the edgy but growing easier relationship they'd developed in the week Clarissa had been living away from home. Chris tried not to question her overtly all the time, but when she felt the mood to reminisce he would listen attentively, encouraging her with his attention. In this way he'd learned that the first place Clarissa remembered living was Fort Worth, with Jean's parents, when Clarissa had been four and Kristen two. Clarissa had liked being with her grandparents but had been aware of a tension in the house, which might have driven her mother away. Home had been only a brief resting place for Jean before she took off again, leaving the girls with her parents for four weeks before she found a place to live in Riverside, California, and sent for them. In Clarissa's memory that month with her grandparents when she'd been in first grade stretched very long, a period of schedules and lessons and meals at certain times that she looked back on wistfully. It had been one of the longest times of security in Clarissa's life.

In California she'd felt isolated and abandoned, with Jean busy all the time, so that the girls grew very close. Clarissa remembered the particular books she'd read to her little sister over and over. She remembered worrying for Kristen as the little girl walked into her pre-school building and being glad the following year when they attended the same elementary school, and could walk there together.

Clarissa had begun talking about that period again this evening, fondly remembering at first but then adding, "I think she got attached to me then and she never got over it. Kristen never was good at making friends. She liked being home. Well, neither of us really had friends, we moved too much. But once we got here I was doing okay. Kristen turned into kind of a pest, she always had to know right where I was, she couldn't—"

Clarissa stopped suddenly, hearing herself criticize her sister. Clarissa would always know where Kristen was now, and wouldn't be bothered by her tagging along.

Chris sat across from Clarissa watching her lip tremble and wondering if he should go hug her. He already knew from very short experience that she would turn away and say she was all right. The girl was a turmoil of feelings, changing so fast no one could keep up with them, even Clarissa herself.

So they sat quietly, only slight tension in the air between them. Chris covertly studied the girl, her shoes kicked off under the table, her feet hooked around the legs of her chair. He remembered sitting like that. Chris couldn't help looking for traces of himself in Clarissa. The resemblances would have to be genetic only, he hadn't been around to pass on habits or mannerisms.

A parent could have told him that one searched in vain for such resemblances, they could only be caught unexpectedly in the flashes of a turning head or a view from an unfamiliar angle.

Clarissa caught him looking and Chris let her catch him. Yes, he was concerned about her. Let her resent that. Chris tried not to press too hard, not to be parental, but certain parental concerns had to be handled. "Is your new school okay?" he asked. "Are they in the same place in the classes?"

Clarissa made a small uninterested shrug. "I'll be okay, don't worry."

"I do worry, that's why you're here."

She knew he wasn't talking about schoolwork. "What can happen, your detective's always there hovering?"

Clarissa sounded annoyed, but affectionately so. He

thought her secretly glad to be the object of his concern. "I could come hang around your office," she added.

Chris had already considered and rejected that idea. The DA's office was no place for Clarissa, and she might run into Olga Zamora and wonder what her classmate was doing there.

He did need to bring Clarissa to his office as part of his investigation. She had been in Raleigh Pentell's house for a month at least; she should know more than anyone about what went on there. So far he had questioned her only lightly. He had to do so much more thoroughly before trial. Probably he should have someone else do it, in a detached professional way.

Later Clarissa used the phone, going into Chris's bedroom for a little privacy. He listened, trying to hear if she was calling Jean or one of her friends, one of the friends who'd gotten her involved with Raleigh Pentell. He walked from the couch to the kitchen and when he passed the bedroom door glanced in to see Clarissa sitting on his bed, talking very softly. Chris's protective feeling surged. But only a few minutes later he had to stand with a sigh and say, "Time to go."

Clarissa looked sullen. "I don't want to go back to that place."

Chris didn't blame her. He had her in a group home, with girls who had been taken from their parents for various reasons. Clarissa must feel freakish and isolated there, but he hadn't come up with a better solution yet.

"It's only for a little while, Clarissa. Until it's safe for you to go home again."

"I'm not sure I want to go back there, either." She stood close to Chris. "Couldn't I stay here with you?"

"I wish you could." Chris put his arms around her. Then the thought that had hovered at the back of his mind for at least a day popped forward, onto his tongue. "Would you like to meet a friend of mine?" he asked suddenly.

*   *   *

When Anne Greenwald opened her front door Saturday
evening, to Chris and Clarissa standing on the front
porch, Anne looked the girl over quite frankly, not coy at
all. "My, what a beautiful girl," Anne said after a moment.

No one could argue with that. Clarissa wore a light-
weight summer dress with thin straps that left her shoulders mostly bare. The blue dress brought out the color of
her eyes and made her shoulders and arms look tanned,
which in turn made her hair seem blonder. Clarissa usually went to school in jeans and bulky sweatshirts or
loose T-shirts, but she hadn't tried to minimize this occasion by dressing down. Chris felt proud of her.

At the compliment from Anne, Clarissa rolled her eyes
and slouched on one leg. Anne continued to watch her,
only touching Chris's arm in greeting to him. Seeing
Clarissa's reaction, Anne said, "Feminists say you
shouldn't compliment a girl or a grown woman for that
matter on her looks, it makes it sound as if that's the most
important thing about her. On the other hand a lot of my
psychology books say you have to reassure teenagers,
girls in particular, that they look all right, because it's the
main thing they worry about at your age, especially since
they're just bombarded with images of unrealistically
beautiful girls. What do you think, Clarissa?"

The long flow of Anne's observation and question
brightened Clarissa's attention. Chris felt nervous about
Anne's directness, but Clarissa looked at her apprecia-
tively and said, "I guess how a person looks is the first
thing you notice, you can't help thinking about it, you'll
have to wait a while to tell me how smart I am. You look
nice, by the way. Is that the first dress you saw in your
closet tonight, or did you think about it for a long time
wondering what kind of impression you wanted to
make?"

"Yeah, that," Anne said. "I was going for feminine, you
know, but not competitive, not like I wanted to dazzle
you."

Clarissa ran her gaze down and up Anne's simple green dress that went to her knees and featured a scoop collar and short sleeves. "Yes, I can see that," she said.

The porch was silent for a moment, Anne smiled and so did Clarissa, and Chris felt out of his depth. "I started to wear a suit . . ." he mumbled.

Anne patted his arm reassuringly. "Yes, you look beautiful, too. Where are we going for pasta? Are you trying to impress Clarissa or does she know some hip kids' place we're going to try?"

During dinner at Boudro's on the Riverwalk, Anne and Clarissa dropped the overt analysis and oneupwomanship, to Chris's relief, but that only meant that their study of each other went subterranean.

"How's your school? Are you going to be able to finish up your classes so you don't lose a school year?"

"Sure, that's the plan," Clarissa said, glancing at Chris. "And I have plenty of time to study, since Chris took me away from my evil friends and these new kids just stare at me. They don't know why I'm here, but they know there's something weird about me."

"There's nothing weird—" Chris began, and Anne interrupted: "What do you think is the weirdest thing they notice about you?"

Clarissa sat blank-faced for a moment; no one had been so direct with her. Then she said with sudden hollow gravity, "Maybe the way I stink of death."

She jumped up and ran from the table. Chris stood, but Anne stopped him with a hand on his. "It's okay, I'll go check on her in a minute. What about the place where she's staying? Anyone she's likely to make friends with there?"

Chris shrugged. "I don't think too many lifelong friendships develop in group homes. But it's the best I can do right now. I can't have her with me."

Anne said soothingly, "I know. What about counseling, is she getting any?"

"Only this conversation she just had with you," Chris said. "And it seems to be going well, doesn't it?"

Anne smiled. "Even I can't solve all their problems over one dinner. Let me go check on her."

Chris sat, feeling very male, for several long minutes until the two returned. Clarissa seemed composed, even smiling. After dinner they walked along the river, standing out from the tourists in shorts and T-shirts, not only by their dress but because Chris and Anne and Clarissa didn't stop to look at the menus posted outside the restaurants or the Mexican folk art in curio store windows. Their attention remained on each other.

Anne went into a tiny drugstore while Chris and Clarissa waited outside. The girl turned confidential, leaning to glance into the shop at Anne.

"I guess your taste in girlfriends has changed since college, huh?" Clarissa asked.

Chris hesitated, trying to figure out the appropriate answer.

Clarissa grinned.

As the three of them drove home, Clarissa's remark about college grew louder in Chris's memory. So Jean had said something to her, something about knowing Chris in college. What exactly had she told the girl? How speculatively did Clarissa watch Chris, while he tried to study her?

At Anne's house he had time to speak to Anne privately, while Clarissa was in the bathroom, spending so long there that she must have been exploring the medicine cabinet and drawers.

"She hates it at that group home, I wish I could bring her home with me. But—"

Anne lounged on her couch, legs crossed at the knees, bobbing one leg up slightly as if giving a small child a horsey ride. "No, you couldn't do that. A sixteen-year-old girl. Besides, this Raleigh Pentell person knows you, knows you're after him. I would think you wouldn't want Clarissa staying with you for that reason."

"But I have to take care of her. I can't let her go back to her mother, and there was no one I could ask—"

He stopped abruptly, realizing that sounded like a hint. He had thought of Clarissa's staying with Anne instead of him, but that might be dangerous and at any rate was too much to ask of Anne.

"Could you get me a pen from my office over there?" Anne asked him suddenly.

A strange request. Like Chris, Anne had a second bedroom that she used as a home office. The door to it, across the living room, was closed. Chris opened it, flicked on the light inside, and stopped dead. In the bedroom, Anne's file cabinet was gone, the desk had been moved into one corner, and the usual piles of papers and journals had vanished. In the resulting space sat a twin bed, neatly made with a dust ruffle around the bottom. There were even thin ruffled curtains on the windows.

Anne had come softly up to stand just behind Chris. "I didn't have time to wallpaper," she said lightly, but with an embarrassed hesitancy.

"Anne—" Chris turned to her but saw Clarissa past Anne's shoulder. The girl walked into the room and glanced around, unaware of the changed status of the bedroom. "You have a roommate?" she asked.

Anne answered, "No, but I'd like one."

Clarissa had a quick mind. She understood at once. "Why?" she said warily.

Chris said rather formally, "It's a nice offer, Clarissa, but it's up to you. Would you like to stay here?"

Anne said, "The one advantage it has over the group home is that there's only one other weirdo living here for you to contend with."

Clarissa drew Chris aside, into the living room. Softly, reaching out tentatively to touch his hand, she said, "I don't want to live with her, I want to live with you."

"I'll come see you every day, Clarissa. I'll take you to school in the mornings, we'll have dinner at night."

Clarissa looked at Anne, who remained in the other

bedroom and casually closed its door, as if to demonstrate the privacy the room could afford. "Why does she want me?" Clarissa asked. "She doesn't even know me."

Chris paused, then said forthrightly, "She's doing it as a favor for me."

Clarissa stared at him searchingly. "I guess she must really like you," she finally said, perhaps making a joke.

Anne emerged from the bedroom, walking quickly as if just passing them by, but Clarissa stopped her. "I guess you've got a T-shirt or something I can sleep in?"

"Check the closet in there," Anne replied, which produced a curious, almost happy look on Clarissa. Anne added, "You'll probably think my taste in clothes sucks, but you can start educating me."

Clarissa didn't brighten entirely, she wouldn't be played easily, but her shoulders unslumped and she walked past Anne into the spare bedroom. Chris looked at Anne for some indication of what she thought.

"Thanks, Anne."

Smiling, she said, "That is a totally inadequate expression of your gratitude."

Chris stayed for another hour, making the transition as easy as he could for Clarissa. His good-byes to the women were awkward because he wanted moments alone with each of them and couldn't manage it. He kissed Clarissa on the forehead and she nodded at him forgivingly.

After Chris left, Anne and Clarissa looked at each other, neither of them minimizing the oddness of their being alone together. Anne kicked off her shoes and reached behind her back to begin unzipping her dress. "Listen," she said, and Clarissa looked wary, as if the instructions were already beginning. Anne went on, "I spend my days delving into the minds and attitudes and psyches of kids. I go off duty at six o'clock and on weekends. So do me a favor and don't confide anything in me, okay? Let's not talk about our childhoods or what's worrying us these days or any of that stuff, all right?"

Clarissa grinned. "Okay." She followed Anne toward

the bedroom. "Let me get a look at your closet and see what my starting point is educating you about how to dress. You do want to learn, don't you?"

Anne chuckled and let the girl go ahead into her bedroom. That quickly Anne had lost her privacy and the solitude that she used to think she enjoyed. "We'll see how it goes," she said aloud.

Later that night, Anne got Clarissa settled into bed, casually said good night, and returned to the living room, leaving the bedroom door half-open. She kept finding herself making compromises like that: Should she talk to Clarissa or leave her alone? Play music or turn on the television? Offer her something to eat or drink or just show her where the kitchen was? The house must be very strange for Clarissa, Anne wanted to comfort her, but obviously she couldn't kiss her good night or tuck her in. Anne had wanted a child, but not a sixteen-year-old. Having the girl there made Anne feel uncomfortable in her own home.

That slight itchiness of the nerves kept her awake for a long time after she went to bed herself. She was just beginning to doze when the soft tread of feet produced a sinister, being-stalked dream that brought Anne awake with a sharp intake of breath. She remembered then that Clarissa might be the object of a criminal's wrath. Quietly, Anne put her feet to the floor and walked to her bedroom door.

A single lamp burned next to the sofa. Close beside it Clarissa's blond head bowed as if she were praying. Or crying. Anne stood for a long moment, not wanting to intrude on the girl, remembering one summer when her own mother had been sick and she'd gone to live with an aunt and uncle. Anne remembered suddenly the feeling of having no corner to herself, and wanting her solicitous aunt and uncle just to leave her alone. Probably Clarissa wanted the same thing. But Anne couldn't leave her there.

She walked out, not quietly, thinking of pretending she'd gotten up for a glass of water herself. *Oh, hi*, she could say casually. But as she moved across the floor Anne discarded that subterfuge, walked directly into the living room, and sat at the far side of the sofa.

Clarissa was hunched over a three-ring notebook with lined pages. "I felt like writing a poem," she said.

Anne just nodded. The girl sat unmoving. Anne said, "I'm sorry about this, Clarissa. Is there anything I can do?"

Clarissa didn't answer directly. Staring at the front door, her eyes lost in time but not tearful, she began talking quietly.

"We moved a lot. We've lived a lot of places. Sometimes it seemed like every few months Mom would get some idea, or . . . Kristen and I got good at packing for ourselves. We knew if we left anything behind it was gone. Then we'd be in some strange place, furnished apartment or somebody else's house. And half the time Mom would be out, finding a job or meeting whoever she'd gone to meet. The first few nights in a new place Kristen and I always slept in the same bed. Sometimes we didn't have any choice, but even if we did we'd sleep together. We didn't talk much. We didn't have to, we were thinking the same thoughts. But I got used to being in new places, it was no big thing for me. Kristen always took longer to get used to things. I felt sorry for her because she was littler, it must've been scary for her. I'd hug her and she'd go to sleep. After a couple of days it would be okay."

Obviously Clarissa missed those nights, missed holding her baby sister close to her. Anne Greenwald, psychiatrist, knew that there is nothing in this world so comforting as giving comfort.

Clarissa's notebook had slipped off her lap, she held her hands folded together in front of her. She gave a quick sidelong glance, showing she was aware of her audience, but she continued to look across the room. "Then three years ago when we moved here Mom got us a house of our own, where we each had a bedroom. I went to bed that first night and waited for Kristen to come to me. I was thirteen, she was eleven, and I remembered being eleven and comforting her to sleep at night when she was nine. And I remembered being nine when she was seven. I even remembered being four and Kristen was two, she could barely even talk, but she slept with me for the first couple of nights.

"Maybe Kristen was thinking about the same thing too, that she was older than I'd been when I started being the big sister. Anyway, she never came to my room. I finally went to check on her and she was asleep. I felt kind of strange, like she'd . . ."

Anne almost suggested an ending for this sentence: *graduated*, or *said she didn't need me anymore*. Instead she let a silence pass and said, "I know how that feels, being left behind."

Now, in this new place, Clarissa obviously still waited for the padding of her little sister's feet coming to her bed. Maybe she even imagined the sound.

Taking a giant risk, Anne moved over a few feet on the couch and put her arms around the girl. The loose hug felt amazingly good. Clarissa leaned her head back on Anne's shoulder for a moment, then said, "I'm okay."

But she didn't pull away.

When Anne did stand up, Clarissa looked uncertain. "Should I—?"

"Stay there if you want. Clarissa, as long as you're here this is your home, too. You can do what you want, within reason. I'm not going to tell you to stay in your room, or stay out of mine. It's your house, all right?"

Clarissa smiled slyly. "So you have nothing to hide?"

"Oh sure, plenty. But nothing somebody could find by rummaging around in my drawers and cabinets."

The girl smiled. Anne went back to bed, feeling a small

sense of having successfully offered comfort. Maybe Clarissa would go poking through the closets and shelves in the next few days. Anne had forgotten her one secret from the world that could be discovered by an explorer of her cabinets.

Ten

Chris received a phone call at his desk from his investigator, Olga Zamora. She sounded furtive, as if afraid of being overheard, but that may have become habitual with Olga because she'd been playing a teenager.

"Chris, I've found out more about that party the night of October twenty-fifth, the day Kristen disappeared. A girl showed up at the party. I think it was her. Some time later Pentell came, too. We can put them in the same room the night she disappeared."

Chris stood up immediately. "I'll get Jack on this. What was the name of the restaurant again?"

"La Coterie. Chris, one more thing. I think your girl Clarissa was at that party, too."

"All right." Chris managed to sound unconcerned, but his hand trembled slightly as he set the receiver down. He had hoped all along that Clarissa had been far, far away from the scene of Kristen's last night on earth.

Raleigh Pentell's world had been deadly even before Kristen Lorenz had wandered into it. Chris hadn't forgotten the murdered drug dealer, Johnny Garcia, he'd been investigating at the medical examiner's office the first day he'd seen the modeled head of Kristen. Chris still pursued the links from that murder to his former Mr. Big, who now had a name and an indictment.

"We can put him on the fringe of that crowd, certainly," Jack Fine said as he and Chris sat in a car parked behind a Target store a few blocks from Holmes High School. Olga Zamora sat in the backseat. She still looked very young, in her dress and in a certain vivaciousness, even as she discussed murder and conspiracy.

"I think so," she agreed about the murdered drug dealer. "But the dealer's name, Johnny Garcia, doesn't mean much to the kids I've asked, and I can hardly show them a mug shot and ask them to ID him. I think that's who they're talking about, though. They saw him some time."

"He was Pentell's supplier and he tried to squeeze Pentell for a piece of the other action, so Pentell killed him," Jack said with the confidence of a veteran investigator used to making leaps of imagination from bits of information. Olga showed a trace of the same expression.

Chris remained skeptical. "We say that, but what does it mean? *Who* killed him? Pentell himself? I don't think so. One of the kids?" Chris's doubts struck at the heart of his murder case against Pentell. Jean had told him, or hinted strongly, that Pentell had murdered her daughter. But why would he have gotten so personal that one time, when his habit was to do things from afar?

"Do we have a schedule of what Pentell did the day Kristen Lorenz was murdered?"

"I know what day your witness Jean says she disappeared," Jack said. He flipped open a spiral notebook. "From Olga we found out about the party that night, October twenty-fifth. It was like the later party in the house in Terrell Hills, but this one was in a public place, the party room of a restaurant. Peter Belasco was showing off again, showing the boys what the good life was like. It seems the victim, Kristen, came there uninvited. Pentell showed up there too, later on. People from the straight world tell us that: waiters and the maître d'."

"You obviously haven't known too many waiters," Olga laughed from the backseat.

Jack ignored her. "That's all we know that night. The next day I've got about half a schedule. Pentell got his hair cut, he had lunch in a restaurant downtown with a business associate, he went home for the rest of the day. As far as I know. Of course I don't have a witness to say if anybody visited the house or if Pentell went somewhere else that night. Nowhere public, that I can tell." Jack flipped a page of the notebook. "By the way, he started going to a different place to get his hair cut after that day."

Chris's eyes widened, but Jack had already investigated that curiosity, of course. "We questioned everybody there. He didn't say anything weird, or act strange at all. Not that anybody remembers. Nothing incriminating fell out of his hair."

"Maybe he just got a creepy feeling about the place," Olga suggested, "going there the day after he'd murdered a little girl. Maybe he saw her face in the mirrors, or heard her voice. With the scissors clicking close to his ear . . ."

Olga gave a little shiver, like a teenage girl who'd spooked herself. "Yeah," Jack said, "let me make a note to go back and ask the haircutter if Pentell wet himself during that last visit."

But Chris was glad that Olga Zamora still had the imagination and the empathy to frighten herself with the thought of murder. "Want us to drop you off?" Chris offered, and she quickly replied, "You kidding?" Somehow he knew she was less afraid of blowing her cover than of being seen with two such squares. She got out and walked confidently away, hugging her schoolbooks to her chest.

Jack also turned to watch her go. "I've got other folks

to talk to, too," he said over his shoulder to Chris. "What about you?"

"Peter Belasco one more time," Chris said. "Make sure he's going to be a witness for us."

"You won't know for sure even when he takes the stand," Jack said, an unfortunately accurate observation.

Nonetheless, Chris returned to jail.

Peter Belasco didn't need much convincing, which made Chris uneasy. Almost as soon as the young man walked into the jail office in his orange coverall he started talking like a member of the prosecution team. "Johnny Garcia?" he said casually. "Oh yeah, that was Pentell's hit. Johnny wanted too much. Course, anything was too much for Raleigh. He didn't hold on to partners long. He wanted Johnny's piece of the action anyway. That was Raleigh's way, learn a new kind of business from somebody, then take him out of the picture. He didn't like paying middle-men. Raleigh definitely hit Johnny Garcia."

"Personally?"

Belasco shrugged. "Wasn't me."

Without naming names or being specific, Belasco described the changing alliances and shifts in power one had to ride to be an "associate" of Raleigh Pentell's. It could have been lifted from TV shows, but Chris found the tale believable. Belasco's story had another indicator of credibility: the tale explained its own telling. No one, even those supposedly deep inside, ever got into their leader's mind. They never knew who might be out of favor next. And being in disgrace usually meant one step from dead. Belasco had already turned on Pentell. Pentell would know it. There'd be no chance of Belasco's working his way back into favor. Peter Belasco's only choice had become open antagonism to his boss.

And there remained the shards of the business to pick up.

"What was going on?" Chris asked. "Something more

than shoplifting and marijuana. That wouldn't pay for what I've seen."

"Hey, some of those jobs were a lot more than shoplifting," Belasco said with odd defensiveness. "Hitting a warehouse for a whole truckload of computers, reselling them a few at a time . . . The thieving paid off, believe me. But you're right, Raleigh was on to something new, that was sure, but he wasn't sharing with anybody. He used at least a couple of the kids, and somebody else. It involved computer records, somebody getting into official records and changing them somehow. He was like farming out the pieces, so nobody'd know the whole scheme."

Chris sat on the deputy's desk in the small office where everything looked metallic. Peter Belasco seemed wired as well. He snapped his fingers while trying to think, his eyes moved jerkily around the sparsely furnished room, not finding anything he sought. "Who would've known besides you?" Chris asked.

Belasco shook his head gloomily, his expression betraying a hint of jealousy. "Only somebody who could put it all together. Maybe that Ryan McClain, Raleigh seemed to use him for errands more than anybody. At first he went through me, but then that stopped. Of course, I guess young Ryan didn't work out for him either." Belasco grinned, sounding like a jealous lover.

Chris had had enough of Peter Belasco. He headed toward the office door to call the guard, but Belasco stopped him with a tight grip on Chris's arm and a stare more intense than he'd displayed before. Sweat stood out on Peter Belasco's unlined forehead, as if the interview had been a great strain for him. "You know why I'm doing this?" he asked.

"Yeah. I know."

"No you don't." Belasco's eyes gripped Chris's, trying to convey sincerity and managing instead an odd fright. "Because you think I killed that girl and I didn't. I would never have been in on something like that. If Raleigh'd told me to do it I wouldn't have. Stealing stuff, who cares? People should take better care of their stuff. But killing little girls? Uh uh."

The moment of manly communion failed, as far as Chris was concerned. He knew from years of hearing stories like Peter Belasco's that people like him acted from impulse, not planning. Even when they claimed there were lines they wouldn't cross, somehow in those bad, confused nights the lines got crossed anyway. Chris nodded so that Belasco would let go of his arm, but his opinion of his new ally didn't rise a millimeter.

Weekends were hard on everybody. In a normal time, with a big trial coming up, Chris would have spent some time at the office, or gone personally to investigate a scene important to the trial. He would also have gone out with Anne. Now, though, he wanted to spend as much uninterrupted time with Clarissa as possible, not knowing how long he might have her close. Clarissa wanted to see him, her friends, and her mother. Jean insisted on having her for a while. Anne wanted both to be with Chris and to stay out of the way of his developing relationship with Clarissa. They were all torn a variety of ways.

It was a Saturday morning in April, still cool in the morning, one of the best days of the year in San Antonio. Chris showed up early on Anne's doorstep, wearing jeans and tennis shoes and a black T-shirt. Anne smiled at seeing him, then gave his outfit an appraising stare. "Are you trying to be cool and hip?"

"Naw, it just comes naturally to me, I don't have to try."

He stepped inside and called, "Clarissa?" but Anne shushed him.

"She's still asleep."

"You're kidding. On a morning like this?" Chris walked quickly to the bedroom door, knocked, and at the sound of a mumble threw the door open. The rumpled twin bed in the corner was empty. Clarissa sat across the room from it at the computer. She turned, smiled hugely at Chris, cleared the screen of her work, and ran toward the doorway, but then stopped short, suddenly shy. Chris pulled her in for a hug, and she responded gratefully.

"Let's go for a breakfast picnic," he said.

"Fine," Anne responded quickly. "You two go ahead, I've got some work I can do around here."

But Clarissa stepped around Chris and said to her quietly, "You come, too. Please?"

Anne and the girl looked at each other while Chris pretended not to study them together, feeling excluded. Anne shrugged, not to make too big a deal of the moment.

So twenty minutes later the three of them sailed out of the drive-through of Jack in the Box, smells of eggs and English muffins filling the car. Food in the car would have made Chris feel very young, except for the genuinely young girl beside him. Clarissa sat with a foot up on the dashboard and an orange juice in her hands, yawning and staring around curiously, as if Saturday mornings were a mystery to her.

Anne lay stretched out sleepily across the backseat, a cardboard cup of coffee resting on her stomach. Without looking out, she asked, "Brackenridge Park?"

"That's for tourists," Chris answered. He turned off Broadway onto Hildebrand, crossed Highway 281, and plunged into Olmos Park. The tall oaks and pecan trees seemed very leafy and overwhelming, still bearing traces of spring's bright green. If they only looked in certain directions and ignored the soccer and baseball fields, they could have left the city behind them.

"Where is this?" Clarissa asked. That's what Chris wanted, to introduce her to something unknown. "Place I used to go when I was your age," he said casually.

He drove past the Alamo Heights swimming pool, not yet open for the season, and pulled to a stop in a circular parking lot behind the pool. A small brick house like a park ranger's information shack marked the entrance to a sort of park within the park, but the shack stood closed up tight, and a sign proclaimed that the Nature Trails were closed, too.

"Closed?" Chris said with evident irritation.

"What?" Anne sat up in the backseat. "Where are we?"

"You don't know this place either?" Clarissa asked, obviously gratified that Chris had never brought Anne here before, either.

They followed Chris out of the car and looked at the woods as he did. Hands on his hips, Chris said disgustedly, "Lawyers are responsible for this. The city doesn't want to be liable for kids going in here anymore, so they call it closed."

"Did you used to spend time here?" Clarissa asked.

"Yeah. Come on, let's go."

"But it says closed," the girl protested.

"You can't close woods. Come on. We might get arrested, but I can pretty much guarantee we won't be prosecuted."

He gathered up the fast food breakfast and walked quickly around the small brick shack. Clarissa followed slowly, looking around. For a girl with her background, she seemed amazingly reluctant to trespass. But Chris was right, there was no obstruction to their entering the woods. There was even an asphalt path that had begun to decompose, blending into the dirt under the trees. In a few steps they found themselves surrounded by nature: tall trees, creeping vines, insects, squirrels, and from somewhere the trickle of running water.

The trees were mostly oaks, tall and twisted. Chris remembered these woods as having been better maintained, but now the area had grown wilder: fallen branches lay everywhere, some of them as large as small trees themselves. They stepped carefully. Chris began to breathe deeply. Clarissa, too, looked around more curiously than fearfully. Anne straggled behind, pretending to find the path slow going but in fact trying to leave Chris and Clarissa alone.

The Nature Trails seemed to go on and on, a miniature

forest in the heart of the city. "You used to come here?" Clarissa asked again, and Chris smiled, feeling proprietary.

"We'd ride our bikes here, up and down these little hills, trying to take off like Evel Knievel, you know, until somebody scraped a knee or popped a tire. You have a bicycle, Clarissa?"

She shook her head. "I have a driver's license."

So Jean had neglected bicycles among other things. Chris felt suddenly saddened. He could close his eyes and feel the wind tugging at his hair and clothes as he flew along these trails.

In the approximate middle of the Nature Trails grew a gigantic oak tree that started out at a sixty-degree angle from the ground before turning and soaring skyward. Chris sat at its base and opened the Jack in the Box bags. Clarissa accepted a Breakfast Jack but remained standing, looking around.

"Where's Anne?"

"She's all right," Chris said, having a good idea that Anne had deliberately left them. But he remembered Raleigh Pentell and for a moment stared around more alertly.

"Mom and Kristen and me were never too big on parks," Clarissa said suddenly. "We do our hiking in malls."

"Really? I'm surprised. Your mother used to like going out in the woods."

Clarissa suddenly crouched in front of him, a light of deep, long-repressed curiosity revealing itself in her eyes. "When was that?"

"When we were in college." Chris said it easily. He didn't want to hide things from Clarissa, but he didn't want to talk in much detail about his and Jean's mutual past, either.

"In Austin?" Clarissa's eager voice made the city sound like a mythical place.

Chris nodded. "I didn't really know your mother very

long. But it seems like we did a lot. Armadillo World Headquarters—that was a music place—the Pedernales River, the Drag." *Lying in bed in Jean's room feeling high above the town, and sometimes higher than other times.*

"She was very special," he said quietly.

Clarissa sat and stretched out her legs. "Sometimes she seems like anybody else's mother—you know, do your homework, go to bed—but other times I think maybe she's this wild woman, or was, or, you know, did things nobody else's mom ever did."

"Well, I wouldn't say that." Actually, he would have, to someone else. Clarissa had used the exact word he'd often thought of to describe Jean: "wild," as if she were a native of a country with entirely different customs. "But she did go her own way. She didn't worry too much what other people thought."

Clarissa looked thoughtful. No telling how she was taking this description of her young mother. Nobody wants a wild thing for a parent; kids want their parents to be straight-ahead average. Most kids, anyway.

"I can see her in you," Chris said quietly. That was what worried him, but he said it as a compliment, and Clarissa smiled slowly and shyly. They walked for a while without talking much, but companionably watchful in the woods, Chris occasionally pointing out a squirrel or a place where the path had gone steeply down, out from under his bicycle tires. The woods seemed timeless; it was a rare occasion when he and Clarissa didn't feel bowed by the pressure of getting to know each other, so that after a while it seemed quite natural for him to put his arm around her shoulders.

"This is an amazing place," Clarissa said wonderingly. "Your own private woods. Even with a sign telling people to stay out. It's like magic. A secret place. Nobody could find us here."

"I've thought of that. If I ever lose my job and have to learn to live off the land."

"This is like where Kristen was buried, but better. Kristen would like this place. We should . . ." Clarissa said, her voice trailing off as she stared around.

"You've seen where she was buried?" Chris asked.

Clarissa answered slowly, as if still infected by the spirit of the woods. "After they told us where she'd been found, Mom and I went to look. We wanted to see . . . what the place was like. Stupid, you know, but we wanted to know if it was an okay place."

Chris, feeling the woods turn colder, didn't answer. The Nature Trails for a moment turned more sinister. He remembered that Raleigh Pentell's killers were looking for Clarissa, and the woods didn't seem sanctuary enough.

But Clarissa seemed enchanted by the place. "I want to come back here again," she said softly, almost to herself. "I want to live here." For a girl who'd done all her hiking in malls, she'd developed a rapid appreciation for nature. Chris wondered if Clarissa's reaction was due partly to the fact that he had brought her here, which made the Nature Trails their place.

"What about your mom?" Chris asked, meaning he couldn't picture Jean living in the woods.

"Yeah, she'd find me," Clarissa said softly, in a tone he couldn't decipher.

Soon they turned back in the direction from which they'd come and went seriously searching for Anne, but couldn't find her. "Do you think she went back to the car?" Chris asked, beginning to worry.

"Only a wimp would do that," came Anne's voice, but they still didn't see her, until a sprinkling of twigs rained down on them. They looked up to see Anne sitting comfortably on a branch ten feet over their heads, sipping her coffee.

"People never look up," she said in a self-satisfied way.

"What are you doing?" Clarissa asked. Obviously it had never occurred to her that trees could be climbed.

"I used to be famous for this," Anne mused, staring out through the treetops. "I would've stayed in Girl Scouts if they'd had a merit badge for tree-climbing. Thanks for bringing us here, Chris, I'd forgotten what this was like."

Chris felt slightly upstaged in his own setting. Clarissa looked at him ironically and he knew what she was thinking: *Still attracted to wild women, huh?* Chris laughed and gave her a quick hug and Clarissa laughed, too.

Anne, listening from above, didn't know what amused them, but felt glad they'd found something in common.

Chris's office felt strange to him. He should have spent long hours there every day, administering the huge law firm that was the District Attorney's Office. But these days he felt that time in his office represented a retreat from the real world. Sitting at his desk he could picture across the room, as if in an old home movie, Clarissa on the brink of tears, huddling into him as she had in Raleigh Pentell's house. Now she was in school, with kids staring at her covertly or openly, turning her into a refugee. Chris wasn't getting any work done anyway, he might as well cruise over to—

His phone rang. His secretary Irma Garcia said, "Some kid on line three," and Chris immediately took the call, expecting to hear Clarissa calling for help. But instead a boy's voice said, "Sir?"

"Yes?"

"This is—somebody who knew Kristen Lorenz."

The boy's decision to make the call anonymous sounded spontaneous. It didn't matter; Chris recognized the voice of Jason Luling, the boy he'd interviewed once already about Kristen. The boy should have known that identifying himself as a friend of Kristen's almost revealed his identity anyway. Hardly anyone had known her. "Yes," Chris said kindly. "What do you want to tell me?"

"I'm not sure." The boy's voice came thinly over the phone line, as if he'd turned his head away. Chris wondered where he was calling from at two o'clock in the afternoon. "Just—I just want to tell you about her."

"Good. Would you like me to meet you—"

"No. This is fine. What I want to tell you, the main thing is—" The boy stopped, then blurted out, "Kristen was very worried about her sister Clarissa, about something she thought Clarissa was getting involved in."

"I see."

"She loved Clarissa, sir. She idolized her. But she thought she had to save her, too."

This wasn't exactly a revelation for Chris, but he was glad to hear it from somewhere else. "Kristen told you this?"

"Yes sir. And she wrote it in her diary."

So Jason Luling was Chris's E-mail correspondent. How did he come to have Kristen's diary? Had she given it to him on the last night of her life, having a premonition that she needed to leave a record? That meant Jason had seen her that night. "You have her diary?" Chris asked quietly. "I need to see it. Let's—"

"Just a couple of pages of it," the boy said quickly. "Kristen gave me copies of these two pages. She wanted to tell me what she was thinking, but she didn't like to say it."

And in giving Jason a portion of her diary Kristen had been making an intimate gesture. Chris could picture that. On the other hand, the boy might be lying, he might have the whole diary but not want to tell the District Attorney.

"I need to see those couple of pages, Jason. They're evidence. You understand I'm trying to put someone in prison for killing Kristen?"

Chris had let slip that he knew the boy's identity, but it didn't impede the conversation. Jason sounded relieved of responsibility when he spoke again. "There's a Kinko's down the street. I could fax them to you after school."

"All right. And take very good care of them."

Chris knew the boy would. They were all that remained to him of Kristen. The pages might be evidence as Chris had said, but they were also surely treasured keepsakes.

Late that afternoon Irma Garcia came into Chris's office with two faxed pages. Chris took them and began reading eagerly. The pages were small, from the kind of bound blank book that could be bought anywhere. They didn't hold much, but it was in Kristen's own handwriting. Chris had gotten messages from the diary, but this was the first time he'd seen the real pages, albeit in a fax from a copy. Kristen had written in large, loopy letters, though the words sometimes got cramped at the ends of lines. He could picture the girl writing these words, thoughtfully but in secretive haste. The first page began in mid-sentence:

> talk to Mom, but she'd never understand being worried about Clarissa. She expects us to be so independent. I think that's what Clarissa's doing, trying to live up to Mom. I try to warn her, but Clarissa would never listen to me, I'm just the baby sister. If I tell her I'm afraid that would just make Clarissa do more of it, to show me it's not anything to be afraid of. Is she really so brave, or does she have to put on a show for me, and for Mom too?

That ended Kristen's thought. The next entry began under a new day:

> I went to church with Jason's family. Church isn't like I thought, all boring preaching. It's nice, it's so pretty, and everybody seems happy to be there. I like church. It was scary, wondering if I'd make a mistake in the liturgy or something, but I'm glad Jason asked me. For a lot of reasons.

It ended there, coyly, showing Kristen's incentive for giving Jason these pages, a shyly directed thank-you note. No wonder the boy missed her so much. Kristen had begun to offer herself to him as much as she could.

So she'd even started going to church. Growing up in Jean's restless, rule-less household, Kristen had begun a transformation in the opposite direction. In other circumstances Chris would have found it funny to picture Jean dealing with this teenage rebellion. The qualities that had attracted a teenaged Chris to Jean—her independence and wildness—wouldn't make her the best of mothers. It must have baffled Jean to have a daughter developing a belief in right and wrong. Church indeed. Where do you get these crazy ideas, girl? Kids today, I swear.

And depending how deeply Jean and her girls had been involved in Raleigh Pentell's underworld, Kristen's burgeoning morality could have scared the hell out of other people.

Jean opened her front door with a wide smile on her face, causing Chris a startling moment of *déjà vu*. He'd seen her like this, fevered with the desire to smash a new idea down on his head. In love with her own mind as much as with him. Jean's smile had always given him a trickle along the spine, down in the nerves where fearfulness felt the same as delight.

But today Chris's arrival didn't inspire Jean's smile. He felt his temperature fall as her face did at the sight of Chris alone on her front porch.

"Where's Clarissa?"

"She'll be along in a few minutes. I wanted to talk to you first."

Jean folded her arms. "It's more trouble than you thought, isn't it, taking care of a child every day?"

"No, it's—" Chris almost said, *It's wonderful*, but stopped short of sharing so much with Jean. "—it's not bad at all."

He walked past Jean so that she had little choice but to close the door and follow him inside. The living room with its sparse, angular style, "modern" in an old-fashioned sense, looked fake to him, a stage set that could be struck at a moment's notice and loaded into a truck headed for another town. Had the girls felt that impermanence about their lives?

Chris stood formally, intending to look official in his dark suit. He thought he had a motive for Kristen's murder now. "You wanted to help me but you hid the truth from me as much as you could," he said.

Jean looked at him with no emotion more evident than annoyance. He didn't scare her. Chris said, "This insurance company you work for, that's bullshit, isn't it?"

"Gee, I hope not. Everybody says what a good company it is. I thought I had a future there. Do you know something I—?"

"You've never had a future, Jean. Not one you planned. I've checked your employment history. It's rather spotty."

"It's true I've had trouble finding my way. My education got cut short—"

Chris refused to take blame. He pressed her harder. "You forget I knew you, Jean. You were a born dropout. You laughed at people who did things the hard way. This insurance job was just a front, like your other jobs. What were you going to do, work there forty or fifty hours a week for twenty years until you earned a pension? Give me a break. You were learning the operation so you could rip them off. Before this you worked at a computer company—for a few months. Then someone robbed them of a big shipment and you quit. You didn't need to work there anymore. That's how Raleigh Pentell operated. Isn't it?"

He'd managed to change Jean's face and win her full attention. Her tongue moistened the center of her upper lip, but she only said, "I wouldn't know."

Chris brushed past her, on his way out of her house. Jean saw his disgust. She grabbed his arm. Chris looked at her coolly and she said, "Maybe I did help a little."

"My God, I should indict you, too. Those boys knew you. You helped recruit them, didn't you?"

"No."

Picturing Jean as a seductress of teenage boys required no imagination on his part. The image devalued his own memories. He wanted to believe her denial but didn't. He turned away.

Again Jean stopped him. She stared at him intently, dipping into their common past. "Believe me, Chris, it wasn't like that. I wasn't a den mother to those boys. That was something completely separate. I didn't even like Clarissa going out with one of them."

So she knew that Ryan McClain had been part of Pentell's crew. Chris said, "If I reach that door I'm gone. You're on your own. Stop lying to me. My God, Jean, whatever you were involved in got your own daughter killed! Don't you understand that yet? Do you want me to be able to convict the man who killed Kristen? Tell me how it worked."

He could see her thinking. Chris shook his head at her to tell her that lying wouldn't work. But habits become character. Lying wasn't just a pose for Jean. She had to change into a wholly other person in order to tell him the truth. After a moment her shoulders dropped, and she seemed to do so. She looked younger and softer, and more than a little scared.

"All right. The boys stole things Raleigh could resell. They worked their way up to big stuff, where Raleigh needed someone on the inside of the company to tell him when a shipment had come in and where it was stored."

"Security?"

"You'd be surprised. Half a million dollars in computer equipment stored in a warehouse without live guards. Just monitors on the walls that the boys would know how to disable."

Chris looked skeptical. Jean shrugged at him. "Or maybe Raleigh'd bought off the guards or had somebody in the security company rerouting them. I don't know.

Nobody knew every bit of the business, that was Raleigh's thing. Only he could know the whole picture. That's why he used kids, they'd pass on and somebody new would take their place and nobody knew enough to give away the whole operation."

How that must have galled Jean. It had taken her more than fifteen years in the underworld to run up against someone who might be smarter than she was. Or who, at any rate, knew more.

"What happened to the boys who graduated? Why did he trust them to keep quiet?"

"Raleigh trust?" Jean laughed harshly, folding her arms. "The boys committed the crimes, they'd be in trouble themselves if they gave anything away. And of course he stayed away from them; they couldn't give Raleigh away."

"What about this car wreck Ryan McClain staged? Tell me the truth, Jean, because I think I know."

She stared at him hostilely. "I thought you said you were trying to find out why Raleigh Pentell killed Kristen."

"I think it's all related. Tell me. Two of the boys had a wreck. Police came and filed a report on it. A car got totaled and someone claimed to be injured, right? And the car was insured."

After a moment Jean said flatly, "Both cars. On paper the injuries looked bad enough to pay out the limit of the liability coverage. Twenty thousand dollars."

Small change for Raleigh Pentell, but it had only been a test run. If Jean could change the insurance company's computer records to reroute the payoff in this small case, she could do it again later. Raleigh Pentell had been forging the perfect crime: no heavy lifting, very few accomplices, with almost nothing existing except on microchips. Next time around he'd probably try the scam with no physical evidence at all, just reports on paper and computer entries.

And Jean the major player.

She watched him without pride or evasion. "He had my daughter, would you remember that?" she said to Chris.

He remembered. "Which reminds me. How did Clarissa know to call me from Raleigh Pentell's house? Did she just look up the District Attorney in the phone book?"

Jean looked a little coy. "I may have mentioned that I knew you, one of those times when we saw you on the news."

Chris wanted to know exactly what she'd told Clarissa, but didn't press her. Maybe Jean had decided to aim Clarissa at him, thinking it would be nice to have the DA on her side if she ever needed him. If so, that had worked. The relationship between Chris and Clarissa had begun in crisis, but had continued to grow stronger, at least on Chris's part.

Shifting the questioning, he said suddenly, "Do you have any amphetamines around here? Diet pills or something that Kristen might have gotten into before she went to that party at the restaurant?"

Jean shook her head quickly. "I'd never have anything like that in the house."

Her denial sounded sincere, but Chris's faith had vanished. "I wish I could believe anything you tell me," he said, and began walking toward the door. "Wait," Jean begged him. "Wait." She sounded frantic. Chris looked back and saw a stricken expression on her face. For the first time in his experience, Jean looked like a woman who needed comforting. Chris watched her cry, immobilized by conflicting desires. Jean looked so alone, as she had been all these years when he hadn't known her. Alone with her children.

Even as he longed toward her, he resisted. "Tell me one true thing," he challenged her.

Jean's tears stopped. In a matter of moments she pulled herself together. Her shoulders drew apart. "I love my daughter," she said quietly.

Chris did believe that. It was the only thing he and Jean had in common anymore. He began walking again.

As he opened the front door Jean said quietly, "My parents took me out of school after that spring."

She'd caught him unguarded. "What?"

"After those few months when you and I were together, Chris. They didn't like that I didn't come home for the summer, they came to visit me in Austin and by that time I was showing. They took me out of school and made me go stay with them until the baby was born. Clarissa."

Chris stood rigidly, feeling chilled all over. Jean was explaining why she'd left him. It hadn't been her choice. He couldn't imagine Jean, even at nineteen, being told what to do by her parents, like a child. But she had been very vulnerable. Maybe it had been a great relief to let her parents take over. Jean hadn't just run out on Chris.

But she hadn't thought much of him either. Jean must have pondered her choices, and Chris had been one she dismissed. In that crisis she had thought he couldn't be much help to her. Even perhaps wouldn't help.

Chris couldn't even say what he would have done sixteen years ago. He only knew what he would do now.

He felt like crying. He wanted to hold Jean close, and he wanted to choke her. Jean saw that she had shaken him. She said, very softly, "You know she's yours, don't you, Chris? Help me protect her."

That was what mattered now. Clarissa. He couldn't revive a life with Jean. That possibility was lost. But Chris intended to do what Jean asked, protect their daughter. He intended to save Clarissa from Jean.

He closed her front door behind him.

Eleven

In the courtroom Chris Sinclair became the District Attorney of Bexar County again. Trial settled around him like the opening notes of an old favorite song. As the jury panel filtered into the court Chris's pulse speeded up but his breathing deepened. He looked at individual faces, beginning to evaluate and to make connections. Twelve of these people would decide a case that was more personally important to Chris than any he had ever tried. And personal connections to the jury would matter, because Chris had also never begun a trial as ill-prepared as he felt for this one. A prosecution should be a tale, logical in its transitions and compelling in its conclusion. Chris's story remained incomplete. He had unreliable witnesses, gaps in his narrative, and a formidable opponent in Raleigh Pentell's defense lawyer Lowell Burke.

In spite of all the problems, Chris wanted to begin the trial. In place of a complete investigation he had a feeling of kinship with the victim. He thought that in many ways he knew Kristen Lorenz better than anyone who'd known her alive. He sensed her presence beside him at the prosecution table. Analytical, practical Chris Sinclair had never had this feeling before, certainly never entered a trial with it: the feeling that he had a spirit guide.

He was first struck by the feeling that he harbored more emotions than his own when the defendant entered the courtroom. The opening of the heavy courtroom doors drew Chris's attention, and when Raleigh Pentell stepped through Chris went stiff with fear. This had not been Chris's reaction at Pentell's house, where Pentell had been backed up by armed men. On that occasion Chris had wanted to go for his throat. But in the courtroom as Pentell walked toward him, the defendant looked frightening. Tall, broad-shouldered, and favored by the sun, Pentell had the look of a Texas land baron. He had not dressed down for this occasion. His dark suit was quietly elegant, announcing its price in its perfect tailoring. Pentell wore a crisp white shirt, a soft blue tie, and an expression of pensive impatience, as if he took the trial seriously but wanted it to be over.

As Chris began to master the unexplained fear Pentell's appearance inspired in him, his gaze went to the defendant's hands. Pentell had large hands, but not threatening ones. They were long-fingered, not roughened by ugly work, the nails gleaming very quietly in a well-tended way. But that was where the fear that had invaded Chris lurked: in Pentell's hands.

"Hello, Chris," defense lawyer Lowell Burke said, extending his hand. To Chris's relief, the defendant didn't offer to shake hands. He only nodded brusquely, as at someone he knew would be bidding against him for an important contract. Chris looked at him, feeling the fear recede. Pentell had an air of complete confidence, as if he would always find a way to win. He took his seat and sat silent, trusting his lawyer.

His trust was not misplaced. Lowell Burke, of the thick wavy hair, broad tanned face, and quick smile, had been charming juries and intimidating judges in San Antonio for decades. The odds are always against the defense in

criminal trials—most defendants are obviously guilty
and the State can dismiss the hard-to-prove cases—but
when Lowell Burke took a case to trial rather than plea-
bargaining it out, the prosecutors knew they were in for
surprises, unexpected defense evidence, or if nothing else
a slow, careful, battering of the State's case.

Judge Paul Benitez, always soft-spoken but quite
clearly in charge of his court, gave the jury panel his low-
key instructions, emphasizing that the attorneys could not
relay during jury selection any specific facts of the case
they would be presenting in trial. But Chris Sinclair and
Lowell Burke both knew ways of skirting this restriction.

Lowell Burke smiled and asked of one potential juror,
"Do you read murder mysteries, ma'am?"

The lady, a white woman in her fifties who looked as if
she might well be a fan of Agatha Christie or Mary Hig-
gins Clark, said slowly, "Yes sir, sometimes."

"Now you see," Burke confided to the panel at large,
while still speaking directly to the woman, "already I
don't want you on this jury. Because you've been trained
to expect neat solutions to mysteries. Police officers like
solutions like that too, and so does this man here." Pointing at Chris, who sat impassively. "But the truth is, some
murders don't have tidy solutions, and if they look like
they do it's because police and prosecutors have neatened
up the facts considerably. I'm not accusing anyone." He
quickly held up a hand, looking like a supporter of law
enforcement. "I count many police officers among my
friends, I've even represented a few, and I was a prosecutor myself for a long time in my younger years. I'm not
accusing people of falsifying evidence, I'm talking about
the way people think in those jobs. How they'll want you
to think, too. If they can cast suspicion on one person,
then show he had opportunity to commit this crime, they
trust you to leap to the conclusion they think is obvious.
When the fact is, they don't know what happened, my
client doesn't know, and at the end of this trial *you* won't

know. And what I want to ask you, ma'am, is this: if the prosecution doesn't prove its case thoroughly, beyond a reasonable doubt, will you do their job for them?"

"No sir," the lady said with a firm voice. In fact, this lady wouldn't get the chance to vote one way or another, she was too far down the list of potential jurors, but the defense lawyer had used her to implant the idea in everyone who would serve on the jury that the prosecution's case was not to be trusted.

Unfortunately, Chris didn't have the evidence to overcome such a suspicion. In vague terms, Burke had described the prosecution case very well.

Chris left most of the questioning of prospective jurors to his young assistant George Stiegers, whose basic decency came across well in his clear, simple questions and the way he listened attentively to answers. Jurors liked George; that had helped him send a lot of men to prison in his relatively short prosecution career. Chris only injected an occasional question, such as after a civil service worker in his forties said that his previous career had been as a high school teacher.

"Why did you quit?" Chris asked curiously.

"A lot of good teachers do, sooner or later," the man replied rather mournfully.

"I've noticed that. Why is that?"

"The kids. I love working with kids, I still spend my Saturdays at the community center coaching basketball. But they're just too hard to deal with day in and day out. One day I found myself about to throw an arrogant little fifteen-year-old snot across the room. I knew it was time to quit."

"Thank you, sir," Chris said, and a little later threw Lowell Burke his first surprise of the trial by not striking the former teacher from the jury. The defense lawyer expected the prosecution to hang much of its case on sympathy for the young victim, so had expected the prosecutor to strike a man with an expressed dislike for certain teenagers. But Chris wanted someone on the jury who understood how a kid could goad a grown man into murderous impulses.

The former teacher sat in the middle of the back row of twelve jurors, looking attentive but not happy to be there. A good expression for a juror. Surrounding him were three Mexican-American women ranging from a young secretary to a grandmother of sixty-eight, two middle-aged Anglo women, two African-American women, and four men equally split between working and professional classes. Chris had wanted parents on the jury and in eight of the twelve jurors he'd gotten his wish. As always, there were at least a couple of jurors who worried him. He hoped the same was true of the defense. Lowell Burke beamed at the jurors being sworn in as if he had personally invited them to the trial.

George Stiegers read the indictment accusing Raleigh Pentell of murdering Kristen Lorenz on a certain date in Bexar County. The defendant rose to respond:

"Not guilty, Your Honor."

The defense lawyer patted his client's arm reassuringly as Pentell resumed his seat, sitting tall. Judge Benitez, who had a boyish face but a strong chin and black eyes that seldom blinked, gave the jury rapid instructions, ending by introducing the lawyers and saying, "These men are very good attorneys. But you do not listen to them. You base your decision on what you hear from here." He pointed at the empty witness chair.

"Call your first witness, please, Mr. District Attorney."

"The State calls Jean Fitzgerald, Your Honor."

Immediately Jean entered the courtroom through the glass doors at the back, walked down the short center aisle, and through the gate in the railing. She passed Chris as if she didn't know him. Chris could barely remember her as his lover of years past. Jean wore a conservative cranberry-colored suit that made her look rather severe. Chris had no idea how she felt about him. Since their confrontation in Jean's house he and she had spoken only in the most professional way about what her role in the trial would be. He needed very little from her in the way of testimony, and didn't know if he would trust anything that came out of her mouth, in or out of a courtroom.

"Please state your name."

"Jean Fitzgerald." Jean spoke in a clear voice, looking at the jurors.

"Where do you live, Ms. Fitzgerald?" Chris saw no reason for anyone in the courtroom to know of his past relationship with Jean. The past that far back wasn't relevant. He would treat her as he would any other witness.

"In San Antonio."

"Do you have any children?"

"I have two daughters," Jean said firmly, emphasizing the present tense. "Clarissa and Kristen."

Jean sounded too tough. Chris would have liked more vulnerability from her, but he would never instruct any witness that way, particularly not this one. He stood and carried an eight-by-ten photograph to the witness stand.

"Can you identify this person pictured in State's Exhibit Number One?"

Jean took the photograph and looked at it quickly but fondly. "That's Kristen. Kristen Lorenz, my daughter. She was fourteen."

Chris had had the photo blown up from one Jean kept on her dresser at home, a picture showing Kristen turning her head, her profile looking surprised, her long neck rather fragile. He passed the picture to the jury and let them study it.

"When was the last time you saw Kristen, Ms. Fitzgerald?"

"On a Friday morning in October of last year. I saw her that morning before she went to school and I went to work. When I came home that evening she had left me a note saying she was leaving. She had taken a suitcase. I assumed she'd gone to visit her father, who lives in St. Louis."

"Why would she have done that?" Chris asked curiously. Jean shot him a sharp look before answering quietly.

"We had the usual mother-daughter problems. Anybody with a teenage daughter could tell you about them. Kristen was always saying she wanted to go live with her father. I assumed she had, and that I'd hear from him soon."

"Did you?"

"No. But that was just like Eddie. We don't talk, at all. He wouldn't take two minutes to tell me our daughter was okay."

"After that Friday in October, did you ever see Kristen again?"

"No," Jean said.

Chris had two more large photographs. He held them close to his chest, not displaying their contents, as he asked, "In January did you receive an official visitor?"

"Besides you, you mean?" Jean asked with a trace of humor.

"Yes ma'am, besides me."

"An investigator from the medical examiner's office brought me some things."

"Was that Monica Burris?"

"Yes."

Chris handed Jean the next photograph, a rather clinical one of a dress laid out on a cold steel table. "Did she ask you if you could identify these clothes?"

"Yes." Jean gave the photo a short, solemn study. "This is what Kristen was wearing that morning before she disappeared."

Chris nodded. Without preamble he passed Jean his last picture. She took it and looked at it in surprise. Chris hadn't told her she'd be seeing this in trial. Jean looked momentarily pleased, then just like a curtain passing over her face her expression turned downcast. The picture shook slightly in her hand. She set it down on the railing in front of her.

"Do you recognize what's portrayed in this picture?" Chris asked.

Jean cleared her throat. "Yes. It's Herbie. A little stuffed dog Kristen always carried and slept with. She called him Herbie." Jean said the name as if Herbie too had been a member of the family. Finally she wore the expression Chris as a prosecutor wanted. Her lip trembled and she put her hand in front of her mouth. Tears stood in her eyes.

Chris hammered it home. "Where's Herbie now?"

Jean tried to clear her throat again but couldn't completely. Her voice came out thickly. "We buried him with Kristen. She always—she always slept with him. We wanted her to have him."

A weighty silence filled the courtroom. Chris turned his back on his witness and walked to his seat, leaving Jean alone with her loss. He did not believe her capable of faking this. She had loved her daughter, there was no doubt of that. Everyone in the courtroom watched her sympathetically.

From his seat Chris said distinctly, "Do you know a man named Raleigh Pentell?"

Jean took charge of herself. "Yes."

"How do you know him?"

Jean shot Chris another sharp look, too quick for anyone else to see. "I met him through business," she said dismissively.

"Did your daughter Kristen know him?"

"Just slightly. She knew who he was."

"Did Kristen like Mr. Pentell?"

"Like?" Jean asked in surprise. She obviously wanted to ask a question herself. Instead she said, "I don't think she knew him well enough to have any opinion about him at all."

Chris nodded as if satisfied with the answer. Beside him, George Stiegers drew a large question mark on his legal pad. Chris ignored him and said, "I pass the witness."

Lowell Burke rose half out of his chair, leaned forward on his fists and said to Jean, "Ma'am, we are very sorry for your loss. All of us here are. I have no questions for this witness, Your Honor."

The soul of courtliness, Burke remained standing as Jean stepped down from the witness stand. He even moved quickly to hold open the gate in the railing for her. Chris remained seated, not looking at her as she passed. Jean took a seat in the audience.

Chris hadn't asked her the nature of her business with Raleigh Pentell, or about Pentell's abduction of her other daughter. Lowell Burke had filed a motion to exclude evidence of other crimes charged against the defendant, which Judge Benitez had granted, unless the other crimes became relevant somehow. So far Chris hadn't thought of a way around this ruling. This trial would just be about Kristen's murder.

George Stiegers questioned the ME's investigator Monica Burris about her investigation of the body in the shallow grave.

"What led you to that location, Ms. Burris?"

"Two people searching for a missing child reported seeing what they thought was a hand coming out of the ground."

"Can you describe the area for us?"

Monica Burris's quiet, authoritative testimony carried Chris back to the woods where Kristen's grave had been found. Outside Loop 1604, in roughly the same part of town as Raleigh Pentell's house, the house where Pentell had held Clarissa hostage to ensure her mother's silence about her missing daughter. It sounded now like the act of an irrational man. How long could Pentell have expected to hold Clarissa? Chris looked at the defendant sitting impassively beside his lawyer, listening to the testimony as if this were the first he'd heard of the shallow grave on the edge of town. Everything Chris had learned about this man told him that Pentell acted very carefully always. But he'd obviously been scrambling desperately the night

Kristen Lorenz disappeared. Anyone would say Pentell's actions indicated the panic after a crime. Whether the jury would call that proof beyond a reasonable doubt was another question. Nothing the investigator had found at the gravesite linked the defendant to the spot.

"How deeply did you find the body buried?" George Stiegers asked.

"Not deeply at all," Burris replied. "The ground was rocky and hard, and I don't think the person who dug the grave had come prepared with tools."

"Object to speculation," Lowell Burke said laconically. Before Judge Benitez could respond, George asked quickly, "Are you just speculating, Ms. Burris?"

"No sir. I found a thick branch at the scene that held traces of the same dirt I found beneath the body. The branch had obviously been used to dig the grave."

The young prosecutor gave a slight smile as Burke took his seat again. George knew Burke's reputation, he considered it a small triumph to have surprised the defense lawyer with news of the branch. He stood and carried one of Chris's photographs to his witness.

"Do you recognize what's depicted in this picture?"

"Yes sir," Burris said quickly. "The little dog. I found him in the grave with the body. Later I showed it to the victim's mother, who identified it for me. That was one of the ways we made the initial identification of the body."

George resumed his seat. "From your investigation, Ms. Burris, do you believe that Kristen Lorenz was murdered there at that scene?"

"No. We searched the area very thoroughly, but found no traces of blood. I don't believe the victim was bleeding by the time she was brought there. She was dead."

A cool breeze brushed by Chris's shoulder and neck, perhaps a stray waft of air conditioning. He thought of lying dead, traveling in a car, maybe in the trunk, lying there growing colder while one's murderer sweated and gasped in the effort of digging out hard ground with poorly improvised implements. Chris imagined Raleigh

Pentell looking down at the small body in that last dis-
tasteful moment when he had to pick it up and carry it to
the shallow grave. Again Chris looked at the defendant.
Pentell seemed to be experiencing no such awful memory. He sat watching the witness as if he had to concentrate on her testimony to understand its implications. He
had been well coached.

When George Stiegers finished with the witness Lowell Burke did not pass up his chance to question her. In a
firm tone of voice that made Burris turn and pay attention
to him, Burke asked, "Have you discovered very many
murder victims buried in graves, shallow or otherwise,
Ms. Burris?"

"No sir. I don't work for the police department, I don't
make most murder scenes. I was sent to this one because
it seemed obvious that forensic evidence would need to
be preserved."

"So at the typical murder scene there's no need for
your services?"

"Well, I do go to some, it just depends on the nature
of—"

"Which is it, Ms. Burris, either you've been to a lot of
murder scenes or you haven't."

"I've been to quite a few," Burris said stiffly.

"And how is the victim usually found?"

"Sir?"

"I mean, is he buried, is he covered, do people carry
him out of the barroom where he got stabbed to death, do
they—?"

"No sir. Usually the victim is found where he fell, on
the floor usually. Sometimes people at the scene have
covered the face, but that's about all."

Lowell Burke nodded as if this testimony were significant, falling silent to let it sink in with the jurors. George
Stiegers stared at him in confusion. Did the veteran
defense lawyer hope to win points for his client because
he'd treated the body more reverently than the average
murderer did?

Chris knew better. He anticipated Burke's next question.

"And how many murder victims have you found, Ms. Burris, buried with their favorite stuffed animal with them?"

Burris stared at him. After a long silence, after the answer had become obvious, she said, "I've never found that before, sir."

Nodding again, Lowell Burke said, "No more questions," leaving nearly everyone in the courtroom puzzled.

Jury selection had taken most of the day, the afternoon had turned late by the time these first two witnesses finished. Judge Benitez recessed trial for the day. Chris turned to see Jean rise from her seat, her eyes downcast. She didn't look at Chris, but didn't seem deliberately to be avoiding him, either. He just wasn't significant to her at that moment. Her thoughts obviously rested with her daughter. She turned and passed slowly up the aisle, ignoring the jostling of the crowd and the questions of reporters.

Chris drove a few blocks to the Santa Rosa Hospital and Anne Greenwald's office, where Clarissa had been dropped off after school. He found the two of them in Anne's office, Anne behind her desk, Clarissa roaming around the room picking up objects and books and talking a mile a minute.

". . . and that one woman, you'd better have security here the next time she comes in. The way she snaps the door open, the way she slaps down the pencil after she signs in, that woman's on a hair trigger. You'd better get metal detectors installed before her next visit."

"I'm not treating her, Clarissa, I'm treating her son. Maybe—"

She looked up at Chris's entrance and smiled.

"How are things going?" he asked innocently. Clarissa smiled at him too, a surprising flash of happiness that in

turn made Chris happy, before the girl's expression grew
more controlled.

"Fine," Anne said. "Clarissa's been sitting in my waiting room and now she's helping me diagnose people.
Some of whom aren't even patients."

"Doesn't mean they don't need to be treated," Clarissa
said quickly. "They just haven't realized it yet. Most cra-
zoids don't, do they?" She smiled to take the sting out of
her words.

Chris put his hand on her shoulder. A small gesture like
that still didn't come naturally to him, but he did enjoy
touching her. Clarissa seemed to accept it, too.

"Let's go to dinner and then see about your homework,
kid. Want to join us, Anne?"

Anne shook her head. "I've got work to finish up. You
can drop her by my house later. Clarissa has a key."

Clarissa walked out of the office and Chris lingered to
say, "Is this okay?"

Anne stood right in front of him, said clearly, "It's
okay, Chris," and surprised him by kissing him quickly.

In the car Clarissa asked, "How did the first day go?"

"About like I expected. Your mother testified."

Clarissa stared out the window at dusk rising out of the
trees of Olmos Park below the elevated expressway and
didn't say anything.

"Clarissa," Chris said slowly, "this trial may not come
out the way you're expecting. I don't have enough evidence that Raleigh Pentell killed Kristen. I'm convinced
of it, but I'm not sure I can prove it. Do you know what
I'm saying? It's not like on TV, the good guys don't
always win."

Clarissa looked melancholy, but she turned to him with
a certain hostile energy. "Why on earth would I think they
do?" She softened her tone. "I know what you're saying.
He might go free, he'd still be dangerous to Mom and me.
So what would you do then?"

Chris had mulled over a variety of answers to that question. He gave her the legal one: "I'd try to prosecute him for something else. One of the crimes you might know about."

He watched the announcement sink in on her: more weight on her narrow sixteen-year-old shoulders. Clarissa nodded, unsurprised. "I don't know much," she said.

"Except about your own kidnapping."

Clarissa remained turned from him, looking out the window. "Well, yeah, that. But I never saw very much. Raleigh stayed away from me, that's for sure."

Chris felt a momentary loneliness. "Even if I win the trial," he said, "what does it change? It gets frustrating sometimes, trying to help victims only after the fact. I wish I could have done something for Kristen before."

"You didn't even know her," Clarissa said quickly, and he turned to see her looking grim.

"No. I didn't. I wish I had." He made an effort to brighten. "At least I've met you."

He touched her shoulder lightly. Clarissa made an attempt at a smile, too. Neither of them did very well.

Trial days are often short, beginning at nine-thirty or ten in the morning, with a long lunch break. That doesn't mean the lawyers in trial lead a leisurely life. During those early mornings and lunch recesses that seem to fly by they must take care of the rest of their lives and plan the ongoing trial.

At eight-thirty the next morning Chris stood in his office with his investigators Olga Zamora and Jack Fine. Now that trial had begun Olga's undercover services should have been over, but she was still dressed for school. "She prefers it to work," Jack growled.

"The kids are buzzing over this trial," Olga replied. "And some of them are testifying for you. Maybe they'll say something different at school from what they say on the stand. Wouldn't you want to know that?"

Jack changed the subject. "What else can we do? Search Pentell's house again?"

"Done that," Chris said shortly. "He wouldn't have taken Kristen there. He wasn't that dumb." Although he had taken Clarissa to his house later. "What about his car?"

"Did that," Jack answered. "You know what we found there. Not much."

"Is it possible he was driving a different car that night? Maybe he took Peter Belasco's or something?"

"That's not what the witnesses say," Jack said. "Besides, do you really want us to find the girl's blood in Peter Belasco's car?"

Chris was spared having to answer by the entrance of George Stiegers trailed by Dr. Harold Parmenter, the assistant chief medical examiner. Parmenter, looking rushed, still wore his white lab coat, which hung on his lean frame.

"Sorry to run late," he said. "Cops called me early this morning wanting an emergency procedure."

"Who died?" Jack asked sardonically. Parmenter only laughed.

He doffed his lab coat. "Can somebody loan me a jacket?"

"Sure," George said, looking up at the tall doctor.

Chris looked too, thinking of telling Dr. Parmenter to keep his lab coat on. It gave him authority, and made him look as if he'd been called away from important work. The lab coat, especially with a nice stain or two, would allow the jury to picture Parmenter at his job, delving into the remains of a human being.

Instead Chris just said quietly, "Don't wear a jacket."

The doctor, lab coat in hand, looked at him blankly, then shrugged acquiescence.

So half an hour later Dr. Parmenter took the witness stand in his long-sleeved light blue shirt and diagonally striped tie, pens in his pocket, his round gold-rimmed glasses shining, with a harassed air of which Chris approved. Lowell Burke looked at him curiously. He had seen the assistant ME testify many times, and expected in this trial that he himself could give the doctor's testimony about as well as the expert could. What struck the veteran defense lawyer oddly was the intense way the District Attorney watched his witness while questioning him.

Chris quickly established the basis for Parmenter's testimony, that he had examined a body later identified as Kristen Lorenz.

"Did you know her, Doctor?" An unusual question.

"No," Parmenter said. He had settled down from the jovial comrade in Chris's office and sat seriously on the witness stand, his long face alert and expressive.

"How could you be so sure of the age of the body?"

"At that age, early teenage years, the bones haven't stopped growing. Certain bony plates haven't quite melded yet. We can be very precise at that age."

Chris would make use of this testimony in final argument. Kristen hadn't even finished growing yet when she'd been murdered.

"What condition was the body in?"

"Rather decayed. The—"

"Objection," Lowell Burke said quickly. "What happened to the body after death isn't relevant. It's a blatant attempt to inflame the jury without offering any probative evidence. The prosecutor—"

"The murderer left her in a shallow grave," Chris said hotly. "At the mercy of the elements and insects and whatever—"

Judge Benitez cut him off. "I'll allow this to the limited extent it pertains to the doctor's relevant testimony." He directed a strict look at the District Attorney.

Chris exhaled a long breath, forcing himself to settle down. The image of the girl in the shallow grave still unsettled him. Though he had never seen Kristen alive, he felt a kinship with her that had only begun after her death, as if she had crept out of that grave and come to find him, drawing him back into her family's life.

He asked, "What day did you perform your autopsy, Dr. Parmenter?"

"January fourth of this year."

"Based on the condition of the body, how long would you say it had been in the ground?"

"Approximately three months. Maybe a little less."

"Do you think there was enough flesh left on the face for someone to identify her?"

"No. And I wouldn't want to put anyone who'd known her through that experience. The condition she was in—"

At a slight cough from the defense attorney Dr. Parmenter trailed off, remembering the judge's warning.

Chris heard a soft sound or a stirring and glanced back over his shoulder at the audience. Spectators didn't fill the seats of the small courtroom. Two or three reporters took the front seats, curious clusters of people scattered over the other eight pews. Near the front on the aisle Jean sat very stiffly. She wore a simple white blouse and dark slacks, as if slowly devolving from the corporate professional she'd appeared to be the day before.

Chris felt shocked and horrified to see her, quickly running over in his mind the testimony he'd just drawn out and what he still had to get from Dr. Parmenter. No mother should hear it. He tried to catch Jean's eye and shake his head at her. She seemed aware of his gaze but stared straight ahead at the witness stand. Chris thought her crazy to be in the courtroom to hear this, but he'd never doubted Jean's bravery. If he could take it she could, too.

He turned back to his witness, revising slightly his planned list of questions. "Could you get fingerprints from the body's hands, Dr. Parmenter?"

"Yes, one. I believe, though, the identification was done through facial reconstruction, and I didn't have any part in that."

"No, we'll get to that," Chris said quietly. "From your examination, could you determine a cause of death?"

"Her neck was broken," the doctor said simply.

"What would cause that?"

Lowell Burke rose to say, "Objection. That calls for speculation, or for a variety of testimony most of which isn't relevant to what actually happened."

Judge Benitez turned to the witness with a question. "Doctor? Do you know, or would you be speculating?"

"I can tell you a few things definitely," Dr. Parmenter replied seriously, and continued as if lecturing. "It's the kind of injury that happens suddenly, not from, say, pressure building up over the course of time. It's quick. The vertebrae snap apart." He emphasized the word "snap," and more than one juror's head jerked back as if emulating receiving such a blow.

"How much force would be necessary to break someone's neck?" Chris asked.

"A great deal. This is an area designed to accept a blow and channel the energy elsewhere. You see boxers get hit tremendously hard, their heads snap back, but their necks don't break. Of course, this was a young girl, not a heavily muscled man, but it would still require a very strong blow to break her neck. Or maybe the neck being slammed against an immovable object, such as a large rock or a tree trunk. It would be much more likely to happen if an implement were used, such as a baseball bat."

Chris turned toward the defendant, who sat as composed as he could under this testimony. Pentell's hands lay folded on the defense table. Chris stared at them, understanding now the fear he'd felt the day before when looking at Raleigh Pentell's hands. Chris felt Kristen's presence near him, and these were the hands that had killed her.

Pentell felt him staring and lowered his hands out of sight beneath the table.

"Did you find any other significant injuries, Doctor?"

"No other broken bones. I have to say no, I didn't find anything else significant to cause of death."

"No bruising, for example?" Chris asked curiously.

Speaking with unaccustomed delicacy, Dr. Parmenter

said, "Bruising is something that happens to flesh, not bones. From the condition of her flesh after so much time had passed, I couldn't tell if she was bruised or suffered abrasions."

"So you can't tell us if she'd been beaten or just suffered one quick injury?"

"No, I can't."

Chris felt Jean's presence behind him, but she didn't make a sound.

He asked, "You also did an internal examination, didn't you?"

"Yes."

"Can you tell us anything out of the ordinary that turned up through that examination?"

"In her liver I found traces of an amphetamine. What's commonly called speed."

A whispered stir rippled through the courtroom. The victim had seemed so pure until now. This bit of testimony seemed a blow to the State's case. Jurors concentrated even more closely on the medical examiner.

"Could you tell how much?" Chris asked levelly.

"I can tell how much reached her liver. Not very much. About like taking a slight overdose of diet pills. Of course, I don't know how long before her death the girl took the drug. Some could have remained in her bloodstream, some could have been worked off or exhaled before she died. She could have ingested a much larger quantity than what I found."

"And can you tell how the speed was introduced into Kristen's body, for example injected as opposed to someone slipping it into her drink?"

"Objection," Lowell Burke said, sounding angry that he hadn't moved faster. "To the District Attorney testifying."

"I'm just asking a question," Chris said innocently.

"Sustained as to the testifying," the judge ruled. "The jury will disregard the prosecutor's remarks. You may answer the question."

"No, I have no way of knowing," Dr. Parmenter said

mildly, knowing the purpose of the question had already been accomplished before he answered.

Concluding, Chris asked, "What was your ruling as to cause of death?"

"Homicide."

"Why, Doctor? Why not accident, for example?"

"The violence of the injury, primarily. Broken neck is a fairly common way that a child dies at the hands of an adult. But I also take into account everything I know about the case, not just the medical evidence. If she had fallen off a ladder and broken her neck, someone would have called an ambulance, or reported her death. Not tried to cover it up by burying her and leaving the death unreported. That's something a murderer does."

Exactly. Chris felt satisfied at having drawn as much evidence as he had from a doctor who'd examined a body that hardly resembled anything human anymore. Slowly they were raising Kristen from the dead.

"Pass the witness."

"People feel guilty even after accidents, don't they, Dr. Parmenter?" Lowell Burke drawled.

"I suppose they do."

"Do you know anything about the psychology of murderers, Doctor?"

"A little. I haven't made a particular study of it."

"Ever known one to bury the victim's favorite stuffed animal with the body?"

"People bury all kinds of things when they're trying to dispose of evidence."

Burke smiled, accepting the evasive answer, inviting the jury to see that his question had gone unanswered.

"This drug you found in her body, Doctor, was it Dexedrine or something like that?"

"Yes."

"Speed, you called it. How would that have affected this girl?"

"They call it speed because it speeds up your system. Your heart beats much faster, you sweat more, become talkative usually. Loss of appetite, that's why they put it in diet pills."

"Would it make a person's movements jerkier?"

"Possibly. Yes, probably. Depends on how used to it a person was."

"Let's hope this nice young girl didn't habitually shoot up speed, Doctor. So the drug would have made her clumsier, is that right?"

Dr. Parmenter saw where the defense lawyer was heading. It wasn't hard, the destination loomed bulkily in his path, so much so that it didn't matter how the doctor answered the question. "Probably," he admitted.

"That would make her more prone to accident, wouldn't it, to tripping, falling, stumbling over something and hitting her head?"

"Now I object to the testimony from defense counsel," Chris said, but the damage had been done. Lowell Burke sat satisfied.

Next the prosecution began its string of boy witnesses, the teenaged members of the theft ring who'd been at the party in October. The picture of Kristen's last night began to emerge.

A sixteen-year-old boy named Joey Flores, with a wispy mustache, an innocent swagger but nervous hands, testified, "It was at this real nice restaurant called La Coterie or something like that. On Northwest Military Drive near Lockhill-Selma. Kind of our part of town, but none of us had ever been there. We had half the restaurant, it had a sign saying closed for private party, and that was us. Private." He smiled.

Though in fact the occasion had been semi-public. George Stiegers asked, "Who gave the party, Joey?"

"Well, Mr. Belasco was there, he was kind of the host, but he told us it was the boss's party, he was doing it for us, for all the work we'd done for him."

"Did you know who the boss was, Joey?"

The boy hesitated, glancing at the defense table. Raleigh Pentell seemed to be trying hard to avoid sneering as he stared at the boy with no sign of recognition. "No, I didn't know. I'd never seen him before that night, or even heard his name. There were rumors, but—"

"We don't need to get into rumors, Joey. What went on at the party?"

"Oh, eating, music. They had kind of a buffet table, with an ice sculpture of a swan, and the waiters kept refilling things."

"What about drinking?"

"Well, the waiters wouldn't serve us anything. Everybody was under age except Mr. Belasco. But he ordered champagne for his table, and anybody could get some when the waiters were out of the room. He gave us other stuff, too, out of his briefcase. Guys would go out into the parking lot, down at the far end, and smoke a joint and then come back."

"Was it fun, Joey?"

"Oh yeah, man." The boy's face glowed briefly at the memory. The evening hadn't been a tragedy for him. It had been a very special occasion. "Everybody was dressed up, the waiters treated us good, the place was beautiful. We felt—" He didn't have a word for it.

"Who all was there?"

Joey's testimony on this point agreed with those of the boys who followed, five of them in all. One thin blond boy named Michael gave the most complete list, counting carefully on his fingers: "Peter Belasco, Damon Whittier, a girl with him I didn't know her name, Ryan McClain and his girlfriend Clarissa, Joey Flores, Raul Hernandez, a girl named Melanie, I'm not sure who she was with, Leo Burns, Victor Cantu, Paul Lewis, Adam Sims. I think that's all. Maybe one or two other girlfriends I didn't know."

Chris questioned this witness. By all accounts this boy Michael had barely been a member of the gang on that night in October and had dropped out soon after. He came from a good middle-class unbroken family, and his parents had been shocked to hear that he would be called as a witness in a criminal trial. After a family conference that Chris hadn't attended Michael had agreed to testify without even a promise of immunity. On the witness stand he listened carefully to the District Attorney's questions.

"Did anything unusual happen as the evening went on, Michael?"

"Yes sir. Kristen arrived. Clarissa's little sister. People acted surprised, like she hadn't been invited."

Chris felt an odd chill at mention of Kristen's name, as if his introducing her into the story was what would get her killed. "Did you see who brought her?"

"No sir. She just walked in to the party. Mr. Belasco went up to talk to her like he'd tell her to go away, but then Clarissa came over to talk to her and it seemed like it would be okay."

"Was it okay?"

"No. Kristen asked Clarissa to leave with her. They were talking by themselves at first, then Clarissa started getting mad, I guess they both did, and Clarissa walked away from her. That's when Kristen started really making a scene. She started talking very loudly about Mr. Pentell."

"About this man?" Chris pointed at the defendant.

"I don't know. I'd never seen this man before that night, or even heard his name. But Kristen acted like she knew him."

"What kinds of things did she say?"

Michael said softly, not looking at the defendant, "That he was a crook. That we were all stupid for working for him. That he was just going to use us and then let us get dumped in jail or killed or something."

"Did people pay attention to her?"

"Well, you couldn't help it. She was so loud."

"Did she drink at the party, Michael? Was she acting drunk?"

"No sir, she wouldn't drink anything. Not even a Coke.

People offered her stuff, to kind of try to get her mind off what she was saying, but she wouldn't have anything."

Jason Luling, Kristen's friend, had helped explain this behavior to Chris before trial. Jason hadn't known about the party, but he knew how Kristen felt about the people there. "She would never take anything they offered her," Jason had said. "She didn't trust any of those people an inch, she was afraid all of them were in on some big plot."

Nevertheless, Kristen had begun acting drugged at the party. In trial preparation Chris had asked Anne Greenwald, "Maybe she had some sort of contact high, from being around those other kids who were doing drugs?"

Anne had answered, "Contact high doesn't leave deposits like what Hal Parmenter found in her liver. She was drugged all right. Oh, she may have talked herself higher than she really was, you know, egging herself on, letting herself go. But she definitely started from a chemical base."

So in spite of Kristen's precautions someone in that dangerous crowd had managed to slip something into her bloodstream. "She got louder and louder," the boy Michael·testified. "She said she was going to go·to Mr. Pentell's house and tell him off. She said that to Peter Belasco."

"Did he look worried?" Chris asked.

"Not at first, but after a while, yes. The manager of the restaurant came in and talked to him and looked suspicious about the champagne and all of us. That's when Mr. Belasco started looking nervous. He got on his cell phone and made a call."

"What happened after that?"

"Mr. Pentell showed up at the party."

This announcement forecast longer testimony and made a good place for a lunch break. Judge·Benitez took it, and the jurors left in the care of a bailiff, who would take them all to lunch together. George Stiegers turned toward Chris to discuss the trial, but Chris moved quickly down the aisle of the courtroom to Jean. She stood up but seemed dazed, as if she didn't know the way to the exit. Chris took her arm.

"Jean, you shouldn't be here," he said urgently. "There's no reason to put yourself through listening to all this."

Jean said quietly, "It's not as bad as my imagination. Or the dreams I've had for the last six months. I'd rather sit here and listen to it than be somewhere else worrying. Don't you—"

She stopped talking abruptly, looking past Chris, who turned quickly to see Raleigh Pentell passing in the aisle. Chris caught the defendant's head moving; he had just given Jean some sort of look, maybe only one of curiosity or sympathy, but from the whitened expression on Jean's face she had obviously taken his attention for something much more sinister. Pentell moved on down the courtroom aisle, staring so stiffly ahead that a vein stood out on the side of his neck.

"Chris," Jean said in a haunted voice. "You have to be very careful. He's vindictive as hell. It's a business tactic with him: you hurt him a little bit, he hurts you back much, much worse. No matter what happens in this trial, he's going to strike back. It won't matter if he's in jail or not. He'll find a way, he'll order someone—"

"Clarissa's okay," Chris said reassuringly. "Believe me, I've got her guarded. And that's why I'm trying to keep her out of the trial, so he won't have any reason to be mad at her."

"I mean you," Jean said, looking at him levelly.

The two of them stood close as the courtroom emptied out. Finally Chris felt again the silent communication the two of them had once shared. Jean watched him closely, taking him in, and he felt her warmth and strength. She leaned toward him, said, "Watch yourself, Chris," then brushed past him and hurried up the aisle.

Chris felt an odd shock that lifted him out of the trial worries that had engulfed him for so long. Jean had been sitting here listening to testimony about her dead daughter, but her thoughts for just a moment at least had focused on Chris. The idea gave him such a mix of emotions that he shrugged off the warning about Raleigh Pentell's need for revenge.

After a long moment he found George Stiegers looking at him very curiously.

In the afternoon Peter Belasco appeared as a prosecution witness. He looked very well groomed in spite of having come from the jail where he'd spent the past many nights. Belasco wore a navy blue pin-striped suit, a very white shirt, wing-tip shoes, and looked like a young executive, which in a sense is what he'd been before arrest had interrupted his career. He took his seat in the witness stand and sat without any nervous twitches or hand movements, glancing once at his former boss. Neither of them showed any reaction to the other.

Chris didn't much like Belasco's appearance, or the apparent lack of recognition in the look he'd exchanged with Raleigh Pentell, that of coconspirators who couldn't acknowledge each other in a crowd. Jack Fine had warned Chris weeks ago that he wouldn't be able to trust Belasco as a witness. It seemed Chris had him firmly in control, but this would be the test.

"Please state your name, age, and address."

"Peter Belasco, twenty-six. Two hundred North Comal. That's the Bexar County Jail," Belasco explained with a trace of humor.

Chris didn't share the witness's casual attitude. "What are you in jail for, Mr. Belasco?"

"Possession of drugs."

"Have you been convicted of that?"

"Yes. I pled guilty."

The convictions weren't complete, since Belasco hadn't been sentenced yet by Judge Willis, but the charges did provide a motive for Belasco to testify falsely in order to gain favor with the prosecutor, so Chris would rather bring the facts forward himself than let the defense do it on cross-examination. He didn't want the jurors to think he was trying to hide information from them.

"Do you know the defendant in this case?"

"Mr. Pentell? Oh yes. He was my boss." Belasco looked at Pentell again, still with a glint of humor. Chris would have liked to ask for a recess in order to slap his witness.

Raleigh Pentell's expression grew even more dour as he stared at his former associate. Chris thought again of Jean's warning. Belasco knew Pentell's nature and habits. He had explained to Chris Pentell's murder of the drug dealer who had been his partner. For Peter Belasco to gaze placidly on an expression like Pentell's, on the face of a man known to kill those who crossed him, took a physical bravery Chris wouldn't have attributed to Belasco.

"Would you describe that relationship more fully for the jury, Mr. Belasco? What do you mean when you say Raleigh Pentell was your boss?"

"It wasn't very formal. He had things he needed done, I did them. Like these boys. They did things for Pentell and I kind of took charge of them."

"What sorts of things did the boys do for Raleigh Pentell?"

Lowell Burke stood quickly and said, "Objection, Your Honor. May we approach the bench?"

Judge Benitez motioned the lawyers forward and pushed his microphone aside. The court reporter leaned in closely to hear. Burke said quietly to the judge, "I object to evidence of any extraneous offenses, Your Honor. They are irrelevant and to the extent they have any relevance the prejudicial effect of such testimony outweighs its probative value."

Burke's objection was a matter of formula. Besides, Judge Benitez had already heard it before trial. Chris answered only briefly. "Without such evidence the whole night of the murder has no context and no motive, Your Honor. It's necessary."

The judge nodded. "I will instruct the jury. The objection is overruled. But no further than you need to go, Mr. Sinclair."

"Yes sir."

Chris and Lowell Burke walked back together, sharing an odd camaraderie. They had embarked on a delicate business. Chris needed to prove the criminal enterprise Pentell had controlled, but to the extent he did so he painted most of his witnesses as just as corrupted. No one on either side of the courtroom wanted to get very specific.

Resuming his seat, Chris said, "You may answer the question, Mr. Belasco. What sorts of things did the boys do for Raleigh Pentell?"

"Steal things, mostly. Pentell'd tell them where to go and what they'd find when they got there, and where to take the stuff."

"What did the boys get in return?"

"Some of the profits, not much. Mostly they got drugs."

"That was part of your job, to supply them with drugs?"

Belasco shrugged. "Part of it, yeah."

"That's what you were doing that night at the restaurant, wasn't it?"

"I gave the boys a little grass and coke that night, yeah."

"That's what you were doing again the following month when you got arrested for drug possession, wasn't it?"

"Yeah," Belasco mumbled, again trying to shrug off his testimony and smile at the jurors. Belasco saw himself as an up-and-coming young lord on the make. Chris didn't mind letting the jurors see him as a low-level thug not bright enough to think for himself in a crisis.

"So you arranged this party at the restaurant the night of October twenty-fifth?"

"That's right. It was a little reward for the boys, give them a taste of the good life."

"Did Mr. Pentell know about it?"

Belasco tried to look commanding. "I didn't have to clear everything through him. But yeah, he knew."

"Was Kristen Lorenz invited to the party?"

"No. She showed up because her sister was there, that other girl, Ryan McClain's girlfriend."

Chris felt momentarily surprised and gratified to hear Clarissa described so peripherally.

"How did Kristen behave?"

"Like a mean drunk. She started shouting almost right away. Telling everybody they were stupid, that Mr. Pentell was using them the way he used everybody and they'd all be sorry they ever met him. Her sister tried to calm her down but when that didn't work it got worse. I went up and talked to her myself. She yelled right in my face that I was the stupidest one. I tried to calm her down . . ."

Actually, according to the other witnesses, Belasco had grabbed Kristen's arm and shaken her. She had screamed, and the maître d' came in. Peter Belasco had a problem then. He couldn't just shove Kristen out of the room, that wouldn't help, the maître d' already thought him responsible for her. He couldn't leave the party unsupervised and he didn't trust any of the boys to take Kristen home. Belasco stood there with a briefcase loaded with drugs in a room full of stoned underaged kids with a yelling girl and panicked.

"What did you do?" Chris asked.

Belasco tried to look cool. "It was Mr. Pentell she was yelling about. I figured it was his problem, so I called him. I told him something bad was coming down and he'd better come deal with it."

"And did he?"

"Yeah." Belasco looked triumphant at having summoned the big man.

At the defense table Raleigh Pentell shook his head, but he couldn't deny having appeared at the restaurant. Too many witnesses had seen him there.

"He came in," Belasco testified, "and the girl, Kristen, attacked him right away. Pentell coming made things worse at first. She seemed to know him, she said something about her mother and him. After Pentell appeared she left the rest of us alone. She just said things about him."

"What did he do?"

"He took her by the arm and tried to shush her just like the rest of us had done, and that worked about as well as giving her a loudspeaker. She got louder and screamed at him not to touch her."

Chris turned slightly in his seat to glance back at the spectator seats. Jean sat rigidly on the aisle, listening to the tale of her daughter's last minutes. She had her head lifted as if looking into a distance.

"The manager came back in and said something to Pentell. That's when Pentell took her away."

"What do you mean by that?"

"He hustled her out to the parking lot and they left in his car. I never saw her again. The next time I asked Pentell about it he said not to worry, the problem had been dealt with."

"What did you take that to mean?"

"Ojection," Lowell Burke said quickly. "Calls for speculation." Judge Benitez sustained the objection.

"At any rate, did Kristen Lorenz cause any more problems for Raleigh Pentell's organization after he took her away that night?"

"No." Peter Belasco suddenly grinned. "Not until today, I guess."

Chris allowed his full contempt for his witness to show. He had no more need for Peter Belasco, felt offended that he'd needed him at all, and handed him over to the defense as if wiping his hands. "I pass the witness."

For a moment triple stares of contempt beamed at Belasco from the counsel tables. Lowell Burke in particular just watched the young man as if there couldn't be much point in questioning him. After a few moments he leaned forward and asked, "After the problem was taken care of, did the party in the restaurant go on into the wee hours of the morning?"

"No. I shut it down pretty quick after that. A few of the kids left right away anyway. I got rid of the rest of them, paid the tab, and left."

"Ever been back to that restaurant?"

"Not that I remember."

"No. When you got arrested hosting the same kind of party a month later it was in a private home, right?"

Belasco shifted uneasily, not understanding the significance of the question. "That's right."

"So at least you learned to keep your dirty business more private. Didn't you?"

The defense lawyer's question could not be answered well. Peter Belasco just stared hostilely at him.

"Where did you go when you left the party?" Burke asked.

"I went by and picked up a girl I knew and we went out. The night was still young."

"You didn't follow Raleigh Pentell and take the girl Kristen Lorenz from him?"

Chris sat up more alertly. Was this the defense theory showing itself for the first time? Blame Peter Belasco for the murder. Not a bad plan, as defense plans go. Chris looked at his witness, who with his gunman's slouch and glaring eyes would be wellcast as a murderer.

"No," Belasco said quickly. "Like I said, I never saw her again."

The defense lawyer insisted, "You said you did things that Mr. Pentell needed to have done. Wouldn't this have fit your job description, taking care of a problem like Kristen? Wouldn't it have been a good way to make up for failing to handle the problem at the restaurant?"

"I told you no. I didn't follow them. I didn't see her again after they left the restaurant. Ever."

"That's right, you went out on your date. This young lady you say you went out with, could you produce her in court to verify your alibi?"

Burke had loaded his question with implications, so many that Chris didn't have time to formulate a precise objection before Peter Belasco answered, "I doubt it. I've been in jail the last few months. We kind of lost touch."

Burke nodded dismissively, as if he'd expected such a weak response. "Let's get to your motives for testifying, Mr. Belasco. You didn't just come forward as a concerned citizen, did you? You had months to do that, and you kept quiet until the District Attorney offered you a deal. Is that right?"

"He made me a good offer on my cases," Belasco said judiciously.

"Specifically in exchange for your damaging testimony against Raleigh Pentell, correct?"

"Specifically for truthful information about what happened to the girl. He seemed very concerned about her."

"So you gave him what he asked for, in exchange for a good deal. And you say you haven't been sentenced yet?"

"That's right. My application for probation is still pending before the judge."

"So the prosecution has something to hold over your head in case you didn't testify the way they wanted today."

"Not really," Belasco said casually. "They've already made their recommendation. Now it's up to the judge."

Burke looked contemptuously at the witness's attempt to spar with him. "And you don't think they'll report to the judge on how cooperative you've been or haven't been?"

"I—I don't know."

"Good answer, Mr. Belasco. As close as you've come to the truth, I suspect. Let's ask about another motive of yours. This criminal enterprise you say Raleigh Pentell organized—you could run it as well as he could, couldn't you?"

"I imagine," Belasco said slyly.

"In fact it sounds like you did run it. You gave the orders to the boys, you paid them off, you collected the profits."

"No. Raleigh got the money."

"Well, we have only your word for that. And now that you've worked out your other cases, it would be nice for you if you could get Raleigh Pentell blamed for this murder and get him out of the way at the same time, wouldn't it?"

Belasco continued to try at cleverness. "Since he's probably going to try to have me killed for testifying against him, yeah, it would be nice if he got convicted for this."

Lowell Burke sat for a long moment staring at Belasco, then glanced at Chris Sinclair as if to remind the jury that this was Chris's witness. Then the defense lawyer stood and said rather formally, "I see no point in questioning this witness any further, Your Honor."

Chris quite agreed.

Twelve

The prosecution finished its case with the testimony of a police evidence technician who had conducted a very thorough search of the car Raleigh Pentell had been driving the night he took Kristen Lorenz away from the party in the restaurant. Defense lawyer Lowell Burke sat very alertly during this testimony, thinking he knew the results of this search, but waiting for a surprise.

"Did you find fingerprints inside the car?" George Stiegers asked his witness.

"Yes, in the places you'd expect. Steering wheel, dashboard, the glass of the windows." Ray Montgomery, the evidence tech, was a man who'd spent years as a patrol officer, had gained enough skills to move up a notch to become an officer who processed crime scenes for evidence, and looked ready to glide from there into retirement in only a few more years. He did his job carefully and testified just as carefully, but without much intensity. He held his report in his large hands, and his slight jowls moved when he looked down at the report and then up again.

Stiegers, the young prosecutor who had been a cop

himself for a few years, seemed deferential to the older man. "Could you identify any of those fingerprints?"

"Some belonged to the defendant," Officer Montgomery said. "Some were unknown, and a couple I matched to people who worked for the defendant."

"Did you have the fingerprints of the deceased, Kristen Lorenz?"

"Yes."

"Did any of the prints inside the car match hers?"

"No," Montgomery said, after scanning his report again as if the needed information might have appeared there since the last time he'd looked.

"When did you conduct your search?"

"Early April, just last month."

Months after Kristen had disappeared, in other words. Raleigh Pentell had had a long time to have the car cleaned of any trace of Kristen's fingerprints. It had hardly been worthwhile obtaining a search warrant for the car, but the prosecution had gotten one tiny little break.

"Did you also check the defendant's car for traces of blood?" George asked.

"Yes."

"How did you do that?"

"First visually," the officer answered. "Including pulling out the seats and looking underneath the floor mats."

"Did you find anything that way?"

"No. So next I used a spray we have called luminol. It can find traces of blood too small to be seen with the naked eye, and reacts to blood by turning green. I sprayed the whole interior of the car and the trunk with it."

"Did that turn up any traces of blood?"

"No. Which didn't surprise me."

Lowell Burke looked even more alert, moving forward to the edge of his chair, as the prosecutor asked, "Why?"

"The original carpeting in the trunk of the car had been pulled out and replaced."

"Objection, objection," the defense lawyer almost bellowed. "There's been no testimony that this man is qualified to determine whether carpet is original equipment in a car. This is entirely speculation!"

"It didn't match the carpet in the interior," Montgomery answered back, showing his first animation. "And I know when—"

"Stop!" Judge Benitez said sternly, bringing a momentary quivering quiet to the courtroom. "It is not up to you to respond to objections," he told the witness. The judge sat a moment quietly thinking. "The objection is sustained. Unless you can demonstrate why the testimony is something other than mere speculation."

Chris whispered quickly to his young assistant, but George didn't need it. He knew the witness better than Chris did. "Officer, what made you think the carpet in the trunk was not original?"

"I pulled it up," Montgomery said rather sullenly, staring at the defense lawyer. "It came up real easy. It was barely glued down. And the glue spots on the metal underneath didn't match the glue spots on the underside of the carpet. It'd been replaced."

George returned to the subject. "So let me remember. Did you find any traces of blood in the trunk of the car, either in the new carpet or on the frame of the car underneath?"

"No. It'd been scrubbed clean."

Surprisingly, this comment drew no objection from Lowell Burke, who sat pondering the witness.

"Did that end your search?" the prosecutor asked.

"No. Next I took off the door panels."

"Inside the car. The panels that cover the door handles and all that?"

"Yes sir. And I sprayed luminol in there."

"Have any luck?" George Stiegers asked overcasually.

"This time I did," the witness said with satisfaction, sitting forward. "Inside the panel of the front passenger seat I found traces of blood. The luminol glowed green."

"How could blood have gotten inside the door panel?" George asked, adding quickly: "If you càn tell without just speculating."

"Well, somebody could've cut himself while he wàs assembling the door. But I did a test with the door and found another way. If there was blood on the inside of the passenger window and somebody rolled it down, the blood would've gone down inside the door panel. Then even if somebody rolled it back up and cleaned it off, some traces would've been left inside the door panel. Or if there were a lot of blood on the inside of the door, some of it could've seeped down inside."

George asked, "Once you'd found the blood traces, did you have them tested for type or DNA characteristics?"

"No. There wasn't enough to test. The luminol spray destroys whatever trace it reacts to. This was such a small amount of blood I couldn't even see it except for the spray."

George Stiegers passed the witness and Lowell Burke didn't say anything for long seconds, watching the witness thoughtfully. Finally he stirred himself and said in a slow rumble, "So this was such a tiny amount of blood you couldn't even see it?"

"That's right."

"And now thanks to your spray it's all gone, so nobody can have it tested."

"I'm afraid that's true."

The defense lawyer leaned forward as if getting intimate with the witness, while his client sat staring rigidly ahead. "Officer, you seem fond of imagining how things might have happened. Let me ask you this: given the accidents and minor injuries that life is fraught with, if you went out and took the twelve cars that belong to these jurors and gave them as thorough a search as you gave Mr. Pentell's, ripping up the carpets and disassembling the cars, do you think you'd find traces of blood in most of their cars? At least in the tiny amount you found in Mr. Pentell's car?"

Chris leaned over to tell George Stiegers to object, but George laid a hand on his boss's arm and kept quiet.

"Yes sir," the police witness said without hesitation. "I bet I would. Probably even more."

Lowell Burke looked at the witness narrowly, thinking he'd won his point but then deciding not to go any further. "Thank you, Officer. Pass the witness."

George Stiegers quickly asked, "What do you mean, Officer, you'd expect to find more blood in most people's cars than you found in the defendant's?"

Officer Montgomery leaned back at ease and said in a folksy drawl, "Well, like this fellow says, people cut themselves all the time, kids lose teeth, whatever. You walk through a little bit of blood without even noticing and then leave traces of it on your car's floor mats and floorboards. Even packages of hamburger bleed through the grocery bag a little bit. Enough that luminol would pick up. I'd expect to find some blood in 'most anybody's car. Most cars haven't been as thoroughly cleaned as this man's was."

The witness stared at Raleigh Pentell, who only rolled his eyes and looked weary. And when George passed the witness and the defense had no more questions, Chris stood and said, "Your Honor, the State rests."

The prosecution should end its case on a high point, after a moment that thoroughly establishes the defendant's guilt. This appeared to be such a moment, when the jurors had been informed that no one had seen Kristen Lorenz again after Raleigh Pentell drove away with her, and now he had blood in his car. But Chris did not feel triumphant. He knew the thinness of his proof of murder.

The afternoon had grown late. Judge Benitez broke for the day, leaving the defense another night to prepare its case. Burke and his client hurried out of the courtroom. Chris turned to see that Jean had left. Maybe the testimony about blood had finally gotten to her.

But Chris was surprised to see one spectator still sitting

in the courtroom, someone he'd almost forgotten about.
Chris walked down the aisle and stood over Jason Luling,
who sat alone, quietly staring into space as if he expected
the show to resume momentarily. His mother must be
somewhere nearby, the ladies' room perhaps. She would
never have dropped him off here alone.

The boy who had been Kristen's friend looked very
small. He was neatly dressed in a plaid shirt and khaki
slacks. His hands rested on the back of the pew in front of
him: small hands with well-kept fingernails and a few
freckles.

"Hello, Jason," Chris said.

The boy looked up, so that Chris saw for the first time
how his eyes brimmed with tears. His cheeks shook
slightly as he nodded a reply.

Here was Kristen's mourner, more obviously aggrieved
than anyone else Chris had seen in the case. "She should
be here," Jason gulped. "She should have come to live
with my family. This is all so—senseless."

Chris sat beside the boy. He remembered that Kristen
had given Jason pages of her diary, probably as intimate a
gesture as the young girl had made to anyone in her life.
The boy seemed peripheral to the case, but he had perhaps lost more than anyone else. The long potential of a
close friend, with no replacement in sight.

"You're right," Chris said. "It was senseless. I can't
think of any good reason why anyone would have wanted
to hurt Kristen."

Jason glanced up at him, then down. Chris frowned.
"Can you?"

A long few seconds of silence passed, then Jason
glanced up again suddenly, as if it had taken that long for
him to realize Chris had spoken to him. "That man," he
mumbled. "The one you're prosecuting. Kristen was
afraid of him, but he should've been afraid of her, too.
She hated him. If she could have teleported everybody in
that restaurant to the moon, she would have done it.
Except Clarissa, of course."

Yes. Except her beloved sister, who had left the party right after Kristen was taken away.

Chris asked the boy, "Did you know Kristen was going to that party? Do you know how she got there or how she planned to get home? Was she going to call you to pick her up?"

"I can't drive," Jason said miserably. The boy looked older now than the first time Chris had seen him, probably considerably older than he'd looked last October. A trace of adult resignation had crept into his face. Chris had forgotten how young the boy was, how young Kristen had been. He took for granted the essential adult skill of driving, but its lack had effectively removed young Jason from events at the restaurant miles from his house.

He could tell that the boy was thinking too, and always would, that he could have saved her somehow if he'd only done something differently that night. Chris had an inkling of the same feeling even though he hadn't even known Kristen Lorenz then—or in fact ever.

"I'm sorry," he said to Jason.

Clarissa had made her usual trek from school to Anne Greenwald's office. Anne left work a little early and took Clarissa home with her. Anne wanted to question the girl in great detail, but knew how ineffective that would be. Questioning made kids clamp down. Instead Anne talked about anonymous patients of hers, about her own teenage years, a flow of talk designed to make Clarissa say, "I know about that," or "Something like that happened to me." But though Clarissa listened attentively, she never jumped in with a personal spin of her own.

At Anne's house Clarissa went into the bathroom while Anne changed clothes in the adjoining bedroom. As Anne slipped on a T-shirt Clarissa emerged holding the testing device from a home pregnancy test. *Damn*, Anne thought.

"You give girls pregnancy tests here in your house?" Clarissa asked curiously.

That would be a good explanation. Anne should have thought of it herself. But she answered truthfully, "No. I never bring patients here."

"Then—" Clarissa studied the small plastic circle with its blue negative line now fading. She shrugged. "Well, at least you dodged this one."

"Yes," Anne replied gloomily.

"I noticed you've got another pregnancy testing kit there in your cabinet," the girl said casually. "You know, they've got very good birth control methods these days. Some of them even last for weeks, you don't even have to worry about it."

"I should be giving you that speech," Anne countered. "Well, not me, but somebody's supposed to tell you, you're not supposed to be telling me."

Clarissa laughed. "Don't worry about me. I will never fall into that trap. Babies are a nuisance."

Anne followed Clarissa out into the living room, remembering how the girl had practically raised her younger sister, with a mother absent from both their lives for long stretches. Clarissa had probably already had enough parental responsibility in her short life.

"But so you want one?" the girl said abruptly, turning to face Anne. "A baby?"

"Yes," Anne said calmly, hoping like hell she wasn't blushing.

Clarissa looked interested and nonjudgmental. She folded her arms, cocked one hip, and studied Anne. "With Chris I assume. But how, with me staying with you for the last three or four weeks?"

"This will come as a shock to a sixteen-year-old, but you don't know everything."

In fact it had been difficult trying to produce a baby when Anne and Chris had already become parents in effect. Anne remembered one noon tryst and a couple of times when Clarissa had been visiting her mother or at school. Chris was cooperating with what Anne wanted. Without further discussion. Even with the events in progress in his life, he was willing to risk parenthood with Anne. She thought of him tenderly.

Now stop that, she told herself. Or she *would* start blushing.

"Listen," Clarissa said, "I could spend the night with one of my friends some night, if you need—"

"Um, thanks," Anne interrupted hurriedly. "But let's not look like we're, you know, plotting anything."

Clarissa narrowed her eyes knowingly. "Got you."

Anne had to turn away, and decided to go to the kitchen to do something about dinner. She felt the girl's thoughts following her. The pregnancy test had made Clarissa think of Anne not only as a person but as a person in Chris's life. Anne thought she understood the complicated nature of that revelation.

She didn't realize Clarissa had followed her to the kitchen until she heard the girl's voice at her back. Clarissa sounded puzzled. "I don't mean to be insulting, but somebody like you, I'd expect you'd want to get married first."

Anne turned to her. "Yes, you would, wouldn't you? But how is that insulting?"

"You know, assuming you're so conventional. Normal."

"Boring?"

"Yeah. I mean, wouldn't it be bad for your position or whatever to be an unmarried mom?"

"Maybe," Anne admitted. She had scrupulously avoided ever asking Clarissa about her mother or home life, but now Clarissa seemed to hear the unspoken question.

Looking off into a corner of the ceiling, as if discussing a hypothetical case, Clarissa said, "With Mom it never mattered. We moved so much she could make up any story for new people. Divorce, dead husband. Whatever. We always went along with whatever she said."

Anne had heard Clarissa make offhand remarks about her mother before, in that tone of contempt with which most teenagers speak of their parents, but Anne could tell the mother-daughter relationship was more complicated than that. Anne didn't want to do anything to injure it. She said quietly, "But she always kept you with her, didn't she? Maybe she gave up a lot for you, Clarissa."

"Mom? Oh yeah, she gave up a lot. Normal jobs, normal life, staying put in one place. But I don't think she gave it up for me."

Clarissa abruptly walked out of the kitchen, but her tone of voice and bitter expression lingered in Anne's mind. The girl strove for sarcasm when she said words like "normal," but she couldn't disguise her longing. The same wistful desire for ordinariness that her sister had displayed in the last months of her life.

Chris, distracted by all kinds of thoughts, took the wrong exit from the expressway. He'd meant to go to Anne's to check on Clarissa, but as he relived the trial day he drove on automatic pilot, passing the Mulberry Avenue exit from 281 and continuing on toward his own. As soon as he exited he realized his mistake, and turned off Basse into one of the entrances to the Quarry Market.

Behind him, a large black Lincoln did the same.

Chris's attention returned to his surroundings as he drove slowly through the large parking lot of the shopping center, watching for shoppers and for other cars pulling out of parking spaces. He also paid more attention to his rearview mirror, which was how he saw the car following him. The driver of the Lincoln had to stay closer in the crowded parking lot than a good tailing car normally should. Chris turned down one parking aisle, paused as if waiting for a parking space to open up, then drove faster toward an exit. The Lincoln hung back then, but not far enough. Chris, instead of heading back to the expressway, drove into Olmos Park, on a narrow, twisting road that made him certain that the black car was following him. And Chris had just turned into a large park, essentially a little-tended forest that was one of the most isolated spots in the heart of the city.

He sped up, past the baseball fields on the left and the park itself on the right. Behind him, the black Lincoln sped up too, the driver obviously realizing he'd been spotted and casting subtlety aside.

Chris drove out of the woods and into the neighborhood of Olmos Park, a wealthy enclave surrounded by San Antonio. Large houses loomed on his right, looking secure and reluctant to recognize his plight. He turned down a residential street. The black Lincoln stayed less than half a block behind. The driver had obviously given up on following Chris to his destination, but remained close. What was his objective now? Chris realized it must be Raleigh Pentell's men in the car, acting on Pentell's orders. First he would have told them to find the most obvious witness against him, Clarissa. But failing that, they could also disrupt the trial by killing Chris himself. *He'll strike at you*, Jean had warned him.

Chris tried to think of a crowded place, then thought perhaps he should keep away from other people, as if he carried a contagion. He tried to think of the nearest police station. He drove almost in circles, stalling for time.

When Chris pulled out onto Hildebrand, the driver of the Lincoln tried to pull up beside him. Chris sped up, but the black car was faster. It almost pulled abreast. Chris abruptly turned right, down the steep street that led to Trinity University and Alamo Stadium, and turned the other direction, onto a narrow street that twisted around to the right. With the black Lincoln out of sight behind him, Chris pulled suddenly into a small parking lot on the right, the parking lot of the animal control facility, closed this time of night. Chris pulled in close to the building and watched to see the black car drive past.

Nothing happened. Chris backed out again and started to exit the parking lot. As he did the large Lincoln suddenly glided across the narrow exit, blocking it completely.

The passenger door opened and a man in a dark suit, with no tie, stepped out. The man had a large bullet-shaped head and shoulders that stretched the suit. Chris knew the man. The last time they'd met, Chris had butted the man in that large forehead.

Casting subtlety aside, the man drew a gun from under his arm and pointed it at the grill of Chris's car. He jerked his head impatiently. If the car moved any farther, the man would obviously disable it, then come after Chris. Chris eased the car into park and opened his door.

"What do you want?" he called through the opening.

"To talk," the man said slyly. "I've got a deal to offer you."

Like hell, Chris thought. The prosecution must have been going better than he'd thought, to make Raleigh Pentell this desperate. The thug put his gun away and made a friendly *come on over* gesture. Chris opened his car door wider and stepped out. At least he hadn't led these killers to Clarissa. He realized that must have been their goal. If Chris's distraction hadn't made him take the wrong exit, he would probably have taken them right to the girl—the one witness Pentell probably feared the most, now that Ryan McClain was dead.

The gunman grinned widely as the District Attorney stepped out of his car. He didn't reach for his gun again. He didn't have to. Chris was quite thoroughly trapped.

Chris took two careful steps, very slowly. Pentell's thug began to look impatient. Stalling, Chris said, "Listen—" The gunman nodded attentively, but then Chris's time ran out. He didn't have to stall anymore.

A park ranger's car pulled off the road, right next to the big black Lincoln. A moment later a San Antonio Police patrol car did the same. The gunman whirled, reached under his jacket, then thought better of the idea as both a ranger and a uniformed cop emerged from their cars, the police officer holding a gun.

When the thug turned back to Chris he had completely lost his joviality. Chris held out the cell phone he had pulled from his pocket. "Times have changed," he said. "You've got to keep up with the technology."

He walked closer as the police officer approached from the other side. "Watch out," Chris said. "This one's got a gun. I'm sure the other one in the car does, too. Now," he added to the gunman. "What's the deal you wanted to offer me?"

But the man had gone silent. He let his glare speak for him. It did so eloquently.

"Well, now I might have a deal for you," Chris said. "We'll talk soon."

The gunman's face said that would not be productive. His face grew even less expressive as the officer put handcuffs on him.

Time passed. Anne and Clarissa chatted inconsequentially. The day grew dimmer, night descending. Anne went into the kitchen to start a teapot boiling for iced tea. When she came out Clarissa had her hand on the clunky black old-fashioned phone in the living room. But she didn't pick it up. She didn't move at all. And a sudden tear rolled down her cheek.

"What is it?" Anne asked in alarm.

Clarissa looked up slowly. "I forgot. I was going to call her, see if she was at Jason's house, see if she needed a ride home."

Memory can be a mean-spirited trickster, tiptoeing away and then rushing back. Even though Clarissa knew she was in an unfamiliar house, not staying at home because of possible danger, even though she and Anne had just talked about the ongoing trial, Clarissa had forgotten momentarily what it all meant. The mind drifted away for a moment and the body remembered its responsibilities: to call the baby sister, drive to pick her up, maybe fix her dinner before Mom got home.

Responsibilities Clarissa would never have again.

By the time Anne reached her Clarissa had recovered. She turned away, sniffed once, then turned back with a rueful smile. "It's okay. I just went goofy all of a sudden."

"Clarissa, I—"

"It's okay!" Clarissa said insistently.

The phone rang, almost under her hand. Clarissa shrank from it. Anne picked up the receiver quickly, then mouthed to the girl, *It's Chris*. "How are things—?" she began with feigned brightness, then stopped and listened. "Uh huh . . . Are you all . . . Okay. Yes. Yes, Chris." She turned her back on the girl and said quietly, "You know I had that alarm installed last year. We'll be fine. Okay, here she is."

Clarissa asked, "What is it?" Anne handed her the phone and said, "He just wants to say good night."

They all had their secrets. Anne looked out her front window at the dark night, then closed the curtains, following Chris's instructions. While Clarissa talked, Anne went to check the door locks.

After his call to Anne and Clarissa, Chris had a quiet evening at home, replaying the trial in his mind and trying to plan ahead. Once he went out for a walk around his complex. In the warm night a breeze toyed with him, just as flickers of thought played at the edges of his mind.

Late that night, after Chris was in bed, his phone rang. He caught it before it finished its first ring, already formulating his questions for Anne. "How did you know—?"

But another woman's voice interrupted him. "Go up on the roof," she said. "The stars are amazing tonight."

"Jean?"

"I mean it. I'm up there now. It's so clean."

They used to make this call to each other on nights when they weren't together. *Go up on the roof*, one of them would tell the other. Years ago in Austin Chris would receive such a call from Jean and afterward climb perilously onto the roof of his apartment building, know-ing that Jean across town had ascended to her own higher roof. She stood at ease on the edge, gazing across town or up at the sky. In an era before cell phones they couldn't talk to each other, but they shared the night sky and in his imagination she lay beside him, surrounded by starlight. After they'd hung up the phones and miles separated them, Jean still filled his senses.

But even then they'd been headed in separate direc-tions, and now they had grown so far apart he didn't trust her.

Her voice drew him back to a past that hadn't been innocent but had been free. If only life could be the way Jean had tried to live hers, free of repercussions. Unbound by these long, long consequences. Lying in bed, he looked up and saw millions of stars, and felt roof shin-gles under his back.

"Go up on the roof, Chris," her voice came ghostly through the phone line, wistfully, almost begging. "It's beautiful out."

The next morning the defense got its turn. Chris had built a strong circumstantial evidence case against Raleigh Pentell. No one had seen Kristen again after he drove away with her. But Chris had no witness to say where they'd gone, and it had taken so long to find her body that Chris couldn't pinpoint the day of her death, through medical evidence. That left a big hole, and the defense drove through it.

When Lowell Burke took over he acted as if the trial had just begun. He made a brisk opening statement, standing close in front of the jury box, his deep, confident voice insinuating itself throughout the courtroom.

"Ladies and gentlemen, we expect the evidence will show that you had better be very careful about giving a ride to hysterical young teenage girls, because if she meets with a terrible, unfortunate accident or is murdered some time after that, you can be dragged into a place like this and have your whole life put in jeopardy.

"The defense will prove that Raleigh Pentell had nothing against Kristen Lorenz and absolutely no motive to kill her. We will prove that he did not kill her. Will we give you the 'real' murderer, like Perry Mason? No. We will only show you other possibilities. We will demonstrate that this murder has not been solved, and may never be solved. Please keep an open mind and listen carefully.

"Your Honor, the defense calls Alicia Green."

Who? Chris Sinclair and George Stiegers looked at each other blankly. While the defense had a right to a pretrial list of the prosecution witnesses, the State didn't enjoy the same privilege of knowing who would testify for the defense. Chris turned to see a lady in her sixties coming up the courtroom aisle, her head held high, her faded blue eyes squinting slightly. She looked familiar, but he couldn't immediately place her. The lady dressed in casual formality, as if for a club meeting, in a calf-length light flowered dress and white low-heeled shoes. She would have looked at home in a hat with a veil, but in fact her head was bare in the courtroom, revealing tightly whorled gray hair. Years of sunlight had lined her cheeks and touched her arms with redness and freckles.

The arms made Chris recognize her as she sailed by him without a glance. The last time he'd seen her she'd been wearing gardening gloves.

The witness sat primly in the witness box and watched Lowell Burke as if he were the only person in the room she trusted.

"Hello, Mrs. Green," he said kindly. "Please state your name and address."

"Alicia Green. Four-six-three-five Heather Mist."

"Mrs. Green, who lives across the street from you?"

"A woman named Jean Fitzgerald," Mrs. Green said with slight distaste.

"Mrs. Fitzgerald has testified in this trial," Burke slipped in. "Does she have children?"

"Two teenage daughters. Although one of them died, I understand."

Burke carried a photograph that had already been marked as evidence to his witness. "Was that this girl, Kristen Lorenz?"

"Yes," Mrs. Green said, with a slight glance at the photo.

"Ma'am, I want to take you back to the night of October twenty-fifth of last year. The last night, as far as we know, that anyone saw Kristen Lorenz. A Friday night. Do you remember that night?"

"Yes."

"Did you see Kristen that day?"

"Early in the evening I did, about six o'clock. Maybe earlier or later than that, I don't know, I didn't take notes. She came out her front door and called something back into the house. She was rather loud, that's what made me notice. But I just glanced out, and when I looked again she was gone. I didn't think anything of it until I heard from you. I didn't know that was her last night." The lady's eyes widened, showing emotion for the first time, though Chris thought it looked rather staged.

"Was that the last time you saw Kristen?" Lowell Burke asked gently.

"Yes."

"Did you see any other activity that night at Jean Fitzgerald's house?"

"Yes. A few hours later, between ten and eleven or so, a car pulled into the driveway over there, and a man got out and rang the doorbell of the house."

"Was it this man?" the defense lawyer asked, pointing at Raleigh Pentell, who gave the witness a small smile.

She didn't smile back. "No," Mrs. Green said emphatically. "It was a younger man."

Burke approached her with a photograph that he had marked as a defense exhibit. "Can you identify this person, Mrs. Green?"

She held the eight-by-ten photo and studied it critically. "I don't know his name, but this is the man I saw talking to my neighbor Jean Fitzgerald that night."

Burke carried the picture casually to the District Attorney, saying over his shoulder, "Your Honor, we ask that Peter Belasco be brought back into the courtroom for identification. Unless the District Attorney is willing to stipulate that the person in this picture identified by the witness is Peter Belasco."

Chris gave the photo a quick study. It was no glamour pic. Someone had taken the full-length photo of Belasco from a slight distance, or from a longer distance with a long lens. The picture showed Belasco wearing dark glasses, stepping out of a car. The young man's wavy black hair appeared prominently, but otherwise the picture didn't show very good detail.

"I'd like to have the witness see him in person," Chris said.

"Very well," Judge Benitez ruled, and George Stiegers stood quickly from the counsel table and hurried up the aisle of the courtroom. Chris followed him with his gaze until he saw Jean sitting in her habitual seat on the aisle. Her mouth had tightened and she stared into space as if thinking of something else, something very sad and troubling. Chris couldn't catch her eye.

Lowell Burke continued his examination of the witness. "You said the young man in the photo was talking to Mrs. Fitzgerald that night, is that right?"

"Yes."

"Could you hear what they said?"

"No, of course not."

"Did you see whether he went inside the house?"

Mrs. Green looked primly disturbed by the question. "No. I didn't stand at my window all night spying on them. I just glanced out that one time and saw them. I believe I went to bed soon after that."

"What time was that, Mrs. Green?"

"Some time between ten and eleven o'clock. I'm not positive. It was months ago."

"Thank you, ma'am. I appreciate your coming here. Pass the witness."

Chris said, "This was some time ago, Mrs. Green, and you said you didn't take notes or pay particular attention. How can you be sure that it was this same night when you saw this man outside the house across the street?"

She must have been prepared for this question, answering quickly, "Because later I realized that was the last time I ever saw little Kristen. The next week was Halloween, and that was when I first noticed she was gone. She didn't come trick-or-treating. I missed seeing her. She always had such imaginative costumes, made out of almost nothing. Nothing store-bought for her. Last year I kept waiting for her and she never came. I finally decided she had just outgrown Halloween, and I thought that was sad."

Chris sat silent for a long moment, the silence filling the courtroom, until a small cough from the judge made him rise quickly and say, "I pass the witness."

Burke had no more questions, either, but asked Mrs. Green to remain available. "Certainly," she promised.

"Call your next witness."

"The defense calls Victor Seuret, Your Honor." This was another name Chris had never heard, and Burke's south Texas French accent made it sound as if the witness had been imported from a more civilized continent.

The heavy man coming up the aisle wore black slacks and a white shirt, the sleeves rolled up two turns to reveal thick, hairy forearms. Chris had seen him somewhere, and soon remembered.

"Mr. Seuret," Lowell Burke asked after the witness had been sworn in, "what is your name and profession?"

"Victor Seuret. I am a chef."

"Ah. Can you tell us some of the places you've worked?"

"I attended cooking school in Paris and did my apprenticeship at a small café there. I worked at La Grenouille in New York City, but then came to San Antonio looking for a warmer climate. I worked at dear La Provence before it closed, and then I was the head chef at La Coserie here."

"Who do you work for now?"

"For Mr. Pentell, primarily."

"This gentleman to my left?"

"Yes." The chef smiled. "He hired me away from my last restaurant. Actually I only work for Mr. Pentell three or four days a week. The other days I like to keep my hand in the pastry business. Mr. Pentell is not very fond of desserts."

Jurors could look from the lean defendant to the jowly witness and believe this distinction.

Burke asked, "Were you at Mr. Pentell's residence the evening of October twenty-fifth of last year?"

"Yes. Earlier he had had a business meeting for which I'd made canapés, and then I also prepared a late dinner for him."

"Did that meal get interrupted?"

"Yes. A little after nine Mr. Pentell got a telephone call. He listened and then told me he had to go out."

"Did he say why?"

"I'm sure he did, but I don't remember."

"Were you also there, Mr. Seuret, when Raleigh Pentell returned to his home that night?"

"Yes. I had been trying to keep the dinner warm, so I noted the time."

"How long was Mr. Pentell gone that night?"

"Not long. A little over an hour, no more."

"How did he appear when he returned?"

"Fine. Perfectly the same."

"Not disheveled, bloody, alarmed, aroused, out of breath, looking over his shoulder as if pursued?"

The heavyset chef smiled at the idea. "No. None of those things."

"Thank you, sir. I now pass you to the District Attorney for cross-examination."

Chris gave the chef his winning smile. He had expected Raleigh Pentell to come up with some kind of alibi witness, but he had thought Pentell would be forced to rely on the easily discreditable testimony of one of the "associates" who worked for him and hung around his house. Chris hadn't counted on the unconcerned-looking man sitting before him.

"Mr.—could you pronounce your name again for me, please?"

"Sooh-rey," the chef smiled, approximately.

"Thank you. Mr. Seuret, have you ever been convicted of a crime?"

The witness smiled again. "No."

"None, are you sure? Even back in Paris? Stealing a loaf of bread, perhaps?"

"No, nothing."

"Why did you decide to leave a position as head chef at one of the finest restaurants in San Antonio in order to devote your attentions to one man?"

"I had grown tired of restaurant hours."

"And yet Mr. Pentell kept you up late occasionally. What time did you say it was when he got back home that night?"

"About ten."

"And what did you do while you waited for him to return? Read, watch television?"

The chef shook his head. "I finished my own dinner and had another glass of wine, while listening to music."

Chris glanced at the defense table and saw Lowell Burke watching his witness closely, prepared to object. Chris pondered.

"Mr. Sueret, I notice you don't wear a watch. Do you usually?"

The smiling witness shook his head again. "I keep track of time by my stomach. In the kitchen I use timers. The rest of the day, time doesn't matter to me."

"Then how do you know what time Raleigh Pentell returned home that night?"

"He told me. He said, 'Victor, don't worry about me. It's almost ten o'clock.' "

"And so you—?"

"I went off to bed. I was very tired after my long evening."

Chris glanced again at the defense lawyer. Burke had been lucky to come up with a witness for Pentell who couldn't be impeached with a criminal record. But that also meant Burke was stuck with this man. In a way he would have been better off with Pentell's thugs, who would do as they were told and follow the script. Chris decided to gamble on the chef's honesty.

"One last question, Mr. Seuret. When Raleigh Pentell returned home, did he finish the dinner that you had saved for him?"

Seuret frowned for the first time. "No. I found it still in the oven the next morning. I suppose it had dried out."

"Thank you, sir. No more questions."

Lowell Burke decided not to risk any more either. As the chef made his slow way up the aisle of the courtroom George Stiegers stepped in from the hallway and nodded at Chris, who turned to the judge.

"We're ready for the identification attempt, Your Honor, if Mr. Burke still wants to try it."

Burke gave Chris a suspicious sidelong glance but said confidently, "We certainly do, Your Honor. Recall Alicia Green."

The thin brisk gardening lady passed Victor Seuret in the doorway, looking like members of different species, then Mrs. Green resumed the witness stand as if eager to reclaim it or to be done with this chore.

Lowell Burke remained on his feet to ask, "Are you the same Alicia Green who testified earlier?"

"Yes, yes."

"Mrs. Green, we're going to have someone step into the courtroom for just a minute—right, Mr. District Attorney? Don't say anything while he's here. I'll ask you a question after he's taken out again."

A bailiff stood at a side door at the front of the courtroom. He unlocked the door with a key on his belt, reached inside the door, and produced Peter Belasco like a jack-in-the-box. Belasco had been delivered to the ground floor of the Justice Center in a van from the jail and brought upstairs through a pattern of elevators and narrow hallways secreted between courtroom walls so that prisoners didn't have to be taken through the public halls of the building. Belasco looked startled, like a man caught at something. He no longer wore his natty suit, he was dressed like all inmates in an orange coverall and flip-flops. Thick dark hair showed below his pale throat.

He looked around the courtroom, waiting for someone to ask him a question or give him direction, but no one spoke. They all just stared at him. It must have been an eerie experience for the cocky young man, as if the world had gone silent. Finally he looked at the witness stand, saw Alicia Green sitting there, and blinked with no sign of recognition.

Judge Benitez made a small gesture and the bailiff pushed Belasco back through the doorway. Belasco began to say something, but the door closed in his face and the bailiff locked him away.

Lowell Burke's voice seemed unnaturally loud as he asked, "Mrs. Green, can you identify that person who was just brought into the courtroom?"

"That was the man I saw talking to Jean Fitzgerald the night her daughter disappeared."

No one gasped. The identification seemed foregone. But Burke passed the witness with a triumphant expression.

Chris asked carefully, "Are you sure, Mrs. Green? Didn't you see other young men at the house across the street from time to time? In fact didn't the older daughter in that home have a boyfriend you may have seen there? Could it have been one of these other young men you saw that night?"

The witness said, "Those are boys. The one I saw that night and in the courtroom just now is a grown man. I'm not so old I don't know that distinction."

"I didn't think that at all, Mrs. Green. Thank you."

Dismissed, Alicia Green left the courtroom more slowly than she'd entered, not looking at her neighbor Jean as she passed her. Chris couldn't tell the impression the defense witness had made. She seemed a bit comical—the snoopy old lady—but her testimony had not been uncertain, and she had certainly messed up Chris's careful pinning-down of Raleigh Pentell as the only suspect in Kristen's murder.

"You have another witness?" Judge Benitez asked the defense lawyer.

"Raleigh Pentell, Your Honor," Lowell Burke said in his rich tones, then turned toward the clock on the wall above the courtroom doors. "Perhaps we should begin after lunch, though?"

The clock hadn't yet reached eleven-thirty, but Judge Benitez took the suggestion as a defense request, and granted it. "Yes. We will resume at one o'clock."

So Burke would have another hour and a half to rehearse his client and patch holes in the defense case. The two of them hurried out. Chris sat while the courtroom cleared out. When George Stiegers bent to say something to him, Chris just said, "I'll meet you upstairs." He sat thinking of Peter Belasco in Jean's driveway, wondering what they'd said to each other, why he had gone there at all.

"He was looking for his boss," said a voice behind him.

Jean stood over him. Chris looked up at her and didn't answer, remembering her voice on his phone last night.

"Peter Belasco came to my house because he thought Raleigh had come there with Kristen. He just wanted to know what had happened. So did I. I told him they hadn't been there. We talked for a minute in the front yard and Peter left. That was it."

She crossed her arms suddenly as if cold. Her arms showed gooseflesh. She looked past Chris and said, "I asked him to call me when he found them. He never did. Nobody did. I sat up all night waiting to hear. All night."

She hugged herself harder, and tears leaked from the corners of her eyes. Chris stood up, put his arm around her, and saw over Jean's shoulder that a single reporter remained in the courtroom, watching them curiously. Chris led Jean to a door behind the judge's bench and took her out of the courtroom into a narrow private hallway that led to the court offices and jury rooms: They stood alone there.

"You knew Kristen hadn't gone to St. Louis," he said, but not accusingly. Jean sighed.

"I didn't know what to think. I didn't. Clarissa came home late and said she didn't know what had happened to her either. I tried to think of who I could call, but I—"

She sobbed harder, remembering more than three months in hellish limbo, her daughter missing. Chris couldn't imagine the horror of wondering every day exactly where Kristen was, whether she was in pain. It must have been unbearable for Jean, always smarter than everyone else, always in control. He saw her hands move helplessly.

Jean slumped back against the wall, then slid down it to the floor. Chris went down on his knees with her. She leaned her head into his shoulder. "I'm so sorry, Chris, that I kept her from you. Back then I wanted to be free of everybody. I thought I could be. I thought I could be completely independent and happy. Just me and my children. That's all I thought anybody needed. God, I wish—" She looked up at him, face streaked with tears. "God would never give me another chance. I wish I could make it up to you. We could have had a life."

He put his arms around her and she clung to his neck. "My baby," Jean mumbled. Chris just held her, so that for a long moment it seemed true that they could have had a life together. It felt as if they had, and his own real past glimmered uncertainly.

Trial resumed promptly at 1 P.M. It now seemed obvious that the defense theory would be that Peter Belasco had met his boss somewhere, offered to take the girl off his hands, and had murdered her himself, then had begun to frame Pentell for the job in order to take over from him.

Chris saw the defense's direction but no way to stop them. Maybe their version was the truth, in fact. The evidence Chris had didn't even convince himself.

Judge Benitez was the self-effacing sort of judge who took the bench so quickly that his bailiff sometimes missed his entrance and didn't have the chance to order everyone to stand. The judge made such a quick ascension to the bench this afternoon, and the jurors filed into their seats even before one o'clock. They looked expectantly at the defense table. Lowell Burke didn't disappoint them. "The defense calls Raleigh Pentell," he intoned with a wave of his hand like a game show emcee introducing the host.

Pentell quickly stood, listened attentively with his right hand raised as the judge recited the oath, said, "I do" loudly, and took his seat, stretching his neck to loosen his collar and then watching his lawyer carefully. He didn't look at Chris Sinclair, who studied him closely. What did Raleigh Pentell look like to someone who knew nothing about him? Chris thought a dangerous man loomed behind the defendant's sun-burnished hair and skin. Pentell had a broad face that would smile handsomely, but his eyes were small and quick. He laced his long, carefully tended fingers around one knee.

"Please state your name, age, and profession."

"Raleigh Pentell. Forty-two. I'm in the import-export business. Machine parts and the like."

"Are you nervous, Mr. Pentell?"

The defendant flashed an abashed grin and his whole appearance changed. One could see the boy he had been, both shy and mischievous. Burke had been wise to induce that face on his client. Smiling shyly, Pentell said, "Yes. I've never testified before."

"Quite all right. You'd be a damned fool not to be nervous at a time like this. Just keep taking deep breaths and you'll do fine."

Pentell nodded, and his shoulders lifted.

"Raleigh, first I want to ask you about Peter Belasco. Does he work for you?"

"No. Not in the sense of drawing a salary. He was more of an independent contractor, I guess you'd call him. Sometimes he brought me bulk merchandise I could sell to my distributors. He always had receipts and a paper trail of where he'd bought the material, but there was something about his manner that made me suspicious. I dealt with him less and less."

"And yet the boys who did work for Belasco knew your name," Burke said.

"Yes. I'm sure Belasco had implied to them that he had a partner, some bogeyman to help him keep the boys in line. And he seized on my name for the role."

Burke frowned as if he would bring all his powers to bear to pick apart his client's story. "But Kristen Lorenz seemed to know you personally. Everyone says she was shouting accusations against you even before you arrived at the restaurant that night."

Pentell nodded. "Kristen did know me. I had been to her home. She knew me because I was dating her mother. Jean Fitzgerald and I had met at a party and started going out. We were romantically involved."

"How long had that been going on?"

"Several months."

"Was it serious?"

Pentell shrugged and looked boyish again as his eyes sought out Jean in the courtroom. "I was serious," he said quietly. "I can only speak for myself."

"So you knew Mrs. Fitzgerald's daughters because of your relationship with their mother. How did you get along with Kristen?"

Pentell chose his words carefully. "I really didn't try to get along with her at all. I wanted her to know I wasn't trying to be a father figure for her or intrude into her life at all. Maybe because of that I was too distant. She did seem to resent me. She would pointedly leave the room when I came in. Her mother told me not to worry about it, it didn't have anything to do with me, it was just Kristen not wanting anyone else to take up any of her mother's time." Pentell coughed diplomatically. "A fairly common reaction in teenage girls, I think."

This tack took Chris so completely by surprise he wondered why he hadn't considered the possibility. He sat without strategy, watching the defendant as if Chris were only another member of the jury trying to gauge Pentell's truthfulness, and found him believable. The defendant looked nervous but sincere.

"So when Peter Belasco called you from the restaurant that night, what did you do?"

"I decided I'd better go. Kristen was disrupting Peter's party and I felt a little responsible."

"So you went not because you were afraid of Kristen's revealing secrets about some mystical criminal enterprise—"

George Stiegers, seeing Chris sit unmoving, stood and objected. "Mr. Burke is making a jury argument, Your Honor."

"Sustained. Please confine yourself to questions, Mr. Burke."

"Certainly, Your Honor. Forgive me for getting carried away. Mr. Pentell, let me put it this way. What was your motive in going to the restaurant?"

"I just wanted to take care of the situation, take Kristen home."

"Were you afraid of what she might say?"

"No. She didn't know anything that would hurt me."

"Were you mad at her?"

"No. I understood. She was a confused young girl. I felt bad that I had in a way helped put her in this situation."

"Did you hate her?"

Pentell shook his head with a slight, sad smile. "Certainly not."

Burke leaned forward intently. "Raleigh, did you have any reason to kill that girl?"

"No. What happened to Kristen was horrible. For her mother, for me, for everybody. A terrible waste. I would never have caused such a tragedy."

"Did you kill Kristen Lorenz?"

"No. Absolutely not."

"What did you do with her?"

"I took her home."

This simple statement stopped the trial dead. Lowell Burke paused to let it sink in. Pentell sat, doing his best to look simple and sincere. Chris turned and found Jean in the audience. Her face had gone white, completely drained of blood so that her hair looked bright red and her blue eyes like holes in her face. No one could feign such shock. She shook her head slowly, then increasingly faster.

Jurors watched her too, until the defense lawyer began another question. "You took Kristen straight home?"

"Yes. Straight home. Where else would I have gone?" Pentell didn't look into the audience. He kept his attention fastened on his lawyer.

"Was anyone home when you got there?"

"Her mother was."

"Anyone else?"

"Not that I saw. I didn't go into the house. When Jean came to the door Kristen bolted inside and I thought it best not to impose my presence on her any longer. I told Jean in a few words what had happened."

"Did you tell her anything else?"

Raleigh Pentell appeared abashed again. He looked down at his hands, twisted together, then up again. "I told her I thought it best that we not see each other anymore, at least not for a while."

Lowell Burke sounded slightly unbelieving and disapproving. "You broke up with her, there on the doorstep? Over something her daughter had done?"

"That's not the way I meant it. I tried to say that Kristen was adjusting so badly to my being involved with Jean that maybe we should cool it for a while. I wanted her to be able to go in the house and tell her daughter it would be okay, that she wouldn't have to see me anymore. But Jean took it more the way you're saying, that I was dumping her because of Kristen. She slammed the door in my face."

"Had you seen her like that before?"

"Objection, Your Honor!" George Stiegers bounded to his feet. "This is completely self-serving, unsubstantiated testimony. It's also irrelevant, whatever way Mrs. Fitzgerald reacted."

Chris would have told his young assistant to keep his seat, if he'd had time to react. Without any response from the defense Judge Benitez said, "Overruled." And now Pentell's testimony would have extra weight, because it looked as if the prosecution wanted it kept from the jury.

"Yes sir," the defendant said sincerely. "Jean had quite a temper. I'd seen her get mad before. There was no reasoning with her when that happened."

"Before she slammed the door in your face, did she say anything?"

"Yes. She said, 'Don't let her come between us.' "

"Meaning Kristen?"

"That's how I took it, yes."

" 'Don't let her come between us,' " Lowell Burke repeated, appearing to write the phrase laboriously on a legal pad; in fact emphasizing it for the jury. "And then after she slammed the door in your face, what did you do?"

"I went home."

"Did you ever see Kristen Lorenz alive again?"

"No sir. Not after that night."

Lowell Burke nodded his head in satisfaction and gave his client an encouraging look. "I pass the witness."

George Stiegers hesitated. They had planned all along that Chris would cross-examine the defendant if he dared to testify, but George had jumped in with objections and tradition held that the lawyer who objected during the direct examination was also responsible for cross-examination. Besides, the District Attorney sat, showing no inclination to ask any questions. George cleared his throat and Chris didn't react. George said, "Mr. Pentell, my name is George Stiegers. I'm going to ask you a few questions now. You and I haven't met before, have we?"

"No." It seemed Pentell couldn't bring himself to call young George "sir."

"When you got the call from the restaurant that night, you immediately left to take care of the situation?"

"That's right."

"What did you think you'd do with Kristen?"

"I thought I'd take her home."

"To her mother."

"Yes."

"Then why didn't you just call her mother to go get her? You knew that letting Kristen see you would probably make matters worse, didn't you? And you did have a relationship with her mother, so why didn't you call her and ask her to go get her daughter?"

Pentell looked momentarily flustered, but during George's lengthy questioning he recovered. "I did try to call Jean."

"You did? I don't remember your cook saying you made a phone call before you left the house. And you just said that you left immediately. Do you want to change your story?"

"No. I called Jean from the car, from my cell phone. She didn't answer."

"But you were already in the car before you thought of calling her. Initially you thought you had to take care of Kristen yourself. Why?"

"I just reacted. Peter called me, so I went to help. It wasn't until I was in the car that I thought of letting Jean pick up Kristen, but as I say, she didn't answer her phone."

"And yet you say she was home shortly after that when you supposedly took Kristen home."

"Yes. I didn't ask her where she'd been."

George didn't write on his legal pad or otherwise let himself get distracted. He stared at the defendant as he questioned him. "Mr. Pentell, let me ask you this. When Peter Belasco called you from the restaurant, did he repeat to you what Kristen Lorenz was saying about you?"

"Yes. Well, the general tone of her remarks. I don't remember if he told me anything specific."

"And what did you think of the idea that Kristen was loudly accusing you of criminal conduct in a public place?"

Pentell shrugged offhandedly. "I thought it was in keeping with her behavior toward me. Kristen had just thought of a new direction."

"It didn't bother you that she was saying these things about you, in a restaurant where you were well known?"

"No."

"You weren't concerned at all that she might be revealing details of your criminal enterprises?"

"No. There aren't any such details."

"And yet you immediately jumped in your car and rushed to the restaurant to take care of her, leaving your dinner uneaten and not thinking of calling the girl's mother? What did put you in such a panic?"

"I wasn't panicked. I just—I was concerned about Kristen."

Chris decided George would be just fine. He looked into the audience again, saw Jean's seat vacant, stood up as quietly as he could, drawing barely a glance from his assistant, and hurried out of the courtroom.

When he emerged he saw Jean at the far end of the hallway, pacing furiously away from him. She pivoted on a heel and came back toward him, unseeing. Jean's face had regained its color, and more. She flushed angrily. Her lips moved, curses aimed at Raleigh Pentell.

When Chris drew near she saw him and immediately began shaking her head. "No," she said abruptly. "He never came near my house that night. Brought Kristen home! The hell he did. I waited and waited. He's lying his ass off. With that little damned concerned expression, like he—Chris, believe me—"

"I do," he said quietly, taking her arm and leading her back toward the quiet end of the hall. "He surprised me, too. I'm going to have to recall you as a witness. Is it all lies, everything he said?"

"Yes! He—"

"I mean about you and him."

Jean suddenly saw Chris in focus. Her fury abated and she looked embarrassed. "Well, not all of it. We did go out a few times. He could call people who saw us together."

"I see." Chris's voice remained quiet. He stared at his long-ago girlfriend, feeling betrayed. A stupid reaction, he thought, but Jean reciprocated by acting guilty. She reached for him.

"It wasn't anything. In fact, at first it was just something to tell the girls about why Raleigh and I were spending time together, because, you know, I didn't want to tell them about our business. But then—I don't know, he got a little bit serious, I guess."

"It doesn't matter."

She kept a grip on his arm. "But I'll say anything else you need, Chris. He called that night to say he was bringing Kristen home, but they never showed up. Something happened. He killed her, Chris, I know he did. I'll testify I saw them together. I'll say I saw it happen."

Jean would look worse than unbelievable as a witness if she suddenly recalled having seen the murder, something she had forgotten to mention during her previous testimony. Chris didn't believe any more testimony would help. Testimony could always be challenged, back and forth as the prosecution and defense had already done, leaving the jury nowhere. "I need something concrete. Some physical evidence he can't refute."

Pentell had an alternative theory he had presented to

the jury and Chris couldn't prove his own version. He only had Pentell's car disappearing into the night, just as the prosecution case was disappearing now.

"If only I could put them together somewhere else later that night. But I've scoured his house. There's no evidence he took her there."

"What can I do?" Jean pleaded.

"Nothing, I'm sorry."

She stopped him as he turned away. Her eyes seemed to have grown larger, magnified by tears. "Chris, can we—No, that can wait until after the trial. Listen. Don't forget what I told you. Raleigh will try to get back at you. No matter what. Be careful."

But at this point it looked as if Raleigh Pentell had little to fear from the District Attorney.

Chris returned to the courtroom to watch the rest of George's cross-examination of the defendant. Pentell's eyes fixed momentarily on the District Attorney as he took his seat. In the black depths of Pentell's eyes Chris's image disappeared. Chris noted again the defendant's elegant posture, the composure of his hands. Kristen Lorenz had broken through Pentell's calm that night in October, but George Stiegers couldn't do the same in the courtroom.

"Can you explain how blood got inside the door panel of your car?" he asked.

"No," Pentell said immediately. His attorney must have advised him it would be better to claim ignorance than to try to sell some excuse to the jurors. "Your own witness said it was only a trace. A cut some passenger didn't even notice or didn't wipe away the slight amount of blood before the window got rolled down. I don't know. A lot of people use my car."

"Why don't you go home tonight and ask them if they're in the habit of throwing beef around inside the car, or cutting themselves and forgetting about it?"

"Objection, Your Honor. That's not a question, it's harassment of the witness."

"Sustained," Judge Benitez said. Chris laid a restraining hand on his assistant's arm.

"Pass the witness," George concluded.

"No further questions, Your Honor. The defense rests."

The words frightened Chris, the announcement that traditionally signaled the conclusion of the case. But Chris wasn't ready for this one to end. The judge looked at him mildly.

"Counselor, do you have rebuttal witnesses?"

"Yes, Your Honor," Chris said hastily, standing. "The State recalls Jean Fitzgerald."

As Jean passed the defense table Raleigh Pentell cast a sympathetic expression on her. She glared back at him.

After a couple of preliminary questions, Chris asked, "Did Peter Belasco come to your house the night of Kristen's disappearance?"

"Yes. Just as my neighbor said. He was looking for his boss, Raleigh Pentell. I told him I hadn't seen Raleigh and Peter left."

"Did Raleigh Pentell bring Kristen home to your house that night?"

"No. That is an absolute lie."

Don't look angry, Jean. Look sad. He took your child.

"Did Kristen come home to you that night?"

"No." Jean's eyes moved off the defendant's face, to Chris's, as if she had to explain herself to him. "She never did. I waited and waited." Her anger drained away, leaving her looking helpless. "I prayed she was okay, but I was afraid. When I found out she'd left the restaurant with Raleigh I knew he'd killed her."

"Objection," Lowell Burke interjected. "To the speculation."

"It's not," Jean said to him. "Do you want me to tell you how I know?"

Jean stared at the defense lawyer, who quietly subsided into his seat without a ruling on his objection.

Chris led Jean through as many refutations of the defendant's testimony as he thought he could safely get from Jean. Partly he was just drawing out the time, and he achieved what he wanted in that regard.

"Ms. Fitzgerald, were you angry at your daughter because she came between you and the defendant?"

"No. That's ridiculous. I would never be mad at one of my children over something like that. If that happened it wouldn't be Kristen I'd blame."

"One more question, Ms. Fitzgerald. Do you have any form of amphetamine around your house? Over-the-counter diet pills or anything of that nature?"

The question obviously took Jean by surprise. She stared at Chris as if asking for the right answer, then said slowly, "I think so. At one time—Yes, I'm sure we do."

"Was your daughter Kristen in the habit of taking them?"

"No. Never. Kristen hated any kind of drugs. She used to say so regularly."

Chris didn't ask how the subject came up. "No more questions."

"I have none, Your Honor," Lowell Burke said, not wanting to give Jean any more opportunities to reach the jurors.

"Approach the bench, please."

The attorneys did so, Chris looking ready to continue. But that look was a fraud.

Judge Benitez asked him quietly, "You have more rebuttal witnesses to present?"

"Yes, Your Honor." Who those might be Chris had no idea. "They're not immediately available, though. I'll have to send for them. I didn't expect the defense to rest this early."

"All right. It's getting late on a Friday afternoon. We obviously will not conclude today, and I want the jury to be fresh when they begin deliberating. We'll recess for the day if there is no objection."

No one objected. The lawyers resumed their seats and Judge Benitez turned a benevolent expression on the jury. "Ladies and gentlemen, the case will not be finished today. We could work late, but then I would have to sequester you in a hotel for the weekend. I think you would much rather sleep in your own beds. But you must remember my instructions. Do not read or watch any news coverage remotely touching this trial. Don't even think about this case.

"Have a nice weekend. Go home to your families."

The jurors looked delighted to do so, shuffling quickly out of the jury box before the judge changed his mind. When they were gone Judge Benitez turned to the trial participants. "I would give all of you the same advice. Go home to your families."

Then he realized what he knew about some of the people in front of him, and how inappropriate his instruction was. He smiled as if in embarrassment and quickly left the room, leaving them all standing uncomfortably in one another's presence.

3

But a cold wind blows into my heart from the past.
For I remember Babylon.

—Arthur C. Clarke

Thirteen

Over the weekend, far from the courtroom, the case finally broke open for Chris Sinclair. It began late Friday afternoon when he got home to the condo and found Clarissa on the phone. Chris wasn't surprised to hear her voice. He'd called her police escort and asked to have Clarissa dropped off here, wanting to see her as soon as possible. He knew Clarissa would like the change too, and felt glad that she preferred his home to Anne's.

Clarissa, talking on the phone in the spare bedroom, standing with her back to the bedroom door, hadn't heard him come in. Chris had a moment's lapse of time when he saw her, one knee bent and hip cocked, arm akimbo on that hip, nearly barking into the phone. She might have been Jean, giving orders to a teenaged Chris.

"You don't know," Clarissa said harshly. "Yes, *I* do. Because I'm the one who's here, that's why."

She turned, caught a glimpse of Chris, didn't overtly look startled, but transformed herself. Her legs drew together, she took her fist from her hip and crossed that arm under her breasts, inclining her head into the phone submissively. As if the change in posture had changed Clarissa's personality too, she lowered her voice, saying softly, "I will. Yes. I promise. Yes, just now. Do you—? All right."

Clarissa hung up the phone, looked directly at Chris, and said as if it explained everything, "Mom."

"Is she okay?"

Clarissa shrugged. "She wants me home. Excuse me." She gave him a hurried kiss on the cheek—something that had become an awkward ritual between them—and went into the bathroom.

Chris wasn't surprised at the transformation he'd witnessed. He knew that Clarissa acted more childlike with him than she must in other places. Her past life would have demanded more toughness than he'd seen, and he'd heard from other sources that she had been a leader among her school friends. Chris hoped that her quiet shyness with him wasn't just a pose, that staying with him allowed the girl to have the childhood that life had denied her.

Clarissa had turned on his computer in the bedroom. Idly he pressed keys, waiting for her to return. In a minute the modem beeped out into the world and found his messages, which he hadn't checked all week. Near the end of the list, recently received, one E-mail address seemed to glow more brightly, immediately drawing his attention: "Krislore."

He cursored quickly down to the message, feeling his heart speed up with anticipation, as if Kristen would be sending him new information.

She had:

Raleigh scares me. I've seen his eyes go so dark nobody could get inside his head. I know deep down inside there he's mean as the Devil. I want Mom to see that. See how scary he is. I want him out of our lives, but he scares me. If I start blabbing his secrets, he'll kill me. I know he would. Kids say he's killed other people.

But he scares me so bad I know I've got to do it, to save Mom and
Clarissa.

"What is it?" Clarissa asked from the living room.

"Nothing. Something from work." Chris pressed the
Print button, folded the message away into his pocket and
deleted it from the computer screen.

"Are you okay?"

Clarissa looked at him with obvious concern, but made
no move to see his message.

"I'm fine. It was just a long day."

"I thought you might have to stay late tonight to finish
the trial. Anne wants you to call her. She and I sort of
made plans to go eat without you."

Clarissa wore a simple sleeveless ribbed white top and
widely flared blue jeans. She was very thin, thinner even
than he remembered her mother years ago, with a long
torso and longer legs. Clarissa's eyes didn't have Jean's
clarity. She studied Chris curiously.

"I talked to your mother, too," he said. "She wants to
see you this weekend."

Clarissa's eyes shifted away and her shoulders
slumped. "Do I have to?"

Her dejected look suddenly shamed Chris anew.
Quickly he crossed the room to her. "You don't have to
do anything you don't want to do, baby." What a lie. But
in that moment he wanted to make it true, wanted to protect Clarissa from any further damage. He put his arms
around her, her head against his shoulder. Clarissa
hugged him back. He felt the crackle of her dead sister's
message in his pocket.

Both Clarissa and Kristen murmured in his ears.

Later, sitting over the remains of pizza with Anne and
Clarissa, Chris stayed quiet, listening to the two of them
talk. He had changed out of his suit into a polo shirt and

jeans, but still felt set apart: the only man in the room, the only lawyer, the only one with responsibility for the two girls.

The E-mail message now lay folded in his drawer, but it still called to him. *If I start blabbing his secrets, he'll kill me.*

Jean, he thought suddenly. She had said she would do anything to help him convict Pentell. The message qualified. Jean had Kristen's diary and had been sending him messages from it. That made sense. She would have searched Kristen's room after she went missing. The diary would have been there somewhere.

"What is it?" Anne said. Clarissa watched him, too.

"Nothing. Just maybe thought of something."

"He's always like this when he's in trial," Anne confided to Clarissa. "He looks like he's here with us, but he's really not. Go ahead, say something to him and see if he remembers it tomorrow." She gazed at him fondly. He would remember that. Her expression. Anne at his table, with Clarissa beside her, their heads close together from their interrupted conversation.

He wanted to ask Anne what she thought of Clarissa, whether she had any insights into the girl, but there was never a chance. At the end of the evening when Clarissa went into the bedroom to use the computer or the phone, Anne took the opportunity to say good-bye. "I'll be glad when this trial is over," she murmured.

In an odd way, Chris wouldn't be. The trial brought Kristen close to him. He bent toward Anne. Her hands moved, one on his back, the other climbing toward his neck. Chris suddenly stiffened.

"What is it?"

"Nothing, nothing. A little twinge. Sorry."

Anne laughed. "You can't get old yet. Not for a long time."

Chris couldn't tell Anne what had really disconcerted him for a moment, the image that had suddenly come unbidden to him as they'd embraced. If he told her he'd been thinking about Raleigh Pentell's hands, she would kill him.

He bent to kiss Anne again, then when he raised his head caught a glimpse of Clarissa, who had returned to the living room and stood there frankly staring at them. Her face looked perfectly bare of expression.

She too came to say good-bye to Anne, and whispered something to her that made Anne shake her head tightly and Clarissa laugh. *What was that about?* Chris wondered, glad to see the two of them communicating so well but not enjoying being excluded from the process.

The next morning Chris met Jack Fine in the parking lot of the Château du Hair on McCullough near Olmos Park. Neither of them had ever been there before; Jack had sent another investigator to check out the place where Raleigh Pentell used to get his hair cut, where he'd had an appointment the day after Kristen disappeared and then never returned. That investigation hadn't turned up anything. The hairdresser hadn't remembered Pentell appearing out of the ordinary or making any memorable remarks.

But Chris had been struck last night with a sudden desire to check the place out. Jack wore a coat and tie. Chris was dressed more like Saturday, in khaki slacks and a short-sleeved blue shirt, but they both still felt out of place when they entered the salon. Not because they were men. Most of the hairdressers were men, and a couple of male customers were being tended in the barber chairs. But a hair salon still held an ineffably feminine atmosphere, removed from the world of business or sports. The winkingly named Château du Hair appeared, in fact, to have little connection to planet Earth. Inside, the air was cool but flavored with the enveloping chemicals of hair prep. The place did not look elegant; elegance held no fashion here. The floor was concrete, painted white and with a pattern of vines. The only dividers in the large room were the stylists' stations with tall mirrors, and industrial-looking black metal trellises that held shelves of oils and unguents.

It was Saturday morning, the place filled with customers. One stylist, a tall man with an earring and his hair cut to stubble length from his chin to his crown, stopped as he hurried by and said, "Help you?"

Jack said, "We're looking for Armando."

The stylist spread his hands and said, "You're a good looker."

Jack, who had never received such a compliment in his life, even ironically, realized that the man meant they'd found their quarry. Jack waited for Chris to begin the questioning. After all, it had been the District Attorney's idea to visit this scene. But Chris gazed around the room intently as if searching for something he couldn't name. Armando, apparently, wasn't it.

So Jack asked, "You used to cut Raleigh Pentell's hair?"

"Oh, sure." Armando resumed his walk and waved them to join him. He reached his station, stood behind a woman with small foil wrappers folded all through her hair, mouthed his customer a kiss in the mirror, and said, "Hasn't someone already asked me about this?"

"Just rechecking. He doesn't come to you anymore, is that right?"

"Check."

"But you went over your records and found that the last time he did was late in October of last year?"

"Check again. I remember I offered to give him a Halloween cut." Armando waited for response and when he got none said, "He had as much sense of humor as you do."

"Do you remember anything he did say?"

"No. In fact he hardly talked at all. He was almost falling asleep in the chair. I've gone over this in my mind again since your guy questioned me and since I've seen about the trial on TV, and he just did not do anything unusual. Believe me, I'd like to help you. If he killed that girl I would not cover up for him. But he just didn't say anything."

"Yet he changed hair stylists after that morning," Jack insisted. "Why? What happened? You raise your prices?"

Armando laughed artificially, glancing at his customer in the mirror. "I am worth every penny. Isn't that right, sweetie? Let's just check the progress here . . ."

"Shit," Chris said suddenly.

"What?" Jack spun to face the interior of the shop, the way Chris was looking, and didn't see anything odd. "What?"

"Always go to the scene," Chris said, walking through the maze. "Isn't that what you taught me, Jack? Always go to the scene yourself."

"The scene of what?"

Instead of answering, Chris continued to lead him through the chairs and stylists and customers. As they climbed three steps into an open alcove and Jack saw their destination, Jack repeated his boss's observation: "Oh, shit."

The manicurist, with bright red hair, plump but tight cheeks, and a small red mouth that opened suspiciously, looked up from the hand she was tending and said, "Can I help you? Need a manicure? I'm pretty booked today, but if you want to wait . . ."

She looked confused when Chris Sinclair said, "Not the hair. He didn't quit coming here because of the stylist."

Jack nodded.

Chris's next break in the case came from an almost forgotten source: Olga Zamora, the investigator he'd placed undercover in Holmes High School. Olga hadn't produced any new information in weeks. Chris vaguely figured she was busy studying for finals.

Sunday afternoon found him uncharacteristically alone. Jean had wanted Clarissa to come home for the weekend, but Chris had refused that, thinking this weekend constituted a dangerous time for the girl. He had announced in court Friday that he had more witnesses, and Raleigh Pentell would spend this weekend wondering who they might be. But Jean had insisted and Chris had compromised by saying Clarissa could spend Sunday with her mother if she wanted and if an investigator stayed close to them throughout the day. Jean reluctantly agreed to the latter condition and Clarissa reluctantly agreed to go, showing little enthusiasm for reuniting with the mother from whom she'd been separated for weeks. "I'd better go," she'd said, hugging Chris as if in prelude to a long departure.

So Sunday afternoon Chris had free time and couldn't remember what people did with that commodity. He had just decided to try Anne's number again and if he got no answer go shoot baskets somewhere, when his phone rang.

"About time," he said into the receiver. "Where have—" then realized abruptly that the caller was not who he'd expected.

Without introduction Olga Zamora said, "Raleigh Pentell has another house."

The afternoon vanished down a swirl of rushed moments: phone calls, a hurried trip to the office to write a search warrant, finding a judge to sign it, calling in investigators and cops from their day off. Olga Zamora joined Chris for much of that activity, filling him in on the run.

"Kids are betting on Pentell to beat the case," she said knowingly, "and they're kind of lining up to get on his team again. Or even if they figure he's going down, then they try to shiver each other with stories about how close they were to him, how it could've been them instead of Kristen Lorenz."

How lovely that would have been. Chris might still be

pursuing the case now, but not feel so personally haunted by it.

Olga sat in the passenger seat of Chris's car, air through the window blowing back her long black hair. She leaned her elbow on the door frame, appearing to relish the breeze and her accomplishment. "So I'm digging for info in little ways, pretending I know some things, trying to get them to top me, and today at EZ's one boy finally does. He says, 'I'm just glad I got out of that hide-out of Pentell's alive.' "

Olga turned to Chris. "In a way it's too bad you took Clarissa out of that school. With Ryan McClain dead, I think she may have known more about the operation than anybody. Assuming her boyfriend told her about things. But it's okay, I'm putting together my own network now."

They drove past Trinity University on their left and Chris turned off Hildebrand onto a much narrower street called Shook, then passed the entrance to the Landa branch library and the long sloping lawn in front of it, turned again and parked on the street across from a tall, wide apartment building that blocked out the sun. Standing in that deep shadow, Chris thought of those stupid characters in vampire movies who somehow don't get organized for their raid on the monster's castle until the sun is just on the verge of setting.

The Bushnell Apartments were old-fashioned in the most pleasant ways, with architectural flourishes and a certain elegance that whispered of refurbishing. A uniformed cop saw Chris and Olga crossing the street and pushed open for them a door that would normally have required them to be buzzed in by a resident. They took a very narrow elevator to the third floor and Olga confidently led the way to an apartment as if she knew the route. Someone had left the apartment door ajar. Inside Jack Fine stood in the living room, slowly turning in a circle, peering in every direction, while calling to searchers in the other rooms.

Olga walked down the entry hall. Today she wore jeans that hugged her thin thighs tightly before flaring out widely around her ankles, a simple white T-shirt and a long black suit jacket, as if transitioning back to adulthood from her teen romp. Her hip cocked jauntily, she looked both young and knowing. Chris wondered how close Olga had gotten to some of the high school kids, especially boys. This was an exciting time for the investigator, working undercover. Chris remembered the excitement of the chase on cases when he hadn't been personally involved.

He walked slowly through the two-bedroom apartment, a place not large but lavishly furnished. In the main bedroom a pedestal bed wore its blue velvet spread voluptuously, the spread half-sliding off. An evidence technician crouched at the black lacquered dresser, dusting the drawers for prints. He gave Chris an encouraging nod.

Another uniformed police officer sifted through the clothes in the closet and asked oddly, "What's the suspect's middle name?"

"William," Chris remembered. The officer pulled out a custom-made white dress shirt and dropped it on the bed to display its monogram: an angular P attended by subservient R and W. Raleigh W. Pentell.

"I think we've got a match here," the evidence tech said from the dresser.

Chris, hands in his pockets, continued his stroll through Raleigh Pentell's hideaway. Dark textured wallpaper made the hallway back to the living room seem narrow. The featured attraction of the apartment was its wide balcony view of downtown San Antonio, gorgeous in the dusk. Except for that view the apartment remained dark and confining. Raleigh Pentell lived larger than this, but he must have kept this place as a retreat, his own Bat Cave. Chris opened a drawer in the small kitchen and found a box of the foreign cigarettes he had also seen in Pentell's house. Pentell's name probably didn't appear on this apartment's lease, but he couldn't deny his presence here.

But that wouldn't mean anything without proof that he'd brought Kristen to this apartment. Returning to the living room, Chris asked Jack, "Any blood? Anything?" Jack shook his head regretfully.

Olga Zamora stalked past, talking into a cell phone. Her eyes flashed angrily. Finding this hideout was her triumphant contribution to the investigation, but the lack of evidence diminished its value to nothing.

"What was that you told me about a room or a closet or something?" she said into the phone, her voice slightly higher and more giggly than her normal speaking voice. "Ooh, cool," she squeaked, rolling her eyes at Chris.

She turned off the phone and said, "There's a closet or something here with a false back wall."

"Who was that?"

"One of the kids."

"How did he hear about it?" Chris asked, but Olga had already hurried out of the room to alert the other searchers.

Five minutes later Jack said quietly, "Here," and they all came running to the front hall closet from which Jack had removed the few hanging garments. Jack knelt against the back wall of the closet, his flashlight lying on the floor shining into a two-inch-wide crack where Jack had slid the back wall upward.

Others crowded into the closet to tap the wall and produce echoing sounds. "Break it open," Chris barked, but Jack grunted, "Just a minute," and slid the wall sideways and out of sight, revealing a narrow space. For a horrible moment Chris pictured a small body lying there, legs scrunched up to fit.

But the space was empty, or almost. Jack shone his flashlight into it revealing a blank back wall and nothing else, until he pointed the light downward. Jack reached triumphantly for a small purse that lay on the floor of the secret space.

"Wait," Chris snapped. He scanned the faces around him and picked out a young uniformed officer wearing an earnest expression. "You," Chris told him. "Pick it up. Carefully."

The officer, wearing thin latex gloves, knelt and picked up the purse. Carefully, his hands out in front of him as if he carried nuclear material, he took the purse to a counter that separated the kitchen from the living room. The other searchers crowded close around him as he turned the fake gold latch and slid the contents of the purse out onto the counter.

The purse held very little. Kristen had been too young for a driver's license or credit cards. Chris felt a collective sigh as the team assessed the evidence's lack of value. He had already begun figuring whether he could use the purse in court anyway—why would a man have a girl's purse hidden in his apartment?—when something more substantial slid out of the purse. A small red book fell onto the counter.

"Open it," Chris breathed. "Gently."

The young police officer with his gloved fingers picked up the book as if it were an ancient text that might crumble at his touch, and turned it over. The book was a volume of blank lined pages such as gift shops sold. Its padded cover gave it a trace of elegance. The officer turned to the first page with handwriting, large shaky print that said, *The Book of Kristen.*

A grand title. Not diary or journal or even "Kristen's book." The girl had invested a lot of hope and grandeur in this small volume. A lot of her identity.

"Turn toward the back," Chris said quietly, and the officer flipped the pages. He came to the end of the written pages and turned back a few. "Stop," Chris said suddenly, and they all crowded around to read the small handwriting. "I'm afraid for Mom," it said. "Afraid of what she's getting into . . ."

Chris reached for the book but stopped short of touching it. "Can you get prints off this?" he asked the technician. Jack Fine looked up sharply at his boss.

"It's hers," Chris confirmed, and walked away from the group.

After the fingerprint technician had done his job and handed the book back, Chris took the young officer who'd first picked it up aside and said, "Study this. Look at it carefully so you can identify it. Mark it inside the back cover. And be in court tomorrow morning at nine."

"Yes sir."

A few minutes later Jack saw Chris pocket the small volume. Jack said, "I think we've got a little more work to do here."

"I'm going home," Chris said shortly.

Chris drove straight to Jean's house to pick up Clarissa. He had no intention of mentioning any of the weekend's new evidence, especially the diary that sat in the glove compartment of his car.

Jean answered the door, and her face didn't fall or brighten when she saw him. "Can't you leave her here?" she asked. Chris shook his head, and Jean didn't insist.

Clarissa appeared quickly at her mother's side. Jean put her arm around her daughter's shoulder and they both looked at Chris, Clarissa studying him more intently. Chris looked back at Jean empathetically, feeling that he carried one of her children in his glove compartment and was taking the other away.

" 'Bye, Mom," Clarissa said suddenly, and kissed Jean on the cheek. Jean hugged her hard, still watching Chris, not angrily, only with deep curiosity.

"Why so quiet?" she asked.

Clarissa said, "Oh, he's always like this when he's in trial," and hurried past Chris toward his car. Jean raised her eyes at him and Chris shrugged.

* * *

Clarissa questioned him too on the drive home, but he didn't say much. When they got out of the car she obviously noticed him slip something out of the glove compartment into his pocket, and looked at him curiously. "What did you find?"

"Nothing."

Inside the condo Clarissa paced restlessly, hugging herself and staring around Chris's rooms as if she had missed his home or was memorizing it for future remembering.

"Would you like to stay here tonight?" Chris asked quietly.

Clarissa turned a childlike lonely expression on him. "Please."

"Fine. I'll call Anne."

"Don't you have to get ready for the rest of your trial?"

He just smiled at her in reply. Chris wondered if Jean had talked about him to Clarissa today, what opinion in fact Jean held of him after all these years. Maybe Clarissa wanted to refute her mother's words with her own experience, or just blot out Jean's presence with Chris's. He didn't want to struggle with Jean over Clarissa, but inevitably he was.

Clarissa changed into a long sleeping T-shirt with an agonized-looking Marilyn Manson on the front. She and Chris talked quietly, avoiding the subject of the trial or Clarissa's family. But just when it was time for Clarissa to go to bed she looked at him steadily and said, "Tell me what you found."

Chris pulled out the small red volume. Clarissa gasped. "Oh, God. Kristen."

Her recognition of the diary surprised Chris. "She showed you this?"

"Little sisters think they have secrets, but they don't." Clarissa took the diary, flipped through a few pages, then held it against her chest. "Can I have it?"

"Not yet. I need it for the trial."

Clarissa moved reluctantly toward her room. "Good night."

"Good night, Clarissa." Chris was anxious to be left alone. As soon as the girl slipped through the doorway of her bedroom he went to the kitchen to make himself a drink, then returned to his cozy reading spot on the couch.

The diary was gone.

He didn't look under the sofa cushions or fall into panic. Chris stood in the middle of his living room floor for a long minute, then walked into Clarissa's bedroom. A blade of light from the living room made the corner where her bed stood even blacker. Chris stepped out of the light and saw her as a remarkably small mound under the covers. He sat on her bed and said her name. Clarissa responded with a mumble that sounded far too sleepy for a girl who had just gone to bed.

"Clarissa, give me the book."

She sat up quickly, clutching the diary in both hands. Voice trembly, she begged, "Just let me keep it tonight."

As Chris's eyes adjusted to the dimness he saw tear tracks down her cheeks. She looked imploringly at him.

Chris put his arm around her and that ruined the last shred of Clarissa's resolve. She buried her head in his chest with enough force to jar his collarbone, and sobbed. He held her closer. She burrowed against him, seeming to shrink. Chris tried to soothe her but she only cried harder, as if releasing all at once the fear she had lived with so long. She had nowhere to feel safe. When she finally spoke she sounded like a little girl. "Daddy, save me," she begged softly.

"I will, darling, don't worry about that."

In the manner of a crying child she started sentences and lost them. "I never meant . . . Don't make me . . . She . . . She . . ."

"It's not your fault. Nothing was your fault, Clarissa. You shouldn't have been put in the middle of all this. Don't worry. I'll be here from now on."

He made shushing sounds as one would make to a

baby, a stage of her life he had missed. Clarissa's fingers clutched his collar. He hugged her and rocked her and she gradually subsided into whimpers, then silence. By the time Chris eased her head gently down on her pillow he felt soaked and drained. Clarissa's breathing deepened. But for a moment when he took the diary from her, her fingers tightened.

Chris returned to the couch, looking around his own condo as if appraising a stranger's home, and settled in for his evening's reading. Trial would resume in about nine hours, the last day. He should be preparing his final argument, but instead he read the young girl's diary. Passages that he'd received as E-mail jumped out at him. Young Jason, Kristen's friend, must have been the sender, Kristen must have given him copies of more pages of the diary than Jason had admitted. No one else could have done it, because the actual diary had been lying in Raleigh Pentell's hidden space for months. Jason must have sent the messages to the District Attorney both to keep Kristen alive in some electronic sense and to try to help in the prosecution of her murderer.

He came to the last page of the diary, an innocuous entry about having too much homework. He'd been looking for more accounts of fights with Jean or fear of Pentell. Something that would wrench the jury's hearts. But he found nothing like that.

He quickly realized what he'd missed, and flipped through the diary again. Kristen hadn't covered all that many pages with entries, he could skim it quickly. The passage he looked for didn't appear, Kristen's fearful writing that she knew she had to confront Raleigh Pentell but was afraid he would kill her. He still had that passage on a sheet of paper, but that had only been an electronic message. For there to be any chance of having the passage admitted in court he had to find it in Kristen's own handwriting.

But it wasn't in the diary. If Kristen had confided that

fear to anyone other than Chris, posthumously, it hadn't been to these thin pages.

The next morning the bright, efficient courtroom felt odd to Chris, as if he were a visitor being given a tour. He had regained Kristen's perspective. Before the jury returned Chris stood at the defense table, leaning over so that Raleigh Pentell looked up at him in surprise. Chris stared at the man's long, well-groomed fingers and understood the fear he'd felt on the first day of trial.

His eyes lifted to Pentell's face and Chris felt his own hands tremble as blood pumped into them with the desire to smash that tanned, arrogant face. Pentell looked fearful for a moment, then his eyes darkened and his lips pursed, holding himself back from speaking. The threat he wanted to deliver remained obvious.

Don't forget him, Jean had warned.

Trial began promptly at nine. Chris had his four rebuttal witnesses lined up in his mind, he didn't need notes. "Marie Portillo," he said in response to Judge Benitez's inquiry.

At the defense table Lowell Burke mouthed *Who?* but knew better than to object. Rules required the prosecution to inform the defense of their case-in-chief witnesses, but not rebuttal witnesses. Beside Burke, his client went a shade paler. Up the aisle came the plump manicurist Chris had met two days ago, her red hair shining under the courtroom lights with bright cheerful falsity. Even though Chris had gone over her testimony with her on Saturday and again early this morning, Marie Portillo appeared puzzled to find herself in a witness chair.

"Ms. Portillo, what do you do for a living?"

"I take care of people's hands."

"You're a manicurist?"

"Oh, much more than that. I treat the whole hand. Complexion, texture, stress. I do nails too, but that's only a small part of it."

"Do you recognize anyone in this courtroom?"

"Mr. Pentell, there across from you. He was a client of mine."

She gave the defendant a welcoming smile, obviously not understanding why he looked darkly back at her.

"Ms. Portillo, at my request have you gone over your records for the last eight months or so to determine when was the last time you tended Mr. Pentell's hands?"

"Yes."

"And when was that?"

"Objection," Lowell Burke said suddenly, on his feet as if someone had poked him. "If this witness has refreshed her memory with records, we're entitled to see those records. Furthermore, I can't fathom the relevance of this testimony. Also the defense was not informed that this witness would testify in this trial, so her testimony should be excluded."

Chris indicated the appointment books that sat on a corner of his table, so Judge Benitez said patiently, "Those appear to be the records, which I assume the District Attorney will proffer to you for cross-examination. Yes? Good. And since this is a rebuttal witness the State had no duty to inform you of her testimony. Finally, if you let her continue her testimony I believe we will learn its relevance."

Burke sat down, angry at himself for objecting ineffectually, clearly thinking that the jury must have realized what Ms. Portillo was about to say just as the defense attorney had.

Chris asked her, "When was the last time Mr. Pentell came to see you professionally?"

"It was October twenty-sixth of last year."

"Do you remember that occasion?"

"Of course. He stopped coming to see me after that, which hurt my feelings." She made a small flirtatious moue at the defendant and failed to see his obvious desire to strangle her.

"Was there anything else memorable about that appointment?"

"Well, the condition of his hands. It was obvious why he'd come to see me. I said to him, 'Honey, don't you have hired people to do this grubby work?' "

"Why did you say that?"

"Because his hands were a mess. I'd never seen them like that before. The nails were all ragged and he had scrapes on both hands."

"Were his fingernails dirty as well?"

"No, it looked as if he'd scrubbed them very thoroughly. In fact his skin looked kind of raw like from strong soap. I thought he might have scraped them with the brush, but there was one cut on the back of his hand that hadn't come from any brush."

"Did you ask him how his hand had gotten into such bad shape?"

"Yes, but I don't guess he heard me. He looked so tired, he just sat there with his head back and his eyes closed. I let him rest, poor dear, while I tried to clean up his hands."

"So he didn't answer your question about what he'd been doing with his hands?"

"No."

"And he never came back to see you after that occasion?"

"No." Again she tried to catch the defendant's eye, but by now Raleigh Pentell stared over her head, trying to hold no expression on his face.

"Thank you, Ms. Portillo. I pass the witness."

Chris had already passed her appointment books over to Lowell Burke, who had been poring over them looking for ammunition for cross-examination. Apparently he'd found none.

"Ms. Portillo, you seem very professional. I assume you have a busy practice of caring for hands."

"Sometimes people have to wait weeks for an appointment," the witness said with satisfaction.

"How many hands would you estimate you've treated in the past year?"

"Oh goodness, I have no idea. Hundreds, certainly."

"And yet you claim to remember the condition of Mr. Pentell's hands on a particular occasion nearly a year ago. In spite of all the hands you've ministered to during that year. You have a remarkable memory. Couldn't you be thinking of another occasion?"

"Hands are my business, sir. I remember hands."

"Well, ma'am, my business is trying cases, but I couldn't tell you what a particular client looked like on a particular date in trial. How can you?"

"I take notes." Marie Portillo looked brightly around the courtroom. Chris gave her a slight smile of approval. He had left the manhole cover off that hole and the defense lawyer had obligingly stepped into it. Ms. Portillo continued helpfully, "It's that third book up from the bottom, if you want to look it up."

Burke didn't accept the invitation. "You say Raleigh Pentell didn't tell you anything in particular he'd been doing with his hands in the days before your appointment?"

"No sir."

"Do you happen to know that Mr. Pentell is an avid gardener?"

"No, he'd never talked about that before." Ms. Portillo looked pleased at learning this new facet of a favored former client's life.

"Well, then," Burke said with apparent triumph. "No more questions."

As the witness left the stand the judge asked Chris whether the prosecution had any more rebuttal witnesses. "Yes sir, three," said the DA, which made the defense lawyer watch him warily. "The next will be Officer Paul Miller."

The fingerprint technician took the stand. A veteran of courtrooms, Miller sat easily, barely glancing at the jurors or anyone else. The witness's face looked as lived-in as his clothes, a creased white shirt and limp plaid sports coat. He quickly identified himself and his special field.

"Officer, did you examine a certain apartment in the Bushnell Apartments yesterday?"

"Yes. A team of us went through the apartment, with a search warrant."

Again Lowell Burke looked at his client for enlightenment. Pentell obviously recognized the address the witness gave, but still appeared puzzled. His shoulders hunched and for a moment he looked like an animal that hears a dangerous sound but can't identify the source.

"Did you take fingerprints in the apartment, Officer?"

"Yes sir. I lifted prints from various locations in the apartment."

"And did you compare those with prints that were known to you?"

"Yes. I compared them with fingerprints of the defendant's that were taken at the time of his arrest in this case."

"What did you determine, if anything?"

"That the defendant, Raleigh Pentell, had left fingerprints inside that apartment."

Chris asked, "Just one print, or a few?"

"No sir. A lot of fingerprints, in every room of the apartment."

"Did you find anything else that indicated that the defendant lived in that apartment or at least had frequent access to it?"

"Yes sir," Miller said, and detailed the other findings, the shirts with the defendant's monogram on their pockets, items linked to Pentell in various ways, even the unusual brand of cigarettes that Chris had found in the apartment's kitchen. "I believe the defendant has a packet of that same brand of cigarettes in his jacket pocket right now. I saw him having one outside earlier, before trial began today."

Lowell Burke glanced at his client and saw no contradiction. Nearly everyone in the courtroom, including the jurors, wore similar expressions: at first intrigued by Miller's testimony, they now waited impatiently for its payoff. *Okay, we get it, you found Raleigh Pentell's apartment. What of it?*

Even the defense lawyer seemed possessed by that impatience, asking no questions of the witness when Chris passed him. "Next?" the judge asked.

"Officer Daryl Tatum, Your Honor."

The earnest young police officer Chris had chosen as his witness took the oath of office briskly, then sat in the witness stand and glared at the defendant as if Officer Tatum carried a personal grudge against Pentell. Pentell looked back blankly, since he had never seen this man.

Chris quickly took the officer through the same apartment, then into the closet with the false back wall. Chris remembered looking around the crowd of witnesses in that hideaway and choosing this one to pick up the diary, meaning he would serve as Chris's witness in court. Chris had chosen well. Officer Tatum was young and fair, not yet hardened by his job. His face flushed as he progressed, conveying the significance of what he would say next.

"Did you find anything inside the secret space at the back of that closet, Officer Tatum?"

"Yes sir, I found this purse."

The purse had already been marked as an exhibit, and Chris and the officer had reassembled its contents. "Was there anything inside the purse to identify its owner, Officer?"

"Only this." Officer Tatum pulled out the small red diary Chris had returned to him this morning, and as Tatum held up the little book he cast his strongest glare of accusation yet at Raleigh Pentell. Everyone began to understand.

The defendant went from looking puzzled to alarmed. He shook his head slowly from side to side. His lawyer whispered to him and got no response.

"Is there a name in that book, Officer? Anything to suggest who its owner might be?"

The young man turned to the first page. "It's a diary, sir. It says, *The Book of Kristen*."

"No!" Raleigh Pentell said loudly, and the judge pointed a warning finger at him. Over murmurs that swept the courtroom Chris said, "Thank you, Officer. I'll offer that exhibit into evidence and pass the witness."

Lowell Burke had had time to recover himself, and went after cross-examination of the police officer with some enthusiasm. He was a veteran at this sort of thing.

"Officer, did you see the lease to that apartment?"

"No, I didn't."

"Any pictures, photographs of the defendant, anything of that nature?"

"No sir."

"Did you ask the apartment manager who had keys to the place?"

"She didn't know."

"Or how *many* people might have access to the apartment?"

"No."

"Do you have any evidence of any kind that Raleigh Pentell even knew about that hidden space behind the hall closet?"

"No sir. I couldn't question him, he's represented by a lawyer. You."

"Well, no one has even asked him, have they? Or informed me of the search for that matter."

"No. We had a search warrant, but no one to serve it on except the apartments' manager. Before we went into the apartment we weren't sure who lived there."

"And in fact the defendant doesn't live there, does he? Do you know that he has a home some miles from that location?"

"Yes, another home," Tatum said angrily.

"In fact," Burke bore down, "do you know how long

this purse may have lain oh so conveniently in that closet, waiting for you to find it?"

"No."

"Who tipped the police to the existence of this apartment?"

"I don't know, sir. Some kids."

"Kids?" Burke shouted angrily. "That's your source, that's the rock on which your accusation rests? Did it occur to you that kids who knew about that apartment could have planted this 'evidence' there?"

"I don't know any reason why they would, sir," Tatum said steadfastly.

And suddenly Lowell Burke had gone too far. Because he didn't know either any reason why unknown children would want to frame Raleigh Pentell for murder. Burke hesitated, having lost his momentum, and concluded with what he thought a crushing rhetorical question: "Do you have any evidence to show that Raleigh Pentell put that purse in that closet, or even knew of its existence?"

"Only that it was his apartment and he was the last one seen with the girl. Sir."

Lowell Burke looked blank, then angry. With a large dismissive gesture he said, "No more questions."

Chris stood quickly. "The State recalls Jean Fitzgerald."

Jean entered the courtroom from the hall, wearing a business suit of deep navy. She looked very pale, as if fading away, and held herself stiffly. Quite obviously Jean would crumble if she let go for a moment. Chris had never seen her look so vulnerable. He wanted to hold her.

He questioned her as gently as possible, only needing two answers from her. "Ms. Fitzgerald, can you identify the State's exhibit on the railing in front of you?"

Jean picked up the purse, turned it over carefully, then held it between her hands as if it radiated heat and she was freezing. "It's my daughter's purse. Kristen's purse."

"When was the last time you saw her carrying it?"

"The last day I saw her. That morning when she went to school. She always carried it. Even around the house, she always had to know where it was, like there was something secret inside."

"Ma'am, would you open that red book, please, and look at some of the pages?"

Jean did so slowly, her face suddenly rocked by a smile when she came to the first page, with the grandiloquent declaration of the book's owner. Then Jean turned a few more pages and stopped to read a passage. One tear leaked out and slid slowly down her cheek.

Chris found himself standing, walking toward her. "Jean, can you identify that handwriting?"

Lowell Burke quickly said, "Objection. This woman hasn't been qualified as a handwriting expert."

Chris whirled on him. "My God, don't you think a mother . . ."

Meanwhile Jean looked up from the page, across the front of the courtroom to where Raleigh Pentell sat stiffly. "You bastard," she said quite clearly, intended for no one else.

"No," Pentell said again.

Chris stood in the front of the courtroom, as if to protect Jean from the defense team. Judge Benitez said, "The objection is overruled," and Chris walked the rest of the way to the witness stand.

"Can you identify the handwriting?" he asked softly.

Jean looked down, but not seeing the page before her. She lost her sustaining anger, her shoulders hunched inward. "It's Kristen's handwriting. It's hers."

"Pass the witness," Chris said, but with a glare at Lowell Burke that defied him to hurt her further. The veteran defense lawyer knew better than to attack a bereaved mother. He simply shook his head. Chris took Jean by the hand and led her down from the stand. She didn't seem to feel him. Chris took her through the gate to a seat on the front row, where a couple of reporters slid over to make room for her. From that spot in the audience Chris said, "That's the end of the State's case, Your Honor. The prosecution closes."

Anne Greenwald pushed her head and neck into the tall back of her padded desk chair, pushing with her arms on the chair arms, trying to drive the tension from her shoulders. Sometimes she thought the worst sessions were when a patient cried, then there were days like today when she knew the worst times were when a kid absolutely refused to cry, fighting to hold everything in. During such a session Anne sometimes felt that something was trying to burst out of her as well, but the kid held them both hostage.

Thinking she couldn't take another one of those today, she reached for her phone to buzz her secretary and ask when her next appointment was, but then the office door opened and a girl strolled casually in.

"Clarissa. Why aren't you in school?"

Clarissa just gave her a look as if the question were so lame it answered itself.

"Well then, why aren't you at the courthouse?"

"I can't be there," Clarissa said, also as if that answer sufficed. She walked across the office, picked up a book, set it down, then turned toward the window, moving with unaffected grace, comfortable in her body. But Clarissa would have been surprised to learn how young she looked, with her thin arms and unlined face. She folded her arms and looked down at the rug, then up again and asked brightly, "Having a busy day?"

Anne interpreted Clarissa's restlessness. She had seen it many times in clients. The girl wanted to be asked something, or told something. She wanted to be drawn out. But it would be a lengthy process. *Nothing*, she'd reply quickly if asked what was wrong. Anne would get a lot of *nothing*s if she started questioning her now, before getting to the problem. At this moment Anne didn't have the energy to delve.

But she could never stop thinking. Speculating about this girl, her sister, their relationship to their mother—always complicated in a teenage girl, in this case impossibly convoluted. Chris had been trying to figure out the mystery of this little family logically. Anne tried to understand it emotionally.

"I would think you'd want to be at the trial. If it were my sister—"

"She wouldn't want me there," Clarissa said quickly. "She was always asking me for some privacy. This is the last time I can give her some. I can stay away and let it be Kristen's show."

Clarissa's eyes looked bright and hot. They wouldn't light on Anne. Anne knew a crisis when she saw one. She also recognized guilt. *Oh God, don't tell me . . .* Standing up from the desk, she ventured, "Kristen never really understood what was going on, did she? She was in over her head, she didn't know what she was doing."

"Oh, she knew," Clarissa answered bitterly. "She was screwing everything up. If she had just stayed out of it everybody would have been okay, including her."

Blaming the victim, another well-known method of evading guilt. But even while classifying Clarissa's responses, Anne didn't look at the girl clinically. That would have been impossible. Clarissa's pain was as visible as a gunshot wound. She pressed a fist tightly against her abdomen while continuing to walk back and forth, her face angry and tight. Clarissa might have thought Kristen had screwed up Clarissa's life: not an uncommon feeling of an older child for a younger one. Clarissa had been close to her mother before Kristen came along. But Clarissa hadn't hated Kristen, she had tried to protect her. In the end, of course, she had failed at that.

Anne stepped out boldly onto dangerous ground. Clarissa was tough, she could take it. "You followed

Raleigh Pentell and your sister that night, didn't you, Clarissa? Did you catch up to them, say you'd take Kristen home?"

"No," Clarissa said quietly. "We couldn't catch them . . ."

But Anne understood the significance of the small, beloved stuffed dog that had been buried with Kristen. "Clarissa, I know you were at her grave."

"*No!!*" Clarissa screamed, putting her hands over her ears and closing her eyes. The sound lingered even after Clarissa stopped. Anne's secretary opened the office door a crack, Anne shook her head, and the secretary went away, used to noises emanating from that office.

Clarissa opened her eyes brightly and said in a perfectly normal voice, "Can we get out of here?"

Lowell Burke, reluctant to place his client in Chris Sinclair's hands again for cross-examination, nevertheless knew he had to recall the defendant to the stand. Burke had done his job well, not only preparing his case but also his client. Pentell sat straight in the witness stand, looking perturbed but guiltless. He picked up the girl's purse and said emphatically,

"I have never seen this in my life."

"And the book, sir?"

"I haven't seen it either."

"Would you please examine it to be sure?"

Pentell flipped through the pages, bending the flexible book almost into a U shape. He showed no trace of recognition, but also didn't realize how two or three jurors glared at his casual treatment of the dead girl's diary. "I'm positive," Pentell concluded.

Burke continued in his fatherly voice, "That apartment in the Bushnell Apartments that the officers described searching. Is that your apartment?"

"My company maintains the lease. I keep it for business guests from out of town."

"But your clothes were there."

"Sometimes when I'm downtown late and have to be back in the office early the next morning I'll stay in that apartment rather than drive all the way out to my house and back."

"Does anyone else use the apartment?"

"Some of my business associates, occasionally, in the same way."

"Does Peter Belasco have a key?"

"I'm not sure. I know Peter stayed there a time or two, and escorted a guest there for me. He could easily have made a copy of the key some time."

Pentell sounded very sincere. His uncertainty as to whether Belasco could have gotten into the apartment was better than a positive assertion that the other suspect had a key. Chris sat with part of his mind admiring the defense lawyer's preparation, while he glared hate at the defendant. Chris had convinced himself of Raleigh Pentell's guilt, whether he'd proven it to the jury's satisfaction or not. He wanted to slap Pentell and tell him to stop lying. But he sat breathing deeply, waiting his turn.

Burke asked, "Let's turn to Ms. Portillo's testimony. Accurate, I'm sure, since she keeps notes. Can you explain the condition of your hands and fingernails back in late October?"

"I'm not sure," Pentell answered wearily but in a puzzled manner, as if he too had been pondering this question. "Can anyone remember the condition of one's hands on a particular day months ago? It was fall, I know I had been working in my yard back then. I remember trying to dig up a tree root that had been bothering me for a long time because it wouldn't let the grass grow over it. I ended up pulling it out with my hands, which I suppose would have messed up my nails and probably scratched my hands. Whether it was around that time I can't say positively. But that is when I'd go see a manicurist, right, when I'd done something to tear up my fingernails?"

Again, his uncertainty made him sound believable.

Lowell Burke nodded in satisfaction and started wrapping up. "Raleigh, did you take that girl, Kristen Lorenz, to your apartment in the Bushnell Apartments?"

"I most certainly did not. I took her home."

"Did you take her purse to your apartment and hide it there?"

"No. Why would I do such a thing? No, I did not."

"Did you kill her, Raleigh?"

"No. I swear. I did not kill Kristen Lorenz."

Burke let the denial hang boldly in the air before passing the witness.

Chris Sinclair didn't sit up straighter. "How big is your house, Mr. Pentell?"

"My house? It's about four thousand square feet, something like that. Two stories."

"Kind of out in the country, yes? How big is your lot?"

"All told, I guess about an acre." Pentell answered in a mild, puzzled voice, looking at the jurors.

"Yet you want these jurors to believe that you, a busy businessman, take care of your own yard?"

"No, I have a yard service. But with this root, I saw part of it sticking out, I thought I could pull it out, it came a little way then it hung on, and I kept digging deeper and pulling at it, until it became kind of a challenge, you know how that is, and I ended up spending an hour and trying to cut it with the shovel and scraping my hands and finally pulled the damn thing out. You know how you get into something casually and then end up putting too much effort into it." He shrugged self-deprecatingly.

"Like the way you went to pick up Kristen Lorenz and she ended up making a much bigger scene than you'd expected and causing you way more trouble than she was worth."

"No," Pentell said quietly. Well coached.

Chris finally sat up straight in his chair, leaning forward, concentrated. "You testified you've never seen that purse before?"

"That's right."

"But Kristen's mother said Kristen always had it with her. Didn't she have it with her the night you took her from the restaurant?"

Pentell hesitated. His denial of any memory of the purse had been so certain. "I don't remember."

"Did you jerk her out of that restaurant so fast she didn't have time to get her purse?"

"No. I mean I didn't see her get the purse. Maybe she did. It wasn't important to me."

"No, what was important was getting her out of sight and hearing of everyone else in the world fast. Right?"

Pentell resisted his urge to deny quickly. "Well, she was bothering the other people. I did want to get her out of there and home quickly."

"But she didn't want to go with you, did she?"

"I—"

"She was afraid of you, Mr. Pentell. You told us yourself that she didn't like you, she didn't like you dating her mother. She certainly didn't want to get in your car with you, did she? How did you make her go?"

"I was just firm with her. I told her it was time to go."

"Did you grab her arm? Think about your answer. Are you telling us she went with you without your using any force at all? This girl who hated and feared you?"

"She didn't *fear* me," Pentell said exaggeratedly, trying to convey with a wave of his hand how absurd the idea was. But he clearly felt hemmed in by the question. Looking more serious, he answered, "I did have to take her by the arm."

"And drag her to the car."

"No, not drag. She became more docile once we were outside."

"Bullshit."

"Objection, Your Honor!"

"Mr. Sinclair," Judge Benitez began sternly.

Chris stood, with no sign of contrition. "I apologize, Your Honor. I'll withdraw that comment and let the jury decide for themselves. Are you saying Kristen didn't resist you anymore once you were outside and there were no witnesses? She climbed right into your car and sat there quietly while you drove her home?"

"Well, not quietly."

"She was screaming in the restaurant. Everyone saw that. She kept screaming at you in your car, didn't she?"

"No. She was upset, but she got quieter."

"Does that make any sense to you? Did you have to tell her in the car to be quiet?"

"I think so. I told her to calm down, something like that."

"Did you slap her?"

"No. Absolutely not. I didn't touch her."

"Picture the interior of your car, Mr. Pentell. You driving, Kristen in the passenger seat. If you had hit her— pushed her, slapped her, something to shut her up—her head would have hit the window, wouldn't it?"

"I can't picture that, it never happened."

"If she had bled, the blood would have run down the window into the door panel, wouldn't it?"

"Objection," the defense lawyer said in an outraged tone. "Calls for speculation."

"I don't think so," Chris answered grimly.

Judge Benitez said in a calming voice, "I'll let the witness answer if he knows."

"I *don't* know," Raleigh Pentell said emphatically. "I can't picture something that never happened."

Chris looked at the jurors and thought, *They can. I hope to God they can picture it.* Chris certainly could. The images blotted out reality. He heard Kristen screaming.

"Pass the witness."

"Raleigh," Lowell Burke asked with quiet emphasis. "Did you have any reason at all to kill Kristen Lorenz?"

"No. None." Pentell sounded just as certain and sincere as he had before Chris had cross-examined him.

"No more questions, Your Honor. The defense rests and closes."

"That is the end of the evidence," Judge Benitez said to

the jurors with evident relief. "I will now give you a short break during which the lawyers and I will discuss the court's charge, then we will hear arguments. Gentlemen?"

As Chris walked forward to the judge's bench, he brushed shoulders with the defendant, returning to the defense table. With the jurors now gone, Pentell turned and glared at the District Attorney. He stopped as if to say something, then his restraint regained control.

Chris remembered Jean's warning. *No matter what happens, he won't forget you.* At this moment, with the case in jeopardy, that sounded like a consoling thought. Chris turned toward the audience and looked for Jean. She stood waiting for him, watching him gratefully and with longing. As soon as the judge dismissed Chris he walked quickly to Jean and led her from the scene of carnage in the courtroom. They had only a moment's respite, though. Final arguments were about to begin.

Fourteen

Anne Greenwald stood close to Clarissa, who slumped limply, looking around the office as if surprised to find herself there.

"You followed Raleigh Pentell when he took your sister," Anne said insistently. "I know you did, Clarissa. You wanted to make sure she'd be okay, didn't you? You knew how much she was afraid of Pentell. You followed them."

Clarissa didn't deny it again. Her eyes went all around the office, as if she heard something other than Anne's voice. Anne asked, "Did you follow them all the way to your house, did you see your mother take Kristen?"

"No. They never got home."

"Did your mother meet Pentell somewhere?"

"I don't know. Why do you think I know anything?"

The girl's eyes, which had gone dead after her scream, began to brighten. She stepped away from Anne but Anne followed.

"I know you were at the grave, Clarissa. Because of the dog. What was his name, Henry?"

"Herbie," Clarissa muttered.

"Herbie. Kristen loved that stuffed dog. Somebody

who knew that buried Herbie with her. That's not the act of a murderer, Clarissa. Not a stranger. And someone kept watch over that grave, because as soon as the authorities found the grave your mother reported Kristen missing. She knew her body'd been found. That means she knew where the body was. Because someone—"

"Stop saying 'the body.' The body, the body. It wasn't just a *body*." Suddenly energized, Clarissa said, "I'm getting out of here."

"Wait. Where are you going?"

"I don't know." Clarissa went out the door, bumping against the door frame.

Anne grabbed her purse and followed. She knew a crisis when she saw one. In this state Clarissa might do anything, including hurt herself.

Anne would have liked to let Chris know what was happening, but she didn't have time. She'd call him later.

George Stiegers outlined the prosecution case in simple terms, trying to make the gap-filled evidence sound straightforward. "Look at the number of people in that restaurant. Some of them perhaps with motives to twist the truth, but some of them completely uninvolved in what happened. And they all said the same thing: Kristen Lorenz accused Raleigh Pentell of crimes. She had evidence against him and she wanted to share it. She got louder and louder, until she was so loud she caused this man himself to appear. He dragged her out of that restaurant still screaming. Even he admits that, since he can't deny it."

George turned toward the defendant, looking him over as if still questioning him. "And then he had her alone, and from that point, with no witnesses to contradict him, he denies everything. But he can't escape the facts. No one ever saw Kristen alive again after she got into his car. Of all her friends, schoolmates, family, neighbors, no one saw Kristen. She disappeared straight from Raleigh Pentell's car into a secret grave. He hoped to hide his crime. He took her purse away and hid it because it was evidence of his crime.

"And the next day he had blood in his car and his fingernails were wrecked from digging that grave."

"Objection, Your Honor," Lowell Burke said briskly. "There was no evidence when that tiny bit of blood appeared in the car. It could have been months after this event."

"Now I object to him—" George began, but Judge Benitez said, "Sustained. Ladies and gentlemen of the jury, remember the evidence as you heard it, not as you hear it recapitulated by the lawyers in this case."

The interruption deprived George of his momentum. Not wanting to take any more time from Chris, he closed quickly. "There's still the matter of his fingernails. Look at this defendant, a fastidious man. Can you picture him digging in the dirt with his fingers, except in a moment of panic? That's what murder is. That's what he committed. Kristen Lorenz threatened him and he killed her. It's as simple as that."

As the young prosecutor took his seat Lowell Burke stood quickly, as if he'd been eagerly awaiting his turn. He moved with barely suppressed delight toward the jurors, as if spotting old friends getting off a train. But he didn't smile. The veteran defense lawyer knew the danger of taking such a case anything but perfectly seriously.

"There are so many holes in the prosecution's case I hardly know where to begin. First and foremost is the question they cannot answer for you. Why? Why would Raleigh Pentell do this? Why would he kill this young girl? She knew nothing about him, she wasn't a danger to him. After taking her out of a restaurant full of witnesses, she could only harm him dead, not alive. Alive, Kristen couldn't hurt Raleigh, but if she turned up dead everyone would remember his taking her away. He knew that. He wouldn't hurt her under those circumstances.

"But someone else might." Burke held up opposing

hands in front of the jurors, who watched him attentively. "Let's look at the State's theory of the case and see if it makes sense, and at the same time look at an alternative theory. First the State's: Raleigh Pentell killed Kristen Lorenz because he hated and feared her. She could wreck all his grand plans by accusing him in public. The fact that she had just done so would make him a natural suspect if she were killed, but he forgets about that and kills her anyway."

Burke shook his head sagely. "Does that make sense? But think of this. Someone else realized that Pentell would be the natural suspect if Kristen were murdered. Peter Belasco, who had been in the restaurant, who would have liked to get Raleigh out of the way in order to take over some of his business." Burke hurried on, not specifying the nature of that business. "Peter Belasco, an admitted criminal, who hurried out of that restaurant and went looking for Raleigh and the girl. He went to Kristen's house, we know that. Why? Why was he so anxious to find her? Because he had a plan.

"And he involved Kristen's mother in the plan, or tried to. What happened between them, what happened when Raleigh Pentell brought Kristen home to them? We don't know. We do know that Raleigh chose that spectacularly inappropriate moment to break up with Kristen's mother."

Burke turned and looked accusingly at his own client, but he only accused Pentell of a boyish indiscretion, a rudeness. On cue, the defendant looked contrite, as if he blamed himself for something for which he really shared no guilt.

"That was stupid," Burke said bluntly. "It made Jean Fitzgerald mad. He'd seen her mad before, he knew how she lost control. She has a redhead's temper. Raleigh didn't want to be subject to it that night, so he left."

Chris turned and saw that Jean had returned to the spectator seats. She sat staring grimly at the defense lawyer, her face demonstrating what he was saying. Lowell Burke had better not walk past Jean when he finished his argument.

"That left only Kristen to receive her mother's wrath. Kristen who had ruined everything, broken up a romance with a wealthy, eligible man. Did Jean Fitzgerald lose her temper? Did she take it out on her daughter? We don't know. But we do know this." Burke held up a finger. "Kristen Lorenz was buried with her favorite stuffed animal. Did Raleigh Pentell do that? Now we're back to the State's theory. Does it make sense to you? Raleigh didn't know about Kristen's dog. That's not the act of a cold-hearted, angry murderer. That's the act of someone who has accidentally killed a loved one and regrets it, and tries to offer her one last comfort when it is much, much too late."

He moved his hands like scales. "Again, which theory makes more sense to you? Now let's go on to what happened afterward. Kristen's purse and diary. The prosecution would have you believe that Raleigh Pentell took them, kept them, kept them in his own apartment just waiting for them to be discovered and used against him. Does that make sense? Would he have done that, or would he have gotten rid of the purse, disposed of it so that it would never be found?

"Again, let's look at an alternative. Someone wanted Raleigh Pentell framed for the murder. Someone who had access to the apartment. Peter Belasco, perhaps Jean Fitzgerald. They hide the diary there, then they tip off the police. 'Some kids' gave the police that tip. The kids Peter Belasco controlled, the ones he supplied drugs to? Probably. Undoubtedly. At any rate, doesn't that theory make more sense than that Raleigh Pentell kept this damaging evidence against himself, kept it until it could be discovered?"

Burke looked the jurors over slowly. He knew his time was almost up and Chris Sinclair would get the last word. "Don't let him sway you. When the District Attorney speaks to you, keep asking yourself, what makes sense?

His strange theory, or one of the alternatives? If they are equally plausible—and you know they are—then the burden of proof requires that you acquit. You cannot find this defendant guilty when these many doubts linger in the case. Don't make it this easy for the real killer or killers. Tell the prosecution and the police, Keep looking until you find them."

He nodded at the jurors as if confident of their continuing friendship, and took his seat briskly.

Chris, on the other hand, stood slowly, lost in thought. He felt oppressed not only by the burden of proof the defense lawyer had mentioned but by his own confusion. He wanted to question Jean privately, but instead he did his job, approaching the jury.

"In jury selection and his opening remarks, Mr. Burke told you the State's case wrapped up this mystery too neatly. Now he tells you our case isn't nearly neat enough. You see that no matter what we proved, he would tell you something is wrong with the prosecution's theory. But he was right about one thing. A murder's solution is never neat. There are always loose ends. Why? Because murder is dark, secret. It doesn't happen on a stage. We don't know exactly what happened, because only two people were in Raleigh Pentell's car. One of them is now dead and the other is lying to save himself. I believe *that* makes sense.

"Mr. Burke tells you Raleigh Pentell isn't the kind of man who would kill a girl. What kind of man is he? What do you know about him?" Chris went to face the defendant. It would have been nice if Pentell had given him that black glare again, but Pentell kept his face controlled, so neutral he almost looked afraid of the District Attorney who stared at him so studiously.

"Raleigh Pentell describes himself as a businessman. That was the truth. His business is theft and for employee bonuses he gives out cocaine. Raleigh Pentell is a high-class fence, that's what he is. The kind of man who poisons a city. He's not evil, just completely amoral. He has

no sense of right or wrong, only of what's good for
Raleigh Pentell. He won't let considerations of lawful-
ness get in the way of business. Once you've dismissed
those human ideas of right and wrong from your life, they
don't come back."

Chris glanced past the defendant to Jean in the audience. She met his eyes. Her face had grown as expressive
as he remembered it. Her eyes glistened, her lips parted.
She stared at Chris, wanting desperately to tell him
something.

"That's the kind of man Raleigh Pentell is," Chris continued quietly. "He made a cold decision that Kristen
Lorenz could ruin him. He took a business action."

He turned back toward the jurors. "Maybe it wasn't
quite deliberate. You heard what Kristen was like that
night: wild, screaming. She must have continued to
scream at him. Maybe even physically attacked him.
Until suddenly he lashed out." Chris's right arm shot out.
His face suddenly contorted, he yelled, "Shut up!"

The jurors flinched. Chris resumed his own persona.
"He did shut her up. Kristen had driven him past the point
where he would suffer quietly. And when you're a man
like Raleigh Pentell, you're not restrained from acting by
even a moment's consideration that maybe this is the
wrong thing to do. He gave up those ideas a long time ago.

"So there he is, in the car with a girl he's just killed.
Broken her neck smashing her head against the window.
Then he did panic. His only thought was to hide the evidence of his crime. He drove to the edge of town, to an
uninhabited place near his house. He dug a shallow grave
close to the road, using his hands because he hadn't
planned this, he hadn't brought a shovel." Chris held up
his hands, inviting the jurors to imagine what such digging would do to a man's hands and fingernails.

"Then he put Kristen in this secret grave and began
throwing her things in after her. The little dog she carried,
her purse . . ."

Chris stopped suddenly, acting out the scene, holding

his empty hands like a guilty man struck by a thought. "But he didn't put the purse in the grave. It could identify her. Whereas if he left her there with no identification, even if she were found she couldn't be traced to him. Believe me, it was only through a fluke that Kristen was identified once her body was found.

"He took the purse away and hid it in a secret place in his secret apartment. There it was barely linked to him. Maybe he forgot it then. Murderers have done stranger things. They go into denial, they try to forget the crime. Raleigh Pentell has made great strides in that direction. From the way he testified, I think he's almost convinced himself that he didn't kill Kristen.

"Look at the defense alternative. Someone else hid the purse in the defendant's apartment. Who? Peter Belasco went to jail soon after that night, and has been there ever since." And Peter Belasco certainly hadn't been sending Chris E-mail messages from the diary. Chris knew more about the case than he could tell the jurors. He wanted the jurors to understand as clearly as he did what kind of man Raleigh Pentell was.

"This doesn't make sense. The defense would like you to think that maybe someone framed Raleigh Pentell for this murder. They cast about for any available suspects. Peter Belasco? He formed a plan that quickly, hustled those boys out of the restaurant and went to kill Kristen so he could frame his boss for it. Did Peter Belasco impress you as that kind of quick thinker?"

Chris searched the jurors' faces for an answer. He saw doubt, and felt the same. Chris turned again, walking slowly between the prosecution and defense tables toward the railing that separated the front of the courtroom from the spectator seats.

"Then who?" he said quietly but in a voice that carried back over his shoulder. "Jean Fitzgerald, the defense suggests. She's available to them as a suspect. Kristen's own mother."

Chris leaned forward on the railing and stared out at

her, his old friend. "Look at this woman," he instructed the jury. "Did she kill her daughter?"

Chris studied Jean as well. She didn't shake her head, but her chin came up, offering her face. She stared back at Chris. He almost heard her voice: *No*. He remembered her face in all its moods: mischievous, passionate, mad as hell. She still wore the same face, full of life and plans. Her daughters shared her expressions. Chris felt lost, but he believed in that face.

Turning his back on Jean, he gestured back toward her. "Did she? If you believe after seeing that woman and hearing her testify that she is capable of killing her own child, over this man"—he sneered the word, dismissing Pentell—"then you find Raleigh Pentell not guilty."

Chris looked as if he had finished, but he stood behind his chair and said one other thing. "And by the way, that defense theory? There's another important reason why it's not true. They say someone wanted to frame Raleigh Pentell for murder, by murdering Kristen themselves? Then why did they let her lie in an unfound grave for months? Why did they remove all identification from her body? If someone had been trying to frame Raleigh Pentell, he would have wanted Kristen's body found right away. That night, the next morning, while so many people remembered that Pentell had been the one who took her away. They wouldn't have wanted the body to lie undiscovered while Pentell had time to try to put together an alibi.

"No. Burying a body and hoping she's never found is the act of a murderer who never wants his deed found out."

Chris turned and looked at Pentell again, and kept his attention fixed in that direction while he resumed his seat. George Stiegers beside him saw the jurors watching the defendant as well, their faces grim, and thought what a bad idea it is for the defense to put forward a theory that the prosecution can take apart. It makes the defendant look like a liar, or worse.

* * *

Anne Greenwald, driving through the late afternoon of a late spring day, noticed changes in the air, a breeze carrying leaves, clouds obscuring the horizon. "Where would you like to go?" she asked.

Clarissa shrugged. Anne had a sense of what parenthood must be like, trying to draw a response from a child who wanted to pretend you weren't there, in fact would be happier if you didn't exist.

"Would you like to go see some of your friends?"

"Why?" Clarissa asked, perfectly guilelessly, a simple request for explanation.

"You haven't been able to spend much time with them lately, have you?"

Clarissa shrugged.

"Seems like you've been spending most of your time with Chris." Anne watched the girl sidelong, wanting to get more personal. She would have liked to ask more bluntly, *What kind of father do you think he is?* Something one could never know about a man ahead of time.

"Does that bother you?" Clarissa asked.

"No, no." Anne stopped herself from asking, *Why should it?* Clarissa would have an answer for that. "I think it's great." Even to herself Anne sounded over-hearty. Clarissa glanced at her scornfully. Why was the girl so ready to be mad? They seemed to have lost whatever closeness had grown between them during the brief time Clarissa had lived with Anne. Clarissa looked like a stranger to her.

Anne had a sudden insight. Jean had protested when Chris removed Clarissa from her house, Chris had said. But Jean hadn't protested much. She hadn't insisted on her rights as a parent. Anne tried to put herself in Jean Fitzgerald's place, failed at that, but thought she understood one thing: Jean had wanted her daughter to stay with Chris, to develop a bond with him. She had wanted Chris to be drawn into her family. Chris himself, or Chris Sinclair the District Attorney?

Anne wondered suddenly if she had a rival.

"What are you thinking?" Clarissa asked.

"Nothing. I'm just driving." But Anne couldn't stop analyzing. Clarissa's life with Mom would have taught her that relationships with men don't last. They weren't as important as . . . As what? Self-reliance? Anne would have thought the same thing a year ago. *Did* think so. Why did she suddenly find herself thinking of Chris?

Clarissa watched her with a slight smile, as if she could read the psychiatrist's thoughts and found them amusing.

As the jurors filed out Chris looked around the courtroom at the spectators and the players in the case. Raleigh Pentell walked away from his lawyer and took out a cell phone. He and Jean didn't even glance at each other.

Chris took Jean by the arm and led her out into the hall and up the stairs toward his office. He talked quietly but forcefully as they walked, as if under the pressure of a deadline.

"Now tell me the rest of it."

"What do you mean?" Jean looked genuinely innocent.

"I may be able to keep you out of prison, but not if you lie to me again. What else happened that night?"

"Just what I said, Chris. Raleigh called me from his car and said he had Kristen. He said I needed to talk to her."

"Could you hear her?"

"Yes. The last time I ever did. I remember what a relief it was to know where she was. I told Raleigh to hand the phone to her, but he just clicked it off."

"He testified that he brought her home."

Jean shook her head. "I told him to and he said he would, but they never got there. I waited and waited."

Chris didn't answer, just mounted the stairs rapidly, until Jean stopped him, pushing him to a halt against the wall of the stairwell. She insisted, "You don't believe what he said, do you?"

Her face remained perfectly open and readable. Her clear blue eyes opened wide. Even the hint of anger in

her expression made her more believable. Jean swept
her hair back from her face one-handed with a gesture
he remembered, which took him back to a cluttered
bedroom in Austin where a girl sat cross-legged on a
mattress, face suffused with pleasure as she made
extravagant plans.

"I know you lied, Jean. So do the jurors if they were
paying attention. Your neighbor across the street—"

"That nosy old bitch."

"Yes, she saw a lot. She saw Kristen leaving home that
evening on her way to the restaurant. And she saw her
turn and yell back into the house. Yell at you, right, Jean?
Or *to* you, saying where she was going. You said the last
time you saw her was that morning, but that was a lie. You
knew she went to Belasco's party."

Jean stared at him with only a slight change of expression. This was a sign of her thinking, her face going neutral for a long moment. Finally she said, "You know why
I lied. I couldn't tell the truth about what had happened to
Kristen, because Raleigh had Clarissa. Remember? Look
at me, Chris. Answer the question you asked the jury. You
think I killed my girl?"

Chris followed Jean's instruction. He looked at her,
with memory and compassion and the habitual distrust
that was part of his job. Jean's eyes shone with loss. Her
full lower lip stood out, unprotected. Chris saw a girl
who'd never had anyone by her side for long, no one she
could trust, only her children to protect. He yearned to
comfort her. He longed for the lost years they could never
recover.

But he only said, "Tell me the rest, Jean. Your business
with Pentell."

Jean's eyes welled with tears. "I was getting out, Chris.
I swear. I saw it was affecting my girls. I put an end to it,
I went into the insurance business."

Mention of Jean's daughters broke through the thin
crust of cynicism he'd been trying to build around himself. If he had been there all these years as he should have

been, none of this would have happened. Thoughts of Clarissa alone—and even of Kristen, the girl he'd never seen alive—broke his heart.

Jean didn't touch him, but she turned a yearning look on him. Her face looked so familiar, as if he'd seen its subtle changes through the years. For a long moment it seemed as if he had. His real past glimmered uncertainly.

Anne took Clarissa to Anne's house, and continued to try to talk to her. Anne Greenwald excelled at her job, much of which involved drawing out children who didn't want to talk. Chris had grown enamored of the idea of having a daughter, and turned erratic with the urgency of protecting her. Anne too looked at Clarissa with great concern, but also couldn't help seeing her as a fascinating case study. Anne had inferred from the few hints Clarissa had dropped how unorthodox Jean's life with her daughters had been—casual to the point of criminality. Anne couldn't help wondering professionally: if you take a child and raise her in an atmosphere of complete disdain for laws and social conventions, what sort of creature would you produce?

Clarissa gazed out the front window and said casually, "You lost my police escort. He must've taken a break, thought I'd be staying at your office until Chris came to get me."

"We can call them in a minute," Anne said, and asked as subtly as possible, "Did you know Raleigh Pentell very well?"

Clarissa shrugged.

"Chris thinks he's involved in the murder of a drug dealer and maybe others, but I don't understand that. If he had a business relationship with them—"

"Those people always fall out on each other," Clarissa said. "They think they're such cunning bandits, like Robin Hoods or something. They think they're such rebels against society, but the basic fact about them is they're stupid. Too stupid to hold a job, too stupid even to protect themselves."

Clarissa had obviously given these outlaw lives a great deal of thought, but she didn't sound like a social scientist. She paced Anne's small living room, again building herself up to anger. Against whom? Anne wondered.

Anne began, "But Raleigh Pentell rose above the crowd, he made long plans. Isn't that what everybody says?"

"He doesn't look so smart now, does he?" Clarissa said flatly.

The jury didn't keep them waiting long. Chris's office phone buzzed, he listened for a moment and hung up. "We've got a verdict," he said tersely to Jean.

They went down the stairs more slowly than they'd ascended. Chris didn't trust a fast jury. That usually meant they hadn't considered all the evidence. As always at this point, he wished he'd given them more. He should have put on evidence of the kidnapping to show that Pentell had tried to cover up his crime. Chris wondered what kind of witness Clarissa would make if that case went to trial, and he thought of her the first time he'd seen her, in that big house in the woods, standing in a barely furnished room, turning toward him as he thought for one instant that he recognized her face.

"What is it?" Jean asked, almost running into him as he slowed down.

"Nothing. Let's get inside."

In the courtroom Raleigh Pentell already stood beside his lawyer, looking concerned but not frightened. Pentell turned to see Chris's entrance with Jean, and a sardonic expression passed over his face at the sight of the two of them together. But by the time Chris took his place at the front of the courtroom Pentell stared straight ahead unseeingly. Chris had seen that blank expression on the faces of other men charged with vicious crimes. They had such a strong sense of themselves that they couldn't actually believe in the existence of other people.

The courtroom was so crowded for the verdict that spectators stood at the back. Chris scanned the crowd and saw a few high school classmates of Clarissa's and Ryan's, but not Clarissa herself. He felt glad she'd stayed away from the trial.

The jurors came in briskly, looking unembarrassed at the attention of the courtroom focused on them. The lawyers watched them closely for the usual signs, but the jurors just looked at the judge until they were told to be seated.

"Do you have a verdict?"

"Yes sir," said a man on the corner of the front row. Jurors nearly always picked a man as the foreman, even when women outnumbered and outsmarted the men on the jury. This foreman was the former teacher, the one who during jury selection had acknowledged how maddening children can be. Had Chris made a mistake leaving him on the jury?

Most judges examined the jury form before letting the verdict be delivered aloud, but Judge Benitez didn't give himself that preview. Waiting like everyone else, he said, "The defendant will rise. Mr. Foreman, please read your verdict."

Pentell stood straight and elegant beside his lawyer. The foreman looked right at him, not needing to read from the paper in his hand, and said in a loud, clear voice, "We find the defendant guilty of murder as charged in the indictment."

A quick smile crossed Pentell's face, the joyful reaction he had been holding back, then he looked stricken as memory played back what he had actually heard. He turned toward his lawyer, and the consoling look on Lowell Burke's face brought the truth home to him. Raleigh Pentell stared, lifted a hand toward the jury, then fell into his chair in a heap.

As if very little had happened, Judge Benitez said

calmly, "It is near the end of the day. We will begin the punishment phase tomorrow morning. Members of the jury, please remember that you are still under my instructions. Be careful driving home."

He waited until the jurors had left, then said with equal calm, "Mr. Pentell, I am revoking your bail. Bailiff."

The uniformed sheriff's deputy took the defendant's arm and almost had to lift him bodily from his chair. The verdict had utterly shattered Raleigh Pentell's composure. The bailiff led him to his desk and began emptying his pockets. Pentell turned a stricken face back to the courtroom and his eyes found Jean. His pleading look smashed to pieces against her stony expression.

Energy suddenly flowed through Chris. He felt the exhilaration of prosecution, a common reaction to a guilty verdict. For a week he had sat next to a man, exchanging glances with him, studying each other and plotting like equals. Now the defendant sat handcuffed in the otherwise empty jury box, on his way to prison while Chris remained free to go on with his life. It felt to Chris like having his life extended.

The exhilaration started his mind working harder, too. He followed the defendant's stare to Jean's face, studied her for a moment, then once again grabbed her and hurried out of the courtroom. The newspaper and television reporters waiting to get a reaction from the District Attorney were surprised at being brushed off. Wasn't the case over? From the way Chris Sinclair rushed down the hallway, he didn't think so.

"Where's Clarissa?" Chris asked Jean as they walked. "I would have thought she'd want to see this outcome. Even some of the other kids came to see it. Where's she?"

"I don't know."

Chris didn't look at Jean as he talked. In a rapid but certain tone of voice, he began to pick apart his own case. "That diary of Kristen's hasn't been lying in that closet all these months. Someone's been sending me E-mail messages straight out of it. Who would do that?"

"What? Someone's been doing what?"

Chris believed Jean's implicit claim of ignorance. Some of the messages he'd gotten had implicated Jean in crimes. She wouldn't have sent those passages.

"I thought that boy Jason might have pages from the diary, but the last passage I got was exactly what I needed to keep me going at the time. Jason wouldn't have known what that was. Somebody else made up that last entry to try to help me with the prosecution.

"The diary was planted to implicate Pentell. Who would want to do that? Someone who wanted to take over his operation, maybe. Someone who wanted him out of the way, certainly. We heard about that apartment of his from kids at school. Again, right when I needed more evidence, it came to me. That's why someone sent me those messages, helping me build a case against him. My God, that's why someone inside the organization sent those anonymous tips to police detectives, the ones who gave me the idea of a Mr. Big in the first place." Chris thought furiously, and more coherently than he had in weeks. "Ryan McClain," he said suddenly. "He was the anonymous informant who led police to that house in Terrell Hills. Clarissa put him up to it, trying to ruin Pentell's organization."

"Clarissa couldn't have—"

"She did," Chris said distinctly. "Right after Ryan was killed, Clarissa said she had killed him. She must have thought Pentell found out that Ryan had been informing police."

"I started to say," Jean said, "that Clarissa couldn't have done that. She was missing then, remember? Raleigh took her to keep me from talking about what had happened to Kristen."

Chris looked at her. "As if you would go to the police. That's amusing. Pentell would know you better than that. Clarissa wasn't kidnapped. Stop trying to play me. When police searched that house after I found her there they didn't find any girl's clothing, any changes of outfits. But she was clean and fresh. They took awfully good care of her, for kidnappers."

Chris remembered other details his mind had been subconsciously processing. The broken window Clarissa had supposedly just broken in an attempt to escape. But the pieces of glass had fallen *inside* the windowsill. The glass had been broken from outside. And that ladder Chris had found oh so conveniently fallen just beneath Clarissa's window. Clarissa hadn't been trying to break out. She had just broken *in*.

"Besides, I saw her during that time when Pentell was supposedly holding her. That night you came to see me at my house, she was out on the balcony, wasn't she? I thought it was your reflection in the glass doors, but she's taller than you. My God, I knew it then, I already knew it in the back of my mind.

"Clarissa wasn't kidnapped. She helped you set up Raleigh Pentell."

A renewed burst of energy carried Chris up the rest of the stairs and through the hallways of the DA's offices to his own office, almost as if he were levitating. He called Anne Greenwald's office and the secretary told him Dr. Greenwald had left, probably for the rest of the day. The woman sounded a little puzzled. Chris understood. He dialed Anne's home number and waited jittering while it rang. The phone rang and rang. Eventually the answering machine picked up and he said her name into uninhabited space.

Clarissa continued to pace around Anne's house, watching the clock as if someone were late to meet her. Anne tried gently to question her but that line had closed. "Shut up!" Clarissa snapped.

She kept her purse clutched close by her side. Dusk was imminent when Clarissa suddenly stiffened and hur-

ried into the bathroom. Anne thought she heard an electronic buzz but didn't think about its possible sources.
Modern life is full of buzzes.

When Clarissa emerged from the bathroom her tension
had only increased. "Let's go for a drive, okay?"

"Where? Chris will probably call here soon, I think we
should wait."

Impatiently Clarissa opened the flap of her purse and
produced a pistol, a silvery automatic. She pulled back
the slide, cocking it as casually as popping a compact
disc into a player. She gave Anne an ironic, still-angry
look. "Okay now?"

Seeing this girl in this condition and carrying a gun,
Anne would have stayed with her no matter what. It
hardly mattered that Clarissa pointed the pistol at Anne
rather than at her own head.

They walked swiftly out of the house and got into
Anne's green Volvo, Anne driving, Clarissa holding the
pistol and tapping it lightly against her thigh, still consumed by impatience. Anne thought the girl might talk
like a speed freak if she only found the right question.

"Who killed your sister, Clarissa?"

Clarissa answered slowly in a dead voice out of keeping with her restlessness. "Raleigh did."

"But why? Why would he?"

"Because of the way she was talking. She was dangerous to him."

Anne leaned toward the girl. "She was dangerous to
everybody involved in the scheme, Clarissa. And how did
she know the things she was saying? How did she learn
things that were dangerous to Raleigh Pentell? She
wasn't in on the business. You knew more about the business than she did."

"What do you think, I killed her? Get on 281, head
north."

Anne steered the car as she was directed, but she continued to talk. "And why was Kristen talking so freely?
Who had slipped her the drug that made her so wild that

night? Just a couple of diet pills, anybody could get those. I know a little bit about pharmacology, Clarissa. From the way people described Kristen, she was already high when she got to the party in the restaurant. She wouldn't take anything from anyone there. But of course she would have drunk anything her mother gave her. Or the big sister she adored."

A troubled look crossed Clarissa's young face, but then she sneered. "Now you're trying to say Mom killed Kristen? You're just jealous of Mom because your boyfriend still loves her. She's had to deal with that her whole life. Women never like people like Mom and me."

Anne stared. Clarissa's identification with her mother seemed solid. Anne and Chris had been wrong. Clarissa and Jean hadn't been separated all this time that Clarissa had been away from home. She and her mother were practically one person. Physical distance couldn't keep them apart.

"Get off here," Clarissa said, gesturing with the gun. They hadn't stayed on the expressway any time at all.

After Chris gave up on Anne's phone number he looked around his office, then through the wider hallways of the Justice Center, and felt almost alone. Jean was nowhere to be found. He couldn't reach Anne, even though a quick call to Clarissa's police escort confirmed that he'd left the girl with Anne. Raleigh Pentell had gone to jail, but he'd had time to make phone calls first. Everyone seemed to be missing.

He won't forget, Jean had warned him about Pentell. *No matter what happens, he'll strike back at you.*

Chris ran down the hall to the investigators' office, found Jack Fine at his desk and said tersely, "Anne and Clarissa are missing."

They could have been at a grocery store or a mall, they could have been on their way to meet Chris right now, but Chris didn't believe in those possibilities, and to Jack's credit he didn't stop to ask about them. Without a word he picked up his phone and called police headquarters.

With a detective on the line, Jack said to Chris, "They must be in Anne's car, right? Give me the description."

Quickly Chris described the green Volvo, including its license plate number. But in his mind he saw the car disappearing or already abandoned on some dead-end street.

Jack hung up, then used the radio on his desk to call two of his own investigators. "Where?" he asked Chris.

"Send somebody to Jean's house, and to Pentell's house. They won't be there, but we have to check."

Chris imagined the small neat suburban home and the sprawling country mansion empty and echoing. Anne and Clarissa wouldn't be either place.

Jean had warned him about Raleigh Pentell's vengeance, but now Jean had disappeared too. She should be here advising him where to look, frantic to find her only living daughter. Jean must have gone to look on her own. What did she know, what places would she search?

"Come on," Jack said briskly, trying to usher Chris out. "Police put out a description of her car, we'll blanket the city . . ."

Chris stood stock still, the energy that still surged through him now directed into imagination. Jean hadn't gone to search. She'd gone to meet her daughter. "It's too late for that," he said dreamily. "I know where they're going."

"How could you?"

He didn't really. Chris only knew one place that had meaning for him and Clarissa, a place she might have suggested, if she had any hand in planning this kidnapping. A place Chris had showed her.

Chris started to run. Jack kept up with him. "If I'm wrong it won't matter," Chris said.

If he was wrong, Anne was dead already.

* * *

After a couple of blocks Anne no longer needed directions from Clarissa, except where to park. "Go past the entrance," Clarissa said. "Turn right here. Now into this driveway. All the way down to the garage." Anne drove by a For Sale sign in a long, sloping front yard. The house apparently stood empty. Clarissa didn't speak again, just reached and took Anne's keys. She gestured with the gun and they got out and walked back along the road, woods on their left, growing quickly dense. Their obvious destination gave Anne both hope and fear.

They entered the Nature Trails from the road rather than walking back to the entrance. Clarissa had obviously returned after their first morning here; she'd known about the vacant house and she seemed familiar with the woods. She listened attentively, but kept the gun pointed at Anne. Dusk stole through the trails, softening the outlines of the woods but expanding the wooded area with long shadows. Anne felt the twisting, reaching limbs of the trees at her back. The air almost trembled with the approach of the unknown: Clarissa had brought her here to wait for someone.

"Why are you helping him?" Anne asked. "The man who killed your sister and your boyfriend. You owe him so much?"

Clarissa looked puzzled, then sneered. "Him? Who gives a damn about him?"

So it wasn't Raleigh Pentell she was helping. Anne understood. But understanding didn't do her much good at this point.

At a spot close beside a tall, thick-trunked oak, Clarissa walked off the path a few feet into the woods, Anne right in front of her. Anne almost tripped but caught herself and looked down at a shallow depression scooped out by erosion. Anne started to walk on but saw Clarissa staring and realized that the hole reminded her of a different, similar spot in another wooded area.

Looking down at the small depression in the ground,

Anne said, "Kristen's grave was your spot, wasn't it, Clarissa?"

The girl didn't answer. Her gun drooped toward the ground. Clarissa clenched her mouth so that the lovely planes of her face stood out starkly. She looked at the hole in the ground with an evident mix of emotions. Hatred showed through most clearly. Hatred does tend to overpower the less fierce emotions, Anne thought, at least in the short term.

"The investigators got mixed signals from her grave," Anne said speculatively. "It was close beside the road, which is where strangers bury people they kill. But someone put that stuffed dog into the grave with Kristen. To keep her company. And someone kept watch over the grave. Someone knew as soon as she'd been found, and reported her missing then. The same person who found her diary, and sent excerpts from it to Chris. Right, Clarissa?"

The hatred had slipped off the girl's face, leaving her unprotected. Clarissa cried quietly, staring around suddenly as if lost. "I couldn't leave her there alone. I came and talked to her . . ."

"How did you know where she was? Did you kill her, Clarissa?"

Clarissa shook her head. "Ryan and I followed Raleigh from the restaurant that night. We saw something happen in the car, he hit Kristen and she fell back. Then we followed him to the woods, staying back so he didn't see us. I wanted to tell somebody all this time, but that would have given away—everything else. I couldn't . . ."

"What else, Clarissa? What else would it have given away?"

The girl looked so young to Anne. She appeared less her mother's daughter. She was struggling to become her own person, as all children did at this age. Clarissa had more to overcome than most. Jean had always used her children. But Clarissa had had the smarts and the toughness to use back. Kristen didn't. Kristen hadn't had time

to develop her own resources and hadn't had to, because
she had always been more protected—by Clarissa.

Clarissa's tears had stopped. She shook her head
fiercely as if fighting off Anne's words, or an inner voice.
Anne stepped toward her to offer comfort, but Clarissa
brought the gun up between them again. Tension made
her neck stiff and the gun shake slightly. Anne watched
her, not speaking, waiting—hoping—for the girl to reach
out to her. She understood Clarissa's torment. She didn't
want to kill Anne. If the two of them hadn't developed a
rapport in the last few weeks, then Clarissa was a hell of
an actress. But she was, Anne knew. Clarissa had had to
be an actress all her life.

Then the world expanded. A breeze stirred the tree
branches, but even above that sound they both heard footsteps crunching along the asphalt path. More than one
pair of feet made little attempt at stealth. They walked
fast, toward the spot where Anne and Clarissa stood.

Clarissa's eyes held on Anne's. For the first time the girl
looked fearful, but of what Anne had no idea. Clarissa
raised the gun again, and gestured into the trees with it.

"Run."

Anne took the girl by the sleeve, but Clarissa shook her
off, turning toward the path. Anne thought she knew what
that meant. Clarissa knew who was coming. She'd
brought Anne here specifically for these people, but had
suffered a change of heart. After another moment's hesitation Anne's instincts took over, and she turned and took
Clarissa's advice, disappearing behind the large oak tree.

As soon as Anne went into the woods, two men
appeared on the road. Clarissa stared at them blankly as
they drew guns.

"Here?" Jack Fine asked Chris, bringing the car to a slow
halt as they passed Alamo Heights swimming pool.

"Yes, here. Don't turn in. Drop me off here and drive
past it."

"Like hell."

"Yes," Chris said crisply. "They might not be here yet, we can't scare them off. Drive on up and hide the car somewhere. Get on the radio and keep the cops from rushing in here like the SWAT team, too. Quiet. Let's all walk softly." Chris didn't really know who might be in these woods, whether Anne or Clarissa was a hostage, so he spoke very authoritatively to Jack.

When he opened his car door Jack said, "Here," and held out the pistol from his waistband holster.

Chris stared at the weapon, small and dark and heavy. "You keep it, Jack. You can do more good with it than I can."

"Amateur," Jack said heavily. "I used to be a cop, remember? I got another one in the trunk."

Chris didn't argue any longer. He took the gun and hopped out, stepping quickly away from the car with its interior light and throbbing motor. As soon as Jack pulled away so that Chris smelled dirt and leaves rather than gasoline fumes he felt somehow safer. A stupid illusion. He didn't see Anne's car, which worried him, but hoped that she too, or Clarissa, had parked somewhere out of sight. He hurried across the parking lot and into the Nature Trails, once again in the woods with Jean.

Or so Chris theorized. If someone had kidnapped Anne instead of killing her—and no body had been found at her home—then Clarissa must be in on the kidnapping. He'd thought of the woods where Kristen had lain buried for three months, but if Clarissa had suggested that as a rendezvous point her partners would have been suspicious, and vetoed the idea. If Clarissa had any choice in the matter, and any mixed feelings, this was the only place Chris could think of where she might have come. He remembered how Clarissa had admired the privacy of the place the day he had brought her. If Clarissa had helped plan the kidnapping, acting on her mother's instructions, she would have chosen these woods.

If he was wrong, then Pentell had simply had Anne killed, for retaliation, and her body already lay dumped somewhere.

Chris stayed off the asphalt path, stepping softly through the trees, picturing Anne's face in the tangle of branches and leaves perpetually before him. She had no place in this mess, it was all Chris's problem. But Anne had a way of involving herself in Chris's problems, along with everyone else's—friends, patients, strangers. As Chris walked and cocked his head to listen, he refused to imagine life without her. He and Anne hadn't been together that long, he'd lived a long time on his own, but now imagination falsely implanted her even into his older memories, as if she'd been watching him all along, waiting for them to meet.

Trees grew in clusters, huddling together and then opening to create clearings. The ground was hard-packed dirt covered by scattered leaves, creating less than solid footing. Night had fallen almost completely, making the woods seem misty. Chris didn't hear any human sounds, nothing guided him, so he just moved in the general direction of the large oak where he and Clarissa had had their breakfast picnic what seemed like a long time ago. Chris moved very softly through the woods, so softly the gunman behind the mesquite tree didn't hear him until Chris almost brushed the man's shoulder moving into his line of sight. But a standing man is even quieter than any walking one, and the gunman wore a deep purple jogging suit that blended into the dark of the woods. Chris only became aware of him when the man's hand moved, and by that time it was too late. The startled gunman didn't shoot, he swung his pistol in a short arc and clipped Chris on the side of the head as Chris turned toward him.

"Unh." Chris dropped his own gun and fell heavily to the ground, banging the back of his head against another tree. Pentell's man in the jogging suit looked at his fallen foe, thinking what Raleigh would want in this situation.

Raleigh Pentell, on his way to prison, had basically instructed his men to burn down the world if they could. The women were the specific targets, but this gunman had a feeling Raleigh would not disapprove of a dead District Attorney as a bonus. He stepped closer to make certain of his shot, bending over Chris to place the gun right at his temple.

Jean, wearing tennis shoes and jeans and a navy sweater, her reddish hair and pale face bursting out of this dark outfit like an exotic flower, stepped up behind the gunman and didn't scream, didn't even breathe hard as she swung the thick branch she'd picked up, and caught the thug in the back of the head and neck, clubbing him unconscious so quickly the man didn't even moan.

Jean stood over the gunman for a moment glaring fiercely, waiting for the slightest movement, then, satisfied, kicked him out of the way and knelt quickly to hold Chris against her chest. His eyes flickered, he remained too groggy even to sit up on his own. "They're after her, too," Jean whispered. "Your Anne. I told you Raleigh'd try to hit you. Don't worry, I'm here."

Chris tried to speak. "I know," Jean said softly. She gave him a small kiss on the corner of his mouth, then patted him comfortingly and let him down again. Then Jean frowned at the quiet of the woods all around her, picked up the gun Chris had dropped, and left him to go exploring. There should have been gunfire by now.

Jean was a city girl, the forest primeval wasn't for her, but she moved through the trees as confidently as she did everything else. Keeping close to the pathways, she saw a vague shape ahead. Jean walked even more quietly, sneaking through the trees that loomed all around. Seeing the shape resolve itself into a woman's figure, Jean raised the gun, but then recognized her daughter, standing beside a large oak tree, her shoulders slumped as if lost in thought.

"Where is she?" Jean asked suspiciously.

Clarissa turned toward her slowly, unstartled. The girl

looked strange in these woods, unearthly pale, as if she came from an ethereal race slightly removed from humanity. Clarissa studied her mother, the girl's pale eyes moving languidly and no apparent judgment appearing in her expression. "I didn't bring her," she said.

"Bullshit."

"I don't do everything you tell me, Mom. Not anymore."

"I know better, Clarissa. Don't you think I have other—?"

A second gunman stepped out from behind a tree behind Clarissa. The sound didn't scare Clarissa, she must have known he was there, he must have been holding a gun trained on her the whole time.

This man dressed better than his partner, in dark gray slacks, a white shirt open at the collar and a navy blazer that his wide shoulders strained. He had a ruddy complexion and the bright, observant face of a successful athlete, perpetually on the verge of smiling.

"She's lying," he reported. "The woman's here somewhere."

Jean nodded. She seemed to know this man, moving toward him casually, headed for the trees behind him. "I'll go—" she said.

"To hell," the gunman said, and shot Jean in the chest. "Raleigh says hi," he added, the smile breaking through.

Clarissa shrieked and fell across her mother, sobbing and clutching at Jean's shoulders. The gunman watched this emotional scene for a moment with a bemused expression, his smile not quite disappearing, appearing surprised by this side effect produced by his gun. The girl ignored him, crying and calling her mother. But in a matter of moments the girl's tears ceased to interest the killer. Obviously Clarissa was one of his targets, too. With a tiny sigh of concentration he took aim at the back of her head.

And Anne Greenwald dropped out of the oak tree onto the man, dazing him. They both fell to earth and Anne's hands scrambled through the leaves on the ground searching for the gun he'd dropped. But the gunman lay on the gun. He groaned, reached under himself to recover the weapon, and pushed himself up. He glared at Anne, surprised to see her, but then gratified, since she'd been another object of his search. His hand found the familiar grip of his pistol.

Anne didn't try to struggle with him for the gun. Instead she picked up a rock and smashed it down on his head. The man looked surprised again, then lost all expression as Anne hit him again. He groaned and once more fell atop his gun, and this time he didn't move.

Clarissa stood behind Anne, holding in both hands another rock the size of a head of lettuce. She and Anne stared at each other, overcome. Clarissa obviously wanted to scream again. She lifted the rock high over her head and hurled it down onto the man's back. Then she cried in earnest, shoulders slumping.

Chris staggered out of the trees, still woozy and too late to save anyone. He saw Anne holding Clarissa and walked toward them, then came into view of Jean lying on her back, a red blossom high in the center of her chest.

"Oh my God." He knelt and held her up as she had done for him a few minutes earlier. Her body felt familiar, solid and tightly wound. Her eyes opened foggily.

"Didn't you know they'd be after you, too?" Chris asked her, verging on anger.

Jean, barely in touch, brightened for a moment. "But I knew that. I had it—"

She lost her breath, and her deep blue eyes darkened and glazed over before she could explain how she'd been smarter than everyone else.

Chris heard motion and turned to see Clarissa standing behind him, solid and upright on her legs, her eyes crazed with anger and grief so overflowing she could not contain them. The girl put her head back and screamed a full-throated shriek, higher and growing even louder before it began to die, her voice following her mother's spirit, both growing thin and eerie and fading into memory.

"Damn you," Clarissa repeated, much more softly. Chris went to hold her but the girl could not be comforted, then or for a long time to come. She stood rigid as a bundle of sticks. Chris stared past her at Anne, who watched them with her eyes welling with tears of sympathy, but had nothing to offer either.

Fifteen

"Jean wanted me dead," Anne said wonderingly. She stood in Chris Sinclair's office at nine o'clock the morning after the night in the woods, and had already said this phrase several times in the intervening hours, with different shades of disbelief or anxiety, until she had come to sound proud. To have someone plan carefully and launch several players in a bid to end one's life . . .

"It's kind of flattering," Anne said.

Chris looked at her as if doubtful of her sanity. "It is," Anne insisted, coming around his desk to stand close to his knees as he sat in his chair. "To you, too. After all these years, she wanted you back badly enough to have somebody killed over you. Doesn't it make you feel kind of . . ." She trailed off, but her hands moved descriptively.

"She wanted somebody," Chris disagreed. "Pentell was lost to her, she'd seen to that, but Jean wanted some other protection. She saw something developing between Clarissa and me, and she thought, how perfect, if she could both take over Pentell's enterprises and have the District Attorney on her side, too. It would've been too cool. It was the scenario that appealed to Jean, not me."

He spoke dismissively, even saying her name with apparent ease, but thinking of Jean did indeed, in Anne's expressive phrase, make him feel kind of . . . Different images of her still flipped rapidly through his memory like a pack of flash cards, Jean's face demonstrating different emotions, different times. Her death killed part of his past as well, making him feel very adult this morning. Not a good feeling.

Anne seemed oddly exhilarated, the common effect of surviving a murder attempt. She continued to gnaw at every aspect of the business. "If Raleigh Pentell had these men who would kill for him, why didn't he call one of them that night to help him bury Kristen? Why'd he ruin his own precious manicure on the dirty business?"

Chris had thought about that, too. "Panic, partly. Plus when you send someone to kill for you, he does the killing. He's even guiltier than you are, so you can count on his not talking. Pentell might have hesitated to let even his 'associates' know that he'd killed someone himself. They would have had something on him then."

Obviously Chris had spent a lot of time thinking about the case. His old lover had spread so many tentacles into his life. Anne watched him covertly, looking for a Jean-haunted vagueness in his expression. She couldn't help her analytical ways. "You think she planned everything just to take over Raleigh Pentell's insurance scheme?" Anne asked.

Chris shrugged. "I don't think she planned, I think she improvised. She knew what Pentell was like. She'd seen him discard business partners he thought had gotten too strong or too demanding. Jean wouldn't let that happen to her. Maybe she had some reason to suspect he was thinking of dumping her, or maybe that's just the way her mind worked constantly, but I think she sent her own daughter to that restaurant, after filling her head with ideas and making sure she'd talk freely, to send Pentell a message that he couldn't get rid of her as easily as he'd done others. She wouldn't go quietly and she'd leave evidence behind. She wouldn't be cut out of the insurance scam. I don't think she meant for Kristen to be killed, I really don't, but she didn't balk at using her death to hold over him. When I accidentally discovered Kristen's body she saw somebody was going to go down for her murder and by that time she'd decided it should be Pentell, she could carry on without him."

"But it was Clarissa who had Kristen's purse and diary."

"And she sent me messages and then planted the diary to seal the case against Pentell. Got her high school friends to leak word of the secret hideaway to my ace investigator like it was a breakthrough in the case." Chris thought Clarissa had had mixed motives in sending him the E-mail messages from her sister's diary. Yes, they'd been intended as part of the plan, but it had also been a way of keeping Kristen alive. Chris thought, and hoped, that Clarissa had also been trying to reach out to him.

He said to Anne, "If you hadn't gotten close to her, if Clarissa hadn't started seeing you as a person, you'd be dead now. She would've helped her mother carry out the killing the way she'd always served as Jean's accomplice. But at least she finally balked at the end. There's definitely a girl worth saving there."

Anne heard the question in his voice and answered solemnly. "Yes, Chris. But don't think she's saved yet. You and Jean grew up in middle-class homes, you had the examples of your parents, conventional morality that you didn't question even if you thought you ignored it sometimes. You could play at being wild, and even Jean who stayed in the kind of outlaw life, you both had underpinnings of morality. Clarissa had nothing. Jean didn't teach her anything except self-preservation. It'll be hard for her to shrug that off." She continued quietly: "Come September a lot of my patients miss appointments because they're home sick. They start back to school, get packed in with all those other kids, and they catch things. Adults, we fight off viruses without even noticing, but kids haven't been exposed enough, they're more susceptible. They catch whatever's out there."

She didn't have to explain her analogy. Chris said, "I needed to be there from the beginning. I would have been, if I'd known."

Anne stepped closer and touched his cheek affectionately. "I know you would."

Anne hesitated, touched by her own guilt, then decided to say it. "I'm sorry, Chris. That I didn't jump out of that tree sooner. I could have saved Jean. But she had a gun too and she obviously knew the man. I was watching from up in the tree and I was shocked when he shot her. If I'd realized sooner . . ."

Chris shook his head and touched her hand. "You couldn't have known. Obviously Jean didn't know herself. You saved the right one. Thank you, Anne."

She looked at him fondly then suddenly drew back, as if embarrassed by her own forwardness. "Well, we've both got work to do." As she turned and left the office she said over her shoulder, "Knock 'em dead," as if to an actor.

Chris nodded. He stood up and straightened his tie, took his suit coat off the back of another chair, and put it on carefully, pulling his white cuffs out of the sleeves. He stood as grimly as a pallbearer.

Entering the courtroom, the District Attorney wore the same expression, until he saw the girl on the front row of the spectator seats. He walked quickly up the aisle and knelt beside her. Putting his hand over Clarissa's, he said, "Are you sure?"

Clarissa nodded. Chris had never before seen her wear anything but jeans or shorts, but today she had dressed for church, or a funeral, in a black skirt almost knee-length and a cream-colored blouse. She looked older than sixteen, as old as her mother when Chris had first known her. "All right," he said, "but you remember Kristen the way

she was. Don't pay any attention to anything lawyers
say."

She nodded again, face stiff, and Chris went forward to
take his seat at the prosecution table. The punishment
phase of Raleigh Pentell's trial began. Chris stood to rest
the prosecution's case without putting on evidence. He
turned and looked at the defendant as he did so. Chris
knew Pentell had had Jean killed, and tried to kill Clarissa
and Anne as well, but he couldn't prove any of those
crimes beyond a reasonable doubt. Certainly he couldn't
have put together sufficient proof in the few hours since
dusk in the Nature Trails. He would work at that case too,
maybe offer Pentell's gunmen deals in exchange for testimony, but for this morning's punishment phase he would
only rely on evidence of the murder of Kristen.

Raleigh Pentell showed no sign he'd heard when Chris
announced that the prosecution had no punishment evidence. He stared straight ahead, his hands flat on the
table. He looked as if he'd been thinking frantically so
long his mind had locked up. Or as if he heard a soft
voice whispering doom in his ear.

In the defense's half of the punishment phase, Lowell
Burke called several associates of his client's, other busi-
nessmen, and the head of a local charity, to testify to Pentell's good character, but George Stiegers managed to
prove in a few questions of cross-examination that these
people hadn't known the defendant very well or very
long. Pentell couldn't call his real associates as witnesses.

As the trial proceeded Chris sat quietly waiting. He
didn't glance again at Raleigh Pentell; he wouldn't give
the man even the slight satisfaction of acknowledging
Pentell's successful revenge scheme of the night before.
Anne and Clarissa had saved themselves and the two gunmen sat in custody, but Raleigh had another victim to his
score.

Long before noon the time came for arguments. The
punishment for murder could be anything from probation
to life in prison, but Judge Benitez didn't give the lawyers

much time to convince the jurors. There was little punishment evidence to summarize. Lowell Burke began, looking pale beneath his tan and trying so hard to hold his real feelings hidden that he appeared rather stiff before the jury.

"You have found Raleigh Pentell guilty of murder and he and I respect your verdict, we really do. You have given him what he most wanted, his day in court. You found him responsible for the death of this innocent young girl. But now comes the time for justice."

The defense always had to respect the jury's verdict, even while hating it, because they had to face the same jury at this moment, when the jury would decide how hard to punish the defendant. Chris didn't envy the defense lawyer his task. Burke briefly painted Kristen's death as an accident, terrible and tragic certainly, but not something anyone had planned.

"You know for a certainty that that horrible combination of circumstances will never be repeated. You don't need to protect society from Raleigh Pentell. Any punishment you mete out will be simply for revenge, and that won't do anything for that poor little girl. But Raleigh Pentell can do good for her. You heard from his associates what good works he has done for this community and his plans to continue, including forming a scholarship foundation to be given in Kristen's name. Now is a time not for revenge but for redemption. Don't throw away two lives."

Ending with thanks, Lowell Burke swept the jury with mournful eyes and took his seat. Chris Sinclair stood at once, but then found himself unable to speak. He turned toward the courtroom and looked over the few spectators. Clarissa sat leaning forward, chin on her hands that rested on the top of the railing in front of her. Chris felt his eyes burn as he looked into hers. Clarissa waited trustingly for him to do something.

Turning back to the jury, he said, "I'm glad Raleigh Pentell has been spending time thinking about Kristen Lorenz. Finally. He never gave her much thought before.

"I too want to thank you for this day in court, but I don't think of it as Raleigh Pentell's day. He's had a lot of days of his own. I think of this trial as Kristen's. Her last, her only, public ceremony. She might have had others in her future, who knows? Awards ceremonies, graduations, a wedding, formal and informal and happy and mournful occasions with her family and some day her own children. But those will never happen."

He cleared his throat. "I feel those unspent days. Somehow they hang heavily in the air of this room. Where did Kristen's potential go? Leached away into the ground where she lay alone? No. I believe it went into the lives she'd touched, the people who will always remember her, and who can only imagine what she might have become. Who will go on remembering and imagining for the rest of their lives. You are now some of those people. I'm sorry we had to put that burden on you. But I'm glad that there are more people who will remember her. I am one of you. I will never forget Kristen."

Chris had turned his back on the defendant to face the jury, and he never turned back toward the defense table, as if Raleigh Pentell had ceased to exist for him. He leaned on the front of the jury box, looked into the faces looking up at him, and continued, "The important question of this trial is: who is responsible for all this shared pain? Kristen's mother? Her sister? Her friends? There is a lot of blame to share in this tremendous loss.

"But the little sins of omission or commission these people committed wouldn't be remembered now except for this man. He alone bears the responsibility for murder. He lost his temper and smashed his fist into the head of an innocent fourteen-year-old girl so hard that he broke her neck. Did he mean to kill her? I think so, but does it matter? Think of the tremendous force of that blow. He certainly meant to hurt her badly. No matter what he says now about his intentions, he is definitely and damnably guilty."

He straightened and again cleared his throat, taking a

moment to look down in silence. The jurors waited quietly, many of them tearful.

"So now we come to your job. The defense has suggested that a light sentence is appropriate, to allow Raleigh Pentell to continue his works." He stared at the jury, saw contempt on two or three faces, and thought the possibility of a short sentence coming out of this box a very small one. He needed just to stop talking.

"Don't waste Raleigh Pentell's life? He's had his life, a good one, three times as long as the life he allowed Kristen. Hers is over for all time. His should be, too."

Chris didn't sit again, but the judge realized the District Attorney had concluded his argument and he dismissed the jury to their deliberating room. The jurors walked quickly, looking eager to begin their last work together. At the defense table Lowell Burke put his head down in his hands and the defendant stared at the ceiling, which looked as blank as his future.

The courtroom almost emptied out quickly. Chris felt lost and alone until he looked out at the spectator seats and saw a girl who looked much more alone. Clarissa now rested her forehead on her hands. Chris walked quickly to her and lifted her face with a gentle hand under her chin. Tears streaked Clarissa's cheeks. She stood, tall next to him, wiped her cheeks and nose and said with a vain attempt at lightness, "Well, I see how you got this job."

"Clarissa, I—"

"Don't worry, you don't have to say anything." The girl sniffed and tilted her head back as if to start her tears flowing backward, back into their reservoirs. She blinked brightly, looking for a moment like her mother. "This trial is almost over and so is everything else. I'll get out of your hair. My grandparents are still in Fort Worth, I'm going to call them today. They'll probably—"

"You can't move to Fort Worth, you'd lose your senior year."

"Well, I don't think the state'll let me live on my own, and they're the only family I've got."

She wouldn't look at him, though Chris's eyes never left the girl's face. He tried hard to take her all in, on her own terms, not an echo of her mother or of him. He saw a tall, pretty girl, with a quick mind and an unusual wealth of experience, but also a large burden of teenage uncertainty. Chris said quietly, "No, they're not."

Clarissa acted as if she hadn't heard him. Chris added, "And you're the only family I've got, Clarissa. I want you to stay with me. Please."

He took her hands, tugging lightly. Clarissa shook her head, still not looking at him. Chris felt uncertain for a moment. Maybe she didn't want him in her life; he would remind her too much of this horrible period, the loss of her family.

Then he pictured her living with grandparents hundreds of miles away, sitting bleakly in a classroom where she knew no one. He pulled her to him, embraced her, and Clarissa offered no resistance. Her hands held his back tightly. She gave herself up to weakness and relief.

But when she pulled back she said again, "No. You're just asking me because you feel responsible—"

"Yes I do. Because I care about you. If you move away I won't be able to do my job, Clarissa. I'll spend all my time thinking about you. I need you close."

She sniffed and rolled her eyes. Chris knew what she was doing, fighting off emotion. He'd spent years doing the same thing. Now in the empty courtroom he cried quietly, and tilted Clarissa's face toward him so she could see.

That got her. She cried afresh, hugged him again, smiled in embarrassment at herself. After a while they sat on the spectator pew of the courtroom, Chris's arm around her shoulders. He gestured around, reenacting some of the trial moments. Clarissa put her head on his shoulder, then looked at him as if he were nuts, or not even real.

"I'm trying to share my work with you," he said with mock seriousness. They laughed, both thinking the same vague thought that they had to make better memories than what they had so far.

Anne Greenwald's desk phone rang. Her hand rested unmoving on a legal pad where she had stopped in the middle of making notes about the patient she'd seen half an hour earlier. She'd been writing something about parental involvement when her mind had drifted. The jolt of the phone's bell made her feel guilty. She answered quickly.

"Are you done for the day?" Chris asked.

"Are you kidding? At two-thirty in the afternoon? I've got to head out to the medical center, I'm supposed to be consulting—"

"Good, I've got to go that way, too. Stop at the Vance Jackson exit and meet me in the park for a minute."

"I don't think I have—"

"Good. Thanks."

He was sitting on the bottom of a fiberglass slide when Anne came walking toward him. It wasn't really a park, just a neighborhood playground for children who would be in school at the moment. Once coming from Westfall Library they'd had an impromptu picnic there after speaking to a group of kids. Between them, for different reasons, Chris and Anne knew a wide variety of parks and playgrounds throughout the city.

He had left his tie and suit coat in his car and looked in his white shirt like a weary out-of-town businessman. But when he saw her coming toward him he smiled and showed a strange light of eagerness in his eyes.

"Jury come back?" Anne asked casually.

"In about twelve minutes. Life. He'll be eligible for parole in thirty years."

"Congratulations."

He nodded, already indifferent to Raleigh Pentell. "What about Clarissa?" Anne asked.

"She said she could go live with her grandparents in Fort Worth."

It was Anne's turn to nod, but as Chris didn't say anything else she looked at him with slight alarm. "You didn't say yes to that?"

He shook his head. "She's back in school. I'm on my way to pick her up now and take her to her house to pack."

Anne looked relieved. "You can't let that girl go off on her own now. Besides, I think you need her, too." She coughed to indicate a delicate subject. "Are you going to, you know, be tested?"

"I asked the medical examiner to preserve a sample of Jean's blood. I can get samples from Clarissa and me any time. DNA tests are fast these days. I could know for sure a week from now."

Anne waited expectantly. "Will you?"

"I don't think so. What difference would it make?"

She nodded in satisfaction. Anne crossed her arms, looking around the small playground with its sandy floor and plastic-bottomed swings. The swings moved slightly in a breeze and she imagined squeals of happiness.

"Now about your project . . ." Chris said.

Quickly Anne answered, "I should never have let Clarissa see that pregnancy test. She probably told her mother and that crystallized Jean's plans. She had to—"

"Yes, but that's all over. Now back to—"

Anne shook her head. "You have enough responsibilities."

Chris, still sitting on the slide, took her hand and said seriously, "I don't think I do. I've had a shortage of responsibilities in my life."

She kept her face averted so he couldn't see her smiling, so when he rose and circled her she had to change expressions quickly, looking contemplative like a scientist.

"Well . . ."

"Let's just see what happens."

Anne cocked her head as if considering, or as if she'd lost track of the conversation because she had so much else on her mind. The posture elongated her neck, so that when he kissed her there it tickled.

"You know," he murmured, "I'm going to have a child living with me. We'll have to sneak around, to places like this."

Anne looked around the playground with an alarmed expression, at the fiberglass slide that twisted halfway down its length, at the narrow plastic seats of the swings, the four-by-four-foot square play fort with a floor of boards separated by an inch or two of free space, at the splintery seesaws. Her arms around Chris's neck, Anne began a sly smile and leaned close against him to say something intimate into his ear.

"Like hell," she said.